LOVE Y♡U

more

NEW YORK TIMES BESTSELLING AUTHOR

JULIA KENT

Cover design: Qamber Designs

Editor: Elisa Reed

Love You More

An icy car accident strands two friends in a snowstorm, igniting an attraction they can no longer resist, until her brother discovers his best friend in bed with his sister. Can they fight family expectations for a chance at true love?

Colleen Luview's love life is cursed. No, *really*. The small-town nurse is notorious in her touristy mountain community. After every third date she's ever had, the guy ends up in her emergency room.

She's untouchable now, and it's not her fault.

Resolved to branch out and find a way to have a life with a partner, children, and meaning, free from being a love pariah in a town devoted to it, she decides to leave her beloved Love You, Maine—where every day is Valentine's Day—to find a bigger dating pool.

And a better nickname than Third Date Colleen.

Moore Mottin hates feeling like damaged goods. Married and divorced twice before age thirty, he has a fifteen-year-old from a teenage pregnancy, was cheated on *during* his second wedding, and now even his best friend, Luke Luview, considers him the butt of every bad-luck joke when it comes to love.

When Luke's sister, Colleen, picks him up from the airport and a freak snowstorm forces them off the road, he rescues her from an icy pond and finds an old hunting cabin for shelter and safety. Vulnerable and shaking, the two give in to their long-simmering feelings for each other, but when they're discovered in the worst way possible, what seemed like a new lease on life turns into a life-altering mess.

Can Moore and Colleen overcome all the obstacles holding them back from a love that's been in front of their faces all this time?

If you're looking for a story featuring two star-crossed lovers doomed by unfair reputations, with a smooth-talking single dad who runs a jewelry store and his best friend's sister, set in a small town in New England, with a calico cat named Sandwich, a heroine with a dry wit and a can-do attitude, and a hero who just wants a good relationship with his estranged child and the chance to find lasting love... then this is your book.

Grab a cup of coffee or tea, and maybe some peanut butter for your burger (What? It's a thing...), and get your happy meter ready as you read the third book (a standalone!) in the Love You, Maine series—where love isn't just a feeling... it's a way of life.

Standalone
One-night stand
Forced proximity
Best friend's sister
Single dad
... and a calico cat named Sandwich

Chapter One

Colleen

Ding!

Colleen Luview's eyes flitted to her phone, secure in a dashboard holder, the text coming through loud and clear as she saw the sign for the airport exit, piles of snow under the sign but the road clear, salt and sand trucks already sprinkling the roads for the pending new snow. Memory reminded her to stay in the right-hand lane for arrivals.

The text was from Tim, the guy she was currently dating.

It's date four tonight. No ER. We're good to go. Can't wait to break the curse officially.

Her sigh stretched back at least a decade.

Ahhhhhh. Life was good.

Dating Tim Fields, the local CPA's son and an accountant himself, was still super weird.

But beggars couldn't be choosers, and when your nickname in your hometown was Third Date Colleen, you took

1

what you could get. Every guy who wasn't a transplant had been part of her life since birth, so her dating pool was more like a wide, shallow puddle.

A good dart player, strong at miniature golf, and a shockingly great kisser, Tim had surprised her.

And now, so had fate.

Her nickname started when she was twenty-one, fresh out of her two-year nursing program, her RN so new, she hadn't even received her diploma yet. After her third date with local handyman Jake Forsythe, she'd gone to bed, woken up the next morning, headed to work in the emergency room of Luview Medical Center–and he'd been her first patient, the victim of a hedge trimmer that flipped when he wobbled on his ladder, earning him seventeen stitches from wrist to elbow and three in his groin.

Because he'd nearly cut off his, um... root.

Jake had the dubious honor of being the first victim of the curse.

He also had a new nickname: *Slicer*.

It was all downhill from there.

Joe Martinez had been bitten by a timber rattlesnake.

Mike McGinty had twisted his ankle hauling stone.

Gerry Jones got food poisoning.

And so on, until old Doc Blythe had finally said, as he wrote up an anti-nausea prescription for poor Gerry, "You really have a pattern, don't you?"

She'd been leaving, about to go off shift, and his comment had stung, though she didn't know why. Moore and Luke were walking in, the three of them on their way to go canoeing.

"What's that, Doc?" she'd asked, not quite sure what he meant.

"You go out with a guy on the third date and he ends up in your ER."

Luke had snorted. Moore had started snickering. Under his breath, he'd stage-whispered, "Watch out for *Third Date Colleen*."

Doc had pressed his lips together. Luke bust out laughing. Colleen whapped Moore on the arm, hard, but it didn't matter.

"Third Date Colleen, huh? You're cursed, young lady," Doc had said as he finished the prescription and gave her a sympathetic look.

All it took was for her cousin Sandy to overhear that, and it spread like wildfire throughout Luview, Maine, the town founded by her ancestors, where love wasn't just a feeling–it was a way of life.

In small towns, once you had a nickname, might as well tattoo it on your forehead.

Tim, though, she thought as she read the text again, taking the exit for the airport.

Tim was the antidote to the curse.

Was he her soulmate? No. Were they falling in love and getting married? Hell, no. Did she plan to sleep with him?

Absolutely.

Because that's the other problem with the curse: No one was willing to have sex with her until date number four.

Which made Colleen cursed *and* horny.

Ding!

Another text, from Tim again.

Just got back from an unexpected business trip. At the airport, on my way to get my car. Can't wait to see you.

Airport?

She was at the airport. Unless he meant Portland? The closest airports to Luview were Portland, Maine and Manchester, New Hampshire, which was where she was right now.

Picking up Moore Mottin.

Sure, she was dating Tim, but Colleen's crush on her brother's best friend had started in eleventh grade and ended, well...

Never.

It had ended *never.*

Which was why she drove two hours and ten minutes each way, totally out of her way, to pick him up at the Manchester airport today.

"Doesn't matter," she muttered to herself as she made the big loop around the arrivals section of the airport, half an eye out for him, the other half on her phone, waiting for Moore's text. "Tim's an anomaly. Not getting my hopes up," she added, as if being down on herself would magically make some other part of her life work.

Like Moore appearing so they could get home ahead of the big snowstorm the radio announcers couldn't shut up about.

Ever since she was a junior in high school and he was a freshman, she'd found herself transfixed by the sight of him, complete in his presence and yet in a constant state of yearning for more.

For *Moore.*

The summer between eighth and ninth grade had been very, *very* good to him, the geeky, awkward boy who was her little brother's best friend transformed into a tall, muscled, hot *guy.*

Young guy, and of course, still a teenager, but the first day of high school that fall had been transformative.

"But *Tim,*" she said aloud, with emphasis, combating the negative voice that always popped up when something good happened. She made herself smile, remembering an article she'd read about how smiling helped to reduce limbic system over-reactivity.

In other words, pretend you're happy and biochemistry might follow.

Tim would be different.

Or at least, she'd finally have some nookie. Different nookie... but as long as it meant getting sweet between the sheets for the first time in way too long, she was happy.

And that made her truly smile.

She read Tim's newest text again and then, with no sign of Moore, took her place in a long line of cars all doing exactly what she was doing. Once she was under the covered area, the snowflakes no longer blocking her view, everything looked grim and gray.

Airport designers must double as prison planners. Nothing but dirty concrete everywhere.

And frowns. Lots of frowns.

Fourth date magic, she texted back to Tim, adding a peach and an eggplant emoji, giggling as she did it, her smile becoming more and more genuine.

The cars were at a standstill, the smell of exhaust strong, coming in through the vent system.

Ding!

Um, don't we need three dates before we get to peaches and eggplants? the text read.

Then she realized she'd sent the text meant for Tim to Moore.

Scrambling to cover her mortification, she replied back with, *That's my shopping list. Peaches and eggplants.*

Add some jello and a mold and you're singlehandedly bringing back 1970s cuisine, he replied, making her guffaw.

Tim asked me out for a fourth date, she typed back, heart pounding faster than it should. For all these years, she and Moore had openly talked about their respective love lives, their friendship spanning both his marriages and countless dating partners for each of them.

She'd been there when he married Cammie Forsythe when they were seniors in high school, unexpectedly pregnant and forced into matrimony by Moore's parents.

Babysat their son, Jordy, for years while Moore busted himself to go to University of Southern Maine and get his degree, all while working as a painter, his parents forcing him to "be an adult" and banning him from the family business until he proved himself.

Proudly watched him get that degree and join Love You Jewelers with the other Mottins.

Been there when Cammie disappeared with his then five-year-old son, Jordy, not long after Moore graduated. Helped him get Jordy back, at least part time.

Been there when he'd married Gia, the sophisticated banker he'd fallen for on a business trip in New York.

Walked in on Gia banging their DJ in the coatroom during the wedding reception.

Held Moore's head while he puked his guts out the next morning.

Nothing bonds friends like a shared trauma.

As Colleen prepared to send her text to the right guy, finding her text stream with Tim and typing, she looked up to see the cars in front of her moving forward.

But then–

SCREECH!

The car in front of her slammed on its brakes, Colleen doing the same, barely avoiding hitting the bumper.

The sight before her was impossible.

Literally impossible.

About two cars ahead, a man wearing a suit and holding a big brown leather briefcase flew up in the air, his arm first, then one leg. The gymnastic twist made her think of Zac Efron in *The Greatest Showman,* except instead of a highly skilled circus performer, this was a businessman twisting midair, flailing reflexively, screaming in horror and shock.

Thump.

And now, pain.

Reflex made her turn off the truck, shove the keys in her pocket, and scramble out, running without thought, the smell of diesel and the sound of car horns fading as her nursing skills kicked in. Luview, Maine, where she was born and raised, was a tiny little mountain town, but she'd worked the emergency room there long enough to have first responder adrenaline in her blood.

The man's head was so vulnerable, and head trauma was bad.

When she reached the body, he was turned away, chin tucked in, his shoulders visible first. But his right foot was angled too sharply.

That was a broken tibia, at best.

"I'm an ER nurse," she announced, the small group of people forming around him parting at her words. "Someone call 911."

At least five people wiggled their phones in the air, the universal signal for *I'm doing that now.*

"Airport security?" someone shouted. "Is there an airport paramedic?"

Colleen heard muted voices, light taps on horns, then the unmistakable crackle of feedback from a walkie-talkie. As long as some chain of emergency medical services was being activated, she could administer early care, then stand down.

Reaching for the man, she said calmly, "Hi, there. I'm Colleen. I'm a nurse. You're going to be fine. Can you tell me—"

"Colleen? Colleen *Luview?*" The groan came from the man on the ground, his words making her pulse race. He knew her? Why would some random stranger at the Manchester airport know her name?

Then it was her turn to be in shock and pain.

But an entirely different kind than poor Tim Fields was in.

"Tim!" she gasped, reaching for his shoulder, blood blooming on his jaw as a fresh scrape turned bright red. Thick eyebrows furrowed over dark eyes that were narrowed with pain. His hair was clipped short, his lips stretched wide below his long nose.

But it was revulsion for *her* that defined the man's state.

"DON'T TOUCH ME!" he screamed. Yes, *screamed*. High-pitched and hysterical, the sound made her flinch then glance around. "YOU DID THIS TO ME!"

"Sir? No, no, sir," said a young man with dark, curly hair, wild eyes, and a painfully guilty look, his phone glued to his ear. His shoulders slumped, the sleeves of his hoodie stretching over his hands. "I did it, sir. She was behind me. I'm the one who hit you and I'm so sorry. So, so sorry! My mom is going to kill me. This is her car! I can't believe I hit a *whole human being* with my car!"

The kid couldn't have been more than twenty, his voice cracking.

"He must have hit his head," said a woman with gray pin curls, her bright red wool coat a shock of color in the dingy airport underpass. She leaned on a three-legged cane and watched Tim with sympathy, lips disappearing as she curled them in. "Poor man."

"SHE IS CURSED!" Tim shouted, trying to point at Colleen with an arm that wouldn't cooperate. She was on her knees on the cracked concrete, absorbing his words as the scents and sounds and overwhelm of everything seeped in.

Colleen knew exactly what he meant.

Dread filled her gut.

"It's not my fault! No! Tim, it's not my fault!" She put her hands on his shoulders, trying to assess his wounds, Tim curling frantically away from her.

"STOP! STOP! Don't let her touch me! She'll kill me!"

The crowd went silent, all eyes on her.

"She's Third Date Colleen! Cursed! CURSED!"

"Do you know this man?" A guy in a Patriots ski cap, his face weathered and creased with the kind of wrinkles that skewed vertical, peered at her intently. "I know you didn't hit him with your car, but why does he think you're trying to kill him?"

"Head trauma," said another man, a tow-headed guy about her age with a goatee, carrying a leather book with a thin rubber band around it. He looked over his shoulder nervously. "I hope a paramedic is coming."

"I'm an ER nurse," Colleen insisted. "And yes, I know him."

Murmurs filled the air.

Tim's eyes were feral, his mouth twisted with pain, neck tendons taut. The angle of that leg looked excruciating. Colleen's own shins were turning to ice as she pressed into the pavement. Tim wasn't in good shape, and this was getting worse.

Time to take charge.

"I am not cursed, I'm not trying to kill you, and your leg *is* broken," she said in her work voice, a matter-of-fact voice designed to be practical yet encouraging.

"Because of you!"

"I didn't break your leg, Tim." Any goodwill she had for him was draining away fast. At the same time, she couldn't help but admire how freaking *hot* he was. The gray suit with a red silk tie was a chef's kiss of perfection, his leg muscles bulging nicely against the fabric.

Or maybe that was a displaced knee cap.

"I should have known better. Every man who ever goes on

a third date with you ends up in your emergency room within days."

The crowd began to murmur. Great. You can take the girl out of Luview, but you can find petty small-town gossipers *anywhere*.

"For the record, you're not technically in *my* emergency room. We can still have that fourth date," she whispered in his ear, his reply nothing but a derisive huff.

So much for that lingerie order she'd made this morning. And she'd paid for two-day shipping, too. Now she'd have to return it, a trip to the post office the last freaking thing she needed. The postmaster, Tim Kurdan, would ask too many pointed questions.

Apparently, her life was nothing but a plague of Tims right now.

"No more fourth date. *Pffft*. I should have listened to Jake."

Cold shot through her veins.

"Excuse me?"

"He tried to warn me. *Hard*. Came to my office after he saw us out on our second date. Said you're some kind of witch."

"Jake thinks that if you drink soda and eat Mentos after taking a Viagra, it'll make things grow even bigger," Colleen replied. She wasn't revealing anything private. Jake had publicly declared this medical "fact" last month, during a heated dart game at Bilbee's Tavern.

"What does that have to do with dating you?"

"Nothing. Just like Jake's opinion, it isn't worth a damn. Why would you listen to him?"

"I didn't! That's the problem! Now look at me."

A long, slow inhale helped center her. Feelings had to come last in moments like this.

Stabilize the patient.

Don't argue with him.

"Let's assess your injuries."

"Because of you, he was nearly castrated!" Tim continued, the words coming out just as a police officer appeared.

There were not enough deep breaths in the world to make this situation better.

"Hello. Officer Tomes here. What's happened?" The cop was in full uniform, hat and all, with a black down coat that dropped to mid thigh. She couldn't tell if he was thirty or fifty, but she knew one thing:

Today was not going as planned.

"Car hit him," Colleen began. "I was two cars behind." She pointed to the kid who actually hit Tim, who was staring at the cop, gape-mouthed and shaking, looking as if he were about to pee himself.

"She's trying to kill me," Tim groaned.

Every police officer has a "work face." Colleen knew this because she'd watched her brother Luke adopt it during law enforcement situations. Seeing it aimed directly at her by Officer Tomes turned the dread in her gut into a flaming explosion of napalm.

"Miss," he said flatly, waving his hand, "would you please move away from the injured gentleman?"

Oh, how he sounded like her brother.

Obeying the order, she lifted her hands in the air and backed away a foot or two, torn between knowing Tim needed immediate medical attention and following the officer's directive.

"I'm a nurse. The only first responder on the scene. I am trying to assess his injuries."

Tomes looked down at Tim and frowned. "He doesn't want you to touch him."

"Because he's in shock."

"BECAUSE EVERY GUY SHE DATES ENDS UP

11

INJURED. SHE NEARLY SLICED OFF A GUY'S WIENER!"

Of all the ways to learn Tim called it a *wiener*. Geez.

She really dodged a bullet.

Letting out a soft laugh, but also genuinely worried about Tim's possible internal injuries, Colleen tried to establish a rapport with the cop.

"I assure you, this is shock. Or he hit his head, hard. Tim's a little..." She twisted a finger in the air around her ear.

"Is that a medical diagnosis?" The officer bent down, putting his hand carefully on Tim's shoulder. "Sir, paramedics are on the way. Is this woman harassing you?"

"YES! She's the reason I got hit by a car!"

Now it was Colleen's turn to groan.

As Tomes stood, his hand went to his belt, fingers brushing a set of zip ties.

"Officer, really, I haven't hurt Tim. We're dating, actually."

"Dating?"

"Not anymore!" Tim called up.

"Yes, sir. We had our third date. And, uh..."

"Third date?"

"And we're about to have our fourth," she continued, but Tim interrupted with:

"SHE HURTS MEN SHE DATES!"

At that, Officer Tomes' entire demeanor shifted.

"So this is a domestic dispute," he said slowly, eyes narrowing.

Backing farther away from Tim, Colleen tried desperately to say the right thing, to say *anything* that would make this horrible mess go away.

"No, sir! Not a domestic dispute. It's actually kind of comical to explain–"

"You're saying that your partner being hit by a car is *comical?*"

Oh, no.

No, no, *no.*

"Not his injuries! Of course not! But the story that led to this is, well, it's full of bizarre coincidences and misunderstandings."

"You think your partner telling me you're the cause of his injuries is a 'coincidence' and a 'misunderstanding'?"

The edges of her vision started to shimmer a bit, as if the light itself were pulsating. The implication of what this police officer was saying began to sink in, layer by layer.

He thought she had hurt Tim, and others.

He thought this was a domestic dispute.

He saw Tim's very real fear of future injury from her.

Trained in how to handle domestic violence situations and very familiar with the procedure for separating an abuser from a victim in the emergency room, it occurred to Colleen that the officer was using his domestic violence training right now.

And he thought *she* was the abuser.

How on earth was she going to clear this up?

"I've never hurt Tim," she began, wincing internally because she sounded like every abuser who begins to get defensive.

"Hey," said a low voice behind her, and a hand touched her shoulder. Turning, she was relieved to see the best person *ever.*

Moore.

His palm was wrapped around the handle of a carry-on bag on wheels, and his thick black dress coat was unbuttoned, flapping as the wind picked up. She knew he's planned his layover in Chicago carefully, to have a short, but important, business meeting there, which explained his formal dress.

Tall and graceful, he was the epitome of a successful businessman, the kind you wanted to relax with over a fine dinner, or talk to while playing eighteen holes on the golf course.

A charmer.

Moore was a *charmer*.

The police officer gave him a hard look that made Moore step back, hands going up a bit.

"Sorry to interrupt," he said, questions in his eyes as they bounced from Tomes back to her. "Is–" He looked down, head snapping back in surprise. "Tim?"

"Moore?"

Before Tim could say another word, men in red jackets appeared.

Paramedics.

Thank God.

"Moore!" Tim shouted up. "You were smart! You never dated her! You're just friends. Stay in the friend zone, man. Don't do it or she'll hurt you!"

Now Tomes glared at her, but turned to Moore. "Excuse me, sir. I'm in the middle of talking to..." He looked at her with suspicion. "Name?"

"Colleen Luview."

As she said her surname, the officer jolted. "Luview? As in Love You, Maine? The town?"

"Yes, sir."

Tomes glanced down at his left hand. A beautiful platinum ring rested on it, the metal textured as if someone had taken thin branches from trees and braided them.

"I was married there." He looked at Moore, tilting his head. "And I swear I know you."

Charm was something Moore had in spades, an easygoing, affable manner he didn't so much turn on as access through his daily life. Colleen felt him go from concerned to engaged as he offered his hand to the cop and said, "Talia. October 2021, right? You're Alberto."

The officer's squint instantly changed to an expression of pleasure while the paramedics began evaluating Tim, who was now groaning in pain and apparently unable to continue accusing Colleen of conjuring the dark arts.

"The jeweler! You're the guy at Love You Jewelry. I'm sorry, man. I don't remember your name."

"Moore. Moore Mottin."

As they shook hands, Officer Tomes gave Moore his full attention, pulling him two steps away from Colleen. Another officer, a short woman with a dark ponytail under her cap, waved at Tomes, who then gestured toward the mess of cars. She immediately began directing traffic, while a third cop talked to the kid who *actually* hit Tim.

You know. The one who *really* hurt him.

Within ten seconds, Moore was chatting up Alberto as if they were best buds who happened to run into each other. Colleen's dad always joked that Moore could climb Mount Everest and find someone he knew at the top.

"Look, man, it's nice to see you again, but this situation is, ah..." Officer Tomes looked at Colleen, then Tim. "You know these two?"

The impish look Moore gave her made it clear he desperately wanted to crack a joke, but now was not the time. In that way old friends have of communicating telepathically, she sent him a stern *no* with three eye twitches, along with some choice nonverbal profanity.

"Sure. Colleen's a nurse in Luview. Her brother is the new chief of police and he's my best friend."

Magic words. Magic, *magic* words.

"Why didn't you say so?" the cop admonished her. "I didn't realize you're practically family."

"I, uh–"

"Don't date her!" Tim rasped as the paramedics stabilized his neck and lifted him onto a stretcher. "Don't do it, bro!"

Officer Tomes held up his left hand. "I'm married."

"I meant Moore! Colleen's playing a long game with you. She'll get you under her spell like she got me. All these years, I thought her ears stuck out a little too much for my taste–"

Colleen reached up and felt her earlobes. What?

"–and when she kisses, she bites–"

"HEY!" she shouted, earning a look from Moore that said this was going to be town gossip unless she paid for all their dart games for the next month.

"–and now she broke my leg!"

Moore rolled his eyes. "She didn't do a thing to Tim."

"Then what's he going on about, that she's evil and cursed?"

"He never said evil."

"He certainly implied it."

"Third Date Colleen," Moore explained as if he were giving him directions to a gas station. "Every guy Colleen makes it to a third date with somehow ends up injured, in her emergency room."

"You're serious?" Tomes gaped.

"No, he's not. Because Tim and I had our third date a few days ago and he's not in my ER," Colleen replied with a sniff.

"But this is close enough to the curse," Moore argued. "Jake sliced himself with the hedge trimmer. Joe got that snake bite. Gerry had food poisoning. Mike–"

Officer Tomes cut him off.

"You're serious? Every single guy?"

"Yep."

"Then why are *you* with her?"

Moore's face went blank with astonishment. "Me?" he said in a two-toned voice.

"Yeah. You two are together, right?"

"Oh, no!" Colleen chimed in. "I'm just picking him up from the airport. I'm dating *Tim*."

"ARE NOT!" Tim called out as the medics slid him into the back of their ambulance, the doors closing on that parting shot.

Tomes laughed softly through his nose. "Sounds like you're on the market again, Ms. Luview."

"Call me Colleen. And besides, Moore and I—no way. We're just friends."

"My wife and I were 'just friends,' too."

The female officer jogged over and Tomes said goodbye quickly. Horns blared behind them and Colleen realized she needed to get back to the truck.

Thank goodness.

Without a word, Moore followed her, shoving his carry-on in the back seat then climbing in.

Heart smacking against her chest like she was clapping at one of her niece's soccer games, Colleen pulled away from the curb as Moore clicked his seatbelt in place, twisting back to get one more look at poor Tim.

"Huh. The only thing worse than that would've been if you were the one to hit him."

"I hate you."

"Is that any way to greet one of your best friends?"

"When it's you with that mouth of yours? Yes."

"'Welcome home, Moore,'" he said in a sing-songy voice. "'It's good to have you back, Moore.'"

"Not when you tease me about—" she waved her right hand in the air in a vague way meant to convey the mess that was her love life. "That."

"Third Date Colleen?"

"You know I hate that phrase."

"Unfortunately, the universe just proved it true."

"Technically," she said, her voice going high and reedy with emotion, "that didn't count."

"Tim got hit by a car after going on a third date with you, Colleen."

"But he won't end up in *my* emergency room. Therefore, it's not part of the curse."

The sound Moore made in the back of his throat did not inspire confidence.

Or make her anger recede.

"If you say so."

"It's true!"

"Just because it's true doesn't mean poor Tim is going out on a fourth date with you."

The words made a salty-sour flavor pour into the back of her throat, tears threatening.

"I know," she said softly, Moore's head jerking to look at her, his expression making this harder.

Because all she saw on his face was pity.

And pity was the last thing she wanted from Moore.

Driving forced her out of her head and heart and into the very real world of vehicles and logistics. No need to add another accident to her day. Remembering the angle of Tim's tibia made her wince.

"I'm sorry," Moore said with a sigh. "I shouldn't tease you like that."

"You always tease me like that."

"Yeah, but it lands different when it's raw."

Her spidey sense went off.

"You sound like you've got something raw going on yourself." She made a left turn, watching cars *whoosh* by, the light flurries causing her to worry a bit.

Moore automatically turned the radio to the local news station. If you learned anything growing up in Maine, it was to always check the weather in winter. Freak snowstorms were a way of life.

"Yeah."

"Jordy?"

"This time, it's Cammie. She's pregnant."

"Again?"

"And getting remarried."

"Dave proposed?"

His ex-wife, Cammie, had a love life that was like musical chairs, and there was nothing Moore could do about the revolving door of men in their life. Cammie's last long-term boyfriend had been Mike, a minor-league baseball player, with whom she'd had a daughter, Jordy's half-sister Soria, who was now three years old.

They'd split up and Mike had virtually no contact with his daughter. Moore never pried, but wondered if Cammie was doing to Mike what she'd done to Moore: block access to his kid.

Then came Dave.

Dave was an actuary. Boring as cardboard, but steady. Cammie and Dave had been living together since Moore's son, Jordy, was nine, which meant Dave had lived with Jordy for longer than Moore had, technically.

Lots of technicalities today.

"No. In fact, Dave dumped her."

"WHAT?"

"Fell in love with a supply chain manager for some auto parts company. According to Jordy, Dave got 'tired of being Cammie's meal ticket for her kids,' which makes me wonder what she's said over the years about money. I pay way more than the required child support, all of Jordy's extras..." He sighed.

"Then who's she marrying?"

"Guy named Locke Enlode."

"Can you repeat that name?"

"Locke. Enlode."

"Huh?"

"First name is Locke. Last name is Enlode."

"Lock 'n Load? No! Sounds like a fake name. Like a porn star name."

"He's a minor league baseball player. Pitcher."

"Oh." Colleen's heart sank.

Then it sank again.

Unfortunately, she couldn't say a word, the opening too good to pass up as cars lined up behind her. Pulling out, she looked at the road and saw enough slush already accumulated to make a mental calculation.

Before she could reply to Moore, the radio announcer cut in:

"Severe storm warning for Lake Winnipesaukee and surrounding areas..."

As they listened to the report, Moore's eyebrows went up, his slow, deep inhale a sign he was taking the information in and processing it. Colleen had literally known Moore since the day he was born, the Mottins and the Luviews being friends in town, but also because her brother Luke was three days older than Moore.

Colleen was two years older than the both of them.

There wasn't an expression, a sigh, a grunt, a laugh that Moore Mottin could make that Colleen hadn't heard before.

Other than a sound of passion.

Cheeks heating up at the thought, Colleen ignored the tingling that raced through her, taking a deep breath to center herself. As she did, Moore's aftershave filled her senses.

And scrambled her inner signals even more.

"Bad storm. Should we re-route?" Moore asked.

"There aren't many options. We're in Manchester. It's two hours either way. We can either go west of Lake Winnipesaukee or east of it and go up through Portland."

"No good option." Moore frowned at the sky, leaning forward. Under the sleek black wool coat, he wore a charcoal suit and dress shoes, and Colleen marveled at how professional and sophisticated he seemed. Moore always dressed like this for work, but usually when she saw him, he was in a t-shirt and jeans, or sweats.

Something about the suit made her pulse race.

Continuing on the road north, she said, "It's the same direction for the first few miles, so we have time to decide."

"Worst case, we get a hotel, I guess. Plenty of them here."

"Is—is the storm that bad?" The thought of sharing a hotel room with Moore instantly charged her up. A thousand fantasies poured through her.

"Last thing we want is to get stuck on the side of the road."

"Well, duh. But we're both good drivers in snow. And I brought Dad's truck on purpose. Six wheeler." She frowned at him. "Since when do you get nervous about snowstorms?"

He sighed, resting his elbows on his knees, scrubbing his hair with his fingers. A very rumpled Moore looked back at her as she eased to a halt at a stoplight, his eyes a bit wild.

"It's not just Cammie. I got dumped mid-flight. By text."

"Hannah dumped you?" Hannah was Moore's latest girl-friend. The guy had been married and divorced twice by the age of twenty-seven, which Colleen knew made him feel like tainted goods. While she loved small town life, she hated how people could be pigeonholed and stuck in an identity they never chose.

Like Third Date Colleen, for example.

Of all the people in town, she was most sympathetic to poor Moore's curse.

"Yep. My phone was off on the second flight. Apparently, she decided to do it while I was somewhere over Cleveland."

"Ouch. I'm sorry. Did she say why?"

"Yes." The word was clipped. Angry. "She had a big work function this weekend, a fundraiser for some nonprofit her paper company contributes to. She said I'm too focused on my kid, and she needs someone who will be more committed to her."

A sharp inhale of outrage was all Colleen could manage.

"That's horrible! She really showed you who she is underneath!"

"Underneath?"

"She always struck me as being very shallow. All surface, no depth. All veneer, no hardwood. All–"

"I get the point."

"Sorry. I'm not one to talk. Tim's on his way to a trauma center in Manchester because of me."

"You didn't hit him!"

"Not with my car. I hit him with my curse."

He snorted, the sound turning into the deep rumble of laughter she enjoyed hearing.

"Tim has no idea what he's missing."

Years of deeply repressed desire formed a hot ball of lead in her stomach, the feeling oh, so familiar.

She was thirty-five. Moore was thirty-three.

Having a crush on him since her junior year of high school meant that half her life had been spent tamping down how she really felt about him.

It was in her bones.

Where it would always stay.

Repressing the truth was the only way for life to stay in balance, the only way to remain a part of his life. Settling for being just friends was better than nothing at all.

"Your only curse is that you date dumbasses who believe there's a curse."

"You date women who need mirrors like a diabetic needs insulin."

The sidelong glance he gave her wasn't just judge-y.

It was a challenge.

"You date men so clumsy and insecure, they create conspiracy theories about you."

"No. Worse. I date men who use the word *wiener*, apparently."

As Moore laughed, Colleen took a moment to hydrate, mentally adding an hour to their drive home. Calibrating her bladder would be a complex math problem for the next three hours.

"Let's stop talking about our failed love lives and talk about Jordy," she said, watching Moore's face in her peripheral vision for signs of how his trip had gone.

"I can't talk about Jordy without talking about my failed love life," he said with a sigh, pausing for so long, she took her eyes off the road to look at him. Stoic and staring straight ahead, he had a bleak look she didn't like.

Silence fell over them like a shroud.

Moore was someone you hung out with. Watched movies with. Talked about the fun details in a game or a song. He showed up when you moved, needed to paint a room, or had to go out of town and couldn't find a pet sitter.

And he worked hard. No, not manual labor, and her brothers often teased him for being "a suit" now, but he was the opposite of sad and bleak, and Colleen wanted to fly to Minnesota, find Cammie herself, and give her a new haircut.

With her fingers.

Wasn't the first time Colleen was driven to violent thoughts when it came to Cammie Forsythe, though. Colleen had been in her associate's degree program for nursing when Luke had come home with the news about Moore and Cammie. Pregnant at eighteen.

Cammie was eight months along at graduation; Jordy was born a week later.

And Cammie had been a terrible mother.

Colleen might not have had any standing to judge, not

being a mother herself, but she'd been raised by one of the finest and had an instinct for caring for other people. When newborn Jordy had been placed in Colleen's arms, she'd felt like an unofficial aunt, eight years before her own actual first niece had been born.

When she'd made abundant offers to babysit, Cammie had taken her up on every single one, which meant Colleen saw how Cammie parented.

And it could be summed up in a single word: selfishly.

In the fifteen years since Jordy had been born, Colleen had experienced a lot, and she had a more nuanced view of the troubles Cammie faced back then. Just eighteen and suddenly a mother and wife. Married to Moore, who was about as exciting to Cammie as a piece of white toast–and he juggled college and working forty hours a week painting houses to pay their new family's bills.

Colleen had offered to help for free, thinking she'd watch Jordy here and there for a few hours.

Instead, she ended up spending every spare hour on a rescue mission. Arriving there to find the baby screaming, his diaper waterlogged, Cammie smoking on the porch and bitching about how the baby "won't even cry himself to sleep" triggered every empathic nerve path in her. After the first few times Colleen came over, Cammie had her act down to a science, suddenly needing milk, diapers, orange juice–and disappearing for hours.

Every single day Colleen was there, which was three to four days a week.

But Cammie was always home before Moore returned, covered in paint flecks and streaks, arms so tired, they shook. On the rare occasions when Colleen was still present, she'd watched Cammie lay into him about how tired she was from "watching the baby all day."

Moore interrupted her thoughts with a throat clearing. "Jordy really likes Locke."

"What?" Colleen shook off her old memories and focused on the present. "Jordy hates everyone!"

"Everyone but you," Moore said slowly, with meaning.

No use in arguing. It was true.

"How can he like someone named Lock 'n Load?"

"Locke gets free tickets to minor league games. And he's working on getting Jordy a spot as a bat boy."

"Wow."

"Yeah."

"Did Jordy actually use the words 'I like Locke'?"

"No."

"Did you tell Jordy about the new performing arts school?" For the last ten years, Moore had hauled himself out to wherever Cammie had moved herself and Jordy—lately, Minnesota—at least four times a year to see Jordy, and brought his son back home more than twice a year. Cammie was hard-nosed on the visitations, but Moore maxed out every single one, never relinquishing a single court-ordered hour.

When the announcement of a new charter school focused on performing arts, including the theater tech work Jordy loved, had hit Luview—the school located just thirty minutes from town—Moore had instantly thought of Jordy.

Part of the trip out there was to trial-balloon the idea of having Jordy move back to Maine and live with his dad. Finally, Moore would have his kid back.

After ten long years.

"I did, but every time I mentioned it, he rolled his eyes and talked about baseball."

"Ouch."

"And the new baby."

"Double ouch."

"And how the only reason he's coming here in a few weeks to visit is because of you."

"Oh, Moore. I'm sorry. He's such a little jerk sometimes."

Moore jolted. "That's my kid you're talking about!"

"Yeah. I know. And fifteen-year-old boys with axes to grind can be little jerks. You love him so much, but Cammie's really poisoned him against you." She sighed. "I wish you'd tell him the truth about what happened when he was five."

"That's not–I wouldn't be a good father if I did."

"You'd be telling the truth, Moore. Not badmouthing her."

The set of his jaw made it clear this well-worn argument wasn't going to be resolved any differently.

Part of the reason Jordy was so negative toward his dad was that Cammie had lied and said Moore abandoned Jordy. That the fictitious abandonment was why he didn't see Moore for a year.

"You know what the psychologist said. Saying anything about Cammie could backfire."

"But it's true! She's been like that since–" Smothering her words with a sigh, she realized she had her own skeletons in the closet.

Because she'd never told Moore that Cammie had not, in fact, "been with the baby all day" so many years ago. She hadn't said anything back then because she knew Cammie would freeze her out of Jordy's life.

And Moore's.

Maybe she shouldn't throw stones when she was riding in a glass truck.

"Whoa!" Moore called out, pointing as Colleen swerved, a car suddenly appearing out of nowhere in the thickening snow.

Heart slamming, she leaned forward, flexing her feet, trying to do anything to distract herself from the close call.

"What was that?" she gasped. "No hazard lights on!"

"The road seems fine. Salted along this stretch. Just a breakdown."

"*I'm* about to have a breakdown." Hand on her heart, she let out a big exhale. "Dang."

"You okay? Need me to drive?"

She shook her head and reached for her water. "I'm fine. Just–that was close."

"On a day when we were both dumped and humiliated, the last thing we need is an accident, too."

"I can't end up in my own ER after a third date with Tim. I'd never hear the end of it!"

As they laughed, she wanted to ask more about how Jordy was handling so much change–new stepdad, new sibling–but she was happy to know he was still visiting in a few weeks.

Snow outside was getting heavier, the need for her head-lights now evident though it wasn't dark yet. As she saw the signs for I-93 North, she gave him a look.

"Should we go down to 95 and go through Portland?"

"It'll be worse there."

"It's faster."

"We always go up through Wolfeboro."

"You just go that way because of the subs at that little café you love."

"Damn right. Is it my fault my uncle got me hooked on them?"

"They are really good. Especially the chicken pesto one."

"See?"

"But worth getting stuck in a snowstorm?"

He gave her a thousand-watt smile that lit up all the gloomy, dark places inside her.

"If I have to be stuck in a snowstorm with anyone, at least it'll be with you."

"That's the sweetest thing you've ever said to me."

"You have great legs."

"Um… thanks?"

"Bet they'll taste good."

"Huh?"

"If I have to resort to cannibalism."

"You're thinking about *eating me?*" The way she said those last two words felt charged. *Too* charged. Moore smothered a smile with his palm, rubbing his chin, letting the moment fade into an unsettling, though not unpleasant, quiet.

That he trusted her to drive meant a lot, but she also knew he wouldn't be as sharp after all that travel, so it made sense to have her at the wheel.

On impulse, she decided to go with the Wolfeboro route, because it would make him happy. Moore needed more happiness. Hannah had been nice enough, though she never hung out with the gang at Bilbee's, and Moore had seemed content, if nothing else, to be with her.

Content was good enough when you were cursed.

"Oh ho ho, I get my sub after all."

"Can't have you gnawing on my tibia."

"So this is an act of self-preservation?"

"Something like that."

"You just like the chicken pesto."

"You don't know me!"

"Actually, I do." The glance he gave her made it clear he wanted to say more.

Focusing on driving, she hoped her heart would calm down so she wouldn't feel so jittery. The only thing worse than driving in heavy snow was driving in it anxious.

"I do know you, Colleen," he continued somberly. "And so does Jordy. Know what he said to me when I mentioned the new performing arts high school?"

"What?"

"He said, 'Colleen could see my sets.'"

"Awww. But you fly out there for every single one of his plays and musicals."

"Sure I do, but it's not enough."

"It's more than enough."

"I mean, I want him here. I want him to know his family. His roots are here in Luview. Mom and Dad aren't getting any younger. The Forsythe family has so many uncles and cousins. Cammie's kept him away for too long."

"You can't push hard, Moore. A kid like Jordy is going to run away if you push."

"I know."

"I know you know."

"You know damn near everything about me. You might as well be my sister, too, in addition to being Luke's."

Every drop of amusement squeezed out of her like an elephant stepped on a tube of toothpaste.

"Ha," she said weakly. "Right."

"You know my favorite foods. My favorite beer. Favorite shows. You have this uncanny ability to stop me from throwing a dart like I'm a squinting drunk. You hate that I eat peanut butter on my cheeseburgers but you always have some at the table for me anyhow. You know that I suck at quarter-round trim installation but–"

"Right," she repeated. "We're friends. We grew up together. You're my annoying younger brother from another mother."

Why wouldn't her heart stop jumping up and down like there was a trampoline in her chest?

"I'm your bonus bro," he said softly, the end of his words coming out with a huff, as if he were about to laugh but felt something other than amusement. Colleen forced her eyes to stay straight ahead, because if she looked at him, what would she see?

Not what she wanted to see in Moore's eyes.

That would never, ever happen. She'd given up long ago.

AC/DC's "You Shook Me All Night Long" came on the radio, which meant only one thing could happen next.

They sang along to it.

Then "Boulevard of Broken Dreams," which Moore made a face at and let Colleen sing all the vocals, followed by "Welcome to the Black Parade" by My Chemical Romance, which made Colleen groan and beg Moore not to do it.

"No! Please!" she shouted as Moore began singing the words, every one with the drama of Gerard Way.

"I can't believe you listen to this crap."

"You know all the words to 'Shake It Off,' Colleen, so don't judge."

And then she was forced to listen to Moore go into the tortured chorus.

"I wish you had an off button!"

"So does Jordy!"

That made her laugh. Moore's son was a delight to her, a fellow baseball nerd who went to games with her to watch the Love You team, the Cupids. No one adored the ragtag, misfit AAA league team more than Jordy, with their pink and white uniforms, hearts on every bat, and hecklers in every bleacher.

Unable to stand it any longer, she snapped the radio off.

"Hey!"

"We were losing the station to static."

"Were not!"

"Then your singing was destroying my aural nerve."

"Sorry to disappoint you aurally."

Blanking, her throat went cold with shock, the rest of her heating up.

Was he... *flirting*?

Awkward silence filled the cab of the truck, or was it just

her? She wished the weird tension in the air didn't exist, but Moore shook his head and seemed the same.

Casual, easygoing Moore. No need to feel uneasy around him. He just did his thing, and seconds turned into minutes, and soon, he was turning the radio back on, shifting from station to station.

Colleen began to feel her wrists tighten and her elbows ache. Her eyes sharpened to take in the falling snow, the fading light, and she tried to stop berating herself for being unable to breathe.

"This is looking bad," he finally said as he landed on an alternative station that was pumping out a Celtic rock fusion song.

"Yeah. But I've driven through worse."

"Me, too. Remember the storm where the deer had her baby right in the middle of the road?"

"You were with Luke when that happened."

"I thought you were there."

"No."

"I guess I'm inserting you into my memories," he said with a quiet speculation that made her heart gallop again. Was she imagining this? What was going on? The skin around her belly began to tingle. For as cold as it was outside, she was heating up fast in here.

A long, slow breath helped center her, but then Moore leaned toward her and she got a whiff of his cologne, which acted like an EpiPen straight to the heart.

Zoom!

"Any chance you have water?" he asked, searching the large center console.

"Yep. Brought two water bottles and two coffees."

"Seriously?"

"You know I always do that."

"I know. I just can't believe you always do that."

"What does that mean?"

"You're always prepared. Not just prepared..." His voice trailed off as he found the bottles, then grabbed a small thermos and opened it, peering in. "This one mine?"

"If it's red, then yes."

He took a sip.

"Milk, no sugar," he said. "Down to the smallest detail. You do these things as if you really care."

"I do these things because it heads off problems down the road."

"Nah. I think it's because you're secretly a marshmallow underneath that tough exterior."

"How dare you!" she joked. "Don't let my deep, dark truth become known! I work hard to keep it hidden!"

"Not hard enough. You're one of the kindest people I know, Colleen."

There it was again. That tone.

The tone she must be imagining.

"I think kindness is underrated," she said sincerely. If he was going to talk like this, might as well join in. The road conditions were deteriorating and she was genuinely concerned. Not enough to stop–yet–and if they could get to Wolfeboro, they had a chance of getting some food and assessing the situation.

Besides, she enjoyed his conversation. Moore had a way of taking sudden verbal detours to places that made her feel better about the world afterwards.

"You're right," he said between sips of coffee, staring straight ahead as she watched her speed. They were on a wider highway now, though two lanes only, but she kept going at 55 mph and looked at the clock, then the odometer.

Well on their way.

Her phone buzzed with a text. She motioned for Moore to look at it.

"What if it's a sexy text?" he joked.

"From who? Tim?" A snort was all she could muster.

"It's Luke."

"Definitely no sexy texts there." She shuddered while Moore laughed and squinted at the phone.

"He wants to know our route. Says the roads are bad up around Fryeburg."

"Ok, Dad," she said, looking at the phone. "Luke is my little brother. He's not supposed to parent me!"

"He's worried. Understandably. Last thing he needs is to lose someone else in a car accident."

Moore could also get morbid. *Fast.*

"I know. Believe me, I know."

Silence filled the cab, but no tension. The weight of Amber's death rested in every molecule. Moore and Colleen had been Luke's rock, filling roles her parents couldn't. They'd both shouldered that responsibility without a second's hesitation, and for that, Colleen loved Moore so much.

Loved him on levels she didn't know people had until they'd gone through hell together.

No matter what, she knew Moore would always be there for the people he loved.

Moore began texting on her phone. "I'll give him the route." He hit Send, and while Colleen wanted to look at the phone, she forced herself to focus on driving.

"Huh," Moore said. "Luke says Wolfeboro is probably safest."

"Good thing, because we're only ten minutes away at the rate we're going."

"He says there's a good chance it'll clear up after that. Told him we'll head up 160 to 117."

"It would be stupid to go south at this point."

"You look tense." Moore put the phone down and

rummaged through the console, pulling out her coffee thermos. "Want some?"

Grateful to be taken care of, she took the thermos that he gently opened and drank greedily, not realizing how much she needed it.

Her phone buzzed.

"Luke again. Says not to take any dumb chances."

"Tell him to check in on Sandwich."

"Your cat is fine."

"My cat needs someone to just peek in on her."

"She's a cat who ignores everyone. You've only been gone a few hours. She'll be fine."

"Just text him." Opening her mouth, she stretched her jaw, a dull pain beginning to settle in there.

Moore did as asked, then frowned at her phone. "He says he can't. A car hit that huge oak right by the Fields' CPA office. Took out the whole building."

"WHAT?"

"Yep," Moore said, squinting harder at the phone. The man needed reading glasses but wouldn't admit it to himself. "Says all hands on deck over there. Power lines down, too."

"Anyone we know?"

"You, uh, were dating Tim Fields until, well..."

"I meant the driver of the car."

Moore texted Luke and waited.

"Message not sent."

Colleen groaned. "We lost the signal?"

Settling back in his seat with an exhale that puffed his lips a bit, he sighed. "Guess so."

"I really hope he can check on Sandwich."

"I think he's a bit busy." Moore searched in the console, the clatter of her dad's CD jewel cases making it clear he was looking for some longer-form music to listen to. Meanwhile,

Colleen was running through every worst-case scenario in her mind regarding her beloved cat.

Someone would check on her. She knew in her bones no one in her family would abandon her sweetie.

Losing the cellphone signal didn't help matters, though. If road conditions were so bad up north that people were sliding into trees and toppling them, maybe she and Moore needed to reassess.

Opening her mouth and suggesting they get a hotel room for the night could be like ending the world, though. Humiliation could kill you. If Moore made a sexy crack, or a joke that made it clear he didn't think of her in a romantic way at all, it would destroy a little bit more of her soul.

She knew there was nothing between them. Never would be. But that was different than hearing it straight from his mouth.

For the next fifteen minutes, they listened to Radiohead and drove on until they hit the center of Wolfeboro.

Which was dead, barren and empty, the way any pragmatic town accustomed to snowstorms would be. One lonely gas station had its lights on and, without a word, she pulled into it, Moore opening his door before she could grab her own handle.

Always fill your gas tank in a storm. You never knew when you'd need it.

Bzzzz

Her phone went nuts, tons of texts coming in suddenly. As she grabbed it, her soundtrack changed from music to the clank and clunk of Moore pumping gas.

Luke's texts were stacked neatly on her screen:

Stay on 28.

Fields' CPA office destroyed by that old oak tree Dad's been eyeing for years.

Single car accident. Fatality. Out of towner.

Colleen gasped at that one and texted back:

Did they make it to the ER?

Her co-workers rarely lost anyone. Normally, if people died, they were dead on arrival.

No. DOA.

She winced.

Were you the first responder?

He replied back instantly.

Rusty

Rusty Johnson was the town manwhore, who didn't even care about her Third Date Colleen status.

Or, as he'd said, "We can just have some fun twice, then." The wink he'd added made her laugh so hard, she'd burst blood vessels under her eyes.

Sadly, there had been nights she'd considered his come-on, but knew damn well Luke would never let her hear the end of it if she slept with a member of the town's police force.

Besides, Rusty wasn't her type.

Can you check on Sandwich? she wrote back.

Mom already did. She's fine. And we're all connected at the camp.

Connected?

Dad put up loose ropes.

Ropes?

Between the buildings.

We're not Little House on the Prairie, Luke! We don't need to tie a rope to Pa when he goes and checks the horses.

Tell that to Dad.

Colleen was laughing through her nose as she heard the loud click that meant the tank was full. Looking over her shoulder, she saw Moore pull the nozzle out, replace it in the pump's holder, and push a button on the electronic payment screen.

Normal. He looked so normal, living life and going about

his business. How many times had Moore filled a gas tank? Bought a candy bar? Delivered a package to the post office, wiped down a kitchen counter, mowed his lawn?

Normal life appealed to her. Fed her. Made the world make sense.

Snowstorms like this were normal, and yet they weren't.

And now she was fighting the rising anxiety that said she was good enough to be Moore's friend, but not to be more.

Who knew that offering to do the guy a favor by picking him up at the airport would be so fraught with emotion?

The passenger door opened and a shock of cold wind and flakes hit her face, making the air in her lungs go icy as she inhaled sharply.

"There," he said. "Someone taped a note to the pump. They left the pumps on for credit card use only. Store closed due to storm."

Instantly nervous, she looked around at the quiet town. "What do you think?"

"I think my favorite sub shop is closed," he said, so morose that she burst out laughing.

Her phone buzzed.

"You have a signal?"

"For now. Luke said Sandwich is fine. Mom checked on her."

"Of course she did. You all live a few hundred feet from each other."

"I know. But..."

"Did he say anything else?"

"Fatality. The car that hit the tree. Single driver. Out of towner."

"Ouch." Moore went quiet. "That's terrible."

"Yes."

"I have an idea. My uncle's cabin."

Her legs turned to jelly.

"Hmm?"

"It's not far from here. He let me use it two summers ago. He never changes the key code. We can head toward it and if the storm keeps up, we can stay there for the night."

Jelly... she was just a heart and a brain floating in jelly.

"Okay."

"I know you're worried about Sandwich, but if the storm's that bad..."

"Sure."

"You have a shift at the hospital?"

"Not until four tomorrow."

"The main roads will be clear by noon, easy."

"Sure." How could he not see that her entire body was quivering before him?

"It's right off Route 28. We don't even have to deviate from our route."

Bzzzz

It was Luke again.

Where are you? he texted.

Wolfeboro, she replied. *Moore's uncle has a cabin near here. He thinks we should head there and maybe ride out the storm.*

"What're you doing?" Moore asked in an amused voice, drinking his coffee.

"Telling Officer Worrywart our plans."

"We might not need the cabin. It's about twenty more minutes north. Gets us closer to Luview, and if it's clear there, we'll just head home."

"Sure."

It seemed that Colleen was now only capable of bland one-syllable words when it came to spending the night with Moore.

If she could reach up and slap herself, she would. How many times had she spent the night with Moore before? Countless sleepovers. Camping trips. Plenty of vacations where Moore tagged along over the years. This was nothing new, she chided herself.

Except... they were alone.

And both were single, suddenly.

And Moore had definitely been flirting earlier.

Right?

"Do we have any food? You brought coffee and water, but if we get stuck?"

"Just the emergency pack in the back. Protein bars and jerky."

"Has to be good enough. Nothing's open here."

A snow plow lumbered by. The scrape of metal on asphalt was followed by the sprinkling sound of sand being spread. That was their cue.

Pulling out slowly, Colleen steered the truck onto the road behind the plow, grateful for the easy path.

"Creep" played on the speakers, Moore's baritone hitting super-deep notes with a mournful tone as they drove, the sound eerie yet calming. Driving behind the snow plow at thirty-five then forty miles an hour, they bought themselves five miles of easy driving until the plow turned off the main route at the town line, where road conditions abruptly became much harsher.

"I'm sorry," Moore said as the song ended.

"For what?"

"For putting you in this situation."

"Because I picked you up at the airport? It could happen to anyone."

"I should have driven myself last week. Then I wouldn't have had to put you out."

"You didn't drive last week because Hannah needed to borrow your car. Remember?"

He muttered a curse word. "That's right. And she dumped me by text!"

"I hope she didn't steal your car."

He pulled out his phone. "No service. Can't even ask her where she left my keys."

"Probably in the ignition. One of the Morgenstern boys has been joyriding."

"Hah." His eyebrows knit, the tips of his lashes almost touching them as she glanced over. "Hannah." Washing his face with his hands, he shook his head. "What a mess."

"Not your mess anymore."

"No. She's not. But ouch."

"Yeah. Sorry."

"Not your fault I can't keep a relationship going."

"It's not your fault, either, Moore! She dumped you because you made your child a priority. Who does that?"

"Maybe I'm somehow doing it all wrong."

"Doing what all wrong?"

"All of it. Parenting. Dating."

"You parent just fine. Better than fine."

"He hates me and I see him a grand total of fifty days a year, Colleen. I'm not parenting 'better than fine.'"

"Those fifty days a year happen through sheer force of will on your part!"

Vehement and outraged that Moore would even entertain the thought that he was a bad father, Colleen unleashed, relieved to let some of her anxiety out.

"But Jordy doesn't want me there."

"Jordy wants you! He's just a teen figuring everything out, and you're a safe target."

"I'm tired of being a target when what I want to be is a dad."

"You are a dad."

"I'm a punching bag."

"Because you're the only parent who loves him uncondi- tionally, so it's safe for him to vent."

Shocked, Moore's face showed it. Colleen felt like she'd scored a point in a game where winning meant nothing.

"You think that's why he's such an ass to me lately?"

"Yes. Cammie makes it impossible for him to talk about his real feelings. She also blocks him from seeing you as much as she can, and she badmouths you. On some level, Jordy wants you to rescue him. You can't, legally, but you still show up, so he's confused."

"How do you know this? Did–did he tell you this?"

"Yes and no. He's still so angry that you 'disappeared' for a year."

Moore slammed his fist on the dash.

"I did not disappear!"

"I know that. You know that. But–"

Black ice is a treacherous demon in the mountains of northern New England, especially under hidden new snow, and when the truck swerved, Colleen instantly knew what she'd hit. A shot of adrenaline, different from anxiety, made her numbness vanish as her senses sharpened. Fishtailing, she turned the steering wheel gently to correct the alignment, her foot lightly pressing the brake to slow down enough but not stop.

Easing off the brake, she hesitated until the wheels touched snow, feeling the traction, correcting the course again with steering.

"Yikes," Moore said softly, once it was clear that the crisis had been averted. "Black ice?"

"Yep. Under the snow."

"I'm not sure where we are, but I think my uncle's place is up ahead. No GPS. I remember an exit with a small pond right there, and the cabin's on the other side of the pond."

"I think we'll be staying there tonight," she said tightly. "And I can't talk anymore."

"No prob."

41

Senses already heightened, Colleen moved into a different state of consciousness. Her eyes fought the dizzying influx of flakes against the windshield, hands gripping the wheel, neck and back tight as she leaned forward and drove.

"I can drive," Moore said quietly.

She shook her head. "If we stop now, we'll be stuck on the road. How much further to your uncle's?"

A sign for Ossipee, the next-nearest town, was almost obscured by attached snow.

"Next right turn!" he announced, in a voice filled with so much relief, she nearly cried.

Slowing down, she worked the brake carefully, the downslope more dangerous than going uphill.

"Here! Turn here."

Her blinker on, she did as told, but nanosecond by nanosecond, everything went wrong.

First, the pressure of the ball of her foot on the brake pedal felt different.

Second, the right wheel began to jump and skitter on the road.

Third, Moore grabbed the arm rest and braced himself.

As the car slid to the right, Moore's arm stretched across her front, as if cushioning her blow. Colleen felt her mind split, part of it going into hiding in preparation for the pain that was about to hit her, the other leaping into strategic action to make decisions about how to move next.

Physics won, though, dominating everything.

It always does.

As the wheels got air, the truck tilted toward Moore, slamming his shoulder into the door. Colleen was pulled by g-force across the center console, the gearshift digging into her lower ribs with a pain she couldn't scream out. It was the kind of blow that could permanently damage your liver, her nurse's mind told her.

A low hum filled her ears, cold air and snow suddenly inside the cab.

"COLLEEN!" Moore shouted. "The water!"

"Water?" There was no water. Just snow, and was he opening the windows? Why would he do that in a snowstorm? Silly man.

Unable to think of anything else as the world tilted on its axis, she searched for the window controls in the door to counteract his stupidity, her hand coming up to open air. The seatbelt cut into her neck, her bones suddenly useless as she hung by the safety belt, her head against Moore's ribs, his shouted words nothing but the vibration of his skin and bone against her ear.

The cab tipped entirely on its side, but one wheel caught the ground, Colleen's foot slipping from the brake to the accelerator, and the truck lurched forward into a strange sort of spin before she could try to press the brake again.

They flipped.

The turnover itself was a blur, but the shock of ice-cold water filling her boots as the truck turned again, Moore suddenly gone underwater, was too much.

Water.

Ice.

Cold.

Shock.

Dark.

Then her face was underwater, too, as she hung mostly upside down, unable to breathe.

Chapter Two

Moore

Damn it.

Think. Think!

On impulse, he'd lowered the windows. He didn't know exactly how deep the pond was, but if they submerged, pressure from the water might make it impossible ever to escape from the truck. In a split-second decision, he'd chosen freedom over restraint, unclicking his seatbelt at the exact moment his side of the truck had rolled over.

Squeezing through the window felt like wearing a cement suit.

A wet cement suit that was forty degrees cold.

As Moore broke the surface, his shoes found muck, but he could stand, the water only four feet deep. Sloshing through it, he moved as fast as he could to Colleen's side, reaching through the half-open window. The truck was upside down and Colleen's entire body was underwater.

He had one minute, if that.

Reaching in blindly, he felt for her lap, but if he searched too low, his face was in the water. His thick coat was an obstacle, but his hands began to shake as he struggled to take it off, fingers suddenly as useful as frozen sausages.

Somehow, he did it.

He had no choice.

Weighed down by his shoes, he went into water rescue mode, kicking them off. Cold feet were nothing compared to a thrashing friend he had to save.

Colleen, Colleen, Colleen, he chanted in his mind as she thrashed, her attempts to unclip herself the same as his. If he went back in through his open passenger-side window, could he unclip her?

A knife. He needed a knife. Slashing the seatbelts would do it.

Panic rose up as he realized she was literally dying, inches from him, and he was debating strategy. Her life was in his hands, and the weight of it crushed his heart.

Desperate, he made his way back to his side of the truck, taking the deepest breath he could before closing his eyes and going in head first, hands seeking hers.

She grasped his, hard, and guided it to the buckle.

He felt the click rather than heard it, just as an enormous rush of bubbles filled the space around them. Hands finding her shoulders, he pulled as hard as he could, using leverage to extract her from his side of the truck.

She was confused and flailing as he changed his plan, grabbed what felt like her waistband, and yanked hard, kicking and pulling back, doing whatever it took to break the surface of the water before it was too late.

You can't die, he thought to himself, the words more chilling than the water. *I haven't told you how much I love you.*

Feet catching the mucky floor of the pond, he now had the

leverage he needed to pull her fully out, turning her face toward the air. An enormous inhale, choking and raw, filled his ear as Colleen gasped hard, the sound frantic and surreal.

"Breathe," he rasped, unsure whether he was telling her or himself, then realizing they both needed to do it.

She passed out, half floating, half in his arms.

Wind whipped the snowflakes at a diagonal, his arms reflexively lifting her up as he trudged through the water to the safety of land. White-out conditions weren't unfamiliar to him, but being in a soaking wet wool suit, in his socks, carrying a limp woman who'd just nearly died, was new.

Up ahead, he saw the dark outline of a house. Was it his uncle's cabin? They were so close.

Even if it wasn't, the laws of basic survival applied here: Without shelter, they would die. Surely any resident would take them in, or forgive them for breaking in. His thigh muscles burned from the strain of carrying her, as well as the violent shivers that had just begun.

"One–foot–at–a–time," he said aloud for no other reason than to hear a voice, any voice. Carrying an unconscious Colleen in his arms meant convincing himself she was fine, the occasional warmth from her breathing compelling him forward.

"You–can't–die," he said, hoping the crazy words would wake her up. "Luke–would–kill–me."

He was approaching a stand of stately pines stretching so high up into the sky that whiteness obscured their tops. The cabin was just beyond, but his feet were blocks of ice, and he was too close to collapsing. Dropping Colleen into a snowbank wasn't just bad manners.

It could kill them both.

History unwound itself in his mind as snowflakes stung his face like little bees. His biceps groaned and a very unstable sense began deep inside him, as if his bones and ligaments had just had a meeting and decided there wasn't a quorum and they didn't have to work together.

"No," he ordered them with a strong huff. "Nope. We're making it."

If Colleen were awake, she'd tell him to toughen up, stop being a wimp, do it for Jordy.

And he *would* survive for Jordy, but he'd make damn sure Colleen survived, too.

There had been very few moments in Moore Mottin's life when his actions literally determined whether someone lived or perished. Working as a jeweler wasn't exactly dangerous business.

But right now, he was just feet that moved forward, arms that cradled Colleen, and one big ball of persistence.

The wind died down slightly, his ears picking up unexpected stillness as the thick trees began to cushion the roar of the storm. Relief set in.

They would make it.

Even if the cabin was unoccupied, he could break a window and get her in.

The joy he felt at spotting a chimney was impossible to describe. Heat. Shelter.

The rest he could figure out in time.

As he reached the edge of the first step leading up to the porch, his foot missed, knee buckling, Colleen nearly spilling out onto the hard wood. Protecting her meant letting his knee absorb the hit.

So he did.

Laboriously, he made the trek up the three wooden steps, and then they were under the porch roof in front of a door he did not recognize.

This was not his uncle's cabin.

And it was definitely not occupied.

Crouching carefully, glutes screaming, he set Colleen

down with a gentle "I'm sorry" murmured under his breath and stared at the lockbox. To the right of the heavy wooden door was a window covered by thick curtains. Below the window sat a flower pot, the top coated in three inches of snow, the top at an angle, the wind sculpting it.

Peeling off his suit jacket, he grabbed the terracotta pot, wrapped his jacket around it, then paused.

Set it down.

Tested the window, lifting it.

Old hunting cabins were locked up but not perfectly secure, and as he rattled the window frame, he could see the ancient thumb lock straining, millimeters away from releasing. A few good shoves and he did it, the window raising with a loud creak. Moore half expected a pane to escape and shatter at his feet, but it didn't.

He was in.

The flower pot came in handy as a step stool, but going in hands first was like climbing back into the truck to release Colleen—only this time, he didn't need to hold his breath.

"Moore?" he heard her cry out just as his shoulder shifted, spilling his cheekbone onto a dusty wooden floor that had last seen varnish during Eisenhower's presidency.

"Hold on!" he shouted, slowly getting to his feet, his body craving warmth. Moving to the door, he found the deadbolt and opened it easily, the outside lockbox not a deterrent.

As he pulled the door open and locked eyes with Colleen, a rush of fear shot through him.

Fear and love.

They were so close. And he'd almost lost her.

"Help," she said. "I can't move." Limbs jerking in funny, erratic patterns, she struggled to sit up but couldn't. Empathy flooded him and he bent down so fast, he forgot his own exhaustion and fell on one side, his hip hitting the scarred wood floor.

"Wha' happened?" she muttered as he leaned into her, righting himself, his brain half fog, half terror. But his arms knew what to do.

They reached for her.

"We skidded off the road," he said gently, though a huge gust of wind blew a mouthful of snow into his face. "Tipped over into a gulley filled with water."

"You saved me," she whispered, her body jerking then going still, eyes on him, wide as hubcaps.

Shaking was good, he knew. It meant the body was trying to pump blood into the extremities.

Going still was bad. It meant all the blood was being conserved for the heart.

"Let's get you inside," he said, reaching down and dragging her in, shuffling backward, her legs twisted but not broken. He huffed his way through moving her, then closed the door.

Ahhh. Blessed relief from the wind and the snow. Shivering enough for the two of them, he looked around and spotted an old Franklin stove, a very dried-out stack of wood next to it.

Tinder. It would burn fast in a few hours, but it was better than nothing.

"Heat. Need heat." Colleen's voice was strong but a bit detached.

"Working on it," he said, reaching for one of the split pieces of wood on the top of the pile.

"I mean me. Blanket... quilt? Something. I'm frozen."

A plaintive quality to her voice made him work faster. Colleen didn't plead.

She *ordered*.

Something was very wrong. She wasn't out of the woods yet.

An old afghan that puffed up a cloud of dust when he

pulled it off a chair was better than nothing, and Moore gently placed it over the cold, still Colleen. She just blinked, unmoving, scaring the hell out of him again.

"I'm getting this fire going." Fortunately, there were plenty of old newspapers, and a small basket of fire starters. Whoever owned this cabin had left it reasonably well stocked. With luck, there would be food and water, too.

Thank God this place existed at all. Worst case, he'd melt snow and they'd be hungry for a night.

Ten minutes ago, he was carrying her here through whiteout conditions and whistling wind that soared into screams.

Fifteen minutes ago, he was under freezing cold water, terrified she was about to drown.

How quickly life could change.

"Moore," she said softly. "Thank you."

"What are you thanking me for?" As he pulled more wood from the pile, searching for smaller pieces to add to the stack of newspapers, kindling, and firestarters, he realized how raw his fingers were. A dull numbness, cold and soaking wet, had settled deep in his bones.

He was a robot.

An ice machine.

But he couldn't fall apart until he had her safe.

"Not shivering," she murmured, the tone making him turn and look at her. Colleen's eyelids were drooping, and a deep gong–a loud, ominous alarm–went off in his head.

Hypothermia.

Damn it.

Right next to the fire starters, he found a big box of blue-tipped matches. With more dexterity than he thought his frozen fingers possessed, he managed to light some edges of the newspaper, careful to spark five different flames. This would have to do to get the woodstove going, he thought as he blew on it softly, then turned to attend to Colleen.

Who was slumped over.

"No!" he called out, moving fast to shake her shoulders, her eyes opening suddenly. Glassy and unfocused, they terrified him. Her sandy blonde hair looked like seaweed against her shoulders and cheeks, a stray strand across one eyebrow.

Pulling her close, he tried to warm her. They were on the floor, about three feet from the edge of an unmade bed.

"Colleen!" he said sharply. She blinked rapidly, then squeezed his arm.

"I'm not shivering," she said slowly, slurring. "Nee' to ge' warm."

"I'm trying," he said, looking at the fire, which thankfully was showing signs of catching. Standing, he scanned the room. A small trunk served as a coffee table, in front of two wood-frame chairs with cheap vinyl cushions.

The chance there were blankets in that trunk was good.

His attention pinged between the trunk and Colleen.

"Sit up," he ordered her.

"Can't."

If he kept her talking, everything would be fine.

"Maybe you just cursed yourself," he told her, trying to get her goat, get a rise out of her, anything to keep her talking.

"Huh?"

"Third Date Colleen. Never thought you'd end up in your own ER after a third date." He lifted the lid of the trunk.

She blew a laugh through her nose. "Too far away from Luview for me to be in the ER."

Score! Two big feather-down comforters, both of them a cream color with a patina that spoke more to their age than to a color palette at a textile factory. His fingers screamed as he gripped the thick, soft fabric, but he grabbed the top one and brought it to her, covering her.

As he started to wrap himself in the other one, he realized he was still soaking wet.

So was she.

Thin hints of warmth began to creep out of the tiny woodstove and he turned his attention to the fire again, blowing on it lightly, then checking the flue.

Whew. All was well. He added a few small pieces of wood he found littering the backside of the woodstack and hoped the fire would continue to take.

"I'm cold. Wet. Brain slow. Mouth slower," Colleen whispered, with a tiny smile.

"Since when do you have a slow mouth?"

"Moore."

His stomach dropped. Looking down at her, his down comforter on his shoulders, he panicked. Stress flooded him like he was underwater again, fumbling for her seatbelt, her life in his hands.

Pressure like that belonged to people like her brother, Luke.

A police officer. A first responder.

Not desk jockeys like Moore.

Heart pounding furiously but missing a beat here and there, as if he had to warm up enough to melt the ice in his bloodstream, he tossed the comforter on the unmade bed and went into the kitchen, opening cabinets frantically.

"What are you doing?" she slurred.

"Looking for alcohol."

"You want to *drink* at a time like this?"

There it was. Everyone had a liquor cabinet in a hunting cabin. *Liquor cabinet* might be too fancy a term, but the bottle of cheap rum was certainly a welcome sight.

In a separate cabinet, he found two mugs, one with the Bilbee's Tavern logo on it–*If we don't have it, you shouldn't drink it*–and the other plain.

Hands shaking so badly, he felt like one of those paint-mixing machines at the hardware store, he managed to pour a half inch in a mug and another half inch on the counter before he stopped and just drank a shot or two straight from the bottle.

The swallow *burned*.

Burning never felt so good.

Walking over to Colleen, he sat gingerly on the floor, his skin no longer a shield, his body a mess, knee screaming from the hit it had taken on the stairs.

But he was better off than she was, so he had to keep going.

For her sake.

"Here." He held the mug to her lips.

"What's that?"

"Rum."

"I don't like rum."

"We're not at Bilbee's and Rider isn't working the bar, so you don't get a choice, Colleen. Drink."

"Moore?"

"Yeah?"

"I'm scared."

"Me, too. So drink this, honey, and let's warm up a little."

The word *honey* slipped out. Her eyes softened with something so close to attraction, he did a double take. Their faces were inches from each other, his body curled around hers. Her breath was hot against his hand.

"Not s'posed to drink alcohol when you have hypothermia."

"Do you?"

"I'm not shivering. Tired. Want to sleep."

"No, no, *no sleeping*!"

"Call 911, Moore."

"I can't, our phones are in the truck."

"Landline?"

He cursed himself. In the rush to get her warm and safe, he hadn't even thought of it. Searching the tiny cabin, though, uncovered no magic landline.

"No luck."

She groaned.

"We—Colleen, this is the best I can do!"

But was it enough? Would it be enough to keep her from dying?

She couldn't die. He would not let that happen.

Pushing the mug to her lips again, he got her to drink a tiny bit. She swallowed slowly, then lifted her head.

"Burns."

"Good. It's something."

"I'm not here, Moore."

"What?"

"I'm not cold. Not in pain. Just... not here."

"You have to be here." Panic zoomed inside him, with a resolution to do whatever it took to snap her out of this. No phone. No help. Just him and Colleen in a cold cabin with a bottle of rum.

The universe had a sick sense of humor.

He returned to the fire. One thing was going right, at least, because it was burning nicely. Adding another piece of wood, a thicker one, was something he could do, and it bought him a little time to think.

Can't feed a fire too fast, he knew. You had to pace it. Too slow and it would starve, too fast and it would smother.

"Moore?"

"Yeah?"

"I need you."

"I'm here."

"No. I mean, I *need* you. There's only one way for me to be okay. I have to start shivering. Have to get warmer."

"You can have my quilt." Standing, he began to pull it off, ready to cover her with it, anything to improve her situation, to make her feel better.

"Not enough. I have to get out of my wet clothes." She flopped a helpless hand against her knee. "I can't move."

"You want me to undress you?"

"Yes. And you, too."

Processing her words was taking far more effort than it should.

"You want me to take both our clothes off?"

"Yes. Naked."

"Naked?"

"I need you to get us both naked. *Now.*"

"You—you want to have sex?" he barked out in disbelief.

"Being naked together is the only way to save my life."

Chapter Three

Colleen

Naked.

It was the best option.

Brain fog was real, her blood like a cherry slushie, moving through her veins at half speed. Nursing had taught her that she was at risk of cardiac arrest right now. Warming up too fast would hurt her. The rum Moore gave her was nice, but not the right treatment.

She needed to drink warm fluids, to be dry, lots of blankets, and Moore's naked body pressed against hers, to slowly heat her to the point of shivering.

Shivering was good.

Shivering would be a relief.

"You want us both naked? Seriously?"

"Heat, Moore. Need heat."

He stood, wincing and moving slowly. For the first time, her slush-filled mind realized Moore was injured, too. Not as bad as she was, but fear surged through her, turning her calm, cold slowness into a more active terror.

They could both die.

No, she thought. *We can't do that to Jordy.*

Or Sandwich.

Flicking a light switch on the wall, Moore scowled at the fixture. "Electricity's off. But I bet they use gas for the stove. No automatic gas generator. Wonder if they're weekenders. Might not have turned the tank off. I'll find a kettle. Get something hot in you."

"Moore." Dark spots filled her vision. "No time. Slow heat. Wet clothes off. Find scissors. A knife." Her capacity for lining up words into full thoughts was fading.

"A knife? For what?"

"Cut clothes."

Alarm flashed across his face, his steps fast as he bent down to her, reaching under the blanket to grab the hem of her sweater. Pulling up, he moved her arms. A dull shock ran through her, heavy and painful, and she made a choking sound.

"Slow. My heart."

"Your heart?"

"Move too fast... heart attack."

"You could have a *heart attack* if I move you too fast?" Incredulity and shock filled his voice as she nodded.

"Cut off. Easier. Safer."

"Safer?"

"I have hypothermia," she said, forcing the words out. "Mild now. Getting worse."

"It can get *worse*?"

"Hard to stay awake. Need warmth. Cut my clothes off, loser!"

A harsh laugh burst out of him at the old insult from when they were kids, but it did what it needed to do, shaking him out of his weird hesitation. He went to the kitchen and pulled out drawers until he found what he was looking for. Striding back to her, Moore took the knife blade and slipped it under her shirt, cutting carefully up to the collar, exposing her bra.

Of all the days to wear her old, overstretched one, the boring beige of function.

Then again, she hadn't exactly been planning to be a Victoria's Secret model today.

Colleen would have laughed if she'd had the energy. Moore was staring at her front-clasp bra, his expression one that had never factored into all her years of fantasies about him undressing her. In fact, this entire scenario had never occurred to her.

"Arms," she said as Moore quickly cut from armpit to wrist, her soaked shirt now off. Moving one arm took all her energy, the black spots blooming like oil spills before her eyes.

She panted, conserving energy, as Moore set the knife down and reached for the button on her jeans.

If only she could feel them, she imagined his fingers would be like icicles.

A wave of heat made her skin hurt fiercely, her attention drawn to the growing fire in the stove.

"Sorry," Moore murmured. "Let me try this." The button unpopped, the zipper lowered, but she felt very little as he pulled her wet jeans down over her hips, stopping to untie her boots. Of course she had to wear her lace-ups today.

"Sorry," she muttered. "Should have worn the zip-ups."

"Next time you plan to flip a truck in an unexpected blizzard, go for Uggs."

Of all the things Moore could have said as he undressed her in the least sexy way possible, this was what made her laugh. The sound was tinny and muted by her chest going tight, pain radiating from a shoulder she was starting to realize she'd injured.

Severely.

Maybe that was why she couldn't move. Not just hypothermia.

Moore gently peeled off her socks, her toes moving slowly by sheer force of will. Couldn't feel the damn things, but she saw movement, which was a good sign.

Then Moore stared down at her.

"Can you lift your hips?"

"Is that your version of dirty talk in bed?"

The way he reeled back in surprise made her smile.

Then he grinned, a light in his eyes she'd never seen before. "*You're* the one who asked *me* to get naked."

"I'll take that as a yes."

Rumbling laughter poured out of him, giving her a chance to really study his movements as she did her best to lift her ample ass. The stroke of his fingers on her chilled skin was something she wanted to feel, but couldn't.

Moore Mottin was taking all her clothes off.

And he had no idea what she was about to propose next.

Clad only in panties and bra now, she looked at him. "Cover me with both quilts."

He did so. She felt a prickly hot sensation in her right shoulder, the injured one. Getting blood to flow would be tough.

And hurt a lot.

"Now you."

"I'm supposed to get naked?"

"Yes."

"And then what? Wrap myself in a blanket?" As he said the words, he fumbled with his top button, struggling so much that he gave up. Hands shaking, thighs quivering, Moore was a motley mess, she realized.

Tears would have filled her eyes if she weren't so tired.

"Just get naked."

He grabbed the placket of his shirt and ripped hard, a button popping off and striking Colleen's cheekbone. As she watched, she realized that his shoes were gone.

"What happened to your shoes?"

"Kicked them off underwater."

"You carried me all the way here in *socks?*"

"Yes."

"That's insane!"

He just shrugged.

And stood before her, torn shirt exposing his chest, the cuffs still buttoned. Reaching for his belt, he slowly opened it, letting the buckle hang as he unbuttoned his pants. The zipper sounded like a sigh when he pulled it down.

Keenly aware of her own body under the down comforter, she felt her ass first.

Of all the places to get sensation back.

A slab of cold concrete, it didn't really feel like part of her body.

Lifting one foot, then the other, he took his socks off. Peeling his pants off was a slog, the fabric tight against his athlete's body. Moore had been a baseball player for years, basketball in the winter, and in his early thirties, he still possessed the fine-tuned lines of a man in shape.

If Colleen weren't so injured, she'd be incredibly turned on by now.

Watching his unscripted striptease might get her blood moving faster, if nothing else, making Moore's undressing the actual act that saved her life.

"Okay. How naked do I go?" he joked, standing before her in tight boxer briefs, shivering.

"Get a blanket."

"You need them more than I do." His words were muted

slightly as he bent down before the woodstove, poking at it, giving her a fine, fine view of his backside.

And that was the moment she knew she would not die. If she could think about sex and lust, she was biologically out of the danger zone.

You couldn't run from a bear and have an orgasm at the same time.

Colleen Luview couldn't drool over Moore Mottin's fine, nearly naked ass while dying of hypothermia.

Another log on the fire and Moore seemed satisfied, turning back to her.

Colleen's left arm worked better now, so she lifted the covers, the shock of cold air making it clear she was warming up, even if it didn't seem like it.

"Get in here with me. I need your body."

"Again, Colleen, these are the worst come-on lines."

"Your heat. I need your body heat. Get in here."

His eyes flitted to a spot behind her. "Would the bed be better?"

"Anything is better than arguing." A spasm, hard and painful, hit her upper arm. Closing her eyes, she bent her head down and sucked in a breath, the cold whistling through her back teeth.

"What's wrong?"

"I don't know. My chest."

Instantly, he was under the quilt with her, hands lifting her up, sliding her forward. She was suddenly in his arms, face against his chest, her cheek cold against his pecs.

"Moving you to the bed. Cold floor isn't helping," he said in a commanding tone she didn't know he was capable of. Laid down carefully on the bed, she watched him disappear, then reappear with the two comforters.

Then he crawled onto the bed on all fours, positioning the blankets, hovering over her. His breath was warm and smelled surprisingly sweet, eyes filled with worry.

"Tell me what to do, Colleen. How do you want this?"

"Now who's throwing out bad pick-up lines?"

Taking the lead, he stretched out next to her.

"As much skin against mine as possible. You're warmer."

"I'm an Olympic athlete compared to you, Colleen. You remind me of one of those wax figures in Madame Tussaud's museum."

"Then your job is to make me melt."

The press of his leg against hers made Colleen wish she could feel more of this, but the pain in her chest and her generally frozen state dominated. This was not how she wanted to die, ninety percent naked in Moore's arms, felled by a heart attack from hypothermia.

Worst of all, she hadn't shaved her legs in a week. Moore's calves were brushing against Bigfoot down there.

And then she realized she hadn't exactly landscaped other parts of her body recently, either.

"Good grief," she muttered to herself as Moore tucked the down comforter around the edge of the side opposite him, her skin going prickly on the soles of her feet.

"What's wrong?"

"Nothing. Just thinking stupid thoughts about stupid stuff."

"Keep thinking them. How's your chest pain?"

"Still there."

He paused, looking down at her with so much caring and love that for a split second, she thought they were together. It was as though he'd always been hers, and the years of not being a couple were a time warp from a different dimension.

Oh, goodness. She was losing her mind.

"You can't die on me, Colleen."

"I know. Luke would kill you."

His hand reached for her chin, tipping it up so their eyes met with an intensity that sparked an emotional fire in her.

"Not just because of Luke."

He wiggled one of his legs between hers, their height disparity enough that he pulled her head onto his shoulder. Then he did exactly what she'd said.

Made sure as much skin as possible was touching.

The edge of her breast, the part spilling out of her bra, was against his pec. His arms encircled her under the thick down comforters. Her nose pressed into his neck, the scent of Moore filling her with a delicious, precarious feeling.

Sure, she might be dying, but she wasn't dead yet, and the tingle between her legs made it clear that some parts of her might have been out of use for a while and a little rusty, but they were still very much alive.

If a bit neglected.

Of all the times to be aroused, this one was terrible. Terrible in so many ways, but the worst was the sense of *duty* she detected in Moore.

He wasn't naked and pressed against her because he *wanted* her.

He was doing this to save her life.

"Well, this is awkward," she said, her lips against the pulse at the base of his throat.

"Is it? I hadn't noticed." A vibration of laughter in his ribs sounded like gemstones in the polisher in the back of his family's store.

"Thank you," she said. The skin pressed against him began to feel like rug burn, a faint pain and sensitivity she knew she'd just have to bear. Nothing was going to help. No first aid kit could get her through this. They were likely stuck here for the night, until town crews cleared the side roads like the one she'd crashed on, found the truck, and began a search. In the morning, Moore might be able to go back to the truck and find a cellphone, but what were the chances it would be dry?

Or have survived through a frozen night?

Control was one aspect of life that Colleen had well in hand. Nothing like her future sister-in-law, Rachel, whose visceral need for control made her a fantastic business development director for their small town and a great match for her laid-back partner, Colleen's brother Kell.

In Colleen's view of the world, you controlled what you could and gave in to the rest.

Reality asserted itself, like it or not, and Moore and Colleen were in the thick of reality, all right.

And speaking of thick, was that, uh... Moore?

"Hey. Don't fall asleep on me," he muttered into her hair. "What do I need to do to help you?"

"Help us both. We should drink warm liquid."

"I prefer mine in the form of rum."

"Start with some tea or just warm water, Moore. We can hit the hard stuff later."

"Later? You're talking about the future, so I'm guessing you don't plan to die in my arms?" The way he squeezed her, almost imperceptibly, made her heart swell.

Her chest stopped hurting.

"My skin feels like the worst rug burn ever, my mouth is dry as cotton, and I'm stuck in bed with the naked man who is responsible for my terrible nickname. If I'm going to die, it won't be like this. I'm going to survive just to spite you, Moore."

"I'll take you however I can get you."

At his words, she looked up, his mouth close to hers, their eyes connecting with a sudden seriousness.

None of this could be real. It was post-car-crash, post-hypothermia talk. Absurd for her to think he was actually attracted to her, right?

He'd had nineteen years to say something. If he hadn't said it before, it was because he didn't feel it.

She must be loopy from the trauma and shock of what happened.

As if on cue, her bladder announced its presence.

Which really sucked, because her limbs needed to work better before she reached this point. No way was she asking Moore for help going to the bathroom, if this cabin even *had* a bathroom. With any luck, there was a composting toilet indoors, but otherwise, this was outhouse territory.

One look at the window, the gap in the curtains showing the wind whipping snow at the structure, and she rethought.

Hush, she told her body. *Not yet.*

Medically, though, this was heartening. It meant her kidneys were working and her body was processing liquids. The trained nurse in her sighed with relief.

Cardiac issues were less of a worry now.

"Colleen," he whispered, voice choked with emotion. "You nearly died. And it was all my fault."

"*Your* fault?" she squeaked, stroking his arm. "No! I lost control of the truck. I should have let you drive when you offered."

"You're a fine driver. No one could handle that road."

Wind whistled sharply outside, as if proving his point.

"You saved me, Moore. You rescued me. I was stuck and panicking, and I couldn't breathe, and the water was so cold. Then I felt your hand." Her fingers brushed the back of his left one, the tendons strong, his fingers long and elegant.

"I needed a knife. If I'd had a knife, I could have cut you loose."

"You did fine."

"No—*you* did fine! You guided my hand to the seatbelt clip."

"And you set me free."

A shudder ran through her, followed by a cold bite across some of her nerves. As her body awoke, it was going to hurt like hell.

Pain never felt so good.

She looked at him again, his eyes closed, the lines of his face so familiar. Neatly-trimmed beard, dark hair, warm eyes, long lashes. His son, Jordy, was a mix of the Mottins and the Forsythes, but Moore was a carbon copy of his father, Leander.

Much younger, and much sexier, though.

Being in his arms, talking about what had just happened, the thrill of his skin against hers, was all too real. A wave of exhaustion rippled through her and she yawned.

"You can't fall asleep on me," he said again in a firm voice that rumbled against her shoulder, his beard tickling her skin. "Not yet."

"That wasn't a hypothermia yawn. That was an exhaustion yawn." The fact that she felt the scrape of hair on her neck was a great sign.

"Good. I don't ever want to hear the word hypothermia again. How's your chest?"

Said chest was currently pressed against his, parts of her breasts snuggled in nicely against his ribs.

"Um, fine?"

"I meant the pain you were experiencing."

A deep breath, long and slow, meant to fill her lungs and belly as full as possible, made her realize the extent of her shoulder injury. The sharp pulling back from the inhale was a sign that she would need an orthopedic consult when they got back to Luview.

Before she could answer him, an enormous wave came over her, a teeth-clenching shiver, her neck going tense and stretched.

Then her elbow. Her knee.

Like a conductor directing a symphony, different pieces of her activated and shivered, tensing to the point of excruciating tightness, then slumped. Moore squeezed her tighter, then loosened his hold.

"Are you—what's going on?"

"My body is waking up." Pins and needles filled her toes, then feet, the sense unbearable. She sucked in air, trying to settle her nervous system.

And failing.

As she shivered, twitching and slumping in a syncopated rhythm, Moore curled his fingers in and released her.

"What should I do?"

"I need that warm tea now. And a bathroom."

"Can you even walk?" he asked, incredulous.

"I don't know, but I do know I'm naked under a down comforter with you, feeling like something out of a Monty Python skit, and I'll be damned if I'll pee the bed!"

Moore released her, tucking the blankets around her again as she began more full body shivers, moving quickly around the little cabin. He disappeared around a corner and she heard, "Aha!"

"What?"

"Composting toilet."

"I'll take it!"

"Do you need help getting up?"

"I need that warm tea first. Bladder second."

"Always triaging, aren't you?"

As her jaw and neck clenched, she couldn't answer. Prickly feelings took over her dormant body parts, skin feeling like it alternated in patches between sticking to her like dead duct tape and floating three inches away, separated by millions of moving ants.

Coming out of hypothermia *sucked*.

Compassion rushed through her as she remembered the

handful of patients she'd had who were in various stages of it. At Luview Medical Center, she'd had a team, equipment, warmers, ventilators–every modern medical advancement in place to help.

And a medevac helicopter in case they needed a trauma center elsewhere.

Here? Here, she had a down comforter, a wood stove, some rum, and the best possible medicine–

Moore.

Who appeared in his underwear, patting her calf with two firm taps that made her shriek.

"Blood flow! Hooray!"

"Don't touch my legs! They're pins and needles."

A gleam in his eye nearly made her laugh.

"Remember when we were kids, how we'd sit cross-legged and make our legs fall asleep, then drag ourselves up and down the hallway of your old house?"

"We only did that on snow days."

A meaningful glance at the window accompanied his reply.

"Well. This one counts."

With that, he went to the kitchen and rummaged around, muttering.

"I was right. Propane." The familiar *tick tick tick* of a gas burner coming on filled the air.

"They didn't shut off their line?"

"Apparently not! We're lucky. Or they were just here last weekend. Who knows? Matches," he muttered, searching the drawers. Quickly, he walked to the woodstove and found them, then went back to the kitchen.

A *plume!* sound, followed by his shout of joyful success, made her smile.

And need to pee even more.

Toes firing away like a faulty spark plug, she groaned as she moved her legs. Assessing her body, she took note:

No more chest pain.

Shivering had definitely kicked in.

Pins and needles sucked.

Her bladder was okay for now.

"Make the tea warm! Not too hot!"

She heard the distinct sound of cabinet searching.

"All I'm finding is coffee. Instant."

"I don't want the caffeine now," she replied.

"Ugh!" He held up an ancient, battered cardboard box. "And licorice tea."

They had a running joke about how awful that stuff was.

"I may be half dead, but I won't drink *that*. Just warm water, then."

The bang of metal on metal was her answer. "Heating it up now. No running water, but there's a five-gallon tank here. I'll boil it, then add some cold water or even snow."

"You gourmet, you."

"Only the finest for my girl."

He turned away, out of sight, drawers opening and closing the only sound she heard. A gust of wind slammed at the door as if begging to be let in.

My girl.

What was he doing?

Did he mean... *what* did he mean?

A cramp, low and twisting, took her out of her thoughts as her ankle turned into Linda Blair's head in *The Exorcist*.

"AUUUUGH!" she groaned, the slide of her bare calf against the comforter excruciating.

Moore was there in an instant, hands on her shoulders. "What's wrong?"

"Cramp!"

"Where?"

"Leg!"

Sliding his hands under the covers, he started massaging her calf.

"Wrong leg!"

"Sorry." Fixing the error, his fingers pressed into her calf, pins and needles warring with spasms. Nothing about her body was going to make sense for a long time, until all the systems were back online and in synch.

"Have to get used to this," she rasped.

"My massage?"

"My dysfunction."

"What dysfunction?"

"My body. It's not the greatest."

For the barest of seconds, his hands hesitated, then his thumbs resumed their slow, steady, deep rhythm in the thick muscle of her calf.

"Your body is great." Long caresses, less urgent, more smooth and silky, made fire run along her skin. Not pins and needles, either.

This was a burning need for *him*.

"It's decided to be more of a one-woman band than a carefully conducted symphony. And I'm falling apart."

"You're healing. It's coming back to life and probably doesn't know what to do."

"I was just thinking that."

The kettle whistle began its early warning and he moved away, the absence of his touch making Colleen feel abandoned.

But if he came back into this bed and touched her again, she would feel the same twin reactions her corporeal self was having as she warmed up:

Touch me!

Don't touch me!

Because Moore's touch was just as excruciating as the

painful tingling of her skin. She wanted it to mean what she wanted it to mean, and it didn't. Wouldn't.

Because Moore didn't love her the way she loved him.

"You go to the bathroom. I'll get you some nice, warm water."

"No, I can wait."

Rolling to her side, she paused for a few breaths, letting her tired muscles figure out what to do next. Moore took her at her word and fussed around the kitchen, coming back for the mug he'd used for rum earlier. Swinging one leg, then the other, off the edge of the bed, she pulled the heavy comforter over her shoulders with her good arm and stopped, her injured shoulder screaming, the pain twisting her muscles and nerves to the point where she couldn't breathe.

Forcing air in and out through the pain was an act of will.

He was right.

She needed to rest first.

Pick me! Pick me! her bladder screamed, refusing to be ignored.

Looked like she had no choice.

Bathroom it was.

When her soles hit the floor, she let out a little gasp. Each foot seemed to have a brick inside the skin, the heaviness pulling her legs down. Sliding forward on her butt a bit, she braced herself.

Other than a racing heart and a flesh suit over her bones that was a heat map of different temperatures, she was just fine.

Well, not really fine, but it was easier to pretend than to think about the truth.

"SCORE!" Moore shouted from the kitchen. "A jar of peanut butter. Expiration date two months ago."

Her stomach gurgled as if responding to the call of her people.

"Moore, the mighty hunter. You found your prey."

"I am a fearless killer of legumes."

"Given how you shoot, a peanut is probably the only thing you could kill, and only in peanut butter form."

"Hey! I'm not *that* bad a shot."

"I've watched you hunt. You couldn't hit Randy the Moose from fifty feet while he was humping Kenny's trailer."

"Why would I ever want to shoot Randy?"

"See?"

"Is this any way to treat the man who brings you sustenance?" Emerging from the kitchen in his underwear, Moore carried a baking tray with two steaming mugs on it, the jar of peanut butter, and two spoons, all on a piece of spread-out cheesecloth meant to be a lace doily. "High tea for m'lady?"

Twisting around to see, she burst out laughing.

Then began to cough.

Hard.

Racking sounds, deep in her chest, registered in her ears. Her lungs wouldn't stop squeezing inside her, like a rag being drained of every drop. Each hollow rebound of her breath made it harder to inhale again.

Her body was no longer hers. It was firmly under the control of the icy water she'd been submerged in, systems working in whatever way possible to recalibrate.

Setting the tray on the wooden trunk, Moore came to her as she slowly breathed, smaller coughs jumping in here and there, interlopers in her attempt to even out.

"You're shivering," he said as she nodded, then acquiesced to Moore's warmth, his body next to hers, arm wrapped around her, joining her under the down comforter. As they sat on the edge of the bed together, Colleen struggled to normalize her breathing.

"Breathe with me," he said softly. "In through the nose, out through the mouth."

Colleen wanted to protest that she knew how, and in fact, she was normally the one saying those words to patients.

She couldn't though.

Because she *was* the patient.

And she needed Moore to take charge.

Chapter Four

Moore

What the hell was he supposed to do now?

Colleen sounded like she was hacking up a lung so big, it would rise up on four hooves and run off into the woods. Her shoulders were slumped, her bare feet turning different shades of purple and blue. As the cabin warmed, her hair had started to dry, the normal soft waves a mess of kinked-up curls that lay flat against her neck. Dark circles were forming under her eyes and she had a hollow look, bleak and exhausted.

It scared him.

All of this did.

Who knew that getting her out of the truck and saving her from drowning would be only the beginning?

"Listen," he said tenderly, pulling her closer, happy every time she shivered in his arms, "you need to just be here. Let me warm you up some more."

"Okay."

"Colleen."

When she looked up at him, tears filled her eyes. A piece of him broke a little.

"Oh, honey," he said, pulling her closer as sobs broke loose, his chest wet, her face buried in his neck.

"I–I–it hurts, Moore! I hurt and I tingle and it's driving me crazy and I nearly drowned and I can't breathe and my lungs feel like someone's carving a marble statue out of them and flinging the pieces up my windpipe and Sandwich is *aloooooooooone*."

Plaintive and soulful, her last sentence made him laugh.

"It's not funny!" Deserving to be smacked, he took her blow with equanimity.

"Colleen. Come on. We've just gone through a near-death experience. We're trapped in someone's cabin with rum and peanut butter for sustenance. You sound like you're gestating gerbils in your throat and giving birth to them via coughing, you have to pee but can't even walk to the bathroom, and you're worried about a *cat*? A pampered cat who lives a few hundred feet away from your parents?"

"Y-yes!"

Rubbing her arm, he was struck by the softness of her skin. It hadn't gone unnoticed by him that when they lay on the bed, the side of her breast rested against his chest, the skin silky and seductive.

No. Not seductive. Colleen wasn't acting out of passion.

She was mostly naked with him because she was a nurse following a life-saving protocol.

No matter how much he wanted this to be about more than that, it wasn't. Colleen had nineteen years to have made a move. If she hadn't done it by now, she wasn't about to start while they were trapped in a blizzard and she was worried about having a *heart attack*.

The part of him that was attracted to her was an asshole.

Now was not the time.

And yet... he couldn't help it. She was soft and vulnerable. Funny and raw. Commanding and endearing. They both had plenty of safety skills to get them through the basics.

If she'd stayed unconscious, he'd have just tried to warm her up by the fire.

Not cut off her clothes and lie naked together.

Sniffling in his arms, she cried and he let her, because he couldn't do anything but just be there for her. Frankly, having her sob like this was wonderful. It meant she was alive. Could breathe. Blood was flowing enough for her to be alert.

And she let him hold her.

Their friendship had always held a hard edge; they shared so many hours together, yet stayed at arm's length from each other. It wasn't just a friendship via shared connection with Luke. It was more than that.

Hard to describe.

Something had always been missing, though. Never able to put his finger on it, Moore had felt the space, nonetheless.

Now, though, that space was gone. They were deeply connected in the present in a way he'd never felt with her before. Maybe it was trauma bonding. Maybe it was shared fear. Maybe it was just compassion.

But as Colleen Luview cried in his arms, he felt stronger. Filled with purpose.

Needed.

Maybe that's what it was. Colleen had never needed him before. In this moment, she needed him, and it felt so good.

"I feel so strange," she let out, the words coming in a rush. "Like we're in a time warp."

"A what?"

"Time warp. Time doesn't exist here. No phone. No way out. All we can do is ride this storm and emerge sometime tomorrow. We'll have to be found, Moore."

"*Shhhhh*. Worry about that later. Not now."

"That's what I mean. My brain is scrambled. It keeps wanting to act, but we don't have the tools to act. Can't call. Can't flag down a road crew. I can't go to work and help with accident victims—I *am* an accident victim!" Her voice went shrill.

"You're fine."

"And the truck! Dad's truck is totaled and it's all my fault. It'll have to be towed, and insurance paperwork will bury us, and there will be a deductible and..."

Pulling away, he crouched down on the floor, inhaling sharply as the cold air hit his skin. Looking up, he locked eyes with her.

"Go to the bathroom."

"What?"

"Bathroom. Now. Then come back and drink your warm water. I'll spike it with a little rum."

"Why are you ordering me around like this?"

"Because you're cluttering your mind with worries you cannot do a thing about. Not one damn thing. So instead of borrowing trouble, take care of your needs."

Her eyes flared at those last words.

"You take care of everyone else first, Colleen. Always have. Let me take care of you, for once." For a split second, he felt the impulse in him.

The impulse to kiss her. To take the comfort up a notch.

To meet his needs, too.

But no.

No.

That would be crossing a line he could never uncross.

And breaking a vow Colleen didn't know existed.

One corner of her mouth twisted up.

"Peeing is how I let you take care of me?" The serious moment was shattered by her sarcasm.

"I... guess?"

"You are so weird."

"But I am remarkably consistent."

"Okay, then," she said, laughing, using his shoulder as a fixed point to lift off from. "Here I go."

Taking one step at a time, it was clear she didn't need help, but Moore stood anyhow, ready to jump in if she fell.

She didn't.

Slumping on the bed, he lay back on it, fingers threaded in his hair, pulling lightly.

"What the hell, Mottin?" he muttered to himself. "What do you think you're doing?"

The memory of his freshman year of high school hit him like a freight train, every scent, sight, and sound rushing through the years until he was there again. His eyes may have been staring at the unpainted wood ceiling of the cabin here in Wolfeboro, but his mind was back in Luview.

Nineteen years ago.

First day of the school year and he'd gone back with Luke to his house, same as most other school days since kindergarten. First day of high school had been surreal after being gone most of the summer, so slipping into the familiar and riding dirt bikes with Luke was an enormous relief.

Until he'd gone to grab a soda from the Luview's garage fridge and ran into Colleen, pumping up her own bike tire.

"Hey," he'd said as she gaped at him, her eyes going wide, eyebrows high with shock.

"Hey. Are you—a friend of Luke's?"

"Hah. Very funny."

"Omigod! MOORE?" she'd screamed, so loud that Luke and their mother had come running into the garage, their black lab Hyacinth on their heels, barking like crazy. A good girl who lived another five years, she'd been their always-companion in the woods.

Instantly self-conscious, Moore had looked around. "Are you pranking me?"

"You—you don't look like Moore! You got tall! And your hair?"

For years, Moore had worn his hair in a shaggy surfer cut, curling over his ears and covering his collar. But while he'd been gone for the summer in Wolfeboro, of all places, growing four inches and adding twenty pounds of muscle, he'd decided to go with a short, sleek haircut.

Over that summer, his uncle had said, "If you're going to work in the family business, you need to look the part." Now fourteen, he would be allowed to work at the jewelry shop, and he was eager to slip into this new version of himself.

Taller, older, more sophisticated.

Plus, the haircut might get him more girls.

Or even *a* girl.

Deanna Luview had laughed so hard. "He's Moore, silly! Your bonus brother, same as ever."

Colleen had flinched at the words *bonus brother*, her cheeks turning a hot shade of scarlet.

"Shut up," Luke told Colleen. "Quit making fun of Moore."

"Thanks, dude."

"That's my job."

The two had wandered back to Luke's room to kill a few more zombies in a game, chugging soda, Colleen long forgotten.

Hours later, deep in the woods, Hyacinth sniffing out a chipmunk's nest, Luke had given him enough glances for Moore to ask, "What?"

"What what?"

"What the hell, Luke? Spit it out."

"Don't—you know. Don't ever date Colleen."

"WHAT?"

Moore's shout scared a bunch of starlings out of a tree, the shade from the enormous cloud of them turning the moment malevolent.

"You heard me."

"Why would I want to date Colleen? Ewww."

"I dunno. I just–"

"What's next, man? Tell me I can't date your dog? Because that's some *true* love there."

Luke had snorted. "If you start dating Hyacinth, you've got bigger problems than I ever imagined."

"No worries. Hyacinth is way too cool. Out of my league. I can't even get a human girl interested in me."

"You swear, though. Right?"

"Swear what?"

"Not to date Colleen."

"Um, sure. You swear not to date *my* sister?"

"Vanessa is ten years older than us and a lesbian, Moore."

"But do you swear?" He'd hooked his pinkie and thrust it at Luke, who laughed.

"What are we? Six-year-old girls?"

"Just go with it," Moore said, earning disdain from Luke.

"I swear."

"Good. Because I'm about as likely to date Colleen as you are to date Vanessa."

"Odds are really, really different there, Moore."

"Can we be done with this conversation? We've covered taboos I didn't know I'd ever talk about with you."

"*Pfft*. You watch more than enough internet porn that–"

The conversation had ended with a wrestling match that took them into poison ivy, forcing them home for Tecnu baths.

All these years, he'd taken Luke's words to heart, even when it had been so hard.

Even when he'd almost kissed Colleen when he was

seventeen.

Even though she didn't know he'd almost kissed her.

Now here he was, mostly naked, alone in a cabin with her, dancing a dance where he didn't know who was leading. The way she rested against him felt so intimate, yet he knew it was clinical.

Skin-to-skin contact was purely for medical reasons. That much he knew, even if Colleen let off confusing hints of more.

He was just reading the signals wrong.

There were no signals.

Just misinterpreted noise.

He heard running water from the bathroom, a thin trickle that confused him. Had he missed plumbing? Nothing in the kitchen indicated that there was any.

Colleen appeared, smiling. "They have a sink in there! Five-gallon fresh water tank. Foot pump. I washed up."

"Feel better?"

"Yes." She made a face. "The hot-and-pricklies are back."

"You sure that's not just your attraction to me?" he joked.

Or not.

Maybe it wasn't a joke.

Desire flashed in her eyes. He wasn't imagining it. The mask of sarcasm returned, though, and she said, "Both feel super creepy and easy to confuse with the other."

Awkward yet again, she stood before him and he patted the bed.

"What do you need right now?"

"More heat."

"I'll add a log to the fire."

"I hate to ask, but..." She reached slowly for a mug and brought it to her lips, the pause killing him. To fill the void, he went to the stove to add the wood.

"Mmmm," she said. "Warm water is really helping."

"No rum in there."

"Save it for later. I'll need it."

"For what?"

"I'm shivering. I think PTSD will kick in next." Wild eyes met his. "I'm starting to freak out."

"Starting?"

"Moore." The crack in her voice made him shove the log he was contemplating straight into the stove, slam the door shut, and pull her into his arms, cradling her as he stretched them both out on the bed again, turning their intertwined bodies into a down-comforter burrito.

Chilled in some places, she was surprisingly warm in others, her now-dry hair tickling his neck as he held her. Their breathing synchronized as they rested on the bed until he couldn't tell the difference between his own and hers.

"You need to drink, too."

"I'm holding out for rum."

"Hydrate."

"Yes, Nurse."

"Whatever it takes, you old lump."

As he reached across her for his mug, her breast pressed against his biceps, the soft fullness of it nearly making him groan. Every part of him yearned for her, but all he was to her was a friend.

And a human heating pad.

That needed to be enough. More than enough. If the only thing he could do in this crazy situation was be the one who saved her, he could handle that. Her presence in his life meant more than being her romantic partner.

Not that he had any choice in the matter.

Risk-reward ratios were part of daily life in his business, managing inventory, going on buying trips, deciding whether a specific gem was worth the investment. Love You Jewelers was a thriving business, but it was also an entirely mainstream business.

Mainstream meaning *boring*. People wanted the same basic things–promise rings, engagement rings, wedding bands, and lots and *lots* of heart lockets, all stamped with the words Love You.

Boring for Moore, but never boring for the people who used these precious items to mark special, first-time events in their lives.

First kisses.

First dates.

First loves.

Proposals.

Weddings.

You name it.

While Moore sold thousands of identical quarter-carat diamond engagement rings each year, each one was unique for the person buying it. Moore pedaled love in a town steeped in it, but he couldn't find his own true soulmate.

Hypocrite? Maybe, but a well-paid one. Plus, he genuinely liked what he did for a living. Everyone came into his store looking for a symbol of love and left clutching one.

As he stroked Colleen's hair, he halted at that thought.

He'd found her.

Just couldn't have her.

"Sorry," she whispered through sniffles. "I'm a hot mess."

"That is not a news flash."

A giggle gave him hope.

"You always know how to make people feel better about themselves, Moore. You missed your calling. You should have been a therapist."

The warm water was boring, too, but it made him feel better instantly. Colleen had drained her mug as well, so he peeled himself away from her, realizing as he got out from under the warm covers that the air had warmed.

"That stove is working."

"Whew. Then we're safe."

Outdoors, the light had taken a turn, and darkness was falling. A wall clock said 5:22, which seemed impossible. Really? Had it only been a few hours since that whole mess back at the airport?

Some chunks of time were denser than others. This one felt like a neutron star. Like osmium. So many emotions and actions and events crammed into such a short space of time. Colleen had been part of his entire life, so how could the last few hours hold more meaning than everything that went before?

Except that wasn't true. It was precisely because of all the previous years that these moments were weighted so heavily. Colleen was precious cargo, clutched in his arms as he pulled her out of the pond and carried her here. Now that she was talking and joking in the warm cabin he'd found, his hands like hot oven mitts as they warmed up, his muscles starting to scream for recognition from all he'd just suffered, Moore felt himself sinking.

Pausing.

Standing down.

"Moore?"

Colleen's voice had an edge to it.

"Hmm?"

"You okay?"

No, he wanted to answer. *No, I'm not. Wasn't okay* before *all this happened. I'm a screw-up and will always be a screw-up. My kid hates me. My latest girlfriend dumped me by text. I couldn't stop the crash we just had. Barely got you out. Now you're in my arms, my body all yours to keep you safe, and...*

And...

And what?

And he was too chicken to say more.

Moore couldn't say... more.

"Sure," he finally replied, shaking himself out of his stupor as he poured them both more water, his hand tremoring so much, he spilled hot water on the counter.

"You just went through an enormous trauma," she said in a voice of dawning awareness. "You're not okay."

"No," he confessed, slow and uncertain. "I'm not."

"I'm so sorry. It's all my–"

"DON'T!" he shouted, his voice big in this tiny space. It felt good to be big somewhere. To take up room.

To *matter*.

"Don't what?"

"Don't say it's your fault! It's not your fault. It's nature's fault. Nature nearly killed us both. No one could have stopped it. Yes, we could have made different choices, maybe gone through Portland instead. Or I could have been in the driver's seat and actually gotten us killed. But no one did this to us, Colleen. It just happened. And you nearly died. You nearly–" Emotion took over, consuming him, his own vehemence unstoppable.

He couldn't shut up if he tried.

"Moore," she said, her voice a thin rasp. "Please come here."

Bracing himself against the counter, he leaned into his palms, feeling his shoulder blades nearly touch, the pain ripping through him as injuries announced themselves. More than a few cuts were stinging on his hands and feet, and that knee was like a big bass drum, thumping hard.

"Right. You need your water," he replied, turning back with the mugs.

His barely dressed state rolled into his consciousness now that the immediate threat was over. Reality check: He and Colleen were virtually naked together. As he approached the bed, she was on her back, hair spilling on the pillow, her cheeks finally showing a little color, her eyes wide open and looking at him with an emotion he couldn't name but felt down to his toes.

Moore might have been in denial, but he wasn't oblivious.

She cared, too.

If she were any other woman, resting on a bed with that look and the words "please come here," a night of very hot, fun, juicy sex would commence.

This wasn't any other woman.

"Here," he said, thrusting the mug toward her. Colleen sat up slowly, seeming a bit amazed by her body doing what she wanted it to.

"Thank you for the water. It really does help. And—and..." Colleen lifted the mug to her lips, looking down, eyelashes long and lacy.

"And what?"

"And I did nearly die. You're right. But..." she said, her hand going to his forearm, short nails glistening, coated with clear polish. Unlike Cammie, Hannah, and nearly every other woman he knew, Colleen didn't have manicured nails. She said she hated the feeling, and long nails ruined medical gloves, so why bother?

The difference added to the newness of the moment.

"But?"

"But we're alive."

"Yes."

Her eyes darted to the bottle of rum he'd left on the small table by the kitchen area. "And that calls for a celebration."

"I thought you said you shouldn't drink alcohol when you have hypothermia?"

"I think I'm out of the danger zone. My kidneys work. I can sit, stand, walk without chest pain. The numbness and tingling is a good sign. And my shivering—" Her whole body began again, as if her words had triggered it.

Tucking the covers around her shoulders, he waited as she

---

finished her water, then gently took the mug from her.

"Then pirates we be, matey," he said in his best pirate's voice.

"You sound like an Australian with a bad case of tongue-tie."

He stuck his tongue out as far as it could go, then curled it up, almost licking the base of his nose.

"I am not tongue-tied, I assure you."

Did she just blush through the shakes?

"I'll handle the shiver-me-timbers part, apparently," she joked as Moore's heart lifted, the mood lightening. On the brink of pouring his guts out, the forcefield he held in place when he was around Colleen had thinned so much, it was almost breached.

Almost.

Nerves shot, his body bare before her, he didn't need to add a dramatic moment of massive rejection to what was already one of the worst days of his life.

Why pile on?

"You're sure it's okay to drink?"

Instead of answering, Colleen picked up the jar of peanut butter, opened it, and dipped a spoon inside. As she licked the peanut butter, her eyes met his.

"Ah ant suffin imah tummick."

"I don't speak peanut butter. Say what?"

"I want something in my stomach," she repeated, "before I have a drink. You should, too."

A loud rumble from his gut agreed with her.

And so Moore found himself dining on peanut butter, sipping water from his mug, and curling under the covers against her still partly chilled skin. As the Franklin stove did its job, he let his guard down.

In his body, at least.

In his heart, not so much. That had been a close call.

"Luke must be going out of his mind," he pointed out. "It's been hours. When you didn't return, I'll bet he went into cop mode."

"He'll find us eventually. Or if he doesn't, someone will."

"You sound so serene about it. Not like the Colleen I know."

"I don't have the energy to be anything but serene right now."

Leaning closer, his face inches from hers, he caught her eye. The peanut butter spoon was in her mouth, upside down, the bottom so clean, he could see his distorted reflection in it.

"I will make sure you're fine."

"You already did."

"I'm going to see this through. In the morning, I'll get dressed and flag someone down on the road."

Coleen looked at her pile of torn clothes. "Uh, yeah. You'll have to. You sliced my clothes off."

"Because you ordered me to!"

"I wasn't making a judgment against you, Moore. Just stating the facts. And speaking of clothes, you should hang yours up to dry."

"My suit is ruined. And my shoes are somewhere back in that pond."

"*Yeek*. Flagging someone down suddenly requires way more sacrifice."

Mulling through the complications of how to find help finally turned Moore to the bottle. Gripping it with authority, he poured a shot into the mug and drank it down.

"Let's take stock. We have a jar of peanut butter. Two-thirds of a bottle of rum. Water. A safe place for the night. Your clothes are useless, and mine will shrink to the size of an eight-year-old if I dry them too fast. I have no shoes. And it looks like we're getting ten to twelve inches tonight."

Did... did her eyes just drift to his *crotch?*

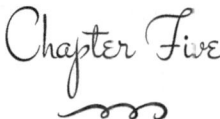

Chapter Five

Colleen

The moment she turned a little porny inside was the moment she knew she was going to make a full recovery.

"Okay," she said slowly. "That's all true."

Moore's brow wrinkled, dark eyes narrowing as he peered at her with an intensity she must be misreading. All the guy was doing was assessing their situation.

"Maybe fourteen," he added, watching her face. Forcing her eyes to stay on his face, she resisted the juvenile impulse to make a penis joke.

Because said penis was currently ensconced only in a pair of very nice boxer briefs, the rest of Moore completely undressed, and if she wasn't careful, she was about to expose her true attraction to him.

Which would be lethal for their friendship.

And worse, her pride.

"Fourteen inches is a lot," she replied, biting her lips and curling them inward to try not to laugh. "Of snow."

"Rum?" he asked, then poured without waiting for her reply.

Looking around, she let his words sink in. "How far is this cabin from the road?"

"Maybe a quarter mile?"

"You carried me a quarter mile in a raging snowstorm? In the woods, without shoes?"

He shrugged.

"Moore. Jesus."

"I'm nothing like him. Other than a beard, but mine's trimmed."

"You went to heroic lengths to save me."

"I did what any decent human being would do."

"Yeah, but–"

His hand went to her bare shoulder, a primal look in his eyes. Nudging the mug of rum against her hand, he said in a gravelly voice, "I don't want to relive what happened outside, Colleen. How about we get drunk and do our best to forget it all, then deal with life in the morning?"

"Drunk?"

"Fine. Not drunk. Just... let's unwind."

"Unwinding sounds good," she answered, slow and unsure of herself, though the food and water was helping. Holding her mug, she raised it a bit, her hand starting to shake.

"To life," he said.

"To you."

"Me?"

"You saved me."

"I had to."

"Right, because Mom and Dad and Luke would kill you."

"Hah." He clinked the rims of their mugs together and

took a sip, eyes roaming around the world as if he were struggling not to say more.

So many questions swirled through her, her muscles beginning to ache as if they were being pulled by some new gravitational force. The tops of her forearms, her calves, the inner thigh muscles—random places made themselves known, her brain calling down and getting reports from below that everything was still in disarray.

Another part down below, though—that part was warm, wet, and beginning to throb.

As they drank their shots, Moore kicking his back in one gulp, Colleen sipping hers slowly, she noticed how quiet the cabin was. Not knowing what else to do with herself, she took a deep breath through her nose, inhaling the light aroma of rum, and closed her eyes.

"How about we make a hot toddy?" she murmured.

"A what?"

"Hot toddy. You know. Tea, honey, lemon, water, and rum."

"I thought it was bourbon."

"Don't get picky."

"*I'm* picky? You just listed a bunch of ingredients we don't have. I can give you hot water and rum."

"Then I'll use my imagination."

"Is this a subtle way to ask me to pour hot water in your mug of rum?"

Shivers radiated in erratic patterns across her legs, her toes so warm, they felt like dough that had been left to rise too long on top of a radiator.

"Yes."

"Hot toddy it is, madame." With a joking flourish, he stood again and went to the stove, reappearing with a battered enamel kettle, the kind Colleen wouldn't even consider buying at a yard sale where everything was a dollar.

But here? It was retro cool.

Moore poured himself a mug full, too. "Wish we had cinnamon. Some kind of tea."

"I'm surprised the owners don't leave more."

"I'm not. Who wants bears and squirrels breaking in?"

"True. But I could really go for a nice cup of chamomile right now."

"Rum a dum dum." Moore tipped his mug up and appeared to drink half of it, jaw moving, giving Colleen a moment to eye him without being seen. If she weren't already shivering, she would quiver with pure desire. Maybe it was the rum. Perhaps it was the way he fiercely protected her. It could even be the coziness of the cabin as it warmed up, the fire granting the space a gentle glow as the wind howled outside.

And it certainly could be nineteen years of pent-up wanting.

But right now, Moore looked so deliciously fine, like a lover about to climb into bed for a night of pleasure.

Oh, dear. The rum was sinking in, wasn't it?

"I probably shouldn't drink this," she said, taking a long sip.

"Because of your heart?"

"Because I'll tell you all my secrets if I drink too much."

Moore picked up the bottle and poured her another shot.

"Hey!"

"What?"

"I just told you I shouldn't do this!"

"You don't have any secrets I don't already know." His saucy grin warmed her up in a way that no woodstove could.

"Oh, yeah? Maybe you're wrong about that."

"I know everything about you. You know everything about me. We've been friends forever—you've literally known me since the day I was born. What important fact could I possibly not know about you?"

Wind pushed hard against the window frames, rattling them like they were Colleen's heart.

At the same time, her limbs were relaxing. A fuzzy feeling began in her skin, and not just because her peripheral nerves were confused. The rum was doing its job, and as she drank the rest of it, she shivered.

And didn't stop.

"Wow," Moore said. "Still that cold?"

"It hasn't been that long."

"Here." Moving behind her, he straddled her back, curling his knees and calves around her legs. Positioning one comforter behind him, he pulled it into an igloo-shaped puff-ball, her head peeking out.

Then he stretched across the bed for the rum bottle and poured them more.

"Whoa, buddy," she said, her words loud in the quiet cabin. Once in a while, a log spit and crackled as it burned, the scent of woodsmoke so comforting. "That's enough."

"Not for me."

"That bad?"

"I really think it's hitting me now. That was a lot, Colleen."

"Yes, it was."

"Plus, it's eerie here. So quiet. Nothing to do. No electricity, no radio, no tv. No phones."

"Want me to put on a variety show?"

"I watched you in the last Love You No Talent show. Taping red glow-sticks in the shape of hearts on your butt, turning off the lights, and dancing to 'Despacito' is *not* a talent."

"It counts!"

"Forcing people to watch your ass bouncing in the dark counts as talent now?"

"You watched, didn't you?"

The long, slow slide of his breath through his nose, measured and heavy, made arousal flare up. All she could do was pull her hands out from under the covers and take another sip of her drink. A loose feeling seeped into her pores now, that gentle moment when the voices in her head that constantly debated everything decided it was time to take a break.

Relaxing back against his chest, she let out a sigh of her own.

One of contentment and release.

Bra straps were no fun in any situation, but being pressed against him meant every part of her body was suddenly up for inventory and examination. As she pulled her knees up, soles of her feet on the mattress, she shook again, inner thighs quivering violently.

"Don't spill your drink," he joked.

"Not enough left in there to spill." Her laugh was bigger, bolder, brasher than normal, and as she loosened, she craned her neck up, looking at upside-down Moore.

Or his chin, at least.

"Is that a request for more?"

"No," she said firmly. "I need to make sure I'm okay." Scooching forward, she tested her legs, which handled the standing maneuver better than expected.

Every breath felt better than the last, but nothing felt as good as having permission to touch and be touched like this.

No, it wasn't intimate, but it was closer than she'd ever been to Moore. Even in crisis, she wanted him. No level of denial was high enough to deny that.

All her defenses were melting away. Maybe it was the trauma. Perhaps she was just too exhausted to fight it any longer. Most likely, the rum was contributing, changing her in a way that felt magical. What else were they supposed to do, closed off from the world, reeling from their narrow escape from death?

Standing up felt good. Moore joined her, hovering like a parent guiding a child's first steps, attentive eyes watching her every move. Chilled a bit, the cocoon of the comforter and Moore's warm body now removed, she shivered again and the sudden twitching of her body threw her off balance.

Instantly, his hand was on her hip, snaked around her waist, providing firm support.

"I'm fine."

"I know you are," he murmured against her hair. "Just making sure."

In any other situation, they'd be making love right now. If they were romantic partners, the accident would be a source of conflict, the cabin a relief, her recovery a blessing, and they'd be celebrating life by connecting in the deepest way possible.

But they weren't romantic partners. She was just a friend, standing in her bra and panties, with another friend standing in his underwear, his arm around her.

The thought depressed her, dread washing over her skin, and her knees buckled from the emotional enormity of it.

"See?" he said as he caught her weight, lifting her gently in his arms, moving her a few feet back to the bed. "Making sure."

"I'm fine."

"Your knees didn't get the message, Colleen."

"My body isn't cooperating. It's being a jerk."

"Bodies can do that."

"Maybe it needs more rum."

The sadness that had just inserted itself into her like an injection faded as quickly as it came. Moore fussed over her, tucking her under the covers again, moving to the stove to feed it another log, this one bigger and thicker than the others. She had to give it to him; Moore knew how to make and tend a fire.

Boy Scouts had served him well.

For a guy who wore suits and talked gems and gold for a living, he was remarkably skilled at basic survival.

Which was yet another reason she loved him so much.

Why hold back? The hazy light and the warm covers made her smile, her eyes on Moore as he finished with the woodstove and turned to the kitchen to get more water. What if she didn't hold back? What if she confessed the truth?

Playing out the scenario in her head, she indulged herself.

And stopped cold at his imagined rejection.

What could be worse than nearly dying in a car accident?

Nearly dying from humiliation.

Shivers began again, this time not stopping, her neck and jaw pulling tight again.

"You need help," Moore declared, voice low and compassionate. He set their mugs on the nightstand and unrolled some of the comforter around her, crawling in as if it were second nature. One arm around her, he stretched the other down, palm resting on her hip.

"Your skin is still so cold."

"You're a furnace."

He laughed. "I'm only warm compared to you. You're an iceberg. I'm just warmed-over slush."

"Warmed-over slush would be water."

"Colleen?"

"Yeah?"

"You're ruining the moment."

"This is a moment?"

"Sure."

"What kind of moment?"

"The kind where you don't nitpick me to death with details."

"I was pointing out a fact."

"You're so practical."

"That's not an insult, you know."

"I never said it was."

"What's wrong with correcting someone when they're wrong?"

"Nothing's wrong with the phrase 'warmed-over slush.'"

"It's a bad metaphor."

"Give me a better one. If I'm not warmed-over slush, what am I?"

Oh.

Body instantly ablaze, she knew the rum was doing its sweet work of relaxing her, because the answers to his simple question were all, well...

The kind that crossed lines.

"Um..."

His chuckle made his chest bounce a bit, her chin slipping into the crook of his neck. He turned so that his thigh slid against hers, her knees shaking so hard, they knocked into each other.

"You're banging your joints together," he observed. "That's got to hurt."

"Blood's finally warming up."

"Here." His knee inserted between hers, the bristly curls of his leg hair sending shockwaves through her. "Does that help?"

Does that *help?*

If he helped her much more, she might orgasm on the spot.

"Sure," she choked out, her body betraying her yet again. First, the damn thing nearly got her killed back in that pond. Now, it threatened to climax on her, here in Moore's arms, as the poor guy was performing advanced first aid.

With his... thigh?

Sighing heavily, he moved slightly, his arm over her head as he retrieved his mug and sat up just enough to take a sip, her hip sliding against his torso, where yet another shock awaited her.

Moore was hard.

Hard as granite.

And not an insignificant amount of granite.

Holding back her reaction, it took every bit of restraint not to snicker, snort, hoot, chuckle, or giggle, impulses that would reveal just how unevolved she really was.

And how much she needed a distraction.

Being pressed against his arousal meant her own arousal shot up into the stratosphere, and Colleen wasn't going to be able to hold back much longer from kissing him.

"Do you remember," he asked after taking his sip, "that huge storm when we were in high school?" His arms came back under the covers, her shaking now settling into little twitches and tingles.

"Which one? There were so many."

"The one where school actually shut down for three days."

Western Mainers were hardy folk. Even a two-foot snow accumulation might yield only a two-hour bus delay. For the superintendent to cancel school was a huge deal, worthy of Armageddon.

"That was your senior year, not mine. I was at the community college then."

"Oh, right, I forgot." His loose chuckle was endearing, his hand stroking her arm as if they were lovers. "I sometimes forget you're two years older. All the memories mash together."

"Mine, too."

"That storm was crazy. Ice underneath snow. Took forever to melt."

"Yeah. The older nursing students were really upset because it happened during practicums and they lost hours."

"We hung out at your house for three days straight. I slept over. Lots of video games and movies."

Memory filled in, like the bloom of watercolor on paper. "Right! And we had that marathon game of Trivial Pursuit!"

"You *do* remember."

"I remember because you guys dominated in the sports category, unless it was baseball. And I nailed entertainment."

"Your mom crushed the history questions."

"That's right! Mom played." She closed her eyes and sank into Moore's arms, any awkwardness evaporating.

"She won. And you were so pissed."

"She's old, she's lived through more history–it's not fair! Plus, I was super competitive back then."

"Back then," he mugged, earning a light slap from her, playful and targeted on his chest.

"I'm not *that* competitive."

"You bet on your brother's relationship with Kylie. You bought three squares in the town betting pool."

"You bought one, too!"

"Yeah, but you tried to sway them!"

"More than four hundred dollars was on the line–I just used every resource available to me."

"You're competitive as hell, Colleen. It's one of your most endearing traits."

"Endearing?"

"Yeah."

"You find me endearing?"

"Yes." The word came out slowly, like a confession, the rasp of the end turning to pure energy, like a wish released to the heavens.

"Oh."

With no electricity to provide white noise, silence dominated. Other than their breathing, the fire's quiet crackle was the only sound inside the cabin.

Meanwhile, her heart beat on in her chest as if nothing were at risk here. As if it weren't walking a tightrope.

As if it weren't exploding from happiness.

As if it weren't quivering in terror.

"I found out Cammie was pregnant the day we went back to school," he said, shattering the part of her that had been drawn to the side of the line where maybe, just maybe...

"Mmmm." Words were gone.

"And just like that, everything changed. I never spent the night at your house again."

She jolted. "Really?"

"I had to 'be a man,'" he said, bitterness seeping in. "My mom and dad said so."

"I remember." Catching her breath, she willed herself to stop feeling with her hormones and start thinking with her mind. His body was here to warm her.

Nothing more.

But for whatever reason, he was also pouring his heart out to her, wandering through memories that they shared.

"I think about that snowstorm a lot. And this one reminds me of it."

"Why?"

"Because it was the last time I was truly free."

"Oof."

"It's true."

"It is."

"Thank you."

"For what?"

"For validating me."

"You don't need me to validate you."

"No, I don't need you to do it. I appreciate it, though. You see it, too?"

"See that you lost your freedom because Cammie got pregnant your senior year of high school? Of course."

"Not just that. I mean, see that I used to be free."

The way he was speaking carried a new tone, a wistful, painful reckoning. Colleen didn't quite understand his point, but she felt the importance of what he was grappling with, and that meant staying present with him through whatever he was going through.

"You used to be free, Moore. Yes."

Did his arms just tighten around her? Were his fingertips stroking her skin with a new, heightened intensity? Dreamy and light, she gave into the sensation, letting herself sigh. As her body stilled, a deep warmth, true and more real than any feeling she'd ever experienced, took over.

"I want to be free again," he murmured against her hair, his leg moving against hers, her fingers on his chest desperate to explore.

"What does that mean to you?"

"It means this."

In all her years of dreaming about him, and many more spent pushing those dreams away, she never imagined it would happen like this—that Moore would simply hold her in his arms, move a few inches, and bridge the gap between them with a kiss. But here it was, and it felt so good.

So right.

So perfect.

Their lips met, his arms curling around her as she turned on her side gingerly, favoring her shoulder, the comforter softer, his muscles harder, the whole of him both familiar and tantalizingly new. Their mouths were soft together, then warm and wet as the kiss deepened, his fingers in her hair now, hers on his shoulder.

Moore's tongue asked for an invitation and she parted her

lips, the line now so thoroughly crossed that there was no line any longer.

Just this kiss.

How could a kiss tell a story so long, so detailed, with so many detours and U-turns? All her wanting was in this kiss, all her time on the sidelines, all the friend-zone moments gathering to watch as Moore kissed her with growing need, their bodies pressed harder together.

They weren't kids. She wasn't his best friend's older sister.

She was a fully grown woman whose life he had just saved, and she had nearly lost the chance to tell him how much he meant to her.

Now? Now she could show him.

Finally.

Chapter Six

Moore

Luke was going to kill him.

But at least he'd die happy.

Two different versions of himself were kissing Colleen, his geeky fourteen-year-old version and the man he was now, and both were enjoying the hell out of the moment.

Because he'd finally done it.

Freedom came in so many different forms. Trapped in a life he didn't choose, because of a stupid mistake he made his senior year of high school, he hadn't felt free since, well...

Since that last night at the Luview's house, all those years ago.

Colleen's embrace, her kiss, the eager way she moved against him, matching him kiss for kiss, stroke by stroke—it added a new layer to their familiarity, made his heart lift, his body harden, and his soul fly.

All these years, he'd wondered.

And it took nearly losing her to finally take a chance.

Lost in the kiss, he became pure sensation. The pressure of her knee against his thigh. Fingertips grazing the swell of her breast. The silk of her hair against the back of his hand. The taste of sweet breath in his mouth. The scent of woodsmoke as he inhaled warmth. The ticking sound of icy snow against the window glass.

The moan of pleasure from the back of her throat.

Keenly aware that they were scantily dressed, so close to being nude, he held back, hands playing in safer zones. But the curve of her ass was too appealing not to cup as she kissed him harder, more fiercely, with more need than he ever expected until finally, she broke away, panting.

Eyes boring into his with a taunt that was purely Colleen, she declared, "Why did you wait so long to do that?"

"*What?*"

Mouth twisting into a smirk, her eyes searched his for answers to questions he suspected mirrored his own. Then her smile faded.

"What was that?"

"A kiss."

"Moore."

"I don't know. What do you want it to be?"

"So this," she said, nudging his erection with her hip, "is just simple biology?"

"Huh?"

Blinking rapidly, she seemed to weigh out what needed to be said next. It gave him a chance to just look at her, in all her beauty. Colleen had no idea how truly gorgeous she was. Beauty could be defined in so many ways, but she was stunning across the spectrum.

Across all the years.

Every single frustrating one of them.

"You took off all your clothes and climbed into bed with me to warm me. That's basic rescue technique."

"This," he said with his own matching nudge, "isn't part of some first aid kit."

Uncertainty made her freeze, and his own inner state scrambled to catch up and get back on the same frequency. The rum had loosened him up, ripping the racing thoughts about what almost happened back at the pond out of him and throwing them aside.

It also made it hard to want to do anything but make love to her.

But that wasn't just the alcohol.

It was so much pent-up yearning.

"What are you saying?"

He leaned in, tracing her jaw, fingers moving to tickle her earlobe as her eyes flared with possibility. Throwing caution to the wind—the literal, howling wind that forced them inside, into this warm, isolated paradise, a no man's land where he could suspend reality and simply be himself with the woman he most wanted that with—he kissed her again.

And again, until he pulled back and said roughly, "I'm saying this, Colleen." Hand going to her breast, he took in the fine line of her body, so precious, so taboo. Every part of him was driven to keep moving forward, keep showing her more and more of what he felt—but at the same time, a voice in his head screamed to stop.

He ignored it. Other parts demanded attention.

It was time for their turn in the driver's seat.

"I like *this*," she responded, biting his lower lip.

Her arms wrapped around him, hands roaming down his shoulders and back, palms at his waist, then a caress of his ass as she grew bolder. The way she kissed him drove him mad, a nip of her teeth on his lower lip tugging for a second, then her tongue dancing against his. Breathy sounds so feminine, such a surrender that he could barely contain himself, filled this new world he'd entered with her.

They were best friends in a new land, exploring uncharted territory. Each kiss was a first. Each touch was a beginning. Every line crossed was the border to a new country with a language that had to be learned.

Their tongues worked hard as they kissed their way to fluency.

Reaching for the front clasp of her bra, he stopped himself, mouth smiling against hers.

"Colleen? May I?"

Breath caught in her throat as she made a little gasp, her hair in her face, draped over eyes he'd seen thousands of times over the years–scores of thousands–but now the light in those eyes was burning for him.

Another first.

"You're asking permission?"

"I am."

"How could I say anything other than yes?"

"You can."

Her hands went to his face, palms on his cheeks, holding him still as she searched his face. "Don't stop now. Please, Moore. You have no idea how long I've wanted this."

Confession may be good for the soul, but he knew how painful her admission was. Colleen lived behind a very high, thick emotional wall, a fortress of sorts, and he'd always been honored to be part of her inner circle.

Though it was never quite enough.

"Trust me, Colleen, I do. I know damn well how long *I've* wanted it. Now let's stop talking about it and–"

"*Shh.*" Her index finger pressed against his lips. "Yes. Permission granted. You said earlier you wanted to be free. Be free with me, Moore. Be free."

The clasp was simple, a twist of the wrist, but it was

symbolic as yet another line was crossed, yet another step taken that could not be undone. So much that lived in his imagination, pure and controlled by him alone, was about to be unleashed.

Every time they touched, it was less his own and more...

More *theirs*.

They had no blueprint, no steady set of rules, no carefully outlined convention for what happened next. His hands were making love to her skin, his mouth licking strokes of love, his body finally allowed to use more than just his voice and platonic hugs to connect with this woman who was as much a part of him as anyone else.

Because she'd been part of his life when he'd needed it most.

"Colleen," he whispered as he kissed her neck, the sweet hollow spot below her earlobe so soft. "What do you want?"

"Everything," she whispered, and he began to give it to her.

"You have high expectations," he replied between kisses.

"You're a hard worker, Moore. Show me what you've got."

And he did.

Nineteen years' worth was a heavy emotional debt, but he began to pay it.

One kiss, one stroke at a time.

Chapter Seven

Colleen

BAM!

BAM! BAM! BAM!

"COLLEEN!! MOORE!!"

Cold.

Ice filled her lungs as Colleen sat straight up, the covers falling off her, disoriented by being startled out of a sound sleep, her shoulder screaming until her neck pulled in and she gasped with pain.

"Wha...? Where are–wha...?"

"COLLEEN!"

She shrieked, wanting whoever was shouting to stop, her head suddenly throbbing hard, so painful that she closed her eyes tight, rotating her shoulder and crying out as it shrieked back.

"ARE YOU IN THERE?" The front door knob rattled as

she looked to her right to find a very confused, very naked Moore in bed with her.

Hold on.

Was this another one of her dreams?

"Well," he said, looking around the room with the same frantic cluelessness she felt. "Guess we're rescued." The one-room cabin with the kitchen to their left, the bathroom to the right, all felt like a condensed cube, as if Luke and Kell were about to peel off the foil wrapper and plunk them in hot water.

"LUKE?" she called out.

"COLLEEN! OPEN THE DOOR!"

"I CAN'T!" she replied before realizing that was the worst possible way to reply to her brother.

The *cop*.

Before she could say a word, before Moore could move, the door came crashing in.

And her brothers Luke and Kell flew into the room.

Luke landed at the foot of the bed, his head snapping up. Kell stood a few feet inside the cabin, looking like an enormous bear who'd just been gored in the butt by a boar.

"MY EYES! MY EYES!" Kell bellowed, turning away and holding his hands over his face, then walking straight into a chair and falling over it head first, heavy tan work boots flailing mid-air.

"Moore? Colleen? What the hell is this?" Luke demanded.

"I can explain," Moore said, leaping out of bed.

Luke stared at him, bug-eyed. "You're naked!"

Moore grabbed the comforter off the bed as Kell righted himself and looked over at them, making eye contact with Colleen.

Who was now completely naked and exposed on the bed, as Moore covered himself with the quilt he'd just taken.

"COVER YOURSELF! MY EYES!" Kell shouted again.

Moore, ever the gentleman, sacrificed himself to toss the comforter back over her. Crouching to find the nearest item to cover himself with, he stood up holding her shredded sweater in front of him.

By this point, Luke had stood up, backed up, and had his hands on his hips, a murderous look on his face as he screamed at Moore, "What the hell did you do to my sister?"

"I think it's pretty obvious what he did *with* her," Kell muttered, clearing his throat suggestively.

"SHUT UP, KELL!" Colleen and Luke shouted in unison.

"Geez. It's like I'm nine again," he snapped back at them, but he took a seat in a chair closer to Moore and wisely shut up, watching the scene intently.

Colleen froze, covered with the comforter now, Moore awkward beyond belief as he covered his crotch with her wool sweater, which hung in ribbons around his thighs.

"EXPLAIN," Luke barked.

"I was driving on Route 28 when I hit some ice. Moore told me his uncle's cabin was–"

"Not you. *Him!*" Luke cut her off and stormed toward Moore, stopping inches from his face, finger pointed at him. "Why are you NAKED, in a BED, with my SISTER?"

"He saved my life!" Colleen retorted, fury building up in her. Still groggy from the abrupt awakening, she was quickly being shocked into full awareness.

"With his penis?" Kell said under his breath.

"SHUT UP, KELL!" they screamed again. Moore just glared at him, tilting his head for emphasis.

Kell simply grinned, crossing his arms over his broad chest and settling in with infuriating amusement. "Wish I had popcorn."

"You can find it back in Luview." Colleen said shrilly. "How about you go get some right now?"

"Make yourself useful and shut the door, too," Luke growled at him.

Kell stood and did as asked, then sauntered back to the chair, clearly not giving up his front-row seat to what was nothing but pure entertainment to him.

Colleen would never, ever hear the end of this.

"I didn't know you two were a thing," Kell ventured, eyes pinging between the two of them.

"They're *not*," Luke said in a deadly voice that made a nerve in Colleen's spine shoot from base to top, settling hard in the back of her skull.

"What we are or aren't is none of your business," she said to Luke, standing up on her knees then losing her balance and falling backwards, her arms and legs sticking out from the covers, shoulder sending nerve pain to her scalp.

Luke looked at her and did a double take, rushing to the bed. His hand went to her ankle, which was covered with bruises.

"You're injured!"

"Badly."

Instead of the expression of sympathy for her truck accident that she expected, Luke just gently released her ankle, patting her shin with a tender touch.

Then charged Moore.

When you've been friends with someone your entire life, from preschool to your thirties, and you've spent all those decades wrestling, fighting, making up, exploring outdoors, and being on sports teams and Boy Scouts together, you pick up on subtle physical signals that otherwise might be missed.

Which was how Moore so readily dodged Luke.

He seemed to know instinctively that his best buddy was

on the attack, and when Luke stumbled into empty air as naked Moore lifted up in a high jump that landed him on the bed, slamming hard on the balls of his feet, it made Kell burst out laughing.

Except that Newton's third law law states that every action has an equal and opposite reaction, and when Moore hit the mattress hard, he bounced Colleen off.

Harder.

Onto the bare wood floor of the cabin, where she felt a distinct snap in her wrist as she made contact.

Screaming felt good, even if pain provoked it, her cry longer and more vibrant than it otherwise would have been. Made of steel and with the pain tolerance of an Amazonian warrior, she normally would have held it in, but this was too much.

The worst day of her life followed by the best night of her life followed by her baby brothers busting in on her *in flagrante delicto* with a man her brother thought he could beat up.

To... what? Save her honor?

That ship had sailed so long ago, it had a pirate flag attached to it.

"LUKE!" she cried out as Kell hovered above her, tossing the blanket over her naked body. "Leave him alone!" She followed this pissed-off declaration with another scream. "You just broke my damn wrist!"

"ME?" Luke yelled back indignantly. Moore was dancing around the table, Luke on the other side of it. Was he baring his teeth?

"Yeah, you! Moore wouldn't have jumped and would someone just HELP ME?"

All three men halted.

"Did you just ask for help?" Kell said in a tone of marvel.

"Yes!"

Luke and Kell made eye contact over her prone body. "She must be really hurt if she's asking for help."

Moore abandoned his table shield and crawled over the bed to the side she'd fallen on, crouching next to her. His hand went to her arm, which made her groan. The white hot, piercing pain was nothing like what she'd felt yesterday after the crash.

This was acute.

And worst of all, unnecessary.

"GET OUT! BOTH OF YOU!" she bellowed between seething gasps of pain.

"But–" As Luke's protest began, Kell's hand went to his shoulder, her youngest brother whispering something into her stupidest brother's ear that made Luke roll his eyes, mouth going flat with contempt. "That's a big crock of–"

Kell whispered something else that shut Luke up. The long-suffering sigh that came out of his invasive, overprotective, busybody mouth made Colleen want to choke him with his police hat.

"You," Luke said to Moore, accusing finger pointing at him. "Get dressed and get outside."

"I'm helping Colleen."

"Oh, you helped her plenty."

"He saved my LIFE, you asshole!" she screamed at Luke, hating her inferior position on the floor, but she didn't have much choice.

Standing would mean being totally naked in front of her brothers.

Again.

"What does that mean?" Luke asked in a gruff voice.

"Just what I said. I'd be dead if it wasn't for Moore."

"Dead?"

"You found the truck, I assume?" she asked as she battled to control her breath, the pain getting worse. "Upside down?"

"It's buried under eighteen inches of snow. Bad angle, too. Even the snowplow guys missed it last night. Hell of a wreck. You totaled dad's truck. Roads must have gotten bad here."

"Upside down in a *pond*, right?"

Kell glanced down at his and Luke's feet. That's when Colleen realized their legs were wet. Both men wore thick down coats, Luke in his bright red Luview police jacket and red cop hat.

"Yes."

"I was trapped in the water. Upside down. Moore got me loose before I drowned. Kicked off his shoes to swim in through the passenger's window and release me. Then he walked all the way from there to here, shoeless, in the storm, carrying me. He found this cabin. *He saved my life*," she spat out, hoping it shamed them.

How dare they barge in here and attack Moore? The guy who saved her, Luke's lifelong friend, who'd been injured in the crash, too.

But *nooooo*. All her jackass brother seemed to care about was some chaotic macho b.s.

Luke had the decency to close his eyes and wince, pinching the bridge of his nose as if regulating the flow of information to his brain.

"How'd you get in this place?" he demanded of Moore. "This isn't your uncle's cabin."

"A window. Easy to jiggle the lock open."

"Breaking and entering? I could have you arrested for this."

"Moore entered someone, alright," Kell said under his breath.

"LUKE!" she screamed again, wishing she had a vase or a shot put or *anything* she could throw at him to cause damage.

Examining the room, Luke prowled around, looking carefully in the kitchen, eyes jumping to the nice, hot woodstove.

While he did his whole cop act, Kell bent down, frowning at Colleen with a look of concern that made him resemble their mother.

"You hungry?"

"We had a lovely dinner of peanut butter and rum."

"Rum?" Luke asked sharply. "You two were drinking?"

By this point, Moore had located his clothes and disappeared around the corner toward the small bathroom.

"I'm okay," Colleen said in a mocking tone. "Thanks for asking. Nearly died of drowning, then from hypothermia. If Moore hadn't taken off his clothes and climbed into bed with me, I'd have died."

"He... what?"

"I wasn't shivering. At all."

Both her brothers went still, knowing the implications of that.

"So you're naked in bed because *all* you did was huddle together so you'd get warm enough to shiver?" Kell asked slowly, eyeing Luke with trepidation, as if trying to see which way the wind was about to blow.

"No," Moore said confidently as he reappeared in his wool pants, now four inches too short, an extremely wrinkled dress shirt with most of the buttons popped off, and socks, holding a balled up wad of fabric that looked like his jacket. He went straight to Colleen and sat on the ground next to her.

A seam in his pants ripped, the sound distinct.

"I need a word with you, Moore," Luke announced, but Moore looked up at him with something Colleen had never seen in him before.

Authority.

"Your sister needs significant medical attention. We just broke her wrist, on top of all the contusions and injuries she sustained yesterday. How about you put your pride or grudge or whatever this crap is aside and do your duty as a family member *and* as a first responder by giving Colleen some compassion and *professionalism*?" His voice rose as the sentence went on, a list of grievances against Luke that Colleen heartily shared.

"Oh, burn," Kell mumbled.

"And *you*," Moore said as he slipped his arm under Colleen to help her stand, keeping the cover over her, guiding her to the bed. He looked at Kell. "You're not funny. Be useful. Do you have food? A painkiller? Clothes Colleen can wear? An ambulance?"

"No signal here. Have to get back to the road," Luke explained, taking a breath in preparation for what was clearly about to be a tongue lashing for Moore.

"THEN DO IT! *NOW!*" Moore boomed at him, his intensity making Colleen's heart race.

Luke's mouth snapped shut like a drawbridge.

"Why have you wasted all this time bickering with me when you could have been out there calling 911 for her?"

Luke's face hardened, nose flaring.

Colleen said, "I don't need–"

Moore pressed his finger to her lips. "You do."

Kell took off out the door, his intent clear, while Luke turned as red as his uniform.

"Who the hell do you think you are, lecturing me about my job, while you're screwing around with my sister?"

"I'm her *friend*."

Moore couldn't have injured her worse if he'd kicked her in the gut with steel-toed boots.

Friend.

Oh, no. *No no no*. Not that word. Not now. Not–

This.

Anything but this.

She was so stupid. How could she have been so stupid?

"Guys," Colleen said, fighting tears, her wrist a mangled,

throbbing mess, her heart even worse. "I need water. Some kind of food would be nice." Breathing was suddenly hard, her chest cracked open and collapsing at the same time.

Luke pulled two protein bars out of a pocket and handed them to her and Moore, who took hers out of her hand, opened the wrapper and peeled it halfway back, and returned it to her hand.

That simple, caring gesture made the tears bubble up in her eyes.

"I have a first aid kit in the truck. There's ibuprofen…"

She shook her head, willing herself not to cry. "I can bear it until the hospital. They might have to give me other things. My shoulder is really hurt from the accident."

"Internal bleeding?"

"I don't know."

A blank look passed across Moore's face at Luke's question.

"That–that never occurred to me."

"Of course not. You sell pretty stones and shiny metal for a living," Luke said with a sneer that made her truly hate him a little bit.

"Just because he's not a first responder doesn't mean you need to be like that, Luke," Colleen said, though her words came out tinny and hollow. "He saved me from drowning."

Emptiness washed over her as if someone pulled her drain plug, whatever emotions she had after all the tumult of the last–the last…

"What time is it?" she asked, biting off a mouthful of what turned out to be a peanut butter bar.

"Two p.m."

"Oh."

Twenty-four hours.

A single day.

Nineteen years of hope.

Now nineteen years of... she didn't have a word for realizing you've spent half your life being a fool, and it's been exposed in a single word: *friend*.

The other f-word.

Maybe because no one was dumb enough to do what Colleen had just done.

Why, why, *why* did she cross that line she'd walked so carefully all this time? It was like crossing the Grand Canyon on a tightrope and then letting herself fall the next day. Kissing him, being with him, being wanted by him felt so good last night.

Better than good.

It was a rich indulgence for a woman who'd been starving for so long, and every taste had been a delight. Even as she sat here, head hung down, her own brother judging her with a look that made her skin feel slimy, she regretted nothing.

Which made her feel even worse.

Moore viewed her as a friend. Last night meant nothing to him. What was he going to say next? It was just an accident? A one-time thing, right?

Hey, we were a little tipsy. Lots of emotions flying around after the accident. These things happen. You know. Let's not make it more than it really was.

Even as he stood inches away from her, she could hear him in her imagination, rejecting her. The script wrote itself, typed out letter by letter on a keyboard made of nineteen years of what-ifs.

The pain in her wrist was nothing compared to the pain in her soul.

Heart of hearts, she knew what was coming was the soft backpedal of the morning after. Never cruel, Moore would simply be increasingly distant and so affable that nothing he said could be taken seriously. During all these years of friendship, she'd seen what he did when he didn't want to be close to someone.

Now, finally, after hiding her true feelings from him for so long, it was about to happen to her.

"Hey." Luke was in front of her now, bent at the knee, his eyes soft, all of his anger gone. "I'm sorry. I—you're more important than anything else, Collie."

Hearing her old nickname out of his mouth made the tears finally come.

"I'm so tired."

"I'll bet."

"And hurt."

Luke's lips formed a line. "Mmm hmm."

The front door flew open and Kell walked in, breathless from the cold and exercise. As he shut the door behind him, he dropped a large duffel bag he'd been carrying on one shoulder.

"Basic first aid. And some old clothes Rachel and I were going to put in a donation box but never got around to it."

"My ass is way bigger than Rachel's," Colleen muttered, earning a grin from Luke and a snicker from Kell.

"So wear my old sweats, then," Kell cracked.

"Guys," she gasped, the word full of everything, nothing, all her emotions and each barren piece within her, time spinning too fast, events merging with emotion and turning her in a gyroscope.

"Oh, Collie. It's okay. It'll be okay." Unaccustomed to being the one being comforted, she let Luke hug her. Supporting him through his wife's death had been second nature, and she'd spent plenty of evenings after he'd put his daughter, Harriet, to bed drinking beer and listening to him try not to cry.

And fail sometimes.

Moore had been there most nights, too. Luke never cried in front of him, though, saving the breakdowns for Colleen.

"D-do Mom and Dad know I'm okay?"

"They know we found you. I'm not sure I can officially tell them you're okay, but they know you're alive and conscious," Kell said. "I called them and the paramedics. Ambulance is going to take a while. Is your shoulder too bad? I can carry you out to the road."

"That's too much for you," she replied, earning a huff from Moore, who gave her one of his friendly smiles.

"I did it yesterday."

"If he can do it, I can do it. Moore's puny compared to me."

Kell's joke hung in the air like a fart.

Too much.

It was all too much, and Colleen couldn't handle it.

"Anyone have caffeine?" she asked, earning another grin from Moore, who seemed to have lost all emotional nuance and decided that just smiling was going to be his mode of communication from now on.

"Caffeine?"

"I haven't had coffee for twenty-four hours."

Rustling around in the duffel bag, Kell held up a small packet of instant coffee. "Better than nothing, I guess."

"Here." Moore took the packet from Kell's hand and busied himself at the stove, heating water.

"How are Mom and Dad?"

"Fine. Dad's working on the tree at the CPA office."

"Luke texted me about that," Colleen said. "Poor Tim."

Luke's eyebrows shot up. "You mean poor Tim because of what happened at the airport yesterday, or because the tree fell on their office building?"

"Both." She grimaced. "And how do you know about what happened at the airport?"

"Third Date Colleen struck again. Word gets around.

Also, Tim called Slicer and Slicer was at Bilbee's playing pool, so..."

"Great. Half the town knows by now."

"Not Tim's finest day," Luke noted.

"Or mine," she said at the same time Moore said it from the kitchen, making them both chuckle.

"I heard Tim embarrassed you in front of a crowd?" Kell said as Luke slowly turned his head to watch Moore.

"Anyone who dates you three times is a goner," Luke said loudly to her.

"You really know how to make your sister feel better," she shot back.

"Sorry."

"No, you're not."

"No, but it's the right thing to say when you're looking so pathetic."

"I don't just look pathetic, buddy. I *feel* pathetic."

"We do have ibuprofen, you know."

"Caffeine is a better drug."

Sex, too, she thought but didn't say, the glow in her blood-stream overriding all the pain for a split second as she remembered last night.

And this morning.

They'd made love twice, the first a frenzy of discovery, the second an act of belonging.

And now—now what?

Friend.

He said *friend*.

In her mind, Moore's failure to make a big, dramatic claiming meant he was uncertain, unsure, or worse—certain and sure.

Certain and sure that last night was a fluke.

Crossing that line had been the hardest thing she'd ever done for herself, an act of self-care that overrode nineteen years of a different kind of self-care. Protecting herself from rejection was different from taking a leap, and in the end, the leap felt so much better.

Until now.

Daylight was a great disinfectant, but right now it was killing all her hope.

Chapter 8

Moore

"Let me help you get dressed," he said to her, unsure how to convey all the feelings inside him, especially in front of Luke.

Who clearly wanted to kill him.

His teenage promise was a juvenile vow that had carried over through getting Cammie pregnant, their marriage and divorce, finding Gia, being cheated on at their wedding reception by her, and all of the guys Third Date Colleen had dated and cursed.

Never, not once, had he even hinted to Colleen how he felt about her.

And now, at the moment he needed his best friend the most, Luke was treating him like a criminal.

"I can do it," she whispered, standing shakily. He hovered, creating an invisible forcefield between him and Luke, because damned if his friend's laser-like glare wasn't enough to split him in half, cauterized neatly.

They were adults. Mature adults who could live their lives however they wanted. Surely Luke could understand unexpected love?

Clutching the comforter around her, Colleen shuffled to the bathroom. Moore followed, carrying the clothes Kell had brought. As soon as they were out of earshot, he whispered, "What an uneventful rescue."

A wan smile was all he got in return.

"Thanks for everything, Moore." Taking the clothes, she turned the doorknob and opened the narrow bathroom door. Briefly, her eyes met his.

Sorrow filled them.

"Thanks for being such a good friend."

A wave of emotion swept over him, unidentifiable but definitely not good. As his brain scrambled to find the right words, he opened his mouth, but all he got was a door shut in his face.

Spine tingling with a deep fear he didn't know his heart could generate, he stood around the corner from his angry best friend and wondered what Colleen meant by that.

He'd been about to kiss her, to reconnect out of sight, and instead she–

"Hey. Moore. Get over here." Luke's order was cold and harsh, punitive and angry. When he was in a mood like this, nothing but time would shake him out of it, but Moore had never been on the receiving end of this much fury from his friend.

Before he turned the corner, he closed his eyes and took a deep breath. An uncontrollable inner trembling began. Three breaths weren't enough.

He suspected a thousand wouldn't be, either.

Rustling sounds from inside the bathroom ended with a couple of grunts of pain from Colleen and he wanted to ask if she was okay, but why ask?

He knew the answer.

No. No, she wasn't. Neither was he.

Did she regret last night? Was it not as important to her as it was to him? Had he misread her signals? Taking the leap felt so good, so huge, so right, and when she'd responded to him measure for measure, beat for beat, with an intensity that made his heart sing and his body so grateful to connect, he felt transformed.

Last night had been a metamorphosis for them both.

Hadn't it?

Kell must have pulled back the curtains, because when he opened his eyes, daylight was streaming in. It wasn't sunny, though, just dull and white. In the distance, he thought he heard the faint sound of sirens. Ambulance and police, likely.

Kell held out a mug of something with steam rising off it, eyes caring.

Unlike Luke, who looked like he was ready to walk Moore to the electric chair, stand back, and enjoy the show.

"Here. Caffeinate. You went through it all, too," Kell said without a trace of joking in his voice.

"I did."

"Thank you for saving her, Moore," Kell said somberly. "We saw the truck—we went into the pond."

"Oh, geez." That explained their wet legs.

"When we didn't find—" Kell paused to clear his throat, "—bodies, we assumed you'd both found a way out. Snow's so thick, it covered your tracks. This is the closest cabin to the crash."

"Yeah."

"Must have been hard to find in the blinding snow."

Moore knew exactly what Kell was doing, laying out all the ways Moore had helped Colleen, trying to force it through Luke's thick skull that he was a good guy and hadn't suddenly become Satan because he'd slept with Luke's sister.

In fact, Moore would have done the same thing, but Kell was handling it just fine, so why interfere?

"It was hard. I did what I needed to do."

"You did *way* more than what was needed," Luke snapped. He rushed toward Moore, so fast and in his face that there wasn't time to take a single breath. "What the hell, Moore? She was injured. She was in a car accident. She nearly died, and you decided *now* was the time to break your promise and sleep with my sister?"

"What promise?" Kell inquired.

"Go away," Luke barked at him.

Kell had a good four inches on his brother, and probably forty or fifty pounds of muscle. When he'd come home at twenty-three from his year in Washington, D.C. and rejected city life, he'd gone full lumberjack, bulking up fast and becoming the biggest man in the Luview family.

But not the most stubborn.

Luke was no shrinking violet, either.

"Not going away. You made a promise not to sleep with Colleen?" Kell asked Moore.

"Yeah."

"When?"

"When we were fourteen."

"Quit talking, Moore," Luke said through gritted teeth.

Moore looked at Kell, who asked Luke, "Why? Why would you make him take a vow at *fourteen?*"

"He broke it."

"You're grown men now! I mean," Kell stroked his beard as if pondering a deep philosophical principle, "I can think of lots of reasons why a man wouldn't want to *schtup* my sister–"

"Gross," Luke growled.

"–and then there's the Third Date Colleen curse–"

"SHUT UP, KELL!" Luke and Moore shouted in unison.

In the silence that fell, they all heard a distinct thump from the bathroom, then a very weak, "Hey, guys?"

All three of them rushed to the bathroom, Luke grabbing the doorknob then pausing.

"Collie? You need help?"

"Yeah," she said weakly. "My legs decided to go on strike."

"Damn it," Luke muttered. "I knew I should have brought one of the paramedics with us. But she's walking and her neck seems fine—"

"Why aren't they here?" Moore asked.

"Out searching. Like us. Kell called them." Luke sighed and asked, "Are you dressed?"

"Mostly."

"Can I come in?"

"Yeah."

Moore's heart cracked in half as Luke carefully opened the door to find Colleen slumped on the floor, her borrowed jeans around her ankles, the rest of her dressed.

"I was fine until my brain had to do the pant cuffs. Shoulder and wrist no worky."

"Is that your official nursing medical term?" Moore joked, but Colleen had lost color and looked like she might throw up.

"I'm fine," she protested.

"You're anything but fine," Luke said, swooping in before Moore could reach her, his buddy's possessiveness of his sister crystal clear.

Luke's two-way radio made a sound.

"The ambulance is here," Luke said. "Taking you straight out there."

"I have no pants on."

"Kell, get the comforter spread out on the bed."

"I'll do it," Moore jumped in, doing what Luke had ordered Kell to do, refusing to be shut out from helping Colleen.

Luke carried her to the bed and set her on the comforter, then wrapped her like a newborn and began to pick her back up.

"I can help," Moore said.

Luke gave him a flat stare. "You have no shoes."

Moore muttered a curse.

"Let me check the truck. Might be some old boots in there," Kell offered.

Luke turned away from Moore, Colleen in his arms, her hand sagging across his shoulder.

"Colleen–" he began, but she didn't even open her eyes.

"Thanks, Moore. You were there when I needed you most."

As Kell opened the door for Luke, the flat white landscape made Moore pause. At least eighteen inches of snow blanketed the ground, cut only by the path Luke and Kell had made on their trek to the cabin. Way off in the distance, through bare trees, he saw a red light flashing rhythmically.

"Ambulance?"

"Yeah. Quarter mile or so."

"Be careful with her," he called out to Luke, looking down at his feet and cursing them.

"Someone has to!" Luke shouted back, making Moore's fingers curl into fists, shame radiating through him. He'd done nothing wrong. Colleen had done nothing wrong. They'd shared a beautiful night–and morning, too–and Luke's asinine complex about this was the last thing he needed to deal with.

"I'll be back, with boots if I have them. Look around, maybe they leave their hunting boots here. Otherwise, find something you can wrap your feet with, unless you want me to carry you out to the truck," Kell said.

Moore looked at him, expecting amusement, but found he was serious.

"You're not carrying me."

"I can if I need to."

"Show off."

Kell headed outside, Luke a hundred feet ahead now, moving slowly.

"Hey, Moore?" Kell said, turning and stepping back up onto the porch.

"Yeah?"

"Thank you. Seriously. Not many people could have done what you did. Blind and in freezing water. When we found that truck, we thought—we just waded straight into the pond, expecting to find you dead."

"I'm sorry."

"Why are you sorry?"

"You know what I mean. No one should go out to find their sister and encounter the truck like that. Then go into icy water thinking you'll, you know. Especially Luke, of all people."

"Right." A big, long sigh rushed out of him. "But we didn't find that. Thanks to you."

"Yep."

"Luke's being squirrelly and angry about whatever this promise you made to him is about. But he's indebted to you, too. Once he comes around, he'll be fine. This has been hard on him."

Stomach sinking, Moore looked over Kell's shoulder, Luke's red-jacketed form like a bloodstain against the white snow.

"Just tell me she's going to be okay. I don't give a damn about Luke's anger. Colleen came too close to dying. Her life was in my hands. I don't save lives for a living like Luke and Colleen do. I just—I just..." A bitter tightness threatened his composure, the bridge of his nose flooding with a rare feeling.

Tears.

No. Hell no. He wasn't about to fall apart now.

"Moore," Kell said, his big hand landing on Moore's shoulder, the press of fingers compassionate and caring. "You went through the accident, too. All of it. In some ways, it was harder for you than Colleen. How badly are you injured?"

Other than my heart? he wanted to ask.

But didn't.

A shaky breath gave him enough fortitude to shake off the vulnerability.

"I'm fine. Nothing compared to Colleen."

"No one experiences a flipped vehicle and rescues someone like that without some kind of damage."

"A few scratches," Moore conceded, unwilling to admit that his muscles were screaming now as the urgency of the whole event receded.

Not screaming as loud as his heart, but close.

"You need to be checked out, too." Kell thumbed toward the ambulance. The flashing lights were still in the distance, but Moore couldn't go with her.

Because he had no shoes.

"Just get me some boots so we can go. I never want to see this cabin again." Moore sighed. "I'll write a note to the owner. We owe them big time."

"We owe *you* big time, too. If Colleen had died..."

"I know."

"Luke couldn't have handled it."

"*I* couldn't have handled it," Moore said quickly, earning a hard look from Kell.

"Look, man, whatever happened between you and Colleen is your business. You two are grown-ups."

"Glad *you* see reason."

"And I don't know why Luke went ballistic like that."

Moore shrugged.

"I just know that you and Colleen have never struck me as

the dramatic type. Whatever's going on here needs to quiet down fast."

"Luke is the drama now. Not us."

"Right. And Luke is about as dramatic as dirt."

That made Moore burst out laughing.

"Are you trying to have a moment here with me, Kell?"

"I don't know what the hell I'm trying to do, so maybe I'll just take all the yelling you guys have done to me and shut up."

"Sounds good." Moore could feel himself withdrawing, closing down, walling himself off. Conserving energy? He didn't know. As Colleen's departure sunk in and real life intruded, he felt unmoored.

And when he felt that way, he always backed off from the world.

"I'll just go get you some boots and we'll pretend none of this ever happened, okay?"

"Sure. Thanks."

Kell shut the door with a finality that made Moore walk to the small dining table and lean forward, shoulders sagging, elbows hard to lock. If he weren't careful, he'd fall face first onto the old wooden tabletop.

Just over twenty-four hours ago, his most pressing problem was finding Colleen in a lineup of cars at the airport, his phone carrying a rejection text, his four days with Jordy an emotional rollercoaster.

"Hah," he said aloud, straightening up and beginning his search for writing materials and boots. "That was nothing."

Except it wasn't nothing. Chills shot through him as he thought of his wonderful, gangly son, the boy who hid his true feelings behind a smirk and a smart mouth, so much like Moore it ached.

Those four days were all Moore had in a carefully controlled, court-mandated world where he got his son for fifty days a year. And by God, he'd take every single one of them, even if it meant hauling himself halfway across the country and spending most of his discretionary funds on plane tickets, hotels, and rental cars.

Worth every penny.

What if he'd died back there with Colleen? How would Jordy have reacted? This long weekend had been fun, even if it meant tolerating Jordy's blistering condescension and teenage rebellion.

Moore, though, was a charmer. He knew how to loosen someone up, and there was no more important target than his own child.

Every time Moore visited, the first day was awkward, with Jordy sparing him no verbal negativity. By day two, they always started to have fun, his child's real smile finally emerging under all the long hair and braces. Joy was a word Moore didn't apply to his life in any situation except this: when Jordy was happy.

And now, he had another joyful situation: making love with Colleen. That had been a different kind of joy.

One Moore wholly owned.

"What have I done?" he groaned.

Finally, a kitchen drawer yielded a few pencils and a notepad stamped with the logo of a local insurance company, scribbled with numbers that looked suspiciously like a Scrabble score. Tearing off a blank sheet, he wrote a grateful and very apologetic letter to the owners, leaving his business card.

Soon, word would get out about the accident and the man who'd carried Colleen through the storm to safety. Knowing most cabin owners, Moore suspected they'd be pleased to have passively provided that safety, rather than being pissed about the intrusion.

If they were summer people from New York or Boston, though, all bets were off.

In the note, Moore asked them to call him. Depending on their response, he'd invite them up to Luview to visit the jewelry store, offer them a gift certificate, maybe take them out for a meal.

A check might be welcome, too. Nothing had been harmed in his and Colleen's time here, but sometimes money and attention went a long way toward heading off problems.

And speaking of problems—what was he supposed to do about Colleen?

Before he could think, Kell stomped up the stairs and threw the door open, holding a duffel bag and wearing an expression of chagrin.

"No boots?"

"No boots."

"Damn. None here, either."

"Yeah. I'll have to get you back to the truck the old-fashioned way."

"What's that?"

"Piggyback."

Moore snorted. "You're—oh, geez. You're serious."

"I can carry you easily."

"I'm not questioning your manliness."

"Then what?"

"I'm trying to preserve mine."

"No one's doubting your strength, Moore. Or your, um, prowess."

"Can you stop bringing that up?" A sick feeling washed over him. Kell was perceptive enough to catch it.

"You're not okay. Let's get you to the local ER."

"Where Colleen's going?"

"No. EMTs decided she needs to go to Manchester. Luke went in the ambulance with them."

"That bad?"

"They want to assess everything. Her shoulder, wrist, the hypothermia..."

"I want to go there, then."

Kell put one of his big hands on each of Moore's shoulders, looking down at him. For years, Kell had been the skinny, tag-along kid brother Moore never had. Luke viewed Kell as an annoying mosquito you just couldn't wave away, but he wasn't allowed to smash him against his arm into a tiny smear, no matter how much he wanted to.

Unlike Luke, Moore was the baby of his family, the "bumper kid," with two siblings who were more than a decade older. Effectively an only child, he'd loved being an unofficial member of the Luview clan.

And now... now what was he? Luke was nuclear. Colleen had seemed so sad as she left, as if she'd made a big mistake.

All these years, Moore had held back because he didn't want to ruin the bedrock foundation of his life, the sense of belonging to the extended Luview family.

Had he really misread Colleen that badly? Was it all just the rum and trauma talking?

"Dude. You're a million miles away."

"Sorry."

Alarm filled Kell's face, those slate gray eyes examining him. "Is it a head wound? Maybe we *should* take you to Manchester, too."

Exhaustion made his spine droop, the muscles along it aching as he took in a slow, sorrowful breath. "You know what, Kell?"

"What?"

"That piggyback ride is sounding pretty good right now. Let's get out of here."

"You have to get medical attention."

"I'll go see Doc Blythe."

"Back home? You don't want to go to Manchester?"

"I want to go home. I need to check in with my parents. Word must have gotten out."

"It has. Everyone's buzzing. I texted Rachel to tell her the whole story."

"The *whole* story?"

"Hell, no! Not the part where you somehow found my sister, of all people, attractive enough to bang."

The word *bang* made Moore's hackles rise.

"Don't talk about her like that."

"She's *my* sister."

"All the more reason to treat her with respect."

"I always respect Colleen!"

Moore didn't have eyebrow muscles strong enough to raise them as high as that comment deserved.

"Just shut up about her and banging."

"You really are just like Luke, aren't you?"

"What does that mean?" Moore moved away, grabbing his ruined suit coat, remembering he had nothing but the clothes he was wearing.

"I made a joke about Kylie once and Luke dropped the hammer on me."

"Did he hit you in the head? Because sometimes you act like it."

Turning away, Kell wiggled his butt at Moore. "Are you going to insult me, or climb on?"

"You sound like one of the ladies at Love You Harder."

"How would you know? You've never gone there." Kell spun around. "Or have you? You and Luke been holding out on me? You have some coming of age story where you lost your virginity to a prostitute at that place?"

"Kell?"

"Huh?"

"Shut up and give me a ride."

"Bet they say that at Love You Harder, too."

Before Kell could open his big mouth and say anything worse, Moore grabbed the guy's shoulders and flexed his knees, willing his aching thighs to leap as high as possible, his banged-up knee protesting but not stopping him. Kell caught his feet and Moore hung on, feeling exceptionally vulnerable and at the same time, whimsically free.

"Heigh ho!" he sang out in the Disney tone.

"No singing!"

"HI HOOOOOOOOOOOOOOO!"

"Ugh," Kell groaned as Moore belted out the seven dwarves' song, or a very butchered version of it, Kell closing the cabin door and wading straight into the deep snow, following the tracks he and Luke had already made.

Cold air shocked Moore's lungs awake. Crossing the cabin threshold took him from surreal to real, and with each lumbering, steady step Kell made, what happened with Colleen faded a little bit more.

Which made his soul ache.

And the line he crossed last night was redrawn, thicker than before, darker and bolder.

Because it had to be, now that he'd had a taste of what could be.

And of what she didn't want.

Chapter 9

Colleen

Two Weeks Later

Even with her arm in a cast, Colleen was here at the monthly meeting of the Luview, Maine, Love Committee, staring at a handout with a heart-shaped penis drawn on it, the diagram covered in what looked like architectural blueprint notes.

"Point eight inches," Anne Petrinelli said loudly from the dais. Five members served on the Love Committee, a quasi-governmental body that had no equivalent in any other New England town, or anywhere, for that matter.

The committee had formed in the late 1960s, when some more-or-less lascivious businesses, capitalizing on the Love You theme, began springing up around the town. Love You Harder, the adult bookstore and under-the-radar brothel, had been founded by hippies in 1968. A head shop featuring heart-shaped bongs and roach clips had gone in at the edge of town next to Fields' CPA office.

More recently, someone had started a hookah bar called Love You Lungs.

Alarmed by the sudden prurient nature of the businesses, Anne Petrinelli and her husband Stan, along with Lucinda and Donald Armistead, had gone to town meeting and proposed a new governing body called the Love Committee.

Their official role: to make certain that businesses and homeowners within the downtown district conformed to specific standards, in order to preserve the general atmosphere that supported the town's goals.

Their unofficial role: to block anything they disagreed with.

Colleen didn't want to be here. And she certainly didn't want to stare at blueprints of penises while Anne talked about tenths of an inch.

But she'd volunteered, as a brake against runaway conservatism on the board. Everyone here was at least forty years older than she was, and the committee needed some new blood.

"I think you're searching for something to complain about, Anne," Lorne Tsaki said loud and clear with a twisted smirk on his lips. Lorne was on the committee for the same reason Colleen was:

To keep people like Anne from going overboard.

Lorne was one of the few farmers left living in Luview proper. His land was more mountain than farm, but his two hundred head of sheep and a small, diversified organic vegetable offering spearheaded by his daughter, Beth, drew people from all over.

But it was their famous pie stand that was the biggest draw. Tiny and neat, the 8'x10' wooden structure housed a hundred pies on any given day, including those of the whoopie variety. Colleen's hips held more than their fair share of maple cream whoopie pies from Beth's Best, as the little shop was named.

Last year, Beth had added a coffee machine, and morning business from tourists and tradespeople who couldn't make it to Deke's Breakfast Diner had made Tsaki's Farm a hopping place.

Rachel was working on getting the electric trolley that carried tourists up and down Main Street to extend the 2.3 miles to the pie shack, but first things first.

The Love Committee had a penis that was eight-tenths of an inch too big to deal with.

"Rules are rules, Lorne," Anne replied, mouth tight, nose flaring, her dry wrinkles folding in on themselves. A cornerstone of the community, Anne and her late husband, Stan, were generations-deep residents, though their respective families weren't related to the Luviews or the Bilbees. Stan had been town manager until his heart attack at the wheel of his car.

The car that struck Colleen's sister-in-law, Amber, who was out for a walk on the side of the road that fateful Thanksgiving Day.

No one blamed Stan, and certainly not Anne, but for years after, Anne had practically begged Luke, over and over, to let her help him. Caring for his daughter was her way of atoning for a wrong that she hadn't committed. It made any conflict a bit tricky to navigate.

And when it came to sign standards in town, Anne was all about conflict.

"Are we really going to argue about the size of the penis, Anne? That's it? You're not upset that there's a, you know... penis?"

"That is secondary," she sniffed.

"Since when are they secondary?" Lorne shot back,

leading to titters in the room. A short man, muscular even in his early seventies, Lorne had a keen gaze that made you feel like he understood all the layers of the world better than you ever would, and he was deeply amused by your fumbling through life.

At least, that's how Colleen felt around him.

Bright red now, Anne pointed at Lorne. The two were on opposite ends of the slightly curved committee table on the dais at town hall. Colleen was smack in the middle. Paula Cuomonelli sat between her and Lorne, doing a crossword puzzle, absentmindedly scratching her gray-haired scalp now and then with her pencil eraser. Paula had been Colleen's ninth grade English teacher.

On Colleen's other side sat old Doc Blythe, whose first name was Marion but everyone called him by his title. Sure, the Luview Medical Center, where Colleen worked, was the region's biggest hospital, but Doc Blythe was the family doctor in town, with hospital privileges. He'd delivered her and all her siblings.

With twenty-five hundred residents in Luview, she'd estimate that he had delivered more than half, which made him the unofficial grandpa for hundreds of families.

She was on the stage with people who not only remembered the JFK assassination, they'd been in high school or older at the time.

Never well attended, the public meeting nonetheless was open to all townsfolk. Tonight, only Nadine Khouri, Lucinda Armistead, and—wait a minute.

Was that *Moore* in the audience?

Like Anne, she turned bright red.

Avoiding Moore had become a second job for her, the emotional pain of what had happened between them almost worse than her physical injuries from the accident. A full exam in the ER at the Manchester hospital had revealed more damage than she'd realized.

Broken wrist.

Injured rotator cuff.

Multiple lacerations.

And, as a nurse who could have been Colleen's twin announced around her chewing gum, "You're wicked bruised and wicked *lucky*. Good thing that guy got you out of there."

That guy.

That guy who was currently sitting in the front row of the audience, legs stretched out, hands in his lap, suit jacket unbuttoned. A new wool topcoat was folded over the seat next to him.

The memory of *that guy's* naked, hot body against hers, how he smelled as they made love under the covers, the cabin warming up as if their passion alone heated it, made Colleen squirm in her seat. Moore wasn't looking straight at her, instead watching Lorne and Anne snapping at each other, one corner of his mouth up in amusement.

A mouth she'd kissed.

A mouth she'd enjoyed.

A mouth that had spent some heavenly time between her legs.

A mouth that–

"Colleen?"

"WHAT?" she practically screamed as Lorne said her name, snapping her out of a hazy, dreamy state that made her want to walk off the stage and sit in Moore's lap.

"Are you–are you sure you're fit to be here? Maybe you need more time to recover," Lorne said slowly, respectfully. Anne gave her a worried look, leaning forward at the table.

"Lorne's right," Anne said.

"I am?" He feigned shock. "You'll quit complaining about the cockamamie eighth of an inch on the co–"

"About *Colleen!* You're right about *her*. Look at the poor woman, she's red as a beet."

Closing her eyes, Colleen pursed her lips and tried to pretend Moore wasn't in the room. She waved her cast-covered arm at Lorne.

"I'm fine. Just distracted."

The second the word came out of her mouth, she knew it was a mistake.

Sharp, rhythmic clacking sounds caught her attention as the back door opened, and in walked a man in uniform.

A red uniform with a black belt, black boots, and an attitude the size of the giraffe that had gotten stuck under a bridge arch a few years ago.

Needle. The giraffe's name was Needle.

"You here to arrest Finola Shaughnessy, Luke?" Lorne joked. Finola, the owner of Love You Harder, generally made herself scarce around town.

"For what?" Luke called out, taking a seat in the same row as Moore, but five spots away.

"For her broken penis sign."

All the men in the room made a funny face at the words *broken penis*.

"Not broken!" Anne called out, annoyed. "Eight-tenths of an inch too big."

Luke blinked. Moore covered his mouth with his hand. She knew these two trixters were dying to make jokes, but she also knew the rules.

No juvenile behavior during Love Committee meetings.

Being part of this board meant talking about anything and everything devoted to love, which led to hilarious and occasionally puerile discussions. For instance, heart-shaped condoms.

Yes. Someone had gone there.

Love You Harder was a constant source of contention, but

it was by no means the only issue. Similar to a zoning board, much of the Love Committee's time was spent making sure buildings conformed to the approved color schemes, that the quaint New England architecture was preserved downtown, that the Love You theme wasn't used in a derogatory manner, and that duplication was avoided.

Next on the docket tonight was Love You Ink, the town's first tattoo parlor.

But first things first: the overly large penis.

"Love You Harder isn't within downtown limits," Luke said slowly, eyes on Anne. "This committee doesn't have control over their signage."

"Then why did Finola submit it to us?" Lorne asked, looking at Colleen, Paula, Anne, and Doc Blythe.

"She looking to move closer to town?" Doc Blythe asked, eyes twinkling with amusement as he watched Anne's face, his question clearly designed to goad her.

"We can't—she can't—we can't have that kind of vulgar establishment in town! Bilbee's is bad enough!"

Whatever grudge Luke was holding against Moore, the two instantly bonded again, their faces hardening with a steely resolve Colleen knew all too well. You could say that Bilbee's was run down and shabby, shady even—and you would be right—but to say that to regulars like her, Luke, and Moore meant getting an earful.

"And what's wrong with Bilbee's?" Colleen asked Anne, leaning forward to look her in the eye. In her peripheral vision, she saw Moore smirk.

"Well," Anne sniffed. "I know it's a local institution, and Rider has done a lot to bring up the culinary quality. But it's still a place where people get into fistfights nearly every week, it's a destination for bikers, and drugs are clearly an issue there."

Luke stood and raised his hat like he was waving a red flag at a bull. "May I speak?"

"*Robert's Rules of Order* says no," Anne replied.

"Robert isn't here, so I'll just go on ahead," Luke said. Anne shut her mouth quickly, clearly uncomfortable with facing off against him. "Bilbee's has been around here longer than the Luviews. Nothing wrong with the place. And if there's illegal drug activity there, please report it to yours truly so I can investigate and keep Luview safe. If you're implying the police department isn't doing its job, Anne, then we need to talk."

She turned as red as his uniform.

"Luke! No. Of course I wasn't saying that! You're doing a fine job, and–"

"Then I don't see what Bilbee's Tavern has to do with a drawing of a penis on a sign being an eighth of an inch too big."

"Rules are rules! You of all people should know and respect that, as an officer of the law! If we don't stick to the rules, anarchy will be unleashed!"

"I'm not sure how you get from a simple store sign to anarchy, Anne," Luke said drolly. "Besides, has anyone taken a good look at Section 17, Point 2 of the sign code?"

Moore caught Colleen's eye and winked. Her whole body flooded with heat.

"Of course we have," Lorne muttered. "And we're trying to explain to Anne that the sign in question will be hung on the porch. It isn't a blade sign that will project out into street view, and as you pointed out, since Love You Harder isn't in the downtown district, it doesn't need to be approved by the Love Committee anyway. Finola submitted her plan as a courtesy."

"It's not just the penis size that's an issue," Anne added,

sticking to her guns. She took a deep breath to get ready for whatever came next.

"That's what she said," Colleen muttered, turning toward Lorne to share a quiet laugh, but she hadn't noticed him re-adjusting the position of the microphone nearest them.

Her words came out like a baseball announcer's.

Moore started laughing, his chuckle rumbling deep, sending a direct electric shock to her belly–and below. Lorne cracked up next, until soon the room was nothing but giggles.

Anne picked up the rarely used gavel and banged it once. "This is unacceptable."

"And that's what she said next."

Moore's eyebrows shot up at Colleen's joke.

Not you, she mouthed to him, and his eyes flared. Her reply came so casually, so easily.

So dangerously.

For the last two weeks, they'd avoided talking about what happened at the cabin. It was surprisingly easy.

Because she'd avoided *him*.

Two nights in the hospital in Manchester, then a trip home with Luke treating her like a fragile porcelain doll, had been infuriating. Her mom had hovered over her, every need supplied. Even Harriet had come over and read Ramona Quimby books to her.

Moore had stopped by, but Luke seemed to have a sixth sense for his presence, always there the second his buddy arrived. Neither she nor Moore had pushed to be alone, which told her everything she needed to know.

Their time in the cabin was an aberration. A fluke. A silly indulgence.

A mistake.

The word *mistake* threatened to spike her eyes with tears, so Colleen did what she knew best:

Deflected.

Standing, she reached for the microphone with her good arm, held it near her mouth, and said, "Here's what I think. The sign will be on a covered porch. No one will see that it's an eighth of an inch too big. If this committee receives complaints from residents–*and committee members do not count*–we reconvene on the matter."

Nadine Khouri stood, glancing around the room, eyes lingering on Luke, who was now her boss. The longtime admin at the police station, Nadine was older than dirt and set in her ways.

"Penises have no place in Luview," she began, but her word choice was poor.

Lorne let out a snort that sounded like a moose in heat. It was already audible, but the microphone turned the room into an echo chamber that practically vibrated.

"You know what I mean! And this is completely in violation of the Love Committee rules. No giggling allowed!" Nadine shouted above the giggles and gasps.

The noise was enough to attract people to the doorway. Kell's girlfriend, Rachel, poked her head in; attending these meetings was part of her job as business development director. Colleen wasn't surprised to see the town manager, Tom Kohl, right behind her. Both wore bewildered smiles.

Anne banged the gavel again. "We will have to go into closed session on this!"

Lorne bellowed above the gavel's din, "Penis issues in Luview should be open to the public!"

If this continued, everyone present would end up in Colleen's emergency room, all needing oxygen and emergency surgery to repair busted guts.

Beyond apoplectic, Anne threw the gavel at Lorne, but he had surprisingly sharp reflexes for a man of his age and the wooden mallet struck the wall behind his head as he ducked. Anne stormed out, with Nadine and Lucinda Armistead, who had not said a word the entire time, following her like a line of angry protesters.

Which was basically what they were.

Paula looked up from her crossword puzzle and exclaimed, "PHALLUS!"

"Yes," Doc Blythe replied to her, tilting his head. He'd laughed along with the rest of them but was looking at his pager most of the time. "Phallus is another word for penis."

"No! I mean, yes, but that's the word I needed to finish the puzzle."

"Were you listening at all, Paula?" Colleen asked her, astounded to see the entire *New York Times* crossword puzzle filled in already. When they'd sat down to start the meeting, it had been blank.

"Pshaw," she said, waving a dismissive hand in the direction of the door, where the three older women had walked out. "Let them rant. The minute I saw there was a sign involving a penis, I knew this would just be another pearl-clutching meeting."

"Aren't they all?" Lorne asked.

"No," Doc Blythe replied. "Sometimes we have to ban the bank drive-thru from offering green or orange lollipops. Heaven forfend the children of Luview learn that there is any color besides red, white, or pink. Protecting young psyches at all costs."

"I cannot believe we spent three hours on that issue," Paula muttered, sliding her clipboard into an oversized canvas purse. "What about kids who like grape? Or orange, or lime?"

"Cast thee out, Satan," Lorne whispered jokingly, eyes narrowed to slits.

"Hey, now." They all turned to see Rachel and Tom in the aisle next to Moore and Luke. "The Love Committee plays an important role in branding for the town. You of all people,"

Tom said, pausing to lend his considerable authority to the situation, "should understand that."

"So much of what we do is silly," Paula said matter-of-factly.

"If you're going to go in that direction, then the whole concept of Love You, Maine–where every day is Valentine's Day–is silly, Paula. That's the point. Our town runs on love. Our economy runs on love. We are a destination that is devoted to a feeling, and we have to shape people's feelings when they're here." Tom folded his arms over his chest, a pen in his front shirt pocket skewing at a rakish angle.

It was, of course, red.

"Because feelings are how you crack wallets open?" Lorne said as he took a long sigh, then a big drink from his thermos.

"Because feelings are how you get people to come back. Over and over. You all know that." Tom's eyebrows shot up. "You of all people, Lorne, understand the concept of building a customer base. Beth's doing an outstanding job with her pies and coffee. You give people what they expect, make them feel what they are seeking to feel, and they come back."

Rachel nodded, eating up Tom's words. "Exactly! My bikesharing initiative is next on the agenda, and that is exactly why I need you all to approve it." She looked at Tom, who made a face. "I promise they'll all be pink, white, or red. I even found heart-shaped red baskets for the fronts of the bikes!"

"Downtown will be littered with bikes everywhere," Paula said with a sigh.

"But it'll cut down on cars–less driving within town. And they won't be free–there'll be a nominal fee to rent them, so it's revenue enhancement. Win-win!"

Colleen grinned at her. Rachel was like a dog with a bone when she was determined.

Just like her.

At that thought, she let herself look at Moore, who was

listening to Tom and Rachel. For two weeks, she'd managed to stay out of his orbit, but now the feeling was building within. While the rest of them argued about pink bikes and lollipop-related cruelty to children, Colleen braced herself for the conversation she knew was coming.

How did she know? Because she was about to initiate it.

Just not anywhere near Luke.

"Hey." Speaking of the devil, her red-uniformed brother touched her elbow, whispering softly. "You okay?"

"I'm fine. Why are you here?"

He looked down at his shoes and her temper flared.

"Mom sent you, didn't she?"

"Yeah," Luke confessed. No use lying.

"I am *fine*," she said firmly.

"Is he harassing you?"

"Who?"

Luke's eyes cut to Moore, who was still sitting in the same seat, watching the lively conversations as if he had nothing better to do.

"What is wrong with you?" she hissed. "The big brother act is bad enough when Dennis is home. I don't need one of my annoying *little* brothers playing the macho jerk on my behalf. Moore and I are fine."

"He keeps coming over."

"So do you!"

"I just..."

"You just what, Luke? Think if you stalk us you'll prevent us from being together?"

Luke's head snapped back in shock. "Together? You two are together?"

"No! But you're annoying me enough to want to sleep with him again just to piss you off!" she uttered between fiercely clenched teeth.

Too caught up in this bizarre conversation, she hadn't

noticed that Moore was now approaching them from one side and was well within earshot of her hasty comment.

He froze.

Then he grinned.

And then he looked at Luke and stopped grinning, the comical erasure of his smile forcing Colleen into a spate of giggles more intense than anything she'd experienced all day.

Luke reached for Moore's arm, fingers digging into his biceps. "Don't."

"Don't what?"

"Just don't."

"That's a very broad order, Officer Luview."

"You know exactly what you shouldn't *don't*."

"Are you okay? Because that's some word salad coming out of you."

"I blame you."

Incredulous, Colleen watched their conversation. With only one good arm, she didn't have the ability to grab Luke's earlobe and drag him across the room like she did when he was twelve and dyed her white Keds with red punch for fun.

"Mrs. Cuomonelli is here and if she heard you say that sentence, she'd make you diagram it and assign you detention homework."

"I wouldn't have to speak in such a twisted way if you two didn't act in such a twisted way."

"Don't blame your weirdness on us!"

"I'm only acting like this because of you."

"Butt out, little bro. What Moore and I do or don't do is none of your business."

"Since when?"

"Since the night I learned that there's no worries about a certain penis being only eight-tenths of an inch longer than desired."

Luke's eyes flew open, the whites so stark against his red

uniform that he looked like the pre-blood moment in the movie *Carrie*.

Moore snickered, the sound ending in a strange gulp-hiccup as he realized she might be talking about *him*.

"We're grown-ups," Colleen began.

"We are?" Moore choked out.

"*I* am," she clarified. "And I've been avoiding you for two weeks." Ignoring Luke, she gave her full attention to Moore, squaring her shoulders to give herself some added courage, then regretting it as her not-quite-healed side flared with pain. "Let's talk."

"That's why I'm here."

Folding his arms over his chest, Luke planted himself firmly in place, as if he had every intention of witnessing what she intended to be a very private affair.

Er... conversation.

Private *conversation*.

So many years of being around Moore made her reaction to him now bewildering. The air between them had changed, and it felt fresh and exciting but chaotic at the same time. Had she misread what happened at the cabin?

After all, she wasn't exactly her best self at the time.

If he wasn't interested, then avoidance made sense, but so many mixed signals had turned her insides into a tornado.

Colleen pointedly stepped around Luke, standing next to Moore, who looked down at her with a grin that made her toes curl. For years, she had hung out at Bilbee's with him, gone to baseball games, painted the new camp with him, gone on countless coffee runs and road trips, spent holidays together... How had she not felt this every moment?

"Stop," she said to Luke, whose hairline moved back as his frown deepened.

"I need to talk to both of you."

"Get in line. Moore and I need to be alone."

"Last time that happened, look where it got you."

"Luke."

"What?"

"Stop it. I mean it."

"That's my line, sis."

"You're really crossing a line."

"*I'm* the one crossing lines?" He let out a huff, eyes pinging between Colleen and Moore, clearly quite certain his outrage was justified.

They both looked back at him with more tolerance than he deserved. Colleen felt deeply connected to Moore, each tick of the clock intensifying her attraction to him.

"MOORE!"

Everyone turned as Moore's nephew, Joey, jogged into the room. Colleen grinned. She loved Joey.

Moore's sister Marissa had moved away, but her only child, Joey, stayed in Luview. Like lots of people there, he was a townie through and through. Moore's parents had been thrilled to have a grandchild interested in the business. Moore would take over when his parents retired and Joey would inherit from Moore.

"The natural order of things," as Moore's father, Leander, often said.

Dressed in a well-tailored suit, Joey stood as tall as Moore but without the early-twenties addition of muscle on his frame. With his dark hair and dark eyes, the kid was a Mottin through and through.

"Hey, Joey," Moore replied, frowning. "Let me guess. Serious jewelry emergency?"

"Life or death," Joey deadpanned.

Luke just snorted and reached for Colleen's arm, pulling her away as Joey and Moore looked at something on Joey's phone. A string of numbers was all she could hear as they moved to a spot closer to the edge of the dais.

"I guess the committee is adjourned," Colleen said dryly as Luke gave her a look so emotional, she felt her heart seize.

"Colleen. Don't do this."

"Do what?"

"Hurt yourself."

She wiggled her cast. "Too late."

"I mean with Moore."

"I told you to butt out, Luke."

"He–he's not your type."

"What's that supposed to mean?"

Looking around the public space, Luke's mouth twisted with distaste. "We should talk someplace else."

"We shouldn't talk about this at all."

"Think about it. Why now? After all these years, now? You guys don't want to ruin your friendship just for a quick lay."

"What makes you think it was quick?"

Luke reddened. "I'm worried about you. Both of you."

"Because you think Moore will get hit by a bus and land in my ER after our third date?"

"Don't even joke like that."

"So you can make fun of Third Date Colleen but I can't?"

"Because neither of you has the greatest track record with love, and I care about you. How can you possibly think this is a good idea?"

Lungs could seize, too, just like hearts.

"You're being an ass."

"I'm being realistic."

"You can't tell me who to date."

"No, I can't. But I can warn you."

"Warn me about *Moore?*"

"About Cammie."

At the mention of Moore's ex, Colleen's blood turned to ice water.

"Cammie?"

"Remember? Part of the reason why she took off with Jordy all those years ago?"

If it hadn't been for the cast, Colleen would have throttled him.

"That was a decade ago!"

"She meant it."

"She was delusional! She thought Moore was in love with me—she threatened me! She told me she'd disappear with Jordy if I–if we…"

"I know. She told me, too. Should have realized it wasn't just some hotheaded venting. She was telling me in advance about her plan."

"What does Cammie have to do with me and Moore?"

"What if you two get together and she holds Jordy back from visiting?"

"You're really pulling that old issue out?" Furtive glances told her Moore was definitely out of earshot now. "And *shhh*. Moore still doesn't know–unless you told him."

"I never told him. Unlike some people, I keep my promises." His eyes cut over to Moore.

"What's that supposed to mean?"

"Nothing. Just… you two have a lot at stake if you end up together. And it seemed like you were both pretty cold to each other when it was time to leave that cabin."

"You–you noticed that?"

"Yeah."

Ouch.

With a long sigh, she leaned forward and whispered, "Stay out of my life."

"Don't kill my best friend."

"*Huh?*"

"The last thing Moore needs is a heart attack after your third date."

If they weren't in public, she'd have started screaming at him, or worse, banging him over the head with her pink arm cast.

"Do I butt into your love life like this?" she began, the question rhetorical. A long list of grievances was forming in her mind.

"You mean like when you ran into Kylie picking up takeout at Mountain Dragon and you warned her not to toy with my heart? At the beginning of our relationship, when she was particularly fragile?"

The tongue lashing she was about to inflict on him quickly turned into her choking on her own tongue. Damn. He was right. She *had* interfered.

But that was different! It was for his own good.

"And before you try to claim that was different, it's not."

Double damn.

"Moore is my best friend. You're my sister. This is gross. Don't make it worse."

"What's worse than gross?"

"Having you two break up and force people to take sides."

"You're seriously reaching here, Luke."

"Am I? No. No, I'm not. You know full well how many family feuds in this town started because two people fell in love and then fell out of it. Generations of fury rest on the whim of two lust-filled idiots."

"Now you sound like Anne Petrinelli on one of her rants!"

"No. I sound like a brother who likes his friend circle the way it is. If you and Moore get romantically involved, when it goes south, it'll suck for everyone. Not only will you be hurt, but playing darts at Bilbee's will never be the same."

"I'm supposed to rearrange my emotional life to make sure you're comfortable during dart night at freaking Bilbee's?"

"You're supposed to think with your head and not with your–" He made a *harumph* sound.

"What the hell, Luke? I'm not allowed to have the full range of feelings every other grown person in town gets? Is that really what you're saying?"

"I'm not saying anything like that!"

"It's exactly what's spewing out of that sewage pipe you call a mouth!"

"Quit using Mom's lines on me."

"Not my fault they're true!"

Catching a whiff of Rachel's perfume, Colleen turned around and there she was, looking at Luke like he was a rabid raccoon and she needed a blanket to throw on him.

"Um, are you guys okay?"

"No!" they said in unison.

"Whatever's going on might be better done outside. We have a zoning board meeting in two minutes." She was clutching a file folder against her hip like a warrior grasping a spear before heading into battle.

"Any penis signs up for review?" Luke asked.

"Given we're talking to a new Christian church, I would expect not," Rachel said diplomatically. The chagrin and embarrassment on Luke's face almost made Colleen soften.

Almost.

What actually did melt her a little was Moore's reappearance.

His light cologne, mingling nicely with the charcoal gray suit he wore, made her recall woodsmoke. Hands on her thighs. Fingertips digging into her round ass.

His face between her legs.

Smiling.

Luke started to say something to Moore, but his walkie-talkie squawked. He listened to something unintelligible as Rachel stepped away. Moving to the committee table, she began neatly centering all of the microphones, the cords parallel to each other, order restored.

An aggravated sigh rushed out of Luke, sounding like a wind tunnel.

"You," he said, pointing in Moore's face. "We're not done."

"How could we ever be done? We're best friends. Cradle to grave. Remember?" Moore held out his pinkie, hooked.

Luke gave him an eye roll to end all eye rolls, hands on his hips, the walkie-talkie sounding like a broken drive-thru microphone.

"You want the grave part of that to happen sooner? Keep this up."

"Keep what up?" Moore asked innocently, making Colleen's skin tingle even more. Suppressing laughter at Moore torturing her little brother was definitely an old, familiar feeling.

Being the object of conflict between them most certainly was *not*.

"Bye, Officer Caveman. Go do your job." Colleen dismissed her little brother with the derisive sneer of a thirteen-year-old girl.

Luke's mouth tightened. The machine on his hip barked at him.

As her brother marched away in his red uniform, the thick red down coat he swung across his shoulders like a blood cape, she flashed back to Officer Tomes at the airport, when Tim called her a witch and the world was so much simpler.

The cop's uniform had looked so strange to her, but Love You, Maine, was the oddity. The sleepy little town followed a different set of rules. Luview made its living peddling visions of love.

Literal visions—the signage requirements were a symbol of that.

"Now that Little Red Riding Luke is gone, can we really talk?" Moore asked her, leaning down to whisper in her ear.

His hand went to her shoulder, the one that was still healthy and worked fine.

His touch nearly made her moan.

When Luke had first donned his uniform, years ago when he joined the Luview police force, Moore had been the one to give him that infernal nickname.

"You started that nickname."

Moore grinned.

"Sure did."

Come to think of it...

"And you gave me my nickname!"

"What nick–oh." He had the decency to wince. "Yeah. I did."

"Third Date Colleen. You're a master at finding the smallest number of words to trigger the biggest amount of shame in someone."

He went still.

"Never thought of it that way."

"I don't think you do it intentionally."

"I–Colleen. I never meant to–"

What had she just done? Turned the conversation in a direction she hadn't seen coming, that's for sure. All the attraction was still there, her arousal too strong to push aside, but suddenly, the moment was serious. A whole new can of worms had been opened.

"Come here," she said to him.

Her impulse was to take Moore's hand but propriety forced her to remember how things were before the accident. Before the cabin. To move through space in public with him as her friend.

Just her friend.

Nothing more.

Which might be true right now, too. Was she just a friend? Having settled for that status for so long, she should have been able to easily slip back into that role. Play that part.

Smile. You're on camera.

Instead, this was excruciating, a different kind of separation from him. From herself. Overthinking every moment around Moore was so much harder than just walling it all off and living a life that wasn't complete.

It had a Moore-shaped hole in it. Yes, he was there, but that hole, that missing piece, had plagued her, forcing her into constant denial.

Denial she couldn't allow any longer.

Not when the memory of him in bed was burned so deeply into her body and soul that she'd never be the same.

Finding a small meeting room, she walked in. The table was just big enough for four people, three chairs in a crooked line along one side. A black office phone with multiple lines sat on the table; the window blinds were closed.

Moore shut the door behind them.

Striding over to the whiteboard on one wall, he picked up a red dry-erase marker and wrote *List of Reasons Why Moore Is a Dumbass* in his crooked, left-handed script.

"We're gonna need a bigger board," she cracked.

His arm was in mid-air, suit jacket askew, ass on beautiful display. He re-capped the marker and set it down, then picked up the eraser and slowly wiped away the words. Turning around, he caught her eye.

Oh, no.

She wasn't imagining a thing.

He burned for her, too.

"Colleen," he began, taking a step toward her. One hand went to his forehead, where his fingers raked his short hair. Dark and a bit wavy, it matched the neatly trimmed beard well. More of his cologne filled the air as he moved, and she realized the room was so tiny.

And her arousal was so big.

"Yes?"

"I keep trying to see you. Talk to you about what happened at the cabin. Luke's made it–"

"Hard."

"Right. But it shouldn't be hard. It should be..." Voice trailing off, he squinted at her, the same face she'd seen hundreds of thousands of times looking at her in a completely new way.

"It should be what?"

"You tell me."

"Oh, no. Not letting you do that."

"Do what?"

"Put it all on me."

"When you left the cabin, it seemed like..."

"Like what?"

"You know."

"MOORE!" she hissed, heart pumping so hard, it shot heated blood to the tops of her knees. "Just say it!"

"Say what?"

"How do you feel about me?"

A rush of raw emotion covered Moore's face, his eyes glittering. Every breath felt like years were filling her lungs, so much shared experience, so many happy moments. But he wasn't her old friend now, he was a man she wanted. Deeply and wholly, but more than anything else, she wanted an answer.

A sense of closure.

A decision.

One way or another, they were going to go down a path. Either they turned around on the path and went back to being friends, or they moved forward through the unknown passages of the heart.

His mouth took hers in the softest of kisses, so featherlight that she gasped, those years she'd inhaled all coming out and surrounding them as if witnessing a vow.

His hands wrapped around her waist, palms and fingers splayed against the middle of her back, pulling her close, his grasp telegraphing his need. As her lips parted, she invited his tongue in, the kiss the answer she'd desperately hoped for.

Still ambiguous, but one part of her confusion was now allayed:

He wanted her.

Whatever happened next, she knew that much.

Wearing a cast while kissing him turned out to invite klutzy drama, because when she reached up to wrap her arms around his neck, passion filling her, she clunked him on the ear with her pink monstrosity.

"Umph!" he said into her mouth, his teeth banging against hers, his hands clasping her tighter as she inhaled sharply.

"I'm so sorry!"

"It's fine," he soothed, laughing. "Comic relief."

"I was rather enjoying the moment. Nothing funny about your kisses."

The look he gave her made it clear her words were warmly received, his new kiss one of determination, the earlier one an exploration.

This one was a declaration.

A claim.

Maybe even a dare.

"Moore," she whispered against his mouth. "I really want you to know that–"

He moved against her suddenly, hips sharp against her belly, the thrust completely out of character. Until he made a small sound of pain, she thought he was joking around, but then she looked over his shoulder, shocked to find her mother standing there, shoving the doorknob into Moore's backside.

Her *mother*.

"Oh, my goodness!" Deanna Luview exclaimed, eyes wide and crawling all over the sight before her. "I had no idea!"

Moore shot across the room as if Colleen had stung him.

"Hi, Mom. Thanks for knocking."

"I–I... you two? What?"

"Mom. Stop."

"This is so wonderful!" Deanna gushed.

Colleen's eyeballs fell backwards into her head, rolled down her cheekbones, kissed her tonsils and landed on her tongue. Moore looked about the same.

"MOM!"

"I mean–why are you kissing in a conference room like this? Is it a secret?"

"MOM!"

"It's just–"

"You. Saw. Nothing! Do you understand?"

"I saw more than enough. Was your hand on his–"

Hampered by her cast, Colleen didn't have her normal dexterity, but pure embarrassment fueled her enough to be able to grab Deanna's arm and pull her close.

"Luke's being unreasonable. Moore and I are figuring stuff out. Now you're invading our privacy–"

"I was looking for you! I'm your ride, remember? You can't drive yet. I went to the committee meeting but Rachel said you'd left, and then I find you making out with Moore!"

Who looked like he was wishing for a magic portal to transport him to another dimension.

He reached into his front jacket pocket and pulled out his phone, fooling no one.

"Uh, text from my dad. Gotta go."

"Liar," Colleen hissed.

"I gotta go."

"Less of a liar."

He closed his eyes for a second, then turned to Deanna with a firm expression. "Don't say a word."

"I–"

"Deanna," he said in a commanding tone Colleen still couldn't get used to. "I mean it."

"What–what is this?"

"Our business," he replied.

"You can't keep this a secret! You're lucky Nadine didn't walk in on you."

All three of them shuddered.

"Mom," Colleen pleaded, changing her tone. "Moore and I went through hell with the accident. Luke's added another layer of purgatory to it. We're just starting to talk. Can you try to understand? We need time. Privacy. Discretion."

Appealing to her mother's mushy emotional core was absolutely the right tactic. Deanna's eyes filled with compassion and mercy. She reached for Moore's face and held it in her hands.

"You. You deserve to be happy," she said to him as he froze.

"I do?"

"Of course! I've been saying for years that you two belong together."

"Who have you said that to? Not me!" Colleen choked out.

"Your father. Luke. Kell," Deanna said matter-of-factly.

"Oh, geez," Moore groaned as he stepped out of her mother's grasp.

"Luke thought I was joking," Deanna said with a wicked grin. "Hah! We'll see who was right now."

"No, Mom. No, we won't. You won't. No betting pools arranged at Greta's. No subtle hints designed to reveal us. We don't even know what *us* is. Don't–*please* don't," Colleen begged, her voice shaking at the end, surprising even her.

"Oh, honey!" her mom exclaimed as Moore moved in closer, his arm going around Colleen's shoulders, protective and team-like. Deanna stood before them, bewildered but also respectful.

"Deanna," Moore began, but her mom cut him off.

"Zipped lips. I won't say a word."

"You are second only to Nadine when it comes to town gossip," he replied slowly, earning a shocked look from Deanna.

"I am not!"

Colleen burst out laughing.

Deanna's mouth formed a straight, angry line. "Fine. But you two better figure this out."

"You make that sound like a threat."

Her mother flounced out of the room, slamming the door behind her, leaving Moore to press his hands against the wall and lean forward, letting out a huge breath.

"That went well," Colleen half joked.

"That was a–"

"There you are!" Moore's nephew, Joey, poked his head in. "What'd you do to Deanna?"

"Nothing," they answered in unison.

Joey gave them a look that said he definitely thought otherwise.

"Moore, the delivery guy from Boston says he was rear-ended on the way here. Some crystal items broke. I know it's after hours but I need your help."

Relief filled Colleen. For as much as she wanted to talk with Moore, and certainly kiss him again, this was all overwhelming. A little space would be welcome.

"We're done here," she piped up, earning raised eyebrows from Moore.

"We are?"

"Done for now. We can pick up where we left off next time."

Joey's phone rang. He answered it while Moore stared at her.

"You sure?"

"*Exactly* where we left off," she assured him.

While Joey took his call, Colleen slipped out the door, walking down the hall to the nearest exit. As she looked around for Deanna's truck, the cool winter air gave her a brisk wake up.

Which she desperately needed.

"What am I doing?" she whispered into the chilly air, as if it had an answer.

It didn't, of course.

And neither did she.

Chapter 10

Moore

Love You Jewelers was the only jewelry store in town.

And as Moore made his morning walk from the back stairs of the apartment above the store around the block to the front door, the Maine spring air still crisp, holding a hint of snow in it, he smiled as he approached.

There were plenty of gift shops that sold cute little baubles, but Love You Jewelers was the only place you could go to find gemstones, gold, silver, platinum, and the perfect ring for your lovestruck needs.

They sold good old standards: promise rings, engagement rings, wedding bands. Gold lockets stamped with the Love You Jewelers logo were a popular item you could only purchase in person, no online sales.

These flew off the shelves every year at Christmas and especially Valentine's Day.

When Moore stepped into the business ten years ago, his

father had told him firmly that absolutely nothing could change. Their bread and butter came from the lovesick tourists who were searching for the perfect item to express their feelings. That item may have been the very same thing that thousands of other people were using to express *their* unique love, but that didn't matter to his father.

What mattered was that every customer who walked through the doors of Love You Jewelers came in with a question and went out with a package.

Moore had followed his father's dictate, but had found a way to quietly subvert—never rocking the boat enough to hurt sales of the old standards, of course. Instead, Moore had slowly expanded the custom design side of the business, which his father had always offered but never seriously promoted.

Moore enjoyed the travel that was required to find good gems, to source high-quality precious metals, and to network in ways that kept their small-town jewelry store in the national spotlight. Location alone wasn't going to cut it, though.

Some of the larger chains occasionally tried to get a toehold and establish a franchise in Love You, Maine, but the Love Committee had been an exceptional ally in protecting Love You Jewelers from outside pressure. Their only competitors were in the neighboring towns.

And so Love You Jewelers continued to be the only place in town to buy a symbol of your heart's true message to the person who made your pulse race, your limbs tingle, and who lit you on fire.

Commissions for custom designs trickled in at first, then began to come in at a steady rate. Moore's father had been forced to recognize that the revenue stream from what Moore was doing was significant enough that he deserved the closest thing his father could give to an accolade:

"Nice to see you can balance both lines without hurting the core business," Leander Mottin had said.

While that terse sentence didn't exactly make Moore swell with pride, he did feel at least a little vindicated. Custom designs would never outpace the thousands of standard mainstream products they sold, but they gave Moore a place where he could be himself within the confines of a life he'd never chosen.

As he jiggled the key in the lock, the deadbolt frustratingly misaligned and difficult to coax into place at times, he heard footsteps approaching and paused, turning around. A very nervous young man in a hoodie and jeans was toeing the concrete about ten feet away.

"Can I help you?" Moore asked, knowing exactly what this guy was here for.

"Uh... yeah, uh... are you, uh, open?"

When the young man pulled the hood off his head, he revealed a baby face. This kid couldn't be more than eighteen or nineteen.

Same age as Moore when he became a father.

"I'm about to be, if I can get this door to cooperate." He shook the keys and went back to his magic act with the lock.

The kid laughed through his nose. "Yeah. That happens all the time at the sub shop where I work. Owner's too cheap to get the lock fixed."

Moore laughed.

The guy inhaled sharply. "Oh–no–I didn't mean to imply that, like, *you're* cheap. I just meant..."

Click

Moore succeeded, the deadbolt sliding back, allowing him to push the door open and turn around.

"It's cool," he said to the kid, who stood under the red awning that covered the storefront. The words *Love You Jewelers* were printed in white on the awning, the letters backward from Moore's viewpoint, looking like a foreign language that made the store more exotic than it really was. "Come on in. I can help you."

"That's okay. It's three minutes until you open, right? Go take your time. Get your coffee. I know how it is."

Moore waved him in. "Get in here. I can make my coffee while you look."

"Really?" He perked up. "'Cuz..." The kid pulled a phone out of his back pocket and stuck it in front of his face. "'Cuz I've only got twenty minutes. I've got to get back for my shift."

"Let me guess," Moore said, looking him up and down. "A promise ring."

"How'd you know?"

"'Cuz I'm psychic," Moore deadpanned.

"Seriously? My mom's super into that since Grandma died."

Moore blinked. Sometimes his smart mouth got him into trouble.

"No, I'm not actually psychic." Mr. Hoodie followed him into the shop and closed the door, flipping the sign from Closed to Open. "I've just been working at a jewelry store for a very long time, and I can spot a promise ring from a thousand feet away. What's your partner like?"

The kid went still.

"She's the best," he said in an earnest voice that made something inside Moore melt a little, an instant flash of Colleen coming into his heart, as if she were the one who'd unlocked a glitchy deadbolt and managed to open the door, flipping the sign from Closed to Open in the process.

The kid's eyes met Moore's.

"You ever feel that way about someone?" His words rushed out. "Where the love just doesn't fit inside you? It just spills out all over, and it's like you have to pick it up and carry it with you everywhere, but it just keeps falling and you can't drop any of it, until finally all you can do is lay in bed and listen to music and stare out into space, and it just takes over and suddenly you're floating in a giant ocean of... *her*."

"That sounds like a lot of emotion," Moore said carefully, the words smooth and professional, even if the rest of him felt like it was drowning.

Drowning in years of love that had indeed been spilling over, all of it for Colleen.

"I'm Moore," he told the kid, reaching out to shake his hand. "What's your name?"

"Elliott."

"Okay, Elliott. Nice to meet you. Why don't we go over to this case and you take a look at the rings while I go get that cup of coffee you were talking about?"

"Cool. You get it. I totally can tell, you get it," Elliott smiled.

"You can?" Moore stumbled. "How?"

"When you know, you *know*."

The cryptic phrase made Moore chuckle and walk away before he said anything so stupid, he couldn't walk it back. As he approached the back room, the smell of pine hit him hard. Last night was the weekly cleaning and their longtime person, Jeanette Fowler, had clearly done her job.

The woman was addicted to pine. She used it, along with an obscene amount of bleach, on the bathroom in the back. Moore turned on the HVAC system and hoped the odor would clear out quickly.

"Hey," he called out to the front of the store, "you want a cup of coffee, too?"

"No, thanks though. I'm gonna hit up Love You Coffee. They've got that drink called the Love Bomb."

"How do you know about the Love Bomb?" Moore called back. "Are you from around here?"

"No, I'm over near Fryeburg, but my girlfriend *loooves* those Love Bombs. I'll get her one on my way out of town."

Moore smiled to himself as he used the carafe to fill the water compartment of his coffee machine. He'd have to make sure to tell Rachel that her custom-designed drink at the coffee shop was *that* popular.

Coffee grounds in place and machine percolating, he headed back to the front of the store, turning on soft jazz that would play at a level so low you only realized it was there in total silence.

Setting a mood for people who came in to buy a luxury item meant creating a luxurious scene, and he had a part to play in that as well. This was why he spared little expense on his business clothes.

Research had shown that there was a sweet spot. If they made Love You Jewelers too high-end, they would lose a lot of the middle-range business. But it still had to be aspirational for that middle-range customer. This was the kind of contribution that Moore had brought to the business ten years ago, painstakingly showing his dad the market research.

As a result, his dad had added a slightly better line of watches and rings, just expensive enough to provide three levels for people coming in, and here's what they had found:

Some people came in with a specific budget, and they could buy the lowest level and that was it; there was no upselling possible.

Some people came in with a specific budget, but they could stretch it, and that's where some of the changes Moore had put in place had worked. To his father's surprise but not Moore's, people often went for the top option when there were three choices.

Aspiration, he had explained to his dad. Adding marketing materials that featured photos of celebrities wearing the higher-end pieces had been one key to their success.

"How's it goin'?" Moore asked Elliott, knowing immediately that this was going to be a low-end sale. That was fine.

When you're eighteen, why spend a bunch of money on a symbol of your love? This kid was so lovesick, he was a walking symbol of what he felt for his girl.

That would be more than enough for her.

That was what he really wanted to say to most of their customers: *I know you want to give a tangible symbol of your love, but your love is enough. The symbol is extra.* Once in a while, he got a customer who was worried that they'd offend the recipient of the special ring or necklace by choosing the wrong piece, and that's when Moore had to swallow his opinions and just act a part.

Because if you were giving someone a piece of your heart in the form of metal and gems and you truly thought that they might reject it because it wasn't enough, then run screaming.

That's exactly what he had dealt with when he was with Cammie.

"What do you think?"

"I don't know." Elliott was puzzling over a tray of twenty or so promise rings. "There's too many to choose from, and I don't have much time."

"Let me help you. This is my job."

A nervous smile was the reply.

"What's her favorite gem?"

"I don't know."

"What's her favorite color?"

"Green!" The kid gained confidence in knowing the answer.

"An emerald might be the right choice." Plucking three little emerald rings from the tray, he held them up to Elliott, who zeroed in on the middle one.

"I think she'd like that one." Holding it up to the light, he rotated it, then looked at the price tag and winced.

"Got anything cheaper?" Shoulders sagging, his entire demeanor changed.

"What's your budget?" Moore asked, and Elliott named a figure. He appeared to be relaxing, and that's what Moore wanted in his customers. Confidence. Excitement. Eagerness.

No one should be anxious and upset when buying something so important. Love shouldn't be so complicated.

And expressing love, even in the form of jewelry, should be joyful.

Elliott's budget narrowed the entire process down. Moore pulled out five different rings.

"Are they emeralds?" Elliott's voice was filled with trepidation.

"No, these are different green gemstones. Peridot, aventurine, and tourmaline. Still beautiful, but less expensive than emeralds." Sliding three from the five, he created a row for the kid to examine. One of the softer skills in working with a customer was budget. A wide selection of merchandise was crucial.

You always offered three items that could work. Just one and they felt like they were settling.

Two felt like they could easily pick the wrong one.

Three was just right. Like Goldilocks.

"Oh, man," Elliot sighed, clearly tortured. He held his mouth a bit tight, one side of his mouth pulled up in a half-smile. "I knew this was going to be hard, but I didn't think it would be this bad."

"Bad?"

"Whatever I pick is, you know... forever."

"Isn't that the point?" Moore smiled.

"Sure. Of course. But when we're old and gray–" Elliot squinted, and Moore realized to his horror that he was checking Moore's head for gray hair, "–she'll still be staring at this ring. It better be good, and I'm a brokeass dude who doesn't deserve her."

"She'll love whatever you pick because she loves you."

"Yeah?"

"Yeah."

"That simple, huh?"

Elliot was killing Moore, as a vision of Colleen's smile made all his words garble in his throat. Clearing it, he pointed to the back and rasped, "Coffee."

"Gotcha. I'll sit here and stare at these until the right one jumps off the glass and begs to be bought."

A thumbs up was all Moore could manage. When he reached the back room, the coffee pot was full and waiting there as if it were a bit impatient that Moore hadn't bothered emptying it of eight ounces or so. A red mug from Love You Coffee – heart shaped, of course – was easily filled with piping hot black coffee. Moore added an ounce or two of cold water to it, a splash of milk, and drank enough to get his throat to stop radiating emotion.

This was a business transaction. Elliot needed a little moral support, but the kid was going to buy.

"Hey, Moore," he called out as Moore held the coffee mug to his mouth, drinking the strong brew. "You ever give a girl a promise ring like this?"

"No. Engagement and wedding rings only."

The kid's eyes jumped to Moore's bare left hand. "But you're not married anymore?"

"No."

Alarm rippled in his eyes. "Didn't work out?"

"Right."

"But–but you loved her so hard, your heart felt like it was in your front shirt pocket, right? Like the whole world looked different because of her kisses. Like–"

"You a poet, Elliott?"

"Naw. Just really in love. You were, too, right? But now you're not."

Every bit of this sale just turned surreal. No one came into

Love You Jewelers to talk about *Moore's* love life. Yammering on about their wonderful beloved, they were always fixated on their own relationship.

Suddenly forlorn, the kid was questioning his own commitment because of Moore?

This was a tragedy.

"You know what, Elliot? I'm not a spill-your-guts kind of guy, and I have an informal rule that I never talk about my own relationships with customers. You don't want to hear about my love snafus."

"Sure I do! Guy like you was more like me thirty years ago, right?"

"Thirty!" Moore couldn't help himself.

"Er, you know. When you were young."

Holding back a grumble about the one-two punch, Moore persisted. "Truth be told, I've never been in love like you're describing."

"Come on. Really?"

"Really."

"But you asked someone to marry you. And then got married."

"Yes." Twice, he didn't add, because why bring on the questions?

"What happened?"

"Elliot, no offense, but what happened to me won't happen to you."

"How do you know?" The plaintive tone made Moore feel so much sympathy for the guy. When he was seventeen, he was in love, too. Not with Cammie.

With Colleen.

And if he'd just spoken up, said something, made a move–*tried*–his entire life since then would be so different.

Maybe.

The maybe always held him back. Because what if he'd

told Colleen all those years ago and she hadn't felt the same way? Instead of taking his shot, he'd thrown it away. Gone to homecoming with Cammie instead. Gotten drunk.

Slept with her.

And a broken piece of latex changed all their lives forever.

Just like a snowstorm had altered current events with Colleen.

In each case, fate had intervened and forced him down a life path he hadn't planned for himself.

Placing a hand on Elliot's shoulder, he caught the guy's eye, staring at him seriously.

"I *don't* know. That's the problem with love. It never comes with a guarantee. No user manual, no road map, no certainty of any kind. Your heart climbs on an amusement park roller coaster that says 'You must be this tall to ride' and then it starts, but suddenly, there are no safety rails. No seatbelts. You're just clinging to each other and hoping the strength of your embrace is enough to get you through the ride."

"That's deep, man."

Moore fought his own internal cringe. Was it? Not really. But to an eighteen-year-old guy who was so deeply in love that he was shaking at the thought of not meeting his beloved's needs, Moore guessed it was.

That whole not-meeting-your-beloved's-needs problem was universal, though. A sick feeling in his gut told him he had to see Colleen today.

Had to.

The kiss at town hall yesterday had been both too much and too little, the prelude to a conversation they were supposed to have later tonight, meeting up at his apartment over the store. For years, he'd fought living downtown, but when the longtime tenants moved out and resettled in a South

Carolina retirement community, his mother had suggested Moore take the apartment.

Now he lived and worked within a stairwell's walk. Every morning, though, he had a ritual: Leave the apartment. Take a walk around the block.

Then enter the store.

Elliot stared at him, increasingly awkward, and Moore shook himself out of his meandering thoughts.

"Deep? I don't know. Love's pretty consistent for us all, isn't it?"

"Consistent?"

"Wrong word," Moore added with a self-deprecating chuckle. "Universal, maybe? You love her so much, right?"

"Yeah."

"When we love too hard, we feel like we might break without them."

"Yes!"

"So here's some friendly advice: Buy the prettiest ring. Someday, if you want, you can get her another one. Your first will always hold meaning for her–and you. It's about the love. Not the price tag."

That line almost always worked.

Elliot's shoulders relaxed a little further, one eye tightening as he surveyed the three rings. "This one," he finally said, voice more certain, choosing a lovely little green garnet and diamond-chip ring. "And it'll remind her of Love You."

"The color is perfect."

"Thanks. And when it's time to propose, I'm totally coming back here."

"Great. We make custom rings, you know. When the time is right, give me a call." Moore slipped his business card into the kid's hand.

He looked at it like Moore had given him a buggy whip.

Centering it on the glass, he used his phone to take a picture of it, then slid it back to Moore.

"Thanks."

Moore had never felt so old.

The front door bell jingled and a couple holding hands walked in, the woman with a beautiful blonde dye job, the man balding but with a perfectly manscaped gray beard. Both grinned like teenagers.

Second or third marriage.

One carat or more.

Custom design.

Revenge jewelry.

The profiling came as second nature to him these days, something to do when he was bored. Competing against himself, he kept score. Seventy percent accuracy wasn't bad.

When he hit one hundred, it was time to retire.

"Be right back," he assured Elliott as he approached the older couple, who introduced themselves as Dick and Linda, asking to be allowed to roam and look.

Taking their cue, Moore returned to Elliott, who was holding his phone and smiling.

"I texted a picture to my sister. She says it's perfect."

"It is."

Elliott looked around, watching the couple carefully. "They're in front of the big rocks. You should spend your time on them. Make more money."

"Don't compare."

"Huh?"

"Don't compare yourself to them," Moore said as Elliott handed him his debit card, which Moore slid into the machine. He found one of the store's red velvet boxes, putting the ring in the little satin slit, closing it all up, and placing the box in a signature red bag with Love You Jewelers in white lettering on the front. "Love can't be compared."

"Wasn't comparing love. Comparing bank accounts."

"You work in a sub shop?"

Elliott looked embarrassed.

"Only for now. Taking classes to become a welder."

"Good line of work. You'll make plenty of money one day."

"I wish one day were now." He signed the receipt, took his card, put it in a beat-up old leather wallet, and beamed at the bag. "She's gonna love it."

"You made a fine choice on both fronts, Elliott. A fine woman and a fine ring."

Tilting his head in contemplation, Elliott asked him, "You always like this?"

"Like what?"

"So positive?"

"I guess so." Trying not to look at the other couple, Moore shifted into closing space, the deal done, the kid interesting but he had other customers now.

"Can't imagine why anyone would divorce you."

An image of Moore and Colleen walking into the coat room at his wedding to Gia, the DJ between her legs, flashed through his mind.

"It's complicated."

"You'll find the right person. I know it. Might have already."

"Huh?"

"Me and Mindy have known each other since kinder-garten. Just didn't really *see* her until last year, you know? Right in front of my face the whole time."

Dick was making eye contact, eyebrows up, the universal customer sign for "We need attention now." Linda was smiling and pointing at a 2.3 carat brilliant-cut diamond set in a pavé diamond band. Her rapturous expres-sion was identical to the look on Luke's daughter's face when Moore had given her a Disney princess tiara for her fourth birthday.

Elliott noticed their signals and reached out to shake Moore's hand. "Thanks, man." He held up the red bag. "For everything. You really helped me."

"You too, Elliott," Moore replied as he waved to Linda. "Thanks for your help."

"What do you mean? I didn't help you."

Moore knew Joey was coming in at noon. His planned afternoon of paperwork could wait.

Telling Colleen how he really felt about her couldn't.

"You helped more than you'll ever know. Elliot. More than you'll ever know."

Chapter 11

Colleen

Painting had a logic of its own, not to mention an odor of its own.

The big lodge at the camp had required lots of not-so-sexy upgrades–like plumbing, wiring, and insulation–before they could start to do the fun stuff like choosing colors and painting walls. Right now, the entire family was busy laying down blue painter's tape to be able to paint trim; first things first. Loud music blasted throughout the high-ceilinged lodge.

Her mom was in the small attached greenhouse, cleaning and sweeping. Some of the glass panes were broken, but her father had temporarily covered the broken windows with clear plastic. Deanna had a green thumb and was determined to make the glass enclosure functional.

Row after row of biodegradable starter pots held seedling plants that had put out tiny shoots. Her mom was growing microgreens and insisted that in the long run, they would be able to use the greenhouse to grow a significant amount of their food. No one in the family was interested in being off the grid or any kind of survivalist, but they were having fun with the space that they had collectively purchased.

Technically, her brother Luke had purchased it, using the life insurance money from the death of his first wife. Their parents had co-signed the loan, lending their good credit to the whole scheme. Everyone pooled their money for the renovations. Many family meetings had led to consensus about how the land and building should be used, how the bills would be divided, and what the future of the space could be.

Deanna had claimed the greenhouse.

"*Mmm*," her mom said, chewing and offering Colleen a tiny handful of what looked like clover. "Kohlrabi sprouts," Deanna said excitedly. "They're quite peppery."

Colleen turned a skeptical eye on the sprouts.

"Um…"

"Kohlrabi. It's a plant, like broccoli."

"I know what it is, Mom. The last time you made me eat sprouts, they practically burned my tongue."

"Those were arugula sprouts, and I didn't know what I was doing back then."

"Are you sure you do now?"

Deanna smacked her arm but smiled. She looked around the big room where Colleen was sitting on the floor, scooching along as she laid the tape.

"This place is going to be magnificent when we're done. Look at that stage."

"I know," Colleen replied. "And once we–"

"Hello."

Interrupted, they turned, and there was Moore. Colleen knew that Kell had asked him to come over and help but, dressed in his business suit, he was clearly not there to pitch in with the painting.

"What's wrong?" Colleen asked.

"Does something have to be wrong?" He marched across the room with so much authority that Deanna took a step back.

"We need to talk," he said to Colleen.

"I have some, uh, alfalfa sprouts to go whisper sweet nothings to," Deanna said, leaving so fast, Colleen felt a slight breeze float past her cheek.

The door between the main lodge and the anteroom to the greenhouse closed, leaving her looking up at Moore with a feeling of awe and a sense of inevitability that turned her skin pink.

"You first."

His eyes dropped to the ground as he thought for a moment.

Her spine began to tingle. This was the moment she'd been waiting for. Not that time in the cabin in New Hampshire after the car accident. Now.

Right now.

"I want to be with you," he said.

In that single sentence, the universe expanded. All she could do was blink. Tormented eyes met hers, vulnerable and raw. Did he really feel exactly what she felt? After all this time?

"I don't give a damn what Luke thinks. I don't give a hoot what your mother thinks. All I care about is what you think. More than that, Colleen—"

His hand went over her heart, palm searing her skin even through the fabric of her shirt.

"—what you *feel*. Do you feel the same way about me as I feel about you?"

She parted her lips to answer, but he pressed a gentle finger against them, eyes boring into hers. He waited a beat and then said, "Don't answer that. I haven't told you how I feel. And I'm about to."

With a long inhale and a swallow that nearly broke her in half, he opened his mouth again. The impulse to kiss him was enormous. To stop the words, to start the touch, to be together again.

But the words mattered. They didn't just have their own basic meaning. They had the meaning that time had invested, and they'd been waiting for all these years.

Now, it was their turn.

"I had a crush on you when I was a kid," he said, slowly smiling as if the past had reached into the present and was witnessing this. "You know that."

She nodded. Words escaped her.

"And then, when we were teenagers, you were the most beautiful girl I knew. I was just your annoying little brother's friend and I knew that, so I didn't have any hope. Snuffed it out a long time ago. And then there was that moment when I was seventeen and you were nineteen."

Jolting out of the soft beauty of his words, she pulled back an inch. It felt like a mile. "What do you mean?"

"Do you remember the weekend before homecoming, my senior year of high school?"

"Yeah. Or no. I mean, it's all kind of a blur."

"You were at the community college, taking your nursing classes," he said, forcing the words out. "And I was spending the night at your house. It was a Friday night, football night. We all went to the game. You remember that?"

"Maybe? All those games kind of blend together." She stopped herself from talking too much, realizing that for him, whatever he was about to say had tremendous gravity to it, a moment that had deep meaning for him but didn't resonate for her. It would in a moment, because he was so serious, so concerned. Every emotion he felt was transferring onto her by osmosis, by choice.

"I asked you to homecoming."

"What?" She gasped. "No, you didn't."

His jaw tightened. His embrace did not.

"Yes, I did."

"Moore. I think I'd remember if you asked me to homecoming."

He closed his eyes. How had she never noticed how long his lashes were?

"We were sitting in the bleachers. It was a home game. The Love You Heartbreakers were playing the Lions."

"Okay."

"It was cold."

"It's always cold at football games in October," she reminded him.

"It was so cold, people brought sleeping bags. Remember?"

Trawling through her memory, she began to piece together a picture of what he was describing.

"My mom pulled out her battery-operated heated socks for that game. Is that the one you're talking about?"

"Yes. The famous cold snap."

"Okay. I still don't remember that you invited me to homecoming."

"We were sitting in the bleachers and Luke was talking about how he was going with Amber—he told me I should find someone. He teased me that Cammie Forsythe was interested in me."

A gong went off in Colleen's head. She did remember this. "You said you'd rather go to homecoming with a rabid dog than Cammie."

"I did."

"Okay..?" Colleen drew out the word, turning it into a question. "What does this have to do with me?"

"Because then I asked you to go with me."

Piecing it together in her mind, she suddenly realized that

what she had thought was an insult, he had meant sincerely.

"Moore." She tightened her grip on him. "You said you would rather go to homecoming with a rabid dog than Cammie, and then you turned to me and said, 'Hey, Colleen, want to go with me to homecoming?' And Luke burst out laughing. Right?"

"You told me that you would sooner go to a dance wearing a ham dress and walk through your cousin Kenny's back forty alone during bear mating season to get there than go to homecoming with me."

"I sure did."

"After that rejection, I didn't know what to do. So I went with Cammie. We had sex that night. I lost my virginity to her and the condom broke."

"And you're blaming me for all of that?"

"Not blaming," he replied, but the complicated look on his face made it clear that some part of him *had* blamed her all these years.

"That was a turning point neither of us knew was a turning point, wasn't it?" she asked, the words pulled out of her like unwinding a tangled ball of Christmas lights.

"I guess so." Their breath filled the air, the sound rhythmic and painful.

In Colleen's mind, this moment was supposed to be a romantic act of unbridled joy, a confession of passion where they'd fall into each other's arms and live happily ever after.

Instead, this was adulting.

Adulting on emotional steroids.

"I was hurt, Moore," she explained, fighting the caustic edge inside her that wanted to cast blame back on him. That piece needed to stand down because there were more important parts of who she was that craved the connection and the love that she had been seeking for so long.

"We were sitting in the bleachers surrounded by all of your

friends with Luke laughing at us, and when you said that about me..."

"About *you*? I didn't say anything about you."

"You said you'd rather date a rabid dog than Cammie, and then immediately turned to ask me! How else was I supposed to take it?"

"The way I intended," he said in an earnest, painful tone. "I meant it."

In all the years that Colleen had held back from telling him how she felt, she hadn't even run through that memory once. For him, it had profound meaning, but for her, it was long forgotten.

How many other missed chances lingered in their past? How often had she misread his signals? How often had he assumed rejection where none crouched ready to pounce?

"Are you telling me that we've been friends all these years and neither one of us wanted to be friends?"

"I've always wanted to be your friend," he interjected. "I just wanted more."

"Same here. That's my point," Colleen said. Frustration was rising in her. Her arm began to itch under the cast, the tender skin just above her wrist driving her nuts.

Maybe it was the body's way of distracting the heart. Make something ache. Make something itch. Force the body to feel, to take some of the spillover from the emotions that the heart couldn't quite handle. Was it a pressure-valve system, the nerves all working together to maintain some kind of homeostasis?

It didn't matter.

Whatever was going on for Colleen was amplified in Moore. She could feel it in the rigid way he held himself, how his hands pressed against her back, but not with connection. She was in a cage in his arms, where he held her in place as if she might flee.

He was a bounty hunter of the heart and now they both had to serve their sentence, for she had committed the same crime he had. Was it as simple as not paying attention, letting fear override everything, just being stupid?

She opened her mouth.

"Are we really this dumb?"

That broke the tension, and he smiled.

"I guess."

"I feel like a grown-up and a kid all at once. I feel like all of the different ages I've been in your presence are standing in a semi-circle around us, and all of yours are on the other side, mirror images, and they're just waiting to be told who we really are together."

He smiled at her, sad but determined.

"I wish I were a man of more emotional courage back then," he confessed. "I wasn't. But I am now. I'm here."

Colleen's admiration for him was growing by the second. Authority and admiration weren't words she would've applied to Moore even a month ago, but now – now she could feel them radiating from him, as if an ancient prophecy had been unlocked inside him and he was fulfilling his true destiny.

Even if they didn't end up together, Moore would be a better person from the power of this mutual reckoning. So would she. She just really didn't want to grow any more without him.

"Can we put aside the past?" he asked.

"It's a big ask."

"I don't mean discard it," he said. Moving one hand from her back, he slid it up to the curve of her jaw. "We have too much good in the interwoven life we've already lived together. You're my best friend, Colleen. I've always said it's Luke, but not anymore. He *was* my best friend, but you *are* my best friend and I want more than that from you. What happened in the cabin was not a mistake. It was not about the alcohol, and it was not about the trauma. Of course, the alcohol and the trauma opened the door to whatever we've both been holding back. But that's just it, we've been holding it back. These feelings have been in there for so long." The skin around his beautiful brown eyes softened as he leaned closer, warm breath on her nose. "Still are."

"Mine are, too." The time for anger was gone. The time for hesitation was gone, too. Now was about clearing the air, sharing their truths, and seeing what the cards on the table said.

The kiss made sense, suddenly, his mouth on hers, tender and hungry at the same time, exactly what she needed to silently answer all the questions that they'd tried to solve.

Lost hopes, lost time, lost causes—all of the uncertainty of the past had to be set aside for this.

The warmth of his wool jacket under her palms. The press of his thigh against her hip. The way his arms curled up and his hands traced the groove of her back as his warm mouth covered hers. It all made this the moment she took all the roles she played and tied them up in the connection between their bodies.

Their hearts.

Their souls.

"I've missed you so much," he murmured against her cheek, teeth on her earlobe, the playful bite making her nearly come on the spot. "I hated the way we parted at the cabin. I wanted to be in that ambulance with you. Wanted to visit you in Manchester. Wanted to come back to your little cabin here and take care of you."

"Why didn't you?"

"You seemed so distant. Cold. When we were at the cabin, Luke was being a jerk, but that wasn't as hard as when you gave me a pained, puppy dog look, like I broke your heart."

"You kind of did."

"How?"

"You called me your friend."

"I–I what?"

"You don't remember? Luke asked you how you could screw me when you're his best friend. You said, and I quote, *I'm her friend.*"

"But... I am."

"Is that all I am to you?"

"Of course not! I wouldn't do *this* if we were just friends."

Oh, that kiss. Already done forgiving him–though he hadn't done anything wrong–the hurt piece of her that froze when Moore said the F-word at the cabin began to thaw. Emotions often made no sense, but they were especially undecipherable around rejection. The perceived slight lingered in her psyche like woodsmoke on flannel.

It would take a long time to air out.

"I wish you'd done that a lot sooner."

"Trust me, so do I." Looking around the lodge as if he'd only just realized where they were, he took a step away from her. "Can we have some privacy?"

"Anywhere but here."

"Your place?"

It wasn't the words. It was the tone.

"Are you propositioning me, Mr. Mottin?"

"Yes."

"How very direct of you."

"I'm tired of opacity."

"See? That's why you're so irresistible. Opacity. Most guys around here would think that's a city where German grandpas live and they'd pronounce it wrong."

"My *vocabulary* makes you hot for me?"

"Your *everything* makes me want you."

Joy was embedded in his features as he took her hand and led her to the door. She pulled away before they went outside.

Luke and Harriet, Kell and Rachel, and her mom and dad all lived at the camp, and while she was tired of hiding her... whatever this was... from them, she definitely didn't want to advertise that they were about to go back to her cabin and have hot sex.

She had standards.

And she hated having her business turned into a spectacle.

Spring snow had become nothing but crust, ragged, pathetic little piles around the fringe of the courtyard. It was two in the afternoon, and Moore was wearing his business attire. Colleen, on the other hand, was wearing her painting clothes and realized she hadn't shaved that morning.

Still.

If the guy didn't mind two weeks ago, he wouldn't mind now, and the electric charge between the two of them made her think that Moore was more focused on getting in her pants than in braiding her leg hair. On her days off, she often waited until nighttime to shower, but this morning she'd run errands around town, tagging along with Kell.

Thank you, Shopping Gods.

All of these random worries shot through her while Moore led the way to her cabin, walking in with an ease of ownership that made her shiver.

On her computer screen, Discord was open, and she saw out of the corner of her eye that Jordy had been messaging her.

"Your gaming set-up is better than any teenage boy's."

"That's because I have more money than a teenage boy."

"I still can't believe you play *League of Legends* with Jordy."

"Moore?"

"Hmm?"

"Are we here to talk about Jordy and *League*, or us?"

"Neither. I thought we were here to do *this*."

Another kiss, this time strong and bold, made her heart

soar. What she thought would be a quiet day checking off to-do list items was turning into a heated lovemaking session with the man she'd wanted for so long.

And who wanted her right back.

The first time they'd kissed, she'd overridden so much. Years of wanting, years of yearning, and years of no.

Just... no.

All those nos had piled up over time, forming an impenetrable wall that had finally been breached by Moore. Sure, the car accident had been the accelerant, but he'd lit the match.

And oh, how they'd burned.

This time, their kiss, her cabin, her bedroom—they had more choice. More time. More of everything, and the deliberate way his tongue played against hers made so many questions dissolve.

There was no *maybe* in his kiss.

She threw herself deeper into it, his hands at her waist, tight and controlled, then unfurling slowly, every inch of skin he touched making her press against him harder. As his palms traveled up her spine, she marveled at how smooth and warm they were. Once he reached her shoulders, one hand curling around to cup her loose breast, she moaned into his mouth and knew that while today's to-do list wasn't getting done...

She was.

"Every day, I want you," he rasped, his thumb sliding against her nipple, twirling with a madness that made her inhale sharply, then go wet. "Every day, you're in my head, distracting me. It's been this way forever, Colleen, but ever since I got a taste of you that night, I can't stop wanting more."

Their next kiss was hard and full, his other hand roaming down to her ass, fingers digging in as he grasped her. All of her was in his embrace, and she wanted all of him in her, to be as close as possible.

"I wasn't sure," she began, but he stopped her, fingers moving to her mouth to hush whatever was about to be said.

"Be sure–I am. More sure about you than I've ever been about anyone in my life. Do you have any idea how long I've craved you? I have said no to myself a thousand times, held back, pulled back, lied to myself to try to stop wanting you."

Her own years of saying no to herself began to fade away, as if they were listening in awe and finally, *finally* could stand down.

All she could do was stare.

And pull him close for another kiss.

This time, though, her hands went to his waist, working the belt buckle, unleashing the belt, and moving on to his trouser button. His hands turned hot and fast, too, pulling off her shirt, leaving her nude and chilled before him, greedy eyes taking her in.

"You're so beautiful," he murmured as he made haste with his jacket, then his shirt, the buttons undone, the cloth set aside, his belt pulled out of the loops, his strong, muscled chest before her. For a guy in the professional class, he was in amazing shape, her hands on his chest as if they had a will of their own, his hot skin against her bare breasts making her moan.

"I want you so much, Moore. I can't believe this is happening."

"What do I need to do to make you believe it? To feel what I'm feeling?"

"I already feel it. I want it all."

"Then let me give you my all."

Kissing her throat, he licked a spot that made her shiver, his hands running down her bare arms, body guiding her to her bed. As the backs of her knees hit the mattress, she melted into it, Moore above her, his fingers making quick work of discarding his pants, then his underwear.

Naked before her, he was glorious. Exactly what she wanted, the stark light of day revealing it all.

Moore moved to her waistband and stripped her pants off, Colleen flat against the bed now as he stood over her, smiling.

"More beautiful than I ever imagined."

"You've seen me naked before. At the cabin."

"That was different," he said as he pulled the covers back, practicality kicking in. Making love on top of the comforter in April in Maine would be an exercise in cold sex. Colleen appreciated the gesture and laughed to herself as they crawled under, his mouth on hers, hands everywhere.

"Why are you laughing?"

"Because I'm happy, Moore."

"Let me make you happy between your legs."

His head disappeared beneath her grandmother's heirloom wedding ring-pattern quilt, the familiar red, white, and pink design looking somehow different and oh, so exciting.

She had never made love under this cover. Never had a man over since they'd moved to the camp.

As his tongue touched her, she reveled in the intimacy, his hot shoulders under her hands. Her mind let go of thoughts like a dandelion in the wind, one seed at a time floating off until she was rising up, finding a rhythm in his hands, their bodies working together for fun and closeness.

What should have been strange and awkward wasn't at all. She found herself thanking the universe for giving her this, Moore's attention so loving and so hot that she felt the familiar peak beginning within.

She wanted him–them–together.

Sitting up, she kissed him, and then his body was over hers, their mouths tangled like the sheets. It was warm and muted under the covers, and she took it all in, their scent driving her to want more.

"Guide me, Colleen," he whispered against her breast

before slowly sucking one nipple in his mouth. "Tell me what you like."

No man had ever said those words to her before. Sex had always involved hints and movements, hips twisted to get the sensation there, hands distracting away from something she didn't like, but never this kind of communication.

So open, so direct.

"I like... this," she said, too many words jumbling inside her, so many levels of unfamiliar terrain making it hard to decide what to say.

Or do.

Moore nipped her nipple with his teeth and she jolted, then laughed, his hand between her legs, thumb tracing circles in a way that made her gasp. "This?"

"Yes."

"And this?" His gentle bites sent sparks throughout her entire body as his thumb intensified its circles.

"Moore," she whispered, reaching for him, finding him hard and thick, pulsing in her palm now. "Please."

"Please, what?"

"Now," she gasped, sliding under him, then suddenly stopping as her mind cleared. "Damn."

She began to sit up.

"What's wrong?"

"Me."

"You want to stop? I'll stop." He pulled the covers off them and the cold air slapped her out of the moment. "Are you hurt? Is it your shoulder?"

"No, I don't want to stop!" she groaned. "It's just... birth control."

"Birth control? I thought you were on the pill."

"I am. But I'm also on antibiotics."

"Okay..."

"Which neutralizes the pill."

He muttered a curse.

"Right. So we need a condom."

"No problem." He kissed her shoulder. "Do you have any? I might have one in my wallet."

"Let me check. They'd be in the bathroom."

Hating the interruption but happy he was handling this so easily, she jumped out of bed, knowing she had a box somewhere. Out of the corner of her eye, she saw him settle against the pillows to watch her, his arms over his head, fingers threaded at the base of his neck.

"I love the view here."

"Oh, stop."

"I do. You have a beautiful body, Colleen."

"You're killing me, Moore."

"What's wrong with complimenting your body? The way your nipples point up, and your breasts rest so gently against your ribs... I could watch it all day."

She gripped the edge of the bathroom sink, reeling. Wet, slick upper thighs, made that way by him, began to tremble.

"All these years, I saw you clothed. Maybe in a bathing suit. But having the privilege of seeing you like this, natural and simple, it's–thank you."

"You're *thanking me* for being naked around you when we're sleeping together?"

"I'm grateful."

"Aha!" She clutched the condom box, pulling one of the three out of the small container and bringing it back to the bed. "Score!"

Moore reached for her, pulling her under the quilt, hands warming her chilled hips and ass.

"You're so cold!" He pressed the length of his body against hers.

"No hypothermia this time."

"Did you come?" he whispered in her ear, the question

churning butterflies in her stomach.

"Not yet."

"How about we take care of that?"

Hand slipping between her legs, he began touching her again, her cheek pressing into his chest, breath suddenly hard to control.

"What about you?"

"I'll get there just fine. I want to make sure you're taken care of first."

"Why?"

"*Why?*" His fingers didn't break rhythm, but his gaze caught hers, holding the look until she felt her self-consciousness melt away under his openness. "Why? Because I want to give you everything. And that means starting with this."

She tore the condom open, trying to remember how to use her hands and breathe while he was touching her like that.

"I want to come with you in me."

"I want that, too."

Reaching down, she found his tip, rolling the condom on carefully as he slipped one finger inside her, hooking it just right, making her gasp.

Then he kissed her, hard and urgent, until she leaned back, wrapped her legs around him, and he entered her, so slowly, so reverently, her mouth captured by his kiss, heart stolen long, long ago.

Each stroke made her tighten around him, her breath coming in gasps as he made low sounds of pleasure, his forehead pressed against her as he slid in and out. She moved her hips, surprised when his hand went between them.

The circles began again.

"That feels so good," she whispered, surprised she could speak at all.

"You've never done this before?"

"Not like—no."

"Do you want to touch yourself while we..." Moving his hand away, he guided hers into place, then shifted slightly, the offer sending a surge through her, skin tingling as her climax built.

"Yes," she confessed, her own touch skilled, and within three strokes she was so close, Moore's body tensing over her, her other hand flat against the small of his back.

"Colleen." His voice was urgent. "Are you close? I'm about to–"

"Yes," she cried out. "Yes!"

They came together and she clung to him, letting go and releasing, as they gave each other the gift of surrender. Moore's heavy breath against her shoulder began to steady, his body relaxing against her, and she felt her heart slow down slightly from its nearly explosive state.

Quietly, Moore stood, walked into the bathroom, and took care of the condom, practically sprinting back into bed.

"Brrr," he said, snuggling up.

"Well," she said, brushing her hair off her face. "That was–wow."

"Yeah. Wow. Nothing like during the snowstorm."

"Was that better?"

"No. Just different. The cold, the rum, the sheer terror."

"So much terror from the accident."

"I meant the terror of crossing the line with you. I had no idea you felt the same."

Propping herself up on her good elbow, she smiled at him as a familiar change in weight distribution on the bed told her Sandwich had just joined them.

"Hey there, girl," Moore purred at her cat, a calico cutie Colleen rescued a few years ago. Gentle and sweet with her, Moore knew just where to scratch Sandwich to get her to close her eyes in luxurious surrender to his charms.

Colleen knew just how Sandwich felt.

"This feels so weird."

"Really? I've petted Sandwich plenty of times."

"Naked, in bed with me?"

"Only in my dreams."

"Hah."

"You think I'm joking?"

"I think I'm incredulous. How could we have both felt this way and not said anything?"

And yet, she knew. She'd had her own reasons for not saying anything.

So had he.

Bzzz

Colleen snorted. "I'm off work, so I don't even have to look at my phone."

"I'm on my lunch break, and Joey's running the store."

"Are there really emergencies when it comes to jewelry?"

"To some of our clients, yes."

"Like what? A dirty diamond?"

He ignored that, rolling over, his bare backside twisting as he bent to retrieve his suit jacket.

Colleen appreciated the view.

Sandwich leaped off the bed and wandered into the bathroom.

"It's Jordy. He's asking about his plane ticket for his next visit."

The grin on his face made her smile right back. Whenever Jordy visited, she felt so complete. Moore always asked her to hang out with them. Over all these years, that had never changed. She knew she helped make things more comfortable between them, and there was a certain pride in knowing she was the only person who could do that.

"Awesome. When?"

"Two weeks."

Bracing her elbow, she tapped her cast lightly against the

nightstand. "This'll be gone by then."

"How's it feel?"

"Fine. Other than not having full range of motion during sex, it's fine."

"I absolutely did not notice a problem."

"That's because you have no idea how much more amazing I am in bed without the cast."

"I can't wait to find out." He was on his back, eyes on his screen, double-thumbing texts to Jordy. Settling back down, she tucked her head into his shoulder, her good hand on his chest. The way her palm fit just so against his breastbone made her sigh, releasing layers of tension she didn't know were still in her.

"Is this real?"

Moore set his phone down, then picked up the covers, looking under them at their entwined, naked bodies. "Sure looks like it."

"COLLEEN!"

They both jolted at the sound of Kell's bellowing voice outside. Colleen's little yelp of surprise made Sandwich hiss, something tipping over in the bathroom. The cat shot across the room and under the dresser.

"The joy of living so close to my family," she muttered.

"I live above the shop," he said with sympathy. "I get it."

"Why did I leave my nice, cozy, private little place to move here?" she grumbled, covering her head with the sheet. "If I hide here, he won't find me, right?"

"HEY! COLLEEN? You have more primer? I ran out in the lodge office."

With one eye peeking out, she saw Kell outside. Within seconds, he was banging on her front door.

Then her phone buzzed with a text.

Freezing in place, she shushed Moore, who looked like he was about to say something. With wide eyes, she made a series of nonverbal gestures and facial expressions designed to get him to be quiet.

He ducked under the covers, planting kisses along her collarbone.

Then her breast bone.

Her navel.

Her–

The gasp she let out turned into a moan she had to suppress as Kell knocked one more time, made an exasperated sound, and finally stomped off. Threading her fingers through Moore's hair, she–

"COLLEEN!"

Moore made his own frustrated sound.

Both their phones buzzed, the cat knocked something else over in the kitchen, and the Discord notification system on her computer dinged.

"The universe is telling us something."

"Yeah. Family and technology suck."

Laughter shook the bed, Moore's body above her now, his kiss soft and sensual. While she normally adored her family, living this new life with all of them right here took some getting used to.

Especially when she was keeping a secret.

"We can't keep hiding this," she said, Moore suspended over her, looking down with a complicated expression that mirrored her own complex feelings.

"Agreed."

"And yet, once we tell people, they'll give us so much flak."

"Flak up to our eyeballs."

"And then there's Luke, acting all weird."

Moore's head dipped down, mouth kissing her nipple. He rolled onto his side and cuddled up to her.

"I know why he's being a jerk."

"Because he's Luke. Duh."

"No. Because I–because he made me promise not to date you. Years and years ago."

"He what?"

"Yeah. When I was fourteen."

"And you said yes?"

"I was fourteen! I never imagined I had a chance with you. And he was so weird about it."

"Luke's always been weird."

"This was extra weird."

"You're telling me my stupid little brother made you promise you wouldn't make a move on me?"

"Yes."

"I'm going to kill him."

"You can't tell him I told you. And I'm sorry. I should have said something. Should have made a move anyway. It's my fault we wasted all those years."

Guilt decided to pick a chord inside her and start strumming a melody.

"If I hadn't let Luke get in my head like that, who knows?" he mused.

"It sure explains why he was so angry at the cabin. And the Love Committee meeting."

"Yeah."

"Immature, though."

"He's got a stick up him about this. And I shouldn't have let it affect me like that. We're both grown-ups. Whatever people said to us in our youth shouldn't have so much power."

That acoustic chord had turned into a heavy metal electric guitar solo.

"Uh, Moore?"

"Yeah?"

"It's not just you and Luke."

"Luke said something to you to keep you away from me?"

"Not Luke. Cammie." Hating the sound of her name in

the heady, sex-filled air, she said it nonetheless. If they were going to confess old truths to each other, she had to come clean, too.

"Cammie? What do you mean, *Cammie*?"

"Cammie told me to stay away from you."

"She WHAT?"

"*Shhh*. Kell might hear you."

"I don't care!" Moore sat up, shoving both hands through his hair, giving her a look that was so raw, so immediate. As his mouth tensed, his forehead muscles pulled back, anger dominating his handsome face. "Cammie told you to stay away from me?"

"It gets worse."

"How much worse?"

"She–she–"

Instantly more vulnerable than she'd ever felt, her nude state not helping, she prepared to finally tell Moore what she'd been holding back for years.

Jordy was old enough now that it wouldn't matter.

Finally.

"Colleen. Did she threaten you? I wouldn't put it past her. She was wicked jealous and she has sharp claws."

"Not physically. No."

"Then what? What could she possibly hold over you? She had no power over you."

"Um, well... it's more like she thought *I* had power over *her*."

"What kind of power?"

"Remember the first few years of Jordy's life? How I babysat a lot?"

"I know you helped out here and there."

"Is that what Cammie told you?"

"What–what are you saying?"

Colleen sighed. "When Jordy was a few months old, I

went to your apartment in your parent's basement. He was screaming, in the crib, and wet as could be. Cammie was on the couch, bawling. I picked up the baby, got him cleaned up, started feeding him a bottle, and Cammie was so grateful."

"Okay."

"She–she asked if she could leave. I said of course. Normally, she'd be gone for a couple hours, or take a shower. She wasn't working then."

He made a sour face. "She never really worked. Ever. She 'did paperwork' for her cousins' handyman company."

"I know. But... after that, she started staying out longer. Pretty soon, she left as soon as I arrived, and came home about fifteen minutes before you did. Then she acted like she did most of the childcare."

His jaw dropped open. "What?"

"I was watching him three or four days a week while you were gone, for... until she disappeared."

"You never said a word."

"I couldn't."

"Of course you could!"

"I couldn't because she said if I told you, she'd never let me see Jordy again."

The breath left his body as if Colleen had just shocked him to death.

"She *said* that?"

"Yes."

"I believe it."

He muttered a string of curses Colleen usually only heard from severely injured farmers or nurses on hour nineteen of an unexpected eighteen-hour shift because of a colleague's call-off. His eyebrows knitted together, face full of so many emotions that had to take fleeting turns, his hand fisting the sheet into a twisted, angry mess.

"But what does that have to do with never telling me how

you feel about me?" he pursued.

"Right before she took Jordy and disappeared, she said she knew you and I were sleeping together."

"We weren't!"

"I know that. You know that. I think she was looking for a reason to leave. Told me if she ever heard even a whiff of a rumor that we were together, she'd make sure no one in town ever saw Jordy again. That she'd take him to California to live their dream life."

"Oh, Colleen."

Tears filled her eyes. "I'm sorry." Sandwich poked her little head out from under the dresser, catching Colleen's eye. "I should have told you."

"I should have told you about Luke, but now your story makes mine look as juvenile as it was."

"Cammie was twenty-one when this happened. Took her two more years before she disappeared with Jordy."

"You never said anything when she took off."

Shame washed over her.

"I wasn't sure if she left because of me."

"Colleen."

"I know! I know. I just... everything about you has been nothing but overthinking for me. Once I realized I liked you, and put it out of my mind that we could ever be together, it's like everything involving you splits my mind into two different realities. I had to live in the actual world with you and make sure I never showed my true feelings to you or anyone else. And then there was my inner reality."

"Which was?"

Reaching up, she caressed his jaw, the closely trimmed beard so soft. Every time she looked at him, she saw all the other ages he'd once been, from toddler to now. The sense of depth in their relationship made her feel more complete.

At the same time, the need to say everything made her

realize some things were still incomplete.

"I was afraid to ask for what I wanted and be told no. How could I face you after that? Be around you, interact at family gatherings? Run into you at Greta's? Feel the t–"

"Tension," he said, just as she whispered the word. Their eyes were on each other, truly seeing each other, Moore acting as a mirror, a doppelgänger, a parallel self.

"We both felt the same way," he said in awe. "And I think I turned my pinkie promise to Luke into an easy–and stupid– justification for not asking you out."

"Me, too, with Cammie. The stakes were too high."

"What she said to you is just so..." He kissed her gently, then looked out the window toward where Kell had just been. Sandwich jumped up on the bed again, walking between them as if they were the interlopers.

It was Colleen who got the view of her butthole.

"Colleen," Moore said, gently pushing the cat aside. Sand- wich, refusing to take no for an answer, curled up against his calves. "I don't know how we live with our eclectic past. We've been friends for so long–I've known you since before I had a memory. You have a better relationship with my own son than I do. Cammie mistreated us both. Now we're telling each other we wanted more than friendship for half our lives but didn't say anything. That car accident kickstarted our life together."

Our life together.

Her heart shot out of her chest as if it could fling itself into his arms.

"I don't want to hide anymore. Not my feelings for you. Not our relationship. We need to be open with everyone, no matter what happens."

"But if Cammie finds out, will she..?"

Moore made a sound of disgust.

"She has no power over us. Jordy's old enough to have his

opinion taken into consideration. In fact, this makes me want to take her back to court to renegotiate the custody arrangement."

"What?"

"I'm capped at fifty days a year because her bulldog lawyer pulled off a miracle nine years ago in California and I didn't fight back as hard as I should have. But now she lives in Minnesota. Different judge, different laws. And Jordy's coming to visit soon. The new theater program is going to entice him."

"Living with you should be enticement enough."

"Not me. But you're part of the draw for him. Imagine how he'll feel if we're together."

Sheer joy filled every cell in her.

"He's so wonderful."

"So are you. And he'll be excited about us."

"I don't know about excited. Fifteen-year-old boys don't normally care about their parents' partners."

"He cares about you."

"You're right!"

"Public it is." Moore frowned. "But... let's wait until he's here."

"Wait?"

"I wouldn't want word to get out before I tell my own son. If Jordy comes back and gets blindsided, that wouldn't be fair."

"Good point. It'll be best if he hears it directly from us."

"Us? I was thinking I'd tell him."

"If we both do, it'll go better."

"He won't be here for two weeks. Can you wait that long before we go public?"

She kissed him again, full and hard.

"We waited all these years. What's a couple of weeks in the grand scheme of things?"

Chapter 12

Moore

"Hey," Jordy grunted.

Watching his son climb into the car at the beginning of a visit was always a thrill.

"Hey, yourself."

Jordy tossed his backpack in the backseat, climbed into the passenger seat, then frowned, brown hair flopping in his eyes as if it passive-aggressively grew longer on purpose just to make Jordy look more sullen.

"Where's Colleen?" As he spoke the words, a flash of his silver on his teeth appeared.

Moore chuckled. "She's not allowed to pick people up at the airport anymore."

The half grin Jordy gave him felt like winning an Oscar, more metal showing.

He snorted. "Yeah. I can see that."

As Jordy closed the passenger door, Moore waited until he

clicked the seatbelt in place. It had only been a handful of weeks, but it had always amazed him how quickly his child changed.

The man-boy in his front seat was all long bones and sharp angles. The little boy was gone. A lump formed in Moore's throat, pushed there by years of never feeling like he was doing enough. Fifty days a year was all he had, but he relished every single one of them.

As he lifted his foot off the brake and pressed the accelerator, his vehicle lurched forward. Jordy's eyes took in the dashboard.

"You know," he said slowly, "I'm a year away from driver's ed."

That lump in Moore's throat grew bigger. The size of a car, even.

"That's right. A year, huh?"

Normally, when he picked Jordy up at the airport, he was greeted with grunts, zero eye contact, and a general contempt that Moore had to brace himself against. He took it all, not so much in stride, but he worked hard not to take it personally.

Jordy was an angry young soul, and Moore viewed his role in his son's life as a person who cared. Even if Jordy didn't like it, he had to acknowledge that Moore showed up, was there, was part of his life–but this was different.

This time felt like a turning point.

"Yeah."

"You know," Moore said, smiling as the words came out, knowing what Jordy would say in return, "while you're back here, I could take you out for some driving lessons."

Joy was not an expression that Moore saw on his child's face very often, not since he was a preschooler.

"Really?" Jordy's voice cracked in half, going higher. "You'd let me?"

"Sure, on some of the back roads. No problem."

"Dad, *really*?" His heart sang to hear the earnestness in his son's voice.

"Absolutely."

"Wow. Cool." Jordy sat back in the front seat, as if he realized his own exuberance was violating some internal policy. His eyes cut over to Moore. "Colleen okay?"

"You talk to her more than I do, on Discord. What do you think?"

"I don't know. We don't talk about her broken wrist on the gaming channel. We talk about the game we're playing."

"You don't talk about your lives?"

"Why would we?"

"What do you talk about when you game together?"

"The game, duh."

Moore deserved that.

"She's fine. Her wrist was in a cast but it's off now. Her shoulder's messed up. Other than that, she's recovering nicely."

A rush of warmth ran through him, his muscles tightening at the thought of what he and Colleen were preparing to unveil. Telling his son about his relationships had always been rocky ground.

For whatever reason, that had never been a problem for Cammie. She just dumped the truth out on poor Jordy. Whether it was Mike the baseball player, Dave the accountant, or Locke the baseball player, Cammie just told Jordy what life was, and their son was forced to accept it.

With Moore, though, it had been different. Always. No woman was allowed access to his son unless Moore thought it was serious, which meant that the only people he'd dated that Jordy had ever met were Gia and Hannah.

"You still dating Tissue Lady?" Jordy asked, as if reading Moore's mind.

"Tissue Lady?"

"Hannah. She always had one tucked in her shirt sleeve."

Jordy made a nasty face. "Kept offering me one. My nose was fine."

"She did?"

"One time she had an entire packet of tissues tucked under her sweater cuff, Dad. You have really bad taste in women."

Moore did not point out that was quite the insult to his own mother.

"No. No more Tissue Lady. She dumped me."

From tight shoulders to a relaxed sigh, Jordy changed. Going casual, he seemed to open up instantly.

This version of his son was new. What was going on?

"Good," Jordy spat out, as if relieved to speak his mind. "It's nice to have a parent who isn't forcing a stepparent on me for once."

"What does that mean?"

"You know Mom's marrying Locke, right?"

"Yeah."

"Now she's all lovey-dovey and it's all about her and the baby and Locke, and once in a while, she remembers Soria and I exist."

"That sounds hard," Moore said carefully. This was completely new territory.

For years, Cammie, Jordy, Soria, and Cammie's last boyfriend, Dave, had lived together. Moore and Dave got along on a surface level, which had seemed to bother Cammie. When Moore came to pick up Jordy, she hid her daughter from him, but Dave was there for a handshake and a few sentences exchanged.

Cammie was constantly trying to trigger drama between the two men, but thank goodness, Dave was stable and steady.

Locke, on the other hand, was a preener.

Moore hated preeners.

He would do whatever it took to get along with Jordy's new stepfather, of course.

Maybe he wouldn't need to put out as much effort as he had in the past, though, because if he could get Jordy to move in with him and finish high school here in Maine, it would change their entire relationship for the good.

And change the power balance with Cammie forever.

"I'm sick of my parents trying to tell me who I have to have a relationship with. I love that you're a confirmed bachelor, Dad."

"A confirmed *what?*" Moore said, confused.

"Hannah dumped you?"

"Yeah."

"Why?"

Moore was not about to tell Jordy that he was, in part, the reason why Hannah ghosted.

"She wanted to spend more time with me than I had."

"Oooo, a clinger?"

Moore just sighed.

"That sucks. People suck. Why have a relationship with them when they're just going to be cruel to you?"

"That's not quite how it all worked."

"She dumped you," Jordy interrupted. "*How* did she dump you, Dad?"

A growing unease centered in Moore's gut.

"What do you mean, how did she dump me?"

"It was by text, wasn't it?"

"Uh..."

Jordy used his hand to brush his hair off his forehead, a choreographed move designed to look cool.

"Oh my God, Dad, she did! She actually dumped you by text. When? You were still dating her when you came to Minnesota last time."

"Well," Moore pondered, buying time as he let his foot off the brake and merged into traffic. "On the plane."

"She dumped you while you were in *mid-air?*"

"Yeah."

"That's so cringe."

This entire conversation was cringe.

"I don't know if it's cringe, but it does suck."

Jordy made a noncommittal sound.

"People suck," he repeated. "Why does everything about people have to be so hard?"

"Hard?" Normally, Jordy climbed into the car, groaned when he realized Moore was alone, and buried his head in his phone.

Actual talking was rare.

Talking about feelings was unheard of.

As he merged onto the highway headed north, he fumbled. As Jordy's dad, he had no idea what he was supposed to say. This wasn't just unfamiliar to him.

It was as if Jordy had teleported him to an alien planet.

His kid was openly talking about his emotional state. Suddenly, all the stakes were higher and Moore was left with the sense that he was operating in the twenty-first century with Paleolithic parenting tools.

"It's hard," Jordy mumbled. "But Locke's cool."

"He is?" Moore asked.

Jordy shrugged.

"I mean, he's okay, I guess."

"He's a baseball player," Moore said, trying to draw Jordy out.

Jordy let out a huff.

"Minor league baseball. He's stressed. Locke thinks he's big shit."

"Hey!" Moore interrupted him. "Language."

"I can't say that word around you? Really?"

Regret flooded through Moore's veins instantly. His own child was finally pouring his guts out to him, treating Moore like a father rather than some object of contempt, and he was policing the kid's language.

"Go ahead. Tell me about Locke," Moore said, regrouping.

"He's... I don't know," Jordy struggled to find the right words.

It was clear to Moore that his son had changed even over the last few weeks. Whatever was going on at home with Cammie wasn't good. A protective streak rose up in him.

"He's not bad." Jordy's dismissive tone was so teenager that Moore almost laughed, but he knew it would be strategically wrong to do so. "He's just so full of himself. You know the type?"

"Yes," Moore said.

"He thinks he's going to hit the major leagues. There's no way. I give him advice sometimes, but he thinks I'm just some punk kid."

Jordy didn't actually play baseball – he just watched a lot of it. Like plenty of hobbyists, he thought he knew better than the people actually in the arena. Nothing wrong with that, but people who were the doers generally didn't listen to the critics.

"Is he excited about the baby?" Moore asked.

Jordy stiffened. Uh oh. Wrong move.

"Mom's fine," Jordy said, a veil falling over his face. "Baby's fine. Soria's super excited, but she gets excited by Paw Patrol, so..."

Hand reaching into his pocket, Jordy went for his phone.

"I didn't ask about the baby, or your mom," Moore ventured. "I asked what Locke thinks about the baby."

"I don't know," Jordy said, leaning away in his seat, his head resting against the window. "He seems fine about it. It's his second kid."

"Second?" Moore sat up so quickly while driving that he almost banged his head on the roof. "Locke has *another* kid?"

"Yeah," Jordy said with a huff. "He's eleven. Key. I've never met him."

An ominous chord vibrated through Moore, as if an unseen phantom of the opera were playing on a creepy organ, each note chosen to provoke the highest level of emotion. How had no one told him Locke had another child?

To be fair, Locke had been with Cammie for less than a year, and Jordy wasn't fond of talking with Moore at all, much less sharing anything about his life. But surely he'd mentioned this to Colleen?

Guess not. She would have told him.

His son was connected to the baby within Cammie's womb, a baby who would be connected to another child that the father had sired. Jordy already had a half-sister in little Soria, who Cammie kept from even meeting Moore.

Compartmentalizing was Cammie's superpower.

"Does Locke have contact with this eleven-year-old?"

"Sure," Jordy said casually. "I don't meet him or anything, but Locke sees him once a month or so."

"Oh."

Jordy glanced at Moore.

"Kind of like you."

"Like me?"

"You only see me when the court requires you to. Same with Locke."

Normally, Moore would have let that comment slide, considering it part of Jordy's inner emotional journey, something he needed to get out. Moore had no problem being the whipping boy.

But not now. Not anymore. Not after what Colleen had told him about Cammie.

Carefully, he pulled the car over to the side of the road, reaching forward to press the hazard lights, then turning to look his son full in the eyes.

"Dad, what are you doing?"

"I don't see you fifty days a year because the court *requires* me to. I see you fifty days a year because that's the limit I'm *allowed*."

Heated silence filled Moore's SUV, Jordy tall enough now that they were at eye level. No more looking down to communicate. His kid was as tall as he was, and maybe Colleen was right.

Maybe he was also old enough to know the truth.

"Oh," was all Jordy said, confusion dominating his face. "Mom always said–"

"Don't believe everything that comes out of your mother's mouth."

A flinch, then raised eyebrows, greeted Moore.

"Whoa."

Knowing full well he'd say something he regretted if he replied, Moore turned the hazard lights off, put the car in gear, and blended back into traffic, Jordy giving him covert glances before shoving earbuds in.

A very, very angry piece of Moore felt liberated.

When Moore was reunited with his son after a year of nothing but pain, he'd made a decision never to badmouth Cammie, no matter how much she deserved it. Jordy didn't need to be put in the middle of them like that.

Cammie could be a jerk, but Moore wouldn't stoop to her level.

As the therapist who'd helped him when Jordy was taken had said, "He'll see the truth when he's older. The hard part is that you have to absorb Cammie's immaturity now."

Colleen thought he needed to tell Jordy the truth about that missing year, but until just now, Moore had never said a cross word about his ex to their child.

Then again, he'd also spent countless years not telling Colleen his true feelings for her. The fear of outcomes from acting had always overridden the lost opportunities from *not* acting.

Time to change all that.

Jordy pulled one earbud out and said, "Grandma and Grandpa are here, right?"

"Yep. Came back from Florida just to see you."

"Last year you took me down there."

"Last year you weren't considering the new school here."

"I probably won't like it."

"I hope you do."

"I'd have to live here, huh?" Chewing on his lower lip, he looked more vulnerable, less jaded, than Moore had seen him in the last few years.

"Unless you can find an easy way to commute from Minnesota, yes."

"More like California," Jordy mumbled.

"What?"

"Mom didn't tell you? Locke might get a shot at a team in California."

Over the last few years, Moore had mastered the art of booking direct flights from Portland to Minneapolis. His flight into Manchester last month had been a fluke.

Now California?

"Where?"

"San Diego."

"Wow."

"Yeah."

"New little brother or sister *and* a move?"

"Right."

Pangs of guilt turned into twisted knots of pain inside him, his little boy torn no matter what he decided. Jordy would have to move wherever his new stepfather took him. Cammie would go along with anything, he knew, as long as she was being financially supported.

Moore's selfish desire to have Jordy move here meant he'd lose access to his only siblings.

"You know, no matter what, I'll always visit. And if you decide to stay here in Luview, we'll make sure you see your mother, Soria, and the baby as much as you want."

"I know. You told me a million times. Colleen has, too."

"She has?"

"Oh, please. Like you didn't put her up to it."

Moore chuckled. "No one forces Colleen to do anything. Ever."

Jordy joined him in laughter. "No kidding. She's the most stubborn person I know."

"Second to you."

"We were playing *League* last week and she completely backdoored their nexus while their whole team was in our base!"

"I have no idea what that means."

"It means Colleen is a badass."

"Yeah," Moore said with a grin. "She really is."

Jordy ignored him after that, settling in to play some kind of game on his phone. The clear roads were easy to navigate. Spring in Maine was a jumble of weather you couldn't quite predict. Other than some leftover piles of old snow lining the roads, everything was melted. The flanks of mud could fool you into thinking that warmer weather was finally here, but a freak nor'easter could dump snow as late as the first week of May.

Predicting the weather was a form of high witchcraft.

"What's Grandma making for dinner?" Jordy asked as they crossed into Luview, the homes instantly changing color until everything was red, white, and pink.

"Pot roast."

"She always makes pot roast."

"But it's really *good* pot roast."

"Locke is vegan."

"He's what?"

"Vegan. Says if Tom Brady can do it and still play into his forties, he can do the same."

"You don't eat meat anymore?"

"No! Locke doesn't. Mom refuses to go vegan, too. Says it's bad for the baby. Then Locke makes a comment about how fat she is and they start screaming at each other."

The casual way Jordy threw that into the conversation made Moore's back teeth grind together.

Hard.

"They fight a lot?"

"More now that Mom's pregnant, yeah. I hate it."

Being overjoyed that his kid was confiding in him while also being horrified by the content of the confidences made Moore's head spin.

"No one likes watching people fight around them."

"Did Grandma and Grandpa ever scream at each other when you were growing up?"

Moore nearly ran off the road in surprise.

"Uh, no. I've never seen them fight."

"Really? Never? You've *never* seen them get mad?"

A flash of being seventeen, holding Cammie's hand in his own clammy paw as they told his parents she was pregnant, ripped through his psyche.

"I've seen them mad, yes. But not fighting with each other."

"Mad at who?"

"Me."

"I can't imagine Grandma getting mad. She's always so happy. And Grandpa's just... there."

"There?"

"Quiet. Boring. He reads the stocks in the newspaper and watches those stupid nature shows."

Laughing at that, Moore had to agree with Jordy's assessment of his dad. "He's never been interested in much other than family, his business, golf, and a good Nat Geo scene where the elk gets shredded by a lion."

"Grandpa's super into those documentaries. Like, extra."

By now, this was more conversation than he'd had with Jordy in the last three years.

"He is, but some of them are interesting. Remember that Joe Exotic one?"

"So stupid, Dad. Like a car accident."

Those two words made him think of Colleen and the cabin.

Taking a right just before the center of town, he drove to the house he'd grown up in. His parents' semi-retirement hadn't made them give up the old homestead, a big colonial with an attached barn that Moore and Luke had spent countless hours playing in as kids.

Most of their time was at Luke's house, though. Unlike Moore, Luke had siblings close in age at his house.

And then there was Colleen...

"Oh. Sorry."

Surprised, Moore looked at his son. "What?"

"Sorry. I said car accident and you went quiet. I keep forgetting you were hurt, too."

A portal to a new dimension had definitely opened up. Jordy never, ever said *sorry* to Moore, and certainly never worried about his feelings.

"Uh, it's okay."

"Colleen's cast is off, right?"

"Yes, but her wrist is still really tender."

There was a pause, and then:

"You were really great, saving her like that."

Those words came out of Jordy as Moore turned into his parents' driveway. They registered in his brain as he pressed the brake pedal, damn near hitting an unexpected car parked before him.

Colleen Luview's car.

"Hey! She's here!" Scrambling out of the SUV, Jordy shot into the house before Moore could kill the engine. As he watched his mom in the doorway, backlit by the glow of the house, Moore slowly bent down and banged his forehead lightly on the steering wheel.

Colleen was here.

Mom must have invited her.

Years ago, Jordy had a meltdown on a visit, insisting on leaving Moore's apartment and going to stay with Grandma and Grandpa. His parents obliged, of course, but it cut Moore deeply. Colleen had stepped in without being asked, acting as a bridge between them, eventually turning Jordy into a giggly tween as the three of them played *Super Smash Bros.* together.

Ever since, his mom had invited Colleen over for a big family dinner at least once every visit.

"And tonight, we come clean," he said aloud, breath fogging in the cool air as dusk showed up to take over from the sun.

The red front door was the same color it had been his whole life, white clapboard siding and black shutters completing the classic New England colonial look. Although his parents spent half the year in Florida, they were always here from Thanksgiving through Valentine's Day, to help in the store with all the major sales periods.

Unconventional retirement, yes. In Florida during much of the time when it was hot, in Maine when it was cold, but they liked it that way.

Flying back here for Jordy's visit was an exception to their schedule.

A welcome one.

As the "bumper baby" of the family, Moore was like an

only child, and an errant one at that. His relationship with his parents had never quite recovered from the colossal shame he'd felt at seventeen, the broken condom on homecoming night shaping the last sixteen years. Between the "tough love" they displayed during Jordy's first five years and then their extraordinary support when Cammie stole Jordy away, his relationship with Leander and Francine was best described as mercurial.

The last nine years had been stable. He was the only one of their three kids to stay in Luview and take over the store, though the addition of their grandchild, Joey, to the business had been a welcome surprise.

One more long, deep breath and he steeled himself for the dinner he was about to walk into. Jordy's negative talk about Locke and his offhand comment about being glad Moore wasn't dating made going public with Colleen even pricklier. He knew she wouldn't say anything to anyone without him there, but how could he explain the emotional tenor of what had just happened with Jordy?

He couldn't. How do you describe a happy heart?

A soaring feeling filled his chest, new and exciting. His son might come to live with him! Be here every day. Fold into the normalcy of each other's lives. Parched for that, Moore felt the world tilt a bit, the chance that Jordy might say no and stay with Cammie an outcome that would hurt more than it did before.

The potential for having his child all to himself was suddenly a viable option.

Nothing could blow his chance.

His phone buzzed in his jacket–Colleen.

Are you waiting for an engraved invitation? Come on! This is the perfect chance to tell them we're together.

She added ten hearts.

Grinning like a fool, he opened the car door, thumbing his reply.

On my way.

With a spring in his step, he jogged to the same front door he'd been going through his entire life, the scent of pot roast, rosemary, garlic, and love infused in the air. The sound of his parents chatting with Jordy in the kitchen filled him with a happiness he didn't know he'd been missing.

Before he made it down the hall, Colleen grabbed him.

"How do we do this?" she whispered, eyes big. "I–I feel shy."

"YOU? Shy?"

She punched his shoulder.

"It's different now. I've been here loads of times as your friend, but never as your... you know."

"My erotic pool noodle?"

"Moore!"

"What, exactly, are we?" he asked, leaning in, inhaling her perfume, a light scent that was more herbal shampoo than anything else. Whatever she smelled like, Colleen was Colleen, and he fell deeper and deeper for her as each moment passed.

His son might move here. The girl he'd pined for most of his life wanted him right back. His parents were hosting them.

This was perfect.

Beyond perfect.

Which made him instantly uneasy.

"Hey," she said softly, giving his hand a squeeze. "You just changed."

"I did?"

"You look worried. Did something happen on the drive with Jordy?"

"Did you know Locke has a kid?"

"You mean the one growing inside Cammie, or–"

"An eleven-year-old."

"Wow. No. Jordy never said a word."

"And he was so glad to hear Hannah dumped me."

"I think we all were."

"I don't mean it like that. He–"

"Dinner!" his mom called out, making him feel like he was twelve again, coming to the table alone, his parents tired and silent as they ate.

Not tonight, though. A lively table awaited them.

"Francine's pot roast is the best," Colleen said with lusty joy.

"Glad you have a good reason to be here."

She poked his rib. "When she called and asked me to come, I wondered if you'd said something."

"No. Not yet. I thought we agreed we would talk to Jordy privately first, then tell our parents."

"Oh. Right. Sure." The way she looked up at him made his body relax. His hand went to her hip, then slid up her back.

"Let's go before they discover us," he whispered, planting a kiss on her cheek, then squeezing her beautiful butt for good measure.

Her laughter led the way as they marched into the kitchen, where Jordy was getting plates out of the cupboard, his shift from arriving at the airport two hours ago to helping set the table as seamless as could be.

Moore's parents were in their seventies, a decade older than Colleen's mom and dad. Francine had been forty-two when she'd had Moore, and Leander was forty-five. They thought they were done.

All his life, Moore had heard his entrance into the world described that way. By the time he and Cammie had nervously sat down with them and explained the pregnancy, his dad was close to drawing Social Security.

Old enough to be a grandfather, but definitely not ready for his high school senior to become a dad.

Shoving all those memories aside, Moore took his place at the table, his mom directing Colleen to sit across from him, Jordy to his left, his dad at one end of the table, herself at the other.

Nose-tickling delights filled the air.

"Meat," Jordy moaned. "Delicious meat."

"Is that a meme?" Francine asked Colleen, perplexed. "Sometimes he makes jokes and calls them memes."

"He's excited to see beef, Mom. Locke has gone vegan."

His dad's eyes got judgmental as he stood, carving a thick slice from the roast. "Vegan! Now, why would a professional athlete deprive his body of proper nutrition?"

Moore could think of plenty of perfectly good reasons why, but he wasn't about to defend the guy.

Jordy shrugged, clearly uninterested in talking about Locke, but he startled suddenly, sitting up, casting an evil glare at Colleen.

"Why did you kick me?"

"I didn't kick you!"

Jordy grabbed a roll from a basket and started to throw it at her, but Francine easily intercepted it.

"No food fights at my table, Jordan."

"Yes, ma'am."

They began serving, the sound of clinking silverware and glasses being filled with water and wine dominating until they were all ready to start.

In his youth, the Mottins had been a family that prayed before meals, but his parents had relaxed in that department as they got older, so his dad just picked up his knife and fork, his mother began buttering a roll, and that was that.

Jordy took a big mouthful of roast and sighed contentedly.

"Mff much a muud ook, Ammaw."

"Excuse me?" his mom asked.

"He said, 'You're such a good cook, Grandma,'" Colleen translated.

Jordy nodded, pleased with himself, swallowing half a cow in one gulp.

"How on earth did you understand that?" Leander grumbled, taking his own bite of meat with a careful fork, tipped just right. Table manners had been drilled into Moore from toddlerhood.

His own son? Not so much.

"I am fluent in teen boy," Colleen replied, taking her own forkful of mashed potatoes into her mouth with perfect timing so she didn't have to follow up.

"Glad someone is," Jordy muttered, busy inhaling his plate.

"What is that supposed to mean?" Francine asked, her voice concerned. "Are you feeling misunderstood?"

No self-respecting teen boy was about to answer that with any authenticity, so instead he replied with, "I'm invisible, Grandma. My replacement is coming in four months. I'm a first-pancake kid."

"Replacement?" Francine frowned. "Oh! You mean your new little brother or sister."

"Sister," he said, then cleared his throat before reaching across the table for the roasted carrots. "Mom's having a girl."

Colleen looked at her plate and took small bites. Moore had no idea what he was expected to say here.

"My goodness! Congratulations, dear. Another sister!" His mom took a bite and smiled at Jordy, who rolled his eyes and shoved food in his mouth.

They all chewed for a minute. The silence was merciful.

Until Jordy looked at Moore and announced, "Good thing Dad's not dating anyone."

Colleen froze.

Leander and Francine looked at each other. His dad cleared his throat and said, "Jordy's right. Your track record with women is..."

"Terrible," Jordy said flatly. "Hannah dumped him by text."

His parents had the decency to just keep eating and say nothing.

"I wish Mom would dump Locke. He's such a dick."

"LANGUAGE!" Leander, Francine, and Moore all called out, which only made Jordy smirk.

Ah. There he was. The kid Moore knew all too well.

"You, Dad, are the best," Jordy declared, knowing full well the words would shock everyone.

"I am?" At this rate, Moore was going to need the Heimlich. "For what?"

"For sucking at love."

"Jordy!" Colleen clapped out. "What do you mean?"

"He and my mom didn't make it. Gia did something really terrible you all think I don't know, but Mom told me."

"She *told* you?" Francine gasped.

"Yeah. Gia, like, slept with the bartender at your wedding reception?"

"The DJ," Moore said weakly, as if correcting the details somehow made it better.

"And now Tissue Lady dumped you."

Tissue Lady? Colleen mouthed at him. He shook his head quickly.

"Face it, Dad. You suck at love. And that means you're my best option."

"Best option?" His mom looked at him with so many questions in her eyes, but hell if Moore knew what was going on. Colleen's foot found his, her nudges making the same inquiry.

"Yeah. You're alone. No stepmother. No live-in mommy

figure. And no babies coming." Jordy's expression made it clear what he thought about babies. "It'll be great living here with you. None of that crap to deal with," he added, happily buttering a roll with what looked like half a stick of creamy goodness.

"Language," Francine said weakly as Moore's heart began to pound, Colleen's eyes big as moons.

"And you don't have a three-year-old I have to babysit every moment I'm not at school."

Francine frowned. "Being an older brother means helping with the younger child. Vanessa and Lucy always helped when Moore was little."

"From the second they got off the school bus until bedtime? And every weekend? Dave used to help, but since Mom's been with Locke, I'm not allowed to be in shows anymore. It takes up too much time, she says."

"What?" Moore gasped. This was new information. "She's making you watch Soria that much?"

"Uh huh. Unpaid, too." The flippant tone was cover for a misery Moore could feel. Colleen closed her eyes, but Moore knew what she was thinking.

Cammie was doing to Jordy what she'd done to Colleen.

"You decided already?" Colleen ventured as she opened her eyes, clearly feeling her way through the minefield this conversation had become.

"Oh, yeah. Easy peasy. The performing arts school is just the cherry on top. Mom already said I could live here if I wanted to."

You could hear a pin drop.

"SHE DID?" all four adults gasped, in various vocal ranges and intensities.

"I think it would be easier for her that way. You know."

Colleen reached across for Jordy's hand. He let her grasp it.

"Did she say that?"

"She says it all the time when we fight. Tells me if I can't shut up, she'll send me back here, but Dad doesn't really want me."

A gasp from Francine and a growl from Leander made the atmosphere so tense, Moore nearly leapt to his feet to get out of the house, clear his mind, breathe in something other than Cammie's toxic air.

Even half a country away, she was poison.

"I *do* want you." Moore stood, the dinner in his stomach bitter and heavy, emotions all over the place but grounded in the very sharp reality that Jordy was hurting. His playful tone was a coverup for what he was communicating with absolute clarity:

Rejection.

Cammie was rejecting him, one emotional papercut at a time.

All while using him unfairly to raise his own sister.

Jordy stuffed a forkful of beef in his mouth, looking down at his plate.

"Yeah?"

"Yeah."

"I'll stay if you promise me one thing."

"Anything."

"Just don't date anyone. Please. Or, at least, don't make me meet them, or have anything to do with them."

Helpless, Moore looked at Colleen.

"Dad?"

"Huh?"

"Deal or no deal."

Leander snorted. "Easiest negotiation Moore's ever faced in his life."

In Colleen eyes, he saw all the conflicted emotions he felt, the tug of his heart in two directions. Surely Jordy would understand, once they told everyone. Colleen was different.

Jordy would make an exception for her.

Right?

"I'm so happy for you, Moore," Colleen said slowly, pulling her cloth napkin from her lap, dabbing her mouth. "You've always wanted this. Jordy's offering you everything you could possibly imagine."

No.

No, no, *no*.

He knew what she was doing. Intellectually and developmentally, catering to Jordy's request was smart. Cammie might pitch a fit if she didn't really want Jordy leaving, which meant that having as much buy-in as possible from him would be crucial.

But—and it was a big *but*—what about him and Colleen?

"I—"

A plea in her eyes shone across the table, the most subtle of hints from the way she nodded making it clear she wanted him to agree to Jordy's request.

"You can work out the details later," she stressed, her eyes flaring, sending silent signals he was scrambling to read properly.

"I can? Are you sure?" Moore choked out, her additional nod a lifeline.

"Mom's going to hate losing my child support," Jordy said, cheeks turning pink as he looked around the table.

Then he grinned.

If the dictionary ever needed a picture below the entry for *schadenfreude*, his son would do nicely.

"Your mother has done just fine for years with what Moore's sent," Leander announced, making Jordy's mouth snap shut.

"And Locke is in baseball. He probably makes great money," his mom added.

"Maybe? I don't really know. He just signed an endorsement deal for, like, thirty thousand dollars," Jordy said, but as he explained the specifics to Moore's parents, a ringing in his ears, ominous and piercing, made their words fade to gibberish.

Despair filled his bones, his eyes meeting Colleen's.

So much for telling Jordy.

So much for a declaration to his parents.

Bye-bye to going public with their feelings.

Jordy didn't realize he was doing it, but he was forcing Moore to choose between his son and his love.

Who was shaking her head just enough to make it clear to Moore that she was putting Jordy's needs first.

Which made him love her even more.

And now he couldn't have her.

Chapter 13

Colleen

This was an x-ray for the unofficial Wall of Fame.

"Is that another one?" Doc Blythe groaned, adjusting his reading glasses. Colleen was back at work full time, her night with Moore, Jordy, Leander, and Francine a painful blur. Today, she was having lunch with Moore if her shift allowed it, and frustration didn't even begin to describe how she felt.

At least she was better off than the poor patient whose x-ray they were currently mocking.

"Yep." Colleen pointed to the flare of gold foil on the screen between the faint images of hip joints. "Heart shaped. I think I can see the word *Harder* in there."

"That's four in the last two years."

"Let me guess," Rhys Morgan said as he changed out the coffee grounds in the staffers' lounge machine. Rhys was a nurse, like Colleen, though he had his bachelor's degree. The two had worked together for the last five years, since he'd moved here with his husband, Kai, who worked as a respiratory tech. "Claims he slipped getting out of the shower."

His dark brown eyes, framed by long lashes, rolled so hard, they might as well have been casters.

"You peeked at the chart," Colleen guessed.

"It was the shower or in the garage on an unfortunately-placed oil spill."

"They always claim that! Any of you ever have an object magically go up inside you like that when you slipped on tile?" Doc asked, the question obviously rhetorical.

Rhys's lips curled in with a grin. "Not a heart-shaped red Christmas ornament with foil lettering that says Love You Harder on it."

"That's not a *no*, Rhys. You're scaring me," Colleen cracked as she poured herself some water from the cooler.

"Okay, no. Definitive *no*," he replied. "You don't get to turn me into a rumor."

"Rectal removal of a *glass* ornament." The old doc let out a puff of air.

"This is number two for the calendar year, right?" Colleen asked, trying not to laugh. Rhys's mugging wasn't helping.

"Three," Doc corrected, "if you include the one that guy from Nordicbeth managed to eliminate on his own."

"Never seen anyone eat so many dates and take so much psyllium in one sitting," Rhys added, chuckling to himself.

"You think it's so funny? You'll assist Dr. Vorchek."

"Me? No! Come on, Doc," Rhys protested.

The old man just waved as he left the lounge, Rhys standing in front of the coffee machine, empty basket in hand, grimacing.

"You just bought yourself a prime spot at an ornament-ectomy," Colleen said with a snicker.

"Gross. I'll trade you any holiday shift you want if you do this for me," he begged.

Colleen held up her uncasted, but still weak, wrist. The ace bandage made her point for her. "Can't."

"It's been five weeks since you broke that thing. You have bird bones? Because otherwise, you're fine."

Colleen just laughed as she grabbed the large can of coffee and continued Rhys's chore. "Have fun!"

Yulia Kosokoff, a fellow nurse, was in the middle of tying her shoes, done with her shift. With a pixie cut that framed her large, dark eyes, she was a runner, well-known in town for going on long treks.

"Hey Rhys. You offering to take holiday shifts? I'm a taker."

"Will you assist Vorchek with an ornament removal?"

"Hah! No way. I'd rather work the next ten Christmases than do another one of those." She shuddered as Colleen cackled.

A tap at the doorway made them both turn. Colleen inhaled sharply in surprise as Moore appeared, resplendent in his charcoal business suit, red tie perfect, as always.

And he was early.

"Moore! Name a holiday Colleen really, really needs off!"

Without missing a beat, Moore said, "Valentine's Day."

Rhys and Colleen snorted. "No one gets that one off. Too many tourists in town."

"Too many people at Love You Harder," Rhys added, looking at the x-ray.

Moore looked, too. He frowned.

"Is that—is that in someone's pelvis?"

"Not exactly." Rhys raised one eyebrow. "Well, technically. Kind of."

"Is it in someone's rectum?" Moore ventured.

"Yes!"

"You say that like I win some kind of prize."

"If you're willing to trade jobs with me, you win a Love You Harder Christmas ornament."

"Why would I want a–" He looked again at the image. "Oh, gross."

"Welcome to the wonderful world of emergency medicine," Colleen said drolly. "Never a dull moment."

"I'll take wiping down display cases and listening to customers complain about our prices over that," Moore declared, peering intently at the x-ray. "It's upside down."

"Yes."

"Point went in first?"

"Uh huh."

"Poor guy slipped getting out of the shower. Ornament happened to be positioned just so. Be careful," Rhys added as he flipped the coffee machine on. "There must be a curse going around."

Moore looked at Colleen with an intensity she'd never witnessed in him before. "You went on a third date with this guy?" He pointed to the x-ray.

"WHAT? No! Of course not. Why would you ask me that?"

Rhys collapsed in hysterics, falling onto the ragged vinyl loveseat next to the fridge.

"He said *curse*."

"He meant this is the third Love You Harder Christmas ornament someone's had shoved up their butt, Moore. I had nothing to do with this!"

"Oh."

Whacking him was easy. Absorbing the emotional blow of his comment was, well...

Harder.

"Are you seriously worried about my stupid third date thing?" she hissed in his ear as Rhys began answering a text on his phone.

"Let's talk somewhere more private."

"You're here early."

"Jordy wanted Greta's for breakfast and I brought you this." In the surprise of his entrance, she hadn't noticed the white bakery bag in his hand.

"Chocolate cherry muffin?"

"You bet."

She wanted to kiss him. Wanted to, but couldn't. If word got out that they were together, Jordy would know in an hour. And after dinner at the Mottin's house last night, it was very clear he did not want his father to be involved with anyone.

Now they had a bigger problem to deal with than just going public. Luke was bad enough, but Colleen could shove his opinion aside and tell *him* to shove it.

Jordy?

Jordy mattered–really, *really* mattered.

"Is this our lunch?" she joked, but caught Rhys's eye.

"You need a break? Go ahead. It's quiet enough. And apparently, I will be assisting Dr. Vorchek." He looked at the bag in her hand. "Any chance there's a brownie in there?"

"It's ten a.m."

"Don't judge my sugar addiction."

Moore held another bag in his hand. Out came a brownie.

"I was joking," Rhys said, but his eyes showed that he was delighted. "For me?"

"Consider it a thank you from the rest of us for your, uh–" Moore's eyes darted to the x-ray, "–service to the public."

"Hah!" Rhys snatched the brownie, taking a huge bite and moaning. "Greta provides the public service. I just help sexually repressed people remove foreign objects from their rectums with minimal damage."

"I got nothin' in response to that," Moore said. "Except a lost appetite."

Colleen reached into her bag and pulled out the muffin, taking a bite while locking eyes with Moore.

"I have zero problem," she muttered around the tasty morsel.

"You're a nurse."

She took another bite.

"And your point is?"

The second Moore's hand went to her shoulder, she melted, the touch familiar and wonderful. Since she'd left his parent's house last night, they had texted but not touched. The connection in public, even if *they* weren't public, felt so good.

"Hey. Go for a walk?"

Her coat was in her locker around the corner. She stuffed the muffin back in the bag and pointed. Gentleman that he was, Moore led the way, opening the locker room door for her as Rhys poured himself a cup of coffee and called out, "Have fun not digging through someone's anus!"

Moore winced.

Colleen laughed.

"You really chose an outstanding career path," he muttered as he held her coat for her, the chivalrous act sweet and caring. As she zipped up, their eyes met.

"Not everyone can inherit a jewelry shop."

"You could have had a tree company."

"I'm not quite built to be a lumberjack."

"You'd look hot in flannel, though. Bulging arms, up high in the tree. Plus, they use ropes. You and ropes. Hmmm." He winked.

She ignited.

The flirting, combined with their excitement about telling Jordy yesterday–an excitement that never got the payoff they were hoping for–left her in a liminal space that was impossible to navigate.

So she found herself desperately wanting to kiss him.

In the locker room.

This would not do.

Grinning, all she could do was walk outside, Moore directly behind her as they went through the outside doors. She scanned the area, finding a quiet bench near the oncology department, a place where family members often came to catch some moments of peace.

In small, rural towns, everything had more than one use. Was it morbid to leap into Moore's arms and kiss him silly in the very space where so many families struggled with complex emotions?

No. Not really.

It was just... life.

So was the kiss she planted on him, his mouth tight with surprise but melting so fast it was if they'd been kissing for hours.

"What's this about?" he asked as she broke away from the surprise kiss, his mouth tasting like coffee. "Greta's muffins make you horny?"

She giggled at the word. "No. You do."

"Feeling is mutual."

"And yet here we are, hiding."

"I know. I'm sorry. Jordy took me by surprise," he said, looking sheepish.

"Me, too."

"This is temporary."

"Is it?"

"It is."

"How long? He's only here for a week."

"I'm sure we can tell him in a couple of days. I just want to wait until he's sure he wants to move here. That's step one."

"And step two is telling him?"

Moore hesitated.

"Step two is telling Cammie."

Colleen gritted her teeth.

"I come after Cammie," she said, the words escaping before she could stop them. Moore's reaction was swift and intense.

"Damn, no. No! That's not how I meant it."

"I know."

"Colleen–this is hard. Confusing. More than I ever expected. I don't want you to feel like you're second fiddle to anyone."

"Except Jordy," she said fiercely. "I have no problem with that."

"I said Cammie because she'll put up a fight. I need Jordy to know for certain he wants this, because taking her on will be that much easier."

"I understand it tactically. Doesn't mean I have to like it."

"Can you just imagine having him live here? Finally? I can teach him the basics at the store. Have breakfast every day, and dinner. Watch him join all the extracurriculars here that I've always missed. He can be in theater productions with our friends' kids. Go to all the festivals on the town common and not just the ones he happens to be in town for. I'll have him for the majority of the year. Colleen..." His voice went from excited to an emotionally charged whisper. "I get my boy back. I have this one shot. He–it's so–"

"Moore," she said, her eyes tight with tears, her arms going around his waist, his cheek resting on her hair. "I am here for it. All of it. Here for you. Here for Jordy. If we have to keep hiding forever, it's fine."

"Forever?"

"I lied. Not forever. But for however long it takes to get you what you want."

"I want you both."

"You get us both."

"Promise?"

"Promise."

This kiss tasted salty, her single escaped tear joining their mouths as Moore kissed her so lovingly, hands cradling her face, body pressed against hers. Fingers curled around the fold of the bakery bag, she couldn't grasp him as hard as she wanted, because she really, really wanted him but there was a chocolate cherry muffin in that bag, and, well...

It was kind of a tie.

"Here," he said, reaching around to take the bag out of her hands, setting it down on the bench. "Now, *really* kiss me."

"How did you know?"

"Because I know you."

"I love that you know me so well."

"I hate that we can't tell the world."

"The world doesn't matter. Jordy does."

Sweeping her into his arms, this time his kiss was deep, hot, so–

Bzzz

"Again?" he groaned. "Why can't we ever have time together?"

"That's *your* hip vibrating. Not mine."

"There are no jewelry emergencies. We have no weddings today. No big proposals. And no one shoves a two-carat diamond ring up their butt."

"Have any women accidentally swallowed engagement rings?" Colleen joked, expecting a no, but Moore surprised her.

"One."

"Really?"

"Billionaire client. One of my uncle Roy's first big commission pieces from the 1950s. Family heirloom. The groom's father called us to explain the whole mess and had his private jet on standby in case we needed to be flown down."

"But what would a jeweler do about a foreign body caught in her digestive tract?"

"We would have handled any damage to the ring or the gem."

"Damage? What can a colon do to diamonds and gold?"

"Billionaire panic is like no other panic, Colleen. Doesn't have to make sense."

Bzzz

Moore stepped back and looked at his phone, then laughed.

"Jordy. Asking if we can do lunch at Bilbee's."

Not wanting the moment to end, Colleen leaned against him. "I love hearing you laugh like that."

"You do?"

"When he's here, you relax more, but it usually takes longer than this. The first two days Jordy's uptight and mean to you, but then he unclenches. This time, it's so different."

Moore nodded. "Something's changed in him. I'm worried he's people pleasing."

"Worried? Don't you mean thrilled?"

"If it's how he's meant to grow, sure. But if he's acting like this because he thinks he needs to please everyone in order to be accepted here, then that's a concern. Hearing him talk about being used as a free babysitter for Soria for all those hours really troubles me. I know he loves her, but no kid should have to do all that. I want him to be a kid himself."

"You really are a great father."

"Sure," he said. "Fourteen percent of the time."

"It's not your fault that's all the courts give you."

He smiled down at her.

"How can so many good things all happen at once? I want to go public with you. Want to tell Cammie to shove it and have Jordy move in. Want to hang out at Bilbee's and play darts and eat that new fried zucchini Rider's selling with the garlic and chive dip."

"We can do all of that. Just not all of it at once."

"How do you think Jordy's going to handle us being together?" he asked, worry making the line between his eyebrows deepen.

"Short term? I have no idea. Long term? He'll be fine."

"He was pretty adamant at dinner last night."

"He's fifteen. He's adamant about which microphone to use when he casts a *League* game."

"I have no idea what that means, but you sure are sexy when you say it."

"It means..." she whispered, kissing his cheek, nuzzling it as she inhaled, taking in his scent. The heat from his body made her remember being under the covers with him, back in the cabin after the accident.

Not the part where he saved her life by getting naked.

The part where he made her night by being naked.

"It means..."

"I miss you," he rasped against her ear, his knee sliding up between her legs, his meaning very, very clear.

"I miss you, too. So much."

"Just because we're not being public doesn't mean we can't be together."

"Is that an invitation?"

"I can't invite you to my place. Not now."

"And if I bring you to my place, the entire family will gather on the porch and have a watch party."

"Or Luke will show up with a shotgun," Moore muttered.

"More like both."

His sigh warmed her cheek, the beautiful push of his tall form against her so appealing, so enticing. "We have to figure this out."

"We will."

His hips pressed against her. "I mean it."

"Oh, you do have a torturous problem there, don't you?"

"It's a medical condition called frustrationitis. I really, really need a nurse."

"This is so bad, looks like you might need a *head* nurse."

The way he looked at her stirred so much inside, every want, every visceral yearning, every pulsing part of her drawn to be as close as possible, as naked as possible, and as uninhibited as could be.

Sex at her place had been phenomenal, but between her work schedule, a trip Moore had made to New York City, and constant interruptions from her family, they hadn't had the time to spend all weekend in bed, lazy and bare, reveling in each other and only each other.

Right now, though, she'd settle for a quickie.

Bzzz

Just as Moore groaned, the sound of footsteps on gravel made her pull away. She was on shift, after all, and they were still keeping their relationship secret.

Doc Blythe appeared, wearing his thick down coat and a guilty expression.

Because he was holding a cigarette.

"DOC!" she shrieked, forcing Moore to step back, clearly stunned by her reaction. "What are you doing?"

A frustrated sound rushed out of the old man.

"Trying to have a smoke in peace."

His glare made Colleen feel like she was nine again, with a BB in her knee, the one she put there herself by accident while trying to shoot Luke in the butt.

Hmm. Maybe she was onto something back then, and not the knee part.

"You can't smoke on hospital grounds!"

"I can if no one catches me," he snarked back, but the hand holding his red lighter didn't move.

"Hey, Doc," Moore said with a two-finger salute.

"Moore. How's that bursitis in your shoulder?"

"Fine. Fine the last time you asked me, and the year before that."

"You're the kind of patient I like, then. I fix you once and you stay fixed."

"How long," Colleen interrupted, "have you been sneaking smokes out here like this?"

"Since before you were born, young lady." He peered at her over the tops of his glasses, looking more like an aging walrus than a human. "What are you two doing out here?"

"Getting advice from her on how to talk to my son," Moore said with his trademark aw-shucks grin.

"Bribing her with Greta's?"

"Something like that."

Doc Blythe wasn't fooled, Colleen could tell, but he wasn't one of the wagging tongues in town. No worries there.

"And why would you ask a childless woman for advice on raising your teenager?"

The word *childless* hung in the air like a bad fart.

"Because she's practically best friends with him. They game together every day."

"That online gaming thing? Where the kids wear those huge headphones and have microphones nicer than professional DJs?"

Colleen gave Doc an impressed look.

"Yes. How'd you know?"

"My granddaughter. Built her own gaming computer when she was eleven, from parts she ordered in the mail. Now she's off at a small college in Pennsylvania. Full-ride scholarship playing those games."

"WOW!" Moore and Colleen said.

"This is David's girl?" she followed up. Doc nodded.

"Yes, Ivy."

"Full ride, huh?" Moore said with a gleam in his eye. "Maybe I should encourage Jordy to play more if it can save me tuition money."

"See? eSports is totally worth it."

Doc nodded. "That's what it's called, eSports. Ivy has to play on three different teams and barely has time for her studies, but she really enjoys it. I never know how to describe it to people, but I'm proud of her for being good at something she loves."

The look on Moore's face was contemplative and pained, as if he yearned for something Doc was talking about, or maybe aspired to it. Putting a mental pin in the moment, Colleen told herself she'd come back to this.

Moore was hers now. Hers to kiss. Hers to sleep with. Hers to care about, and care *for*.

This new landscape they navigated meant rethinking every single premise upon which their dynamic was built and realigning. Reading his signals as a friend and being supportive was one part of this.

"Proud. Right."

Bzzz

Moore's phone interrupted the moment. He read the message and groaned.

"This time, it's work. Joey."

"Let me guess. A diamond broke."

"Diamonds can't break." Moore scowled in confusion.

"That was a joke."

"But a mounting prong broke and a two carat diamond is falling out of its setting. I'm the only one who can fix it, and the customer is coming in this afternoon to pick up their special order." Moore leaned toward her as if to kiss her, but stopped short. Doc was watching.

"See you later?"

"Of course. Opening game of the season coming up. We have tickets."

Doc's eyes bounced from Moore to Colleen but he said nothing.

"All right," Moore said awkwardly. "See you then. And thanks, Colleen."

She wiggled the bakery bag. "No, thank *you*."

A wave was his reply, then a nice view of his back as he walked away. Doc stood holding the lighter in one hand, flicking it but not lighting the cigarette.

"You know you shouldn't do that," she admonished him.

Doc glanced toward Moore.

"People shouldn't do lots of things."

Her wrist began to itch, and controlling her reaction to Doc's obvious poke took more restraint than she expected.

"How many of those do you smoke?"

He sighed. "Only when I lose a patient."

The instant sympathy that flooded her felt like emotional whiplash. Doc Blythe was a firm but kind man with a moral core that never wavered. He tried so hard, and every loss hit him in the gut.

"I'm so sorry. Go ahead."

Only then did she realize his hands were shaking.

"I probably shouldn't."

"Who's the patient?"

"Belinda Mullins."

"Oh." A long sigh filled Colleen with deep sadness. Belinda was fighting her third form of cancer in twelve years. Diagnosed with breast cancer in her daughter's first year of life, she'd refused to move to Portland or Boston for treatment, wanting a normal life for Kelly.

"Yeah. Hung on all these years. She just passed away. I feel like I used duct tape, chewing gum, and faith I didn't know I had to keep her going this last year."

"Is that why you're here in the oncology garden?"

"Yes."

A well-placed hand on someone's shoulder in a moment of grief is an immeasurable comfort. When she touched him, Doc's shoulders dropped, his hands slowly going still, his sigh so full of caring that she teared up.

"Rural medicine is a calling, Colleen. I'm not from here, but I'm *of* here."

"You've been practicing medicine in Luview for almost half a century. You're absolutely *of* here."

"Thank you. I take that as the highest of compliments."

"You should."

"But I'm getting old." He squinted at the cigarette. "I'm mortal."

"We all are."

"And I need to know the town will be in good hands when I'm gone."

"Gone?"

"Yes, gone. Like I said, I'm mortal."

"You got something you want to tell me, Doc? Is something wrong?"

"Other than losing one of the sweetest, nicest patients ever? No. I'm seventy-four, Colleen. Most men my age retired long ago."

"You're planning to retire?"

"Someday. Maybe. I don't know." His vulnerability surprised her. Pleased her, too. Knowing that someone so strong and stable could turn to her as a person to confide in made her feel good. "But I need to know this medical center, and this town, will be okay when I'm gone."

"I'm not sure what that means."

He squared his shoulders. "You have your RN."

"Yes."

"But only an associate's degree."

"I have a few classes toward the bachelor's, but you know..."

"I know. Amber died, you stepped in to help Luke, and never went back."

"Right."

"I think you should go back. Get that BSN. Maybe a master's in nursing or a physician's assistant degree."

"What? *Me?*"

"The BSN is no problem for you, and advanced training would be a breeze. You're a Luview and Luviews are smart and encouraged by family. And you're a devoted, responsible nurse. This town needs you for the next thirty or forty years."

"But I don't have the money. I sank it all into buying the camp."

He waved that off with the hand holding the unlit cigarette.

"You can get scholarships. There are government programs for additional nurse training, with loan forgiveness."

"You sound like you've been researching this."

"I have."

"Wow. Me? You really think–me?"

"If I thought I could convince you to go to med school, I would."

"I can't be a doctor!"

"You can, Colleen. I just don't think you'd ever take that kind of time away from your family."

"Huh?"

"You are a caregiver. It's in your blood. I saw how you helped Moore and Cammie with Jordy when he was little. How you jumped in after Amber died and took over with Harriet. Thank God Moore was there to rescue you right back in that car accident."

It had never occurred to her that Doc Blythe was paying

one whit of attention to the events in her life, other than when they were on shift together at the hospital.

"Problem is, you'd have to leave for a while if you went to school on one of the bigger scholarships. They often have field requirements in underserved areas. Native American clinics, urban medical centers, that sort of thing. But you get paid and tuition is covered."

Her head spun.

"Doc, this is a lot. Going from learning that Belinda died to you telling me I should be a nurse practitioner or a PA."

"You should," he said firmly. "We need more people with advanced training here. You'd be a pillar of the community. Plus, your dating pool would broaden."

"Excuse me?"

"I see what's going on with you and Moore. Why is he hiding you from the town?"

"*Excuse me?*"

"I don't generally butt into people's business, but–"

"For someone who claims not to, your butt is definitely in, Doc."

"All I'm saying is that when a man really cares for a woman, he makes it loud and clear."

"It's not like that."

"Then what is it like?"

Trying to explain the Jordy situation felt too big. Too–

Bzzz

Both their pagers went off.

Tractor accident at Tsaki's farm. Early spring hayride. Four injuries.

Dropping the unlit cigarette, Doc rushed to the door first, Colleen on his heels.

"You deserve to be treated as a whole human being," he said, huffing as they hurried. "You don't need to truncate your life for others."

"I had no idea you were a therapist, too, Doc!"

He snorted as they crashed through a set of doors to the ER.

"You work in this town long enough, you don't have a choice. Think about what I said."

And then Colleen did what was in her blood.

She cared for the people of Luview.

Right alongside her mentor.

Chapter 14

Moore

"Dad!"

"What?"

"Why'd you just ult?"

"What's an ult?"

"OMIGOD, Dad!"

In an effort to be closer to Jordy and Colleen, Moore had finally relented and joined them in a game of *League of Legends*. *League* was a journey that required precision and intense teamwork, and gave you a chance to screw up and try again. With phenomenal music, calibrated sound effects, and a genuinely fun world, it drew Moore in. Even better? It gave him a shared experience with the two people he loved best in the world.

Also in his effort to get Jordy to move to Maine, Moore had bought him a brand new gaming computer.

Which meant Moore got his old one.

The two of them in his living room were quite the sight. Jordy had insisted on setting up their game computers in parallel, two folding tables replete with electronics, giant monitors dominating. His place looked more like the command center for a spy agency than a jeweler's living room.

The thick noise-canceling headphones they both wore gave Moore an eerie sense of surreality, half in the electronic world of play, half grounded in real life. He could certainly see the appeal, though his gaming tastes were older.

Super Smash Bros. was really more his speed.

Jordy screamed at the screen and shouted with glee–all long, thin limbs and antsy, bouncing knees–and a flashback hit Moore.

He'd been spending the night in a friend's dorm room before an early-morning class at the University of Southern Maine, a rare night away from Cammie and the baby. For that one night, Moore had hung out like a regular college student, having a few beers, eating junk food, playing video games, and just being something other than a teen dad, a young husband, and…

A screw-up.

For five years, he busted his ass to get his bachelor's degree and earn his way back into the good graces of his parents. To prove himself worthy of working at Love You Jewelers. To take care of his son and wife and give them a stable life.

And then he graduated. He did it. Mission accomplished.

A month later, Cammie disappeared with Jordy.

The mind wanders through the landscape of memory when it's gathering pieces to put together into a whole and, for some reason, Moore took the recollection of that night at Lance's dorm in Portland and slapped it right onto Jordy being taken away.

Moore swallowed hard, willing away the emotional wave rolling over him. His son couldn't be stolen again. He was right here next to Moore, reeking of teen boy and pixelated adventure.

"Moore? You there?" Colleen asked, her voice reassuring through the headphones.

"Yeah. What'd I do wrong?"

It was a sentence he asked himself ad infinitum.

Colleen cut in over Discord, her voice filled with laughter. "An ult is a big ability you're supposed to save for the right moment."

"But Dad just blew it!"

"Uh, sorry? What do I do now?"

"You'll just have to play safe, then," Colleen explained.

"Safe?" Moore asked, expecting invective from Jordy, who was currently red with frustration.

"Just play under your tower."

"Yeah," Jordy grumbled. "Dad can't screw that one up."

"HEY!" Moore nudged him with his knee. Clad in an old Mumford & Sons concert t-shirt, jeans so faded they were practically cotton balls, and covered in Cheetos dust, Moore glanced over at Jordy, who had chocolate milkshake stains on his Love You Cupids t-shirt.

They were practically twins.

"Sorry," Jordy muttered.

"How about I kill a bunch of the gnomes?" Moore tried.

"MINIONS, Dad! They're called MINIONS!"

"But they're not yellow with big eyes," Moore replied, genuinely confused now. Seeing kid movies had always been a way to bond with his son, so at least he knew every major animated movie character. "And where's Gru?"

"Moore," Colleen interrupted. "Just kill the little things. You earn gold that way."

"What do I do with the gold?"

"You buy stuff," Jordy explained quickly, as if conserving words. His hair fell across his eyes and he shoved it away.

"Do I get another ult?"

Jordy exhaled with aggravation. "Yes."

"Hey, Jord," Colleen said. "He's teachable. Remember that!" Encouraging but firm, she used a voice Moore knew all too well.

It was the same tone she used when her brothers were losing at darts at Bilbee's Tavern.

Moore spent the next five minutes killing a bunch of gold-earning critters and ignoring Jordy's heavy sighs.

"Now where are we going?" Moore asked as Jordy's character began to walk away from his character.

"Going upriver," Jordy said tightly, eyes focused on the screen.

"Like, on a river cruise?"

"DAD!"

Colleen explained, "You have to go to dragon."

"What's dragon?"

"COLLEEN!" Jordy shouted. "PLEASE JUST PLAY WITH ME!"

Now it was Moore's turn to let out an aggravated sigh.

Moore's phone buzzed. It was a text from Colleen.

Don't let him get to you.

He set the phone against his hip, far from Jordy's line of sight.

"Jordy," she said on Discord. "Sportsmanship. If you ever want to play on an eSports team, you can't be a jerk like this."

"But–"

"Especially not to someone who's just learning the game."

"Fine. Just keep farming for now," he said to Moore, eyes glancing at him for a split second.

Farming means getting gold, she texted.

He texted back: *Killing minions?*

Right.

For five whole minutes, Jordy didn't treat Moore like a moron. His phone buzzed again.

Don't use your ult, she texted.

"You have your ult back, Dad. Don't blow it again."

"Okay. How do I know when to use it?"

"When we fight."

"Sounds good."

Colleen texted: *Aim for the AD Carry.*

What's that? he texted back.

"Who are you texting, Dad? Eyes on the game."

"Sorry," he lied. "Work thing. Can't help it."

Jordy grunted his disapproval.

Didn't you bother reading that beginner's book on League *I sent you? Or the YouTube videos?* Colleen chided him via text.

I didn't get around to it.

Men. You never read the manuals.

"Man, my monitor's refresh rate is so high. I can see so smoothly," Jordy said as he killed more minions. "This is lit."

"Enjoying the new system?"

"Yeah. Thanks," Jordy grunted out.

Moore texted Colleen: *That's his version of I love you, Dad. Right?*

She texted back a heart.

On screen, Colleen's and Jordy's characters began heading toward the dragon. Moore followed.

"Stick with us, Dad. We're going to secure the dragon."

"Okay."

Aim your ult at the AD Carry, Colleen texted.

Do I shoot now? Moore replied.

NO!!

The enemies appeared on screen, making Jordy's entire body tense.

"They're coming back from reset," he announced.

"We're going to have to fight," Colleen said, her voice coming over the earphones.

"Do I use my ult now?" Moore asked.

"NO!" they called out so loud, he nearly pulled off his earphones.

"They're engaging on us!" Jordy screamed, a big beefy person appearing onscreen. The figure jumped on Jordy's character, stunning Jordy.

Use your ult now! Colleen texted, Moore glancing at his phone then shifting instantly back to his computer, launching his ult.

"OH, SHIT!" Jordy shrieked, laughing.

"LANGUAGE!" Moore shouted. "Just because I screwed up doesn't mean you get to swear at me."

"You didn't screw up! You saved me!" Jordy's hand went to Moore's shoulder, shaking him in brotherhood.

"I did??" Moore gasped. "Hot damn!"

"LANGUAGE!" Jordy and Colleen shouted in unison, both descending into giggles over the Discord channel.

Colleen's character took the dragon, her battle cry over the audio making Moore laugh even harder.

Jordy bounced in his chair. "They surrendered! WOOT!"

Moore watched the game chat onscreen, the opposing team writing "gg" over and over. He turned to Jordy and asked, "Good game?"

"For a beginner, sure."

"No, I mean, 'gg' means good game?"

"Yeah."

"See?" Colleen piped up. "Teachable."

"I can't believe you're so good at *Super Smash Bros.* and so bad at *League*," Jordy said to him as he reached for a handful of chocolate popcorn.

"You think I'm good at something?" Moore joked with

him, but the look Jordy gave him spoke to the deeper message under Moore's tone.

"I, uh, yeah. You're really good at *Super Mario Brothers*, too."

"Thanks. I'll practice more with *League*. Do more with you guys."

"That'll be fun!" Colleen said in an overly enthusiastic voice.

Moore wished she were here, hanging with them. He'd suggested it, but she'd backed off, countering with the offer to play online. Probably didn't hurt to have some distance between them.

It was getting harder and harder not to touch her. Be affectionate. Show how much he cared for her.

Crossing that line in his own apartment with Jordy there might blow up what little progress he'd made with his son.

He hated being pulled in two different directions, though. Long term, the delay was worth it, and that's all this was, he assured himself.

A delay.

"Colleen? Gotta go." Jordy pulled off his headphones and used both hands to feed himself enormous amounts of sugar and chips.

"Moore still there?" Colleen asked.

"I am. Jordy's headphones are off."

"Oooo, does than mean we can have Discord sex?"

Moore nearly did a spit take with his soda.

"Is that a thing?" Moore rasped.

"It's ten-thirty," Jordy said, standing, grabbing the empty snack bowls. "At home, this is bedtime. But I don't have school in the morning."

"Hang on, Colleen," Moore said into his mic.

"I'll just start undressing," she replied, his body revving at the thought.

"Dad?"

"You have the tour of the new school at eleven tomorrow."

"Yeah. You're just dropping me off, right? Like we said? Not coming in."

"Of course not," Moore said as he imagined Colleen peeling out of her clothes—as opposed to having them cut off by him with a knife to save her life. "I won't intrude."

The grin he received from his kid was so genuine, it went straight to Moore's heart.

"Awesome."

As Jordy left the room, Moore said to Colleen, "Don't start something you can't finish."

"You want me to finish? I can do that. My hand is going between my legs and I–"

Jordy reappeared and grabbed his headphones, about to put them back on.

"NO! JORDY! WAIT!" Moore shouted as his son gave him a *wtf?* look, sliding the headphones on.

"Hey, Colleen?" he started, at the same time she said, "– am touching my–"

The rest of her words turned into unintelligible gurgles.

"Touching your what?"

"My cat."

"Your cat? What's wrong with Sandwich?"

"She's lonely," Colleen said in a quiet voice. "Really lonely. Needs some extra touching."

Moore was about to die on the spot.

"Oh, that's easy. Just give her more love than she can ever possibly need. That'll satisfy her."

Cold, sputtering silence filled the air between the three of them.

"What?" Jordy asked, looking at Moore. "What's wrong?"

"Nothing," he and Colleen said at the same time.

Completely flummoxed, Moore pulled his headphones off and was assaulted by all the tiny sounds the device had muted.

"Uh huh," Jordy said. "Okay. Bye." Tossing his headphones on the chair, he said, "Colleen says goodnight. She has to deal with her cat. Give it lots of attention so it'll be happy and go to sleep."

"Gotcha." Moore pretended to yawn. "I need to go to bed, kiddo."

"It's only ten thirty!"

"I get up early."

"You're getting boring."

"I just played *League* with you!"

"Fine."

"Tell you what. Get up early with me and we'll go to Greta's."

Jordy's face lit up. "Seriously?"

"Sure. The high school tour isn't until eleven. Plenty of time."

"Cool." Jordy walked down the hall to his bedroom. The door closed softly.

Moore dropped to the couch, slumping, staring up at the ceiling. What the hell were he and Colleen doing?

And how could he get her to do more of it–in person?

* * *

Moore appreciated the fact that Greta's son, Wolf, didn't do what some of the townspeople did. Being greeted with, "Hey, Jordy, you in town again?" always made Moore feel like a guest parent, rather than a real parent.

The fifty days a year he got with Jordy, half of them here in Maine, were the only moments he had to find normalcy with his son. Walking into Love You Bakery meant being treated like a typical dad.

JULIA KENT

When Luke came to Greta's with Harriet, no one said, "Hey, Harriet, you in town?" because he raised her.

Moore was raising Jordy, too, just in a different way.

"Jordy!" Wolf shouted.

The place was surprisingly quiet. Nine-thirty on a weekday was the right time to come in. After his promise, Moore had made sure they were here, starving and ready for whatever yummy goodness Wolf was serving up. Some of his newest items included heart-shaped red velvet Belgian waffles, strawberry pancakes, and sage chicken fried steak, but Jordy was fixated on one offering.

"Hey, Wolf. Got any chaffles?"

"Sure do. That keto lady writer who came through here last year did me a favor. Between these new bacon and cheese chaffles and Rachel Hart's Love Bomb over at Love You Coffee, we're becoming a boutique café in a foodie town."

"Got to include The Food Alchemist in there, Wolf. Blake and Sheila would be hurt if they weren't mentioned."

Wolf snorted. "Anyplace but Bilbee's."

Moore made a thoughtful face.

"Rider is trying, with those pop-up chef events."

"I'll give him credit for that, but only that."

"Fair enough."

"Two bacon and cheese chaffles, home fries, and rye toast?"

"Yes, sir. Coffee for me."

Wolf nodded, then grabbed a mug, gesturing for them to pick the counter or a free booth. Jordy led them to the counter, where they chose stools and settled in.

"Can we also get loaded brownies for later?" Jordy asked. "And I want a coffee, too."

Moore startled.

"You? Coffee?"

"Yeah." Shifty eyes met his. "Half a cup?"

260

"I thought you weren't allowed. Cammie says so in her emails to me whenever you're here."

"I drink Starbucks sometimes with my friends. Mom doesn't know."

Wolf let out a whistle.

"Never, ever say the S word in front of the crew at Love You Coffee. You'll get stoned to death."

Jordy smiled, his grin all metal. The braces would be gone the next time Moore saw him. Two more months and counting, he knew.

Which meant Moore's payments would stop, as well.

"Can I, Dad?"

Yet again, the sheer normalcy of the moment rocked Moore internally. Fifteen-year-olds pushing boundaries, wanting to be more grown up. Cammie's rule about caffeine rolled through his mind, but damn it, he was Jordy's parent, too.

He didn't have to defer to her.

"Sure."

Wolf poured them their coffees, filling Jordy's halfway. Then he topped it off with decaf.

As Moore drank his back, he watched Jordy pour... and pour... and *pour* sugar from a heart-shaped container into his heart-shaped mug. Six creamers later, and Jordy had a very nice drink.

In no way did it resemble actual coffee.

As they sipped from their respective mugs, Moore looked around. A couple he didn't know was sitting in a booth behind them, and then three more customers came in, the bell at the door ringing. It made him think of the jewelry shop and how glad he was that his nephew, Joey, was manning the store this morning.

The drive to the new school would take about thirty minutes, more like forty-five in winter. It was a drive that

Moore would have to learn and work around if Jordy came and lived with him. Those two or three hours in the car every day would be a joy. Eventually, Jordy would have his license, and the captive hours in the car would have been just a phase.

But a phase Moore got to experience in full.

"It's really nice to be here, Dad," Jordy said unexpectedly. He was halfway through his coffee and looking around, just like Moore. "Every time we come here, I feel like I'm at home."

"You are at home."

Jordy shrugged. "Not really. This isn't where I live."

"Luview is your home, Jordy. You're a townie, just like everyone else."

"How?" Jordy's voice wasn't defiant or defensive, which was new. "How am I part of Luview if I'm only here a few weeks a year?"

"We take what we can get, kiddo. You can change that, you know."

"Can I?" Jordy took a sip of his coffee as the scent of their chaffles made Moore's stomach growl. Jordy's decided to join him, as if they were singing a duet. It made them both laugh, breaking the seriousness of the moment, but Moore didn't want to lose this thread.

"I don't know how hard your mom would fight. You said earlier that she told you to go ahead and move in with me."

Jordy let out a snort.

"She says that, but you know Mom."

"I do indeed."

The silence that buffered those words said so much: fifteen years of pain all rolled into that which was unspoken.

"I'm fifteen now, and I'm behind. You guys held me back a year."

"*I* didn't hold you back a year, Jordy," Moore began, but his son put up his palm.

"I know. I know how it works. That year I was gone is why I'm behind."

"Right," was all Moore could say.

"I've got four years of high school left, and I'm really into theater. It's my jam, Dad. There's something about it, and *League*, that makes me feel like I'm finding my place."

Moore went still. He got the sense that Jordy was ready to say more, open up more, share more. Any interference could screw this up, so he took a sip of coffee and just listened.

"I don't know what to do. Mom's having a baby, my second little sister, and I want to be part of her life. Soria's a pain in the butt, but I love her, too. I can't stand Locke, though. Then there's this really cool school here in Maine, and I never really got to live with you all these years. I barely remember when you and Mom were still together and we lived in the basement at Grandma and Grandpa's house."

"You don't have memories?"

Jordy shrugged. "I guess they're more memories that come from the pictures that Grandma shows me every time I visit. I have a few. I mostly remember Colleen."

"Colleen?"

"Yeah, I mean, she was with me all the time."

Colleen's confession about helping take care of Jordy while Cammie claimed all the credit boiled Moore's blood. He wanted to say something, correct the record, but he played it cool.

"Really?"

"Yeah, I mean, I can remember being three or four and going to preschool. Colleen walked me there. She was always the one who was there to pick me up."

"Right."

Jordy shrugged. "I remember you sometimes, and I remember Mom. Most of what I remember is you and Mom arguing."

"You do?"

"You'd get home from school, because you were always at school or work. But I remember Grandma and Colleen always telling me that your school was so important, but not more important than me. I didn't understand how something that *wasn't* more important than me took you away, though."

Moore let out a big breath.

"Oh, Jordy."

Jordy's eyes went wide as they locked with Moore's.

"I'm not supposed to say this, am I?"

"No, no." Moore reached over and covered Jordy's hand with his. To his surprise, his son didn't move. "This is exactly what I want to hear from you. There is nothing you can't talk about with me."

"Chaffles!" Wolf announced, standing in front of them. The look on his face made it clear that he thought he was walking over to one situation and had encountered a completely different one. Plunking the large heart-shaped plates on the counter, he gave Moore a *sorry, dude* look and asked, "Need more coffee?"

Moore covered his cup with his palm after letting go of Jordy's hand. "I'm good."

Jordy avoided eye contact and just dug into his food. Wolf walked away, giving Moore an appraising glance. Wolf was definitely among the people who understood how hard parenting is, as the father of two girls who had turned out beautifully, a little bit older than Jordy.

Food was the great equalizer and conversation ender, a relief for both of them. Jordy was clearly going through something developmental, testing the waters, trying out some kind of emotion other than contempt.

And Moore was here for it.

He wanted more than anything right now to tell Jordy the truth about that missing year. Colleen had urged him countless times to fill in the blanks for the poor kid, once Jordy was a teenager.

Cammie had poisoned him, Moore knew, but it felt wrong to say something negative about her.

Jordy had to spend the majority of his time with his mother and Moore didn't want to create conflict, the internal kind that eats away at you. Putting his son through that just so that the record could be cleared felt like an added burden for a child who should have more emotional freedom.

Maybe, though, Colleen was right. Jordy was obviously struggling with memories that didn't add up.

Shame filled Moore as he took another bite of the delicious breakfast in front of him. Stomach twisting, he paused and set his fork down.

He never regretted having his son, but if events had unfolded differently when he was seventeen, so many lives wouldn't have been disrupted.

Then again, his son wouldn't exist.

"Dad, you okay?" Jordy never checked in on him, so that alone made Moore do a quick head shake.

"What?"

"You okay? You look weird."

"Weird?"

"Like something's wrong. Am I upsetting you by talking about this?"

"No. It's not bad. My head is just really full."

"A lot going on at work?"

"You could say that."

"Dad, I don't ever want to work at the jewelry store. I mean, you know, summers or helping around the holidays from Christmas to Valentine's Day, sure. But even then, I was thinking about getting a job at Love You Chocolates. They'll hire me even though I'm only fifteen."

Moore gaped at Jordy.

"What?"

"Yeah." Jordy turned away and began eating the pile of home fries on his plate. Golden, crusty potatoes with seasoning and grilled peppers and onions mixed in. All of the peppers were red, of course, to fit with the red, white, and pink theme of the town.

"Why are you mentioning this now?"

"For when I move here."

"You really have decided?"

"I said so."

"I know you said so before, kiddo."

"What? You didn't believe me?"

"Honestly, no."

"Because Mom's right and you don't want me here?"

"Of course not. Because I thought you'd need more time to decide."

"Being here these last two days means I've already decided. I want to move here."

"Whoa." Wolf happened to walk up with a coffee carafe at the exact moment that Jordy's words rang out. His eyebrows shot up, and he looked at Moore, then Jordy.

"More coffee?"

Moore lifted his hand.

"I need it."

"How're the chaffles?"

"Good." Jordy was chomping on his final bite. "Can I get a loaded brownie, too?" He looked at Moore, who just nodded.

Wolf poured the coffee and walked over to the bakery case, bagging the brownies.

Moore's appetite came back. Suddenly, everything smelled amazing. As he took bites, Jordy pulled his phone out of his pocket and started thumbing texts. Ignoring his dad now, he pushed earbuds in. In the silence, Moore could hear his ears popping as he swallowed, and he marveled at how life turned in a second.

The car accident with Colleen had been proof of that, and here was another moment. Why did so much of life get crammed into such short periods of time when long stretches of nothingness and routine prevailed? If he could take some of the excitement of the last month or two and spread it out, he would gladly pace it.

Adrenaline raced through him as the implication of Jordy's words sank in.

This was real.

There were lawyers to call, custody arrangements to make, and conflicts to be had with his ex-wife. There were long-term travel plans to coordinate so that Jordy could truly know his little sisters. By moving in with Moore, Jordy would have a relationship with his siblings akin to the relationship that Moore had been forced to have with his own son for the last decade.

There was no way around it.

Either Jordy continued to have a strained, limited relationship with his dad, or he had a strained, limited relationship with his sisters.

Short of convincing Cammie to move back to Luview, Maine, which he knew was never going to happen, Jordy couldn't have it all, and that hurt Moore the most. He wanted his son to have every possible emotional joy and he couldn't give it to him.

No matter what.

Wolf dropped the bakery bag on the counter and went back to the cash register with Moore's credit card. A small line had formed and as the door bell jingled, Moore looked up to see Luke walking in with his daughter, Harriet, who was now eight.

A pang of emotion hit him in the gut. Luke had been

avoiding him. Yes, he had Jordy in town and always spent every possible moment with his son, but this was different. His best friend was mad at him, and Moore knew when he was being frozen out.

It hurt.

"Jordy!" Harriet squealed, racing across the small café to launch herself into his arms. He pivoted quickly and caught her.

"What are you doing here, Fairy Girl?" he asked, brushing her thick, dark curls with his hand. Sure enough, glitter sprinkled to the floor.

"Daddy and I are here to get loaded brownies," she announced.

"I thought you had school?" Jordy questioned her with a pretend adult scowl. "Are you skipping?"

"No, I had to get a shot." She pulled her sleeve up to show the colorful band-aid on her shoulder.

"Ouch," Jordy said in commiseration. "Shots stink."

"Yeah, so Daddy's getting me a loaded brownie."

"I think that's a fair deal."

"Hey, Moore." Luke walked over and sat on the stool next to him looking at the remnants of his breakfast. "You guys headed over to the new school?"

In Love you, Maine, everyone knew each other's business.

"Yeah, Jordy has a tour at eleven. I'm dropping him off."

Jordy and Harriet chattered animatedly about some new anime kids show that they were watching as Luke leaned in and said, "How's it going with him?"

The normalcy of this conversation made something in Moore loosen and ache less.

"It's going great," he confided. "Jordy just told me he wants to move here. Full stop."

"Whoa. Even before he tours the school?"

"I don't think this was ever about the school. I think it's about Cammie being pregnant with his little sister."

"They know it's a girl?"

"Yeah. And Cammie's been making him take care of Soria way more than any teenager should have to."

"So he has to choose between being close to you and being close to his sisters?" Luke had a way of getting to the heart of matters with a Scud missile-like precision.

"That's right." Moore took a sip of his refreshed coffee.

"That's hard." Luke said, nodding. "You can't give him everything, can you?"

"No." Moore's eyes drifted over to Harriet, realizing that Luke understood that better than almost anyone else. "All we can do is love them and try our best."

"That's more than a lot of kids get," Luke replied.

Jordy and Harriet each dug into their respective brownie bags and took a big bite.

"Yum," she mumbled, chocolate frosting at the corners of her mouth.

"Double yum," Jordy agreed.

"Sugaring up the young folk, I see," said a rumbling voice from behind them. Old Doc Blythe had walked in and put one hand on each man's shoulder. "Those brownies are–"

"Diabetes in a bag," they both said in unison. Doc's words were well known in town.

He laughed and winked at them. "And I'm about to eat one, too. *Shhhh*. Don't tell Michelle." Michelle Blythe was Doc's new wife.

"New wife" meant they'd been married for seventeen years. His first wife had left him two decades ago, for a woman. Poor Doc knew exactly what it was like to be the object of gossip, and he kept a low profile, working long hours to provide for the citizens of Luview and staying out of the limelight.

"Michelle still on that vegan kick?" Wolf called out from the grill.

"Yeah. You have anything vegan here?"

"We do." He thrust his chin toward a case behind the men. "All the gluten free and vegan stuff is in there."

"Getting fancy," Luke noted, nodding with approval.

"We're trying. People come to our town to get their needs met, right? That's how we keep them coming back. Moore knows that all too well."

"Meeting the right needs," Doc said with a wink that made Moore's radar go haywire. Was he alluding to catching him and Colleen outside at the hospital?

Wasn't only Moore's radar that went off, though. Luke's eyes narrowed as he looked at them both.

"Dad?" Jordy was looking at his phone. "We need to get going."

Doc looked up at him. "When did you get so tall?"

"Why does everyone ask me that?" Jordy groused. "What'm I supposed to say? I grew so tall when I was caged in the basement and force fed nothing but pie?"

"Is that a life option?" Doc replied smoothly. "Happy to trade places with you."

The unexpected *bon mot* made Jordy burst out laughing, giving the doctor a fist bump that the old man took with a smooth motion that impressed Moore.

"Hope you stick around, Jordy. We need more character in this town."

"Thanks, Doc." Wolf lifted Moore's credit card in the air, the transfer easy and smooth, like everything in his stable, steady little town.

Moore led as they walked out, calling goodbyes to everyone, Harriet squeezing Jordy's torso with a bear hug. She looked up at him.

"You'll come to our new house and play, right?"

Jordy smiled down at her. "Of course! You're my unofficial sister." Jordy looked at Moore. "Harriet is to me what Colleen is to you."

"Huh?"

Luke snapped around and looked at Jordy sharply.

"You know. An unofficial sister?"

"That's right," Luke said in an arch tone. "Jordy makes a great point."

Sensing zero positive outcome if he tried to argue or explain, Moore defaulted to his typical mode: affability.

"I'm just glad you two get along so well," he said to Jordy and Harriet, their comments ringing in his ears. As he and Jordy sauntered out, Moore looked back in through the window. Luke and Doc were talking as Wolf rang up new customers, Harriet's face smeared with more brownie.

Turning on the engine, he pulled away while Jordy put his earbuds in, goofing off on his phone.

Unofficial sister? No.

More like, unacknowledged love interest.

Moore was being handed what he'd wanted for so many years: his kid living with him, and Colleen.

So why did this all feel so wrong?

Chapter 15

Colleen

"Thank you for meeting me here," Colleen said gratefully to Rachel, who was settling into her chair on the opposite side of the table. She'd specifically chosen Love You Coffee as the place for this meeting because she knew how much Rachel enjoyed the drink that she had created.

The famous Love Bomb.

Half almond milk, half two percent, with espresso and a teaspoon of ground vanilla bean. It had taken over as the dominant drink in the town's coffee shop after Rachel had stormed into town a couple of years ago and ordered a hand-crafted version of it for herself, and Reef Matthews, the manager of the shop, had put it on the menu.

Instant hit.

Clutching her cup in a perfectly manicured hand, Rachel took a sip and rolled her eyes behind closed lids. Colleen laughed at the sight.

"I think you're only supposed to make a face like that in the privacy of your own bedroom," she whispered.

Rachel turned a furious red and looked away. "Sorry, but I need caffeine that badly."

"Bad day at work?" Colleen asked.

"You have no idea. This whole mess with the Love Committee and the sign requirements is making it more difficult for me to bring in business."

"What do you mean?"

"Word is getting out. A couple of possible prospects are tired of some of the more rigid policies that the board enforces."

"You mean they're sick and tired of Anne?"

Rachel shrugged. "Business owners these days are different. They want streamlined. They want simple. They don't like delays, and with e-tailing, they have way more options. They aren't as dependent on the local consumer market for sales."

"Sure, but Love You, Maine, has a special character to it. We have to attract a certain kind of business owner."

"Of course," Rachel agreed, taking a long sip of her coffee as Colleen did the same. "But some businesses can fit in here or anywhere, and some businesses just aren't going to make it in this tiny town. Some, frankly, are turned away by the cheesiness of the town's concept."

"Well, then, we don't want them," Colleen replied tartly.

Rachel shook her head. "You are a Luview through and through."

"Yes, I am. It's in my blood and bones."

"I'd like to see the town get bigger," Rachel said.

"Of course. It's your job."

"It's not just that it's my job. I think there's something so special about Love You, Maine, that the message the town puts out there needs to be heard by more people."

"What message is that? Love?"

"It's not just love–or anyway, it's not just the idea of love. When you come here, you feel accepted."

"You feel that way because you fell in love with one of the town founders' descendants."

"I don't feel that way *just* because of Kell," Rachel countered. She took another long sip and looked around. "Check out this coffee shop. I've been in hundreds of coffee shops over the years, especially in L.A. and D.C., and none of them are like this."

"You mean covered in red, white, and pink?"

Rachel laughed. "The decor definitely stands out."

Police lights flashed, and both turned to see Luke driving by in his pink police cruiser, the red and blue lights flashing as he drove slowly but determinedly through town.

"And then there's that." Rachel pointed.

"The pink cars?"

"Yes."

Colleen shrugged. "It's part of the appeal."

"Exactly," Rachel agreed. "Why not encourage more of it?"

"We don't want Luview getting *too* big. Part of the appeal is how small it is."

"Why not let the market determine that?"

"Ugh," Colleen groaned. "The market?"

"There's nothing wrong with the free market system."

"No, there's nothing wrong with it, Rachel. But we don't want big corporations coming in here."

"I didn't say anything about big corporations."

"You used to, though. That's the whole reason you're here, right?"

"I'm here because of Kell," Rachel said softly, her eyes glimmering with love. "Moved here because I fell in love with him."

"I know." Colleen reached for her hand and gave it a squeeze. "And we're so glad you did."

"Speaking of falling in love." Rachel started, and Colleen's hand froze. "Why did you really ask me out for coffee?"

Blinking hard, Colleen just stared at her. Early on in the time that Kell and Rachel had been together, Colleen had thought of her as a bit shallow. No, she was never going to admit that to anyone, but Rachel Hart, the daughter of a fading Hollywood star and a high-powered entertainment attorney, had arrived in Luview determined to help the local artisan chocolate company get bought out by the mega corporation she worked for, and that first impression had left a bit of a bad taste in Colleen's mouth.

In the time that Rachel had spent settling into the town and into their large extended family, Colleen had learned that she was anything but shallow. Still, Colleen was slow to warm. Having Rachel call her out on a matter of the heart was surprising. They weren't best buddies, and this was definitely crossing a privacy line and a confidentiality boundary that Colleen held firmly.

"I can see it in you, Colleen."

"Did my mom say something to you?" Something flickered in Rachel's eyes. "She did, didn't she?"

"I haven't said a word to Kell," Rachel replied, her hand up in defense. "I swear to God."

"My mother cannot keep a secret," Colleen hissed. "She was not supposed to tell you that she caught Moore and me kissing."

Something about Rachel's affect made Colleen pause. Staring people down was a special gift she possessed. As the seconds ticked by, Rachel predictably became more and more uncomfortable, and then Colleen realized the deep, dark truth.

"My mother told you that I kissed Moore, but *Kell* told you that I–"

Rachel jumped in. "He told me what happened at the cabin."

The slam of her palm against the table was complete impulsivity, the sound making people turn toward them, their drinks almost spilling. Rachel grabbed both coffees before they could topple.

"I'm going to kill him," Colleen said calmly.

"Your little brother is a foot taller than you and outweighs you by a hundred pounds of solid muscle."

"Doesn't matter. I will climb him like a tree and I will cut his heart out."

"I would really rather you not do that," Rachel said primly. "I've grown a little fond of him."

"He really told you about what happened after the accident, he and Luke barging in and finding us in bed?"

"Yes." Rachel grimaced. "He still talks about needing brain bleach. I thought you invited me out for coffee to talk about this."

"I didn't know you already knew! This changes the whole tenor of the conversation. I thought I was sitting down with you and having a bonding moment where I was going to confess this big, deep, dark secret of mine, and instead, you not only know part of it, you know the whole freaking thing!"

"That doesn't have to change the bonding part," Rachel said with a sigh. "I would love that. I'm touched, Colleen. I thought you viewed me as shallow."

Colleen jolted.

"What? No!" she lied. "I would never think that of you."

One perfectly threaded eyebrow arched on Rachel's face.

"You're a really bad liar, Colleen."

Colleen started laughing. "You're right. I am." She took a giant gulp of her cooling coffee.

Rachel's other eyebrow rose, and she tipped her head down. Her look said, *I'm judging you so hard.*

"That's okay. I've always thought of you as small minded and a little bit stuck up."

"Hey!"

Rachel shrugged with one shoulder.

"If we're confessing our true feelings, why not air it all out? Put it on the table, then we can move beyond it. You must be desperate for a friend if you're turning to me."

"That's not true," Colleen said, though she struggled. "It's just..."

"Come to think about it," Rachel ventured, "You don't have many friends."

"I have plenty of friends."

"But not really, Colleen. You have your family. You have Moore. You have your colleagues at the hospital. And other than that, you have–who?"

"I have Jordy."

"Jordy's great. He's your gamer friend, but he's more like your son or your nephew."

At the word *son*, Colleen's skin began to tingle. Rachel was giving her a rundown she didn't expect, and the only way to stop it would be to tell her what she'd really been feeling.

"You're right. You know who my best friend is, Rachel?"

"Who?"

"Moore."

"Oh," Rachel said softly. "I see. You can't talk to him about any of this, can you? And that's got to hurt."

"It does," Colleen confessed. "I can't really talk about this with Mom. And Luke is completely off his rocker when it comes to me and Moore. There are a couple of people down at the hospital, but whenever I try to talk about my romantic life, they just make Third Date Colleen jokes. I need somebody to talk to."

"And Kylie was busy." Rachel said flatly.

"No, I wanted to talk to you first."

"Me?"

"Kylie's great, but she's kind of contaminated by Luke."

"Contaminated?"

"I don't know what the right word is. Every time I think about talking to her, I just imagine she's going to go tell Luke and then that's going to make this worse because Luke seems to think that Moore and I aren't together."

"So you *are* together?"

"Not publicly together, but privately together."

"That's the same thing, Colleen."

"No, Rachel. Trust me, it's not."

"I see. You guys are hiding it?"

"Yeah."

"Because of Luke?"

"No. Yes. I don't know. Mostly because of Jordy."

"Jordy? Why would you hide your relationship from *Jordy*?"

"We weren't going to. We were going to be completely transparent. Go public, deal with all the flak from the town, the whole bit. And then Moore picked up Jordy from the airport, and Jordy started talking about how much he doesn't like his new soon-to-be stepfather. How he was glad that Moore got dumped by his ex-girlfriend, Hannah. How he was excited to have a parent who didn't force a stepparent or a parent figure on him, and it scrambled Moore's brains."

"Sounds like it scrambled his heart."

"Yeah." Colleen sighed and sipped her coffee. "That, too."

"Hey." Reef, the manager, was standing beside their table with two taster cups in his hands. "I need victims."

"Victims?"

"I mean, test subjects."

"For what?" Colleen asked, instantly suspicious.

"We're trying out a new drink."

"You already have the best drink in town." Rachel said, smoothly. "My Love Bomb."

Reef's mouth set into a firm line. "Just because you were the first person to order that drink doesn't make it yours."

"Yes, it does."

"No, it doesn't."

"Yes, it does."

"No, it–" He held up one finger. "I am not arguing with you, Rachel. We're testing some new drinks. Skylar wants more than her own opinion before we add things to the menu."

"I think that's fair." Rachel said. "You're doing proper product testing, focus groups, all of that."

"No." Reef scowled at her. "We're just asking you two."

"Fine." Colleen took the taster cup out of his hand. "Is that a new tat?"

She pointed to a red streak on his wrist and he pulled the cuff of his shirt down.

"Yeah." He obviously didn't want to talk about it.

As she raised the taster cup to her mouth, her nose explored the drink.

"Coffee, cinnamon, ginger, and something deeper. Is that... cardamom?"

"Just try it. I'll tell you what's in it after you taste it."

"How about I'll taste it after you tell me what's in it." Rachel replied.

All she got in return was a glare.

Colleen took a tentative sip, her taste buds dancing as the flavors her nose had detected hit her tongue, along with a rich creaminess.

"Mmm," she said, "This is amazing."

"What do you taste?" he asked.

"Like I said, cinnamon, ginger, cardamom. A little burnt sugar?" she probed.

"That has to be coconut cream," Rachel said, but he shook his head. "MCT oil?"

"And something peppery," Colleen added.

"You got almost all of it right. You're missing the black seed oil."

"What's black seed oil?" Rachel asked. "I thought I was up to date on coffeehouse culture. Every time we go back home to L.A., I make sure I go to the trendiest places."

"Why do you have to go to the trendiest places there when you can come here?" Reef shot back.

"It's got more bite than I expect when I drink a cup of coffee."

"That's the black seed oil. It's black cumin, ground up just the tiniest bit. Some people like their Mexican mochas with the cayenne pepper giving that little extra jolt when it hits your tonsils. This is similar, but without the after spice."

"What are you calling this?"

"Electric Chai."

"Ooh," Rachel said, "I like it."

"All right, then." He turned to Skylar, who was racking mugs, and gave her a thumbs up. She jumped up and down, squealing, clapping her hands, pressing her palms up against the air like she was dancing in the middle of a nightclub.

Colleen drank more of her coffee as her mind went back to her problem. An unsettled feeling grew in her. Rachel knew about the cabin? Her mom had told her about the kiss at town hall? Word was going to spread soon.

Sure, Deanna and Rachel were a closed loop, but if they knew, it meant Kylie knew. And her dad. Now the whole family was aware of her and Moore, and all it would take was one misstep before Nadine Khouri was practically announcing it during Town Meeting.

"Great," Reef said. "Now we can take the Love Bomb off the menu and put the Electric Chai on there."

"What?" Rachel shouted. "You can't remove my Love Bomb!"

"Watch me."

"It's your most popular drink!"

"No," he said calmly, seeming to enjoy the conflict. "It's *your* favorite drink. Big difference."

"Everyone I know tells me they come here and get it and love it!"

"That's not everyone in town, Rachel."

One corner of Reef's firmly set mouth twitched, a tell.

He was messing with her.

"Reef, the Love Bomb is worth keeping."

He scratched his chin. "Maybe we could just rename it."

"Why would you do that?"

"How about we call it the 'Don't Tell Me How to Run My Business'?"

Deflated, Rachel took in a deep breath, regrouping.

"I'm not trying to tell you how to run your business."

His snort would have made a rhinoceros jealous.

"I just think there's room for two original drinks on the menu! Why don't you have a contest?"

"Contest?" Skylar piped up from behind Reef, evidently eavesdropping.

"Put out two tip bowls. One labeled Electric Chai and the other labeled Love Bomb. Let customers decide by tipping. It's win-win. You find out which drink is more popular, and I'll bet tipping increases."

Skylar's eyes were huge. "Or we could do a fundraising drive for Mel's animal sanctuary!"

Reef seemed to like that idea more.

Probably because it didn't come from Rachel.

"Yeah," He said slowly. "Let's do that."

"I'll make the signs!" Skylar was artistic, with the ability to hand-draw fonts like no one else.

The front door suddenly filled with a gaggle of college girls, probably up from Portland. Reef nodded and left them, Rachel looking smug.

"Hah. He really doesn't understand how much I'm helping him make more money."

"Money isn't the only reason people are in business here."

An O of surprise was all Rachel could muster, and Colleen burst out laughing.

"Making money is the reason people go into business! Otherwise, they'd just be someone's employee."

"*I'm* someone's employee. Nothing 'just' or lesser about that."

"I didn't mean it that way!"

Taking a deep breath, Colleen fought the irritation inside her. Being defensive was her instinctive response whenever something Rachel said seemed demeaning. Was it fair? No. Was it Rachel's fault? Absolutely not.

But was it real and something Colleen needed to manage inside herself?

Yes.

"You're right. I'm being oversensitive."

Surprise filled Rachel's eyes. "You are?"

"I need help."

"Anything! How can I help you?"

"I need to know how you know when to leave home."

A slow blink. The closing of her mouth. The scrape of her fingernail against the table. Small details like these were what Colleen observed in Rachel as seconds ticked by, time meaningless. The words had been spoken, said aloud, unable to be walked back.

"*What?*" Rachel gasped. "You want to leave Luview?"

"*Shhhhh,*" Colleen hissed, pulling Rachel's hand. "Don't spill all my secrets!"

"But why?"

"I don't *want* to leave. And if I do, it won't be for long. Doc Blythe put this crazy idea in my head."

"Crazy enough to make you leave? You just helped buy the camp with the whole family!"

"And I would keep my place there. That's forever."

Rachel's relief was palpable.

"Thank goodness! Deanna would lose it if you ever left."

"I've been thinking. A lot. Doc said I'd make a good nurse practitioner or even a physician assistant. And I can't get that kind of education here."

"Oh! So this is about your career!"

"Mostly."

"What about Moore?"

"What about him?"

"If you two are together, does he support your leaving town?"

"We're not *together* together. We're just... undefined."

"Sounds pretty defined to me. You're sleeping with him."

"But we're still hiding. And then there's that whole Third Date Colleen nonsense. Plus, my ovaries have an expiration date, you know?"

"That's... a lot to unpack right there, Colleen."

"My life feels like there's too much to unpack."

"Is this about the accident?"

"Huh?" As if called forth by a spell, her shoulder began to ache.

"You're reflecting and re-evaluating your life? Lots of people do it after a near-death experience."

The words *near-death experience* evoked images of soft light, mystical beings, and peaceful music. None of that had happened to her in the icy pond where Moore saved her.

She suddenly felt a little cheated.

"Near death, huh? Hadn't thought of it that way. I didn't hear angels sing or tell myself to turn away from the light."

Expecting laughter, Colleen was surprised when Rachel leaned forward, serious, and said, "You've been through a lot. Both of you."

"You mean Moore?"

"Kell told me how destroyed the truck was. How it felt when he and Luke came upon it. How they expected to find your bodies in the water. The sheer panic of thinking you were both dead. The walk to the cabin, and then how, uh..."

"How they actually found us."

"Right."

"We were definitely wet," Colleen joked, laughter bubbling up from her belly as Rachel made a confused face, then reacted.

"Oh, geez."

"Sorry. Dark humor."

"You need to think these things through. Add in the fact that Moore won't go public with your relationship, and you must be reeling."

"Hold on. Moore and I both made the decision, together, not to go public. For Jordy's sake."

Rachel took a big gulp of her coffee.

"I understand. There's no one right choice here. But why hold your life back at a time when you just got a second chance at it?"

"Because Jordy might–"

"Jordy is fifteen. He's already decided to move here, right? That's what Deanna told me."

"Yes."

"Then what are you two waiting for? Tell him. Then you can be free." Rachel studied her. "Or maybe you *do* want to leave? Go study and try out a life away from Luview?"

"I want Moore," Colleen said firmly.

"That's what I mean! You deserve more. And maybe you'll find more out there, in the big world beyond the town line."

"Moore is right here."

Rachel scowled, then her eyebrows went up.

"Aha! I think we're having a 'Who's on first?' moment. When you said 'I want more,' you were using his name. Not m-o-r-e."

"Right. Oh! Then that's what you meant when you–"

As they both began to giggle at the misunderstanding, Rachel suddenly did a double take, looking out the window.

Mel Chassi, the local animal sanctuary operator, was walking an old yellow Lab on a service dog harness.

With a parrot riding on its back.

Wearing a red snow vest.

Slowly, surreptitiously, Rachel took out her phone and snapped photos.

"This is going to be so quaint and quirky for the town website!" she gushed.

"What on earth is Mel up to now?" Colleen muttered as Mel caught her eye and changed direction, entering the coffee shop.

With the dog and the parrot.

"LOVE BOMB!" the parrot squawked. "LOVE BOMB!"

Rachel looked over at Reef with a triumphant grin.

"Did you tell Mel to train that thing?" he called out.

"I trained McPirate!" Mel shouted back. "It's my favorite drink!"

"You know that thing's not allowed in here," Reef grumbled as he began pulling espresso, casting suspicious sidelong glances at the animals stacked like a double-decker.

"Service animals are permitted anywhere humans can go. Don't you dare try to block Caramel from coming in!"

"I meant the bird."

"McPirate is Caramel's emotional support animal."

"*Dogs* have emotional support animals?" Reef groused. "Now I've heard it all."

"HURRY UP!" the parrot snapped. "NEED CAFFEINE!"

"That bird's been hanging around you for too long, Mel. Picked up on all your bad habits."

"I don't scream at people like that!" she yelled.

"DARREN IS A STUBBORN ASS!" McPirate shouted.

Darren Chassi was the local veterinarian and Mel's ex-husband.

"Yeah, right."

Mel ignored Reef with a wave and turned to Colleen. "You heard from Dennis lately?"

"Den? Sure. Last week on our family video call. Why?"

"He asked me about taking a retired military dog. Haven't heard from him in a week."

"He's on a mission. Something he can't talk about. He goes quiet like that."

"Ah. Makes sense." The parrot pecked at the old Lab's fur, but gently. The dog's left shoulder relaxed a bit, the bird lifting its feet and setting them back down.

"Is that parrot seriously an emotional support animal?"

"Yep. Can't separate them. Tried to adopt Caramel out. She's an old service dog but still workable. McPirate escaped and found her. Twice. The foster family was going to take Caramel but refused on McPirate, so..."

"Now they're both part of your zoo?" Reef cracked, delivering a Love Bomb to Mel.

"My *family*," she corrected him. Reef went back to the counter and rang up Mel's order on the iPad. Most of the townies had their credit cards on file. Mel slipped a dollar bill into a tip cup.

"Maybe you'll find someone who will take them both," Rachel said excitedly.

"That's my hope."

Colleen pulled out her phone and texted Dennis:

We're at Love You Coffee. Mel's asking about a military dog you contacted her about. Hope you're safe.

She added a heart. Her big brother hadn't lived in Luview for decades, but he was still part of the emotional fabric of daily life. Weekly group video calls and the occasional trip home, plus Mom and Dad's big Germany trip a few years ago, kept Dennis a part of their lives, even though he'd taken himself out of Luview.

"There. I texted Dennis."

"Thanks. Worst case, I figured I could sic Deanna on him."

"Whoa now. Let's not call out the cavalry."

Mel grinned at her and took a sip of her Love Bomb, moaning with pleasure.

"Rachel, thank you. Best improvement you've made to the town yet."

"What about the trolley? The parking meters? The–"

"Nope. This," Mel called back as Caramel led her to the sidewalk, McPirate riding along like the king of the world.

The pink Love You, Maine, electric trolley let out a series of bells, the sound it made when entering a stop zone. A moment later, a group of female shoppers, all part of a large tour making its way through town, descended on the coffee shop.

Reef got busy making some welcome tourist dough, the women *ooohing* and *ahhhing* over the red mugs, the heart-shaped everything, and quite a few eyeing Reef himself as if he were a souvenir they'd like to take home with them.

Finishing their respective coffees, they sat in amused silence until Rachel finally said, "I don't know how you know when it's time to leave. I never felt planted firmly in place like you Luviews do. Leaving L.A. was easy."

"Leaving this place is not."

"So don't."

"I'd have to, in order to get the education I want."

"How badly do you want it?"

"Not sure."

"It sounds to me like you're still in the information-gathering stage. Not the decision-making stage."

"Hadn't thought of it that way."

"Sometimes you have to make a choice because there's a deadline. But sometimes you have loads of time to collect your input and see where the information takes you. Why not view this phase that way? You don't have to know where you're going, or when. You just have to know that you're interested in a journey with a specific endpoint, but maybe lots of different ways to get there?"

"Kell's right."

"About what?"

"You have a unique, sharp way of organizing things."

"No, I don't. Anyone can do it."

"Not true. Don't sell yourself short."

"Right back atcha, sister."

Rachel's words hit home. There was no looming deadline before her. No huge conflict. All she really had to do right now was learn what her options were.

"Thanks."

"For what?"

"Listening. Hanging out. *Being discreet*," she said pointedly.

Rachel looked down at her Love Bomb. "Was this a bribe?"

"Did it work?"

"Yes!"

"Then it was a bribe." Standing, Colleen reached out for a hug, happy to have a sister figure in her life. Both her younger brothers had now found their soulmates, and that meant Colleen got the sisters she'd never had growing up.

Both men had chosen well for her.
And she knew that with Moore, she'd chosen well.
How?
Because he was already Luke's best friend.
And yet...

Chapter 16

Moore

"Uh-huh. Yeah, Mom. Yes. Sure."

Moore overheard Jordy talking to Cammie, tension building between his shoulder blades as he hand washed dishes that didn't need the level of attention he lavished on them. The tour of the new high school had gone incredibly well, exceeding Moore's highest expectations.

When he had picked Jordy up, he'd been asked to come inside and talk to the principal, *with* Jordy.

To be acknowledged by his son as an actual human being was shock enough, but to watch him gush with unabashed pleasure about the new school was a whole other level of happiness.

"It's a lottery system," the principal explained. "So Jordy's name would need to be entered, and we would let you know, as soon as next month, whether you're accepted. Our first class here had an easier time getting in. Next year's class will be a little tighter. However, Jordy, there is one advantage you have."

"What's that?"

"Technically, while you'll be coming from Luview, you are an out-of-state transfer. That's unique, and in the interest of diversity, the school is favoring some people with your profile."

"Awesome," Jordy said, giving his dad an excited look. Moore beamed back at him.

"It sounds like all things are a go here," he said to the principal, who nodded.

"Just take care of the paperwork on the parenting end, and we'll let the system do the rest."

"Thank you so much," Moore said, before Jordy dragged him down the hall to take a look at the stage design and props section.

"Dad, they have this huge space for everything, and all of this equipment. At my school, we just have to wing it. There's no real budget. We're lucky if our director gives us twenty bucks. And this place helps us get into special camps and summer repertory theater. This could launch everything I want in life."

"You've really been giving this a lot of thought, haven't you?"

"Yeah."

But as Moore washed the dinner dishes, he listened to his son go from enthusiastic to increasingly quiet while talking about the new school with his mother.

"Uh, sure," he heard Jordy say, fear creeping into his child's voice. "I can put him on."

Moore braced himself, closing his eyes as he dried his hands on the kitchen towel. Here it came.

The big confrontation.

Jordy's eyes were wide with fear as he handed the phone

off. A hand on his son's shoulder, designed to connect them and calm his child down, seemed to help.

It's okay, he mouthed.

"You go play." He pointed to Jordy's new gaming system, knowing that a few rounds of whatever game he chose would help him to relax.

"Hey," Moore said into the phone.

"What do you think you're doing?" Cammie snapped at him.

"What do you mean?" Fighting to stay calm, Moore drew on years of experience with her.

"You think you're going to convince Jordy to come live with you? *You?*" It wasn't so much her words, but the voice. Cammie wielded an acidic tone like a weapon.

"He came here to look at the new high school, Cammie. Everything went incredibly well. He's excited. If he wants to come live with me so he can have a phenomenal opportunity, in a career path that—"

She cut him off. "Career path? Listen to you. He's fifteen. Last year, he wanted to be a video game designer. Now he wants to be a theater tech. Next week, he's going to want to fly a dragon. You're going to take what a fifteen-year-old says about his career path seriously?"

"Yes."

"You're stupider than I remember."

Moore's tongue rolled in his cheek, working hard to loosen the tension in his jaw and failing.

"Cammie," he said softly, knowing that sometimes going the appeasement route could work. "I know you have a lot on your plate. The baby, getting married, a move."

"Jordy told you?"

"He did."

"He wasn't supposed to."

Damn. Moore knew that he should have compartmentalized better. Now Jordy might incur her wrath for having told him.

"It's my fault," Moore said, throwing himself under the bus to save his kid. "I pried it out of him."

"You can't keep yourself out of my affairs, can you? We haven't been together for ten years, and you just can't let me go."

"That's right," he said dully. "You hit the nail on the head."

"And you think you can just waltz in and take Jordy away from me, at a time when his new little sister is about to be born? This is a time when I need help, Moore. I don't need you taking things away from me."

Aha. What she really meant was that she didn't want to lose the child support.

"Listen, Cammie. For the first year he's here, I'll continue to pay you his full child support."

The phone went quiet.

"Why would you do that?" she asked, her voice a monotone, no emotion attached to it.

"Because I don't want you to worry," he said.

"That's weird."

"How is it weird?"

"Why would you be so nice to me, Moore?"

"I'm being nice to Jordy," he said, unable to stop the words from coming out of his mouth. "This way, you get what you need and Jordy gets a year here, to see how it feels to live in Maine for his freshman year."

"And then what?"

"I don't know, Cammie. Give the kid a year here. You can have him as often as you want. I'll fly him out there. He can spend the summer, you can have him at Christmas and Thanksgiving, all the major holidays."

"If you think I'm going to settle for having Jordy only fifty days a year, like you did..." The gut punches kept coming.

"We can negotiate an acceptable deal."

She snorted. "You mean our lawyers can."

"We don't have to take this to lawyers, Cammie."

"We sure as hell will have to, because you're trying to steal my child."

"No," he said, unable to control his voice, getting louder, "I'm trying to give him something he's never had before: a parent who treats him like an autonomous human being with wants, needs, and his own ideas about how to live his life!"

Jordy looked up from his game, startled, and ripped off his headphones.

"Don't you dare talk to me like that!" she shrieked.

"Don't you dare treat my son the way you've treated him all these years," he thundered, hands shaking. As a decade's worth of frustration poured out of him.

Some piece of him felt safe with Jordy here, with Jordy being fifteen, with Jordy wanting to live in Maine. The knot inside him was a little less tight.

The part of him that had walked a line with Cammie for so long was finally ready to let his foot cross it.

"You are such a–"

He cut her off. "You have no power, Cammie."

Jordy's jaw dropped comically at Moore's words. Thankfully, he could only hear half of the conversation.

"What did you just say to me?"

"You heard me. You have no power." His voice settled, going into a calm register, almost hypnotic. "If you want to lawyer up, we'll lawyer up, and this time I'll win."

"I can't believe you're upsetting a pregnant woman like this. Do you know what stress does to a developing fetus?"

Her pivot didn't shake him at all.

"If you're so concerned about your developing fetus, then maybe you shouldn't be provoking stressful situations like this."

Jordy shut his mouth with a snap, eyes laser focused on Moore. He swallowed hard, his teenage Adam's apple bobbing.

"While he's there, he may be saying that he wants to stay with you, but he's going to come home and change his mind. Soria's so attached to him, he has a baby sister coming, and his stepfather is a baseball player, Moore. You're just a jeweler. You live a boring life in our podunk little hometown, and you don't–"

"Is there anything else you want to talk about, Cammie? Because otherwise, this is just boring. *You're* boring." Her gasp was satisfying. "And if you continue to heap verbal abuse on me–"

Cammie hung up on him.

He gave Jordy his phone back, hands shaking, then turned and splayed them on the counter. Leaning down, he rolled his shoulders until his neck cracked, then took in a long, deep breath.

"Holy shit, Dad."

"Language," Moore said softly.

"That was a lot. If there's ever a time I'm allowed to curse, this would be it."

"Maybe."

"You stood up to her! I've never heard that before."

"I stand up to her all the time."

"You do?"

"You don't see it, kiddo, but I do."

"When? Where?"

"Mostly in court. Or through our lawyers."

"Oh."

"Look, Jordy, your mom and I have a... complicated relationship."

"I know. You hate her."

Moore jolted.

"What did you just say?"

"You hate her," Jordy repeated, this time with less confidence. "That's what she tells me all the time. You hate her, and because I remind you of her, you..." His voice trailed off.

"She says that to you?" Moore's ribs began vibrating with outrage, though he hid it, knowing that the last thing Jordy needed was to deal with Moore's emotions.

"Sometimes. Yeah."

"She's wrong."

"You don't hate her?"

What the kid meant was, *You don't hate me?*

Moore wanted to address that head on, but he also knew this was very fragile ground. If he could get this just right, it would build the foundation of trust that Moore had craved for years.

But first, he had to get it right.

"I have never hated Cammie. Remember that we were married for six years."

"She says you left her alone with me every waking moment that you possibly could because you couldn't stand being a husband and father."

None of this was new information. What was novel was hearing it out of his son's mouth. Cammie had claimed all of this, and so much more, when she tried to justify taking Jordy away without any warning, forcing Moore to spend a year tracking them down and fighting for custody in the courts. While Moore had been working and going to college to support his family and make life better, Cammie had been swallowed by the internet.

Where she found Mike, the baseball player.

Then Dave, the accountant.

If she'd stayed in Luview and simply tried to divorce him, they'd have had each other's families directly involved, with her brothers and cousins all weighing in, and his parents and far-flung siblings all expressing opinions.

Cammie evaded all of that by leaving.

And cut Moore to the bone by disappearing.

"I loved being a father. Still do. And I want nothing more than to settle down and be married to my one true love."

"That's sappy, Dad."

Moore shrugged. "Call me sappy."

"Mom wasn't your true love. She was someone Grandma and Grandpa forced you to marry when you knocked her up."

The language patterns made Jordy sound exactly like Cammie. He wondered how many scripts she'd implanted, and how much pain and grief the young man would experience if he ever had the chance to unravel the difference between what his mother had told him and the truth.

"It's true that Mom and Dad pushed me to marry her. And we were barely dating when your mom got pregnant. But I did love Cammie, Jordy."

"You did?"

"Yes. I came to love her. She's a good mother, overall." That last part was true. Moore wasn't the kind of person who viewed people as all good or all bad, and even he found the good in her, though as more truths came out about her, he found himself with so much to process.

Some deep wound inside his ex-wife must have driven her to hurt so many people, Jordy most of all. He could despise the pain she'd caused so many people while also recognizing that it was her own demons that drove her to do it.

"She's—I guess? I don't know. I mean, I have a place to live. My own room. Nice clothes. She complains you don't send enough money."

Moore told him how much he sent every month.

Jordy's eyes bugged out. "Really?"

Again, new territory. He'd never talked about this with his

son before. An antsy, nervous feeling filled his gut, but he persisted.

"Really. And extra for your theater camps, events, all that."

"Mom says you don't!"

"I do. Like that *Christmas Carol* theater workshop you wanted to do last winter. I guess you decided not to go?"

Pain and fury filled Jordy's eyes.

"You—you sent the money for that?"

"Of course. You asked to go and I sent it to Cammie. Then when I asked you about it, you were really angry and said you decided not to go."

"I was angry because Mom told me you refused to pay for it!"

"No. Jordy, I sent the $450 to her. It's not part of regular child support, so it's not through the courts, but I sent a check. Like I always do." Moore felt his stomach sinking. "I paid her for it."

"She—she—sucks! She told me you never sent the money. And then I asked if we could do it anyway and she said she had to save up to fly to Fort Myers to watch Locke do some stupid baseball thing!"

"Did she go to Fort Myers?"

"YES!"

And that was how Moore realized he'd financed his ex-wife's baseball fun with her soon-to-be husband.

"Wow."

"I have a lot of words, Dad, and *wow* isn't one of them!"

Tell him about that stolen year, Colleen's voice, invading his thoughts.

"What else don't I know? What else has she been keeping from me?" Jordy grabbed his phone, tapped, and started to scroll. "She's going to pay for this."

"Hold on there, bud. Don't call her in anger."

"But, Dad! She—she—"

Jordy burst into tears, shoulders slumped, phone sliding out of his hand onto the couch. All Moore could do was wrap his gangly teen in his arms and let him sob. Something had cracked open between them.

Truth.

Not all of it, but enough to make a difference.

Enough that they could never go back.

"I really wanted that winter camp! And she told me you refused to send the money. Spent a bunch of time with me on the couch, bingewatching *Star Wars* shows instead. I mean–Dad, I was mad at you. *Really* mad. And when you came to visit me last time, I didn't want to see you because–because–"

"I get it, buddy. I understand now. I'm so sorry this is all going on."

I'm so sorry your mother is manipulating us both is what Moore wanted to say, but didn't.

"You know," Jordy began through sniffs, his face pressed against Moore's shoulder.

Another year and he'd be taller, probably stopping at two inches above his old man. Moore hadn't hugged his son like this in years, not since Jordy was ten or eleven, before the attitude kicked into gear.

"Yeah, Jord?"

"What else has Mom been telling me that makes me mad at you and maybe you don't deserve it?"

It felt just like that moment back at the cabin when Moore stood on the edge of a line and had to make the decision to cross it, knowing the consequences were so enormous that it would alter the trajectory of his life.

Here he stood again.

Only this time he stepped back.

"Why don't we focus on calming down and letting what we've learned settle a bit," Moore said diplomatically. "We can talk to your mom later when you're more collected and after she's cooled down from my conversation with her."

"Okay." Jordy's response was small, almost meek. "All these years, Colleen's been telling me that I shouldn't be so mean to you. That you're really a good dad. Underneath, I knew it, but I didn't know how to say the things that I needed to say because of what Mom's been telling me."

"I know, sweetie. I know."

"Did you just call me *sweetie*, Dad?" Jordy let out a snort as he pulled back, stepping out of the comforting embrace and back into full-blown teenage boy.

"I guess I did," Moore chuckled.

"I'm not a little kid, you know."

The defensive shield was coming back up. Internally, Moore had to acknowledge his relief. They had gotten very close to a part of their relationship that he wasn't quite ready to deal with.

Jordy's phone buzzed and he looked at it. "It's Colleen. She wants to do a campaign."

"Now?" Moore said.

"What? It's only nine o'clock and I don't have school in the morning because there is no school."

"True." Moore's phone buzzed as well.

You guys okay? her text read.

Sure, he replied. *Just fine.*

Want to play League?

Every nerve in his body felt like a superhero had picked it up and flung it off a cliff one by one until all of him vibrated out of frequency.

I'm good, he replied. *You and Jordy have fun.*

Is something wrong? she texted back.

No. It's just been a long day. I had a fight with Cammie.

His phone rang instantly.

"You had a fight with Cammie?" Colleen gasped into the phone.

"Yes."

"Did you finally tell Jordy the truth?"

"Not all of it," he said carefully.

"Jordy's in the room, isn't he?"

"Yes."

"What happened?"

"I stood up for myself," he said, struggling to find the right words to describe the situation.

Colleen let out a howl of joy.

"Finally!" she said. "Good for you."

His breath rushed out of him in a mighty wave.

"It doesn't feel good."

"It doesn't?"

"Part of it does, but..."

He kept one eye on Jordy, who was setting up, sitting down in his gaming chair, and throwing his headphones on. He pulled one earphone away from his head and said to Moore, "Don't keep Colleen too long."

"I won't."

Moore took that as permission to leave the room, wandering down the hall to his bedroom. Not that he needed permission, but the emotional aftermath of both of their discussions with Cammie put him on guard.

"What did you say to her?" Colleen asked.

"She started doing her twisted version of events and I called her on it."

"How?"

"She told me that there was no way Jordy was going to move in with me and that his expression of needs about the new school didn't matter. That sort of thing."

"Classic Cammie," Colleen replied. "She hasn't changed one bit."

"No," Moore said with a sigh. "If anything, the claws are sharper now that she's pregnant."

"Did she say any of these things to Jordy?"

"Not that I'm aware of."

"How did Jordy take it, listening to you two fight?"

"Surprisingly well, but then he fell apart. I had to hold him while he cried."

"Oh, Moore."

"Yeah. Not our best day."

"Actually," she responded, "it sounds like a great day. Jordy got to tour the school and enjoy it. He expressed to Cammie what he really wants out of life. You stood up to Cammie. Now it's clear Jordy wants to live here."

"And I'm about to lawyer up. Cammie flung that in my face."

"She doesn't have the kind of power over you that she used to."

"She does," Moore countered. "I still don't want Jordy to know what happened ten years ago. Cammie's stubbornness could get worse if she thinks everyone's against her."

"Everyone *is* against her," Colleen pointed out. "Because she deserves it. Brought it on herself."

"But she's still Jordy's mother. I don't want to turn my child against his own mother."

"She's turning herself against him, or him against her. I don't know. It's all getting so confusing," she said, her burst of emotion catching him by surprise.

"Colleen," he said quietly, "are *you* okay?"

"I'm just tired of hiding. I'm tired of having my life on pause because of other people."

"You mean Jordy."

"I mean Cammie."

"Cammie will be dealt with. I'll hire my lawyer again and we'll bang it out in the courts."

"And if you lose?"

"I'm not going to lose this time. Jordy knows damn well what he wants and I'm here to support that."

"But shouldn't he know the full truth?"

"That's for me to decide. Not you."

Silence swelled in the space.

"Right," she said with a resignation that sounded vaguely ominous. "I don't really have a role in his life, do I?"

"What's that supposed to mean?" Moore said. "I never—"

"You didn't have to say it, Moore. I get it. I know why you're waiting and I know why you don't want Jordy to know about what happened in the past, but for the record, I think you're wrong."

"Can we talk about this tomorrow?"

"Sure." But there was something in her voice that sent a spike of fear through him. "We can talk tomorrow. I think it's time we got our priorities straight."

"I'm hungry," Jordy announced loudly from the other room.

Moore walked back to the kitchen and watched him rummage in the fridge until he pulled out a big bowl of strawberries, finding a fork in the drawer. One thing Moore had to give Cammie credit for: Jordy ate plenty of junk, but he defaulted to fruits and vegetables in a way that made it clear good habits had been instilled in him.

"Okay," Moore said into the phone.

"Okay. I'm off to play with Jordy."

"Thank you."

She ended the call before he could say more, their exchange unsettling.

"You're not dating anyone now, right?" Jordy asked out of the blue.

"What?"

"I don't know how you ever handled being married to Mom."

"Um..."

"Because like I said, I'm glad you don't have anyone else here. Locke's a jerk. Gia was a mess. Hannah was okay except for the tissues, but I don't want a stepmother."

"Uh..."

"Women suck."

"Hey, now. That's *not* okay to say."

"Is it okay to say *some* women suck?"

"It's okay to say some *people* suck. I don't think being a jerk is limited to a specific gender."

"Right. Locke's a big old jerk, too."

Moore had no idea what to say to that.

Jordy resettled in front of his gaming computer, headphones on.

"But it sure is nice not dealing with someone else here."

And just like that, Moore was full. Done. Drained.

Between Cammie and Colleen, he was spent.

Yet it was all for Jordy. If he could keep his eye on the prize, he'd be fine.

But at what cost?

Chapter 17

Colleen

The FaceTime call was completely unexpected.

And a little disappointing.

Because it wasn't Moore.

"Hey, Dennis! What's wrong?"

Those big blue eyes, framed by thick eyebrows, stared her down.

"Why does something have to be wrong?" Seeing his smirk, she remembered how much he looked like Luke, only bigger. Thicker and more intimidating.

"You never FaceTime me."

He sighed, the sound tender and definitely out of character for her Army officer brother who worked missions he couldn't talk about.

"I need your help."

"Me? How can I possibly help you?"

"Need your advice."

Colleen clutched her chest.

"You–you–what?"

"Cut it out."

"Wait, I need to pick my heart and jaw up off the floor."

"After you do that, look around for your sense of humor."

"Hah!"

"Seriously. I have to tell Dad and Mom something big, and I don't know how."

"You got a girl pregnant in Germany?"

"What? No!"

"You married a stranger?"

"Nope."

"You did some genetic research and learned we're descended from royalty?"

"Why are you doing this?"

"Spill it, then!"

"I'm retiring from the Army."

"*What?*"

Silence. Dennis was always good at wielding silence as a weapon.

"Wow. You're really doing it?"

"Yep."

"What are you doing next?"

"Coming home."

"Of course. But after that?"

"That's just it, Colleen–I'm coming *home*. For good."

"For good?"

"I paid into the camp. Have a cabin. I plan to come home and live in it."

"*Live* live in it?"

"Yes. So here's my question: How deep are Dad and Kell in the tree service business?"

"Dennis."

"Hmm?"

"You're hitting me with too many big issues here. Are you asking because you want to work in the business?"

"No."

"Then why?"

"I'm asking because I'd like to take over from Dad. Run it. But if Kell's deep in, I won't interfere."

"Kell's trying to figure out how to get out. His poison ivy-pulling company is killing it."

"Good for him. Too bad I'm allergic."

"Dad and Mom are going to die from happiness. You're retiring and moving back to Luview?"

"I am."

"You always said you'd never move back home!"

"I said I wanted to see the world, and I have."

"You said that Luview is a consumerist b.s. veneer over a town full of small-minded, adventure-phobic worrywarts."

"Same thing."

Colleen took in a deep breath, debating whether to confide in him. All their life, they'd been close, but now Dennis kept everyone at a distance. This was an outpouring of emotion from him—as measured as it was—and Colleen found herself feeling more vulnerable than usual as a result.

"Why are you really coming home, Dennis? What happened?" she inquired softly, the flare of his eyes telling her she'd hit the mark, but then those eyes went flat.

"Can't a guy retire and live out the rest of his life peace-fully in his hometown?"

"Too bad you're finally coming home just when I might be leaving."

Her turn to shock him.

"You?" He laughed through his nose, the genuine smile spreading his features from a tight ball of self-protection to relaxed, brotherly love. "You'll never, ever leave Luview."

"Maybe I need a change."

"That would be a big one."

"I'm not getting any younger."

"You and me both, Colleen. You and me both." He paused, then asked, "Still dealing with that third date b.s.? Is that what you're thinking?"

"Yeah. Hard to find a life partner when no one will touch me after two tries."

"Life partner?"

"I want the whole dream. Soulmate, kids, perfect life. My needs are modest."

Dennis had the decency to laugh politely.

"You really would be the best mother, Colleen, if that's what you want. It's like you're already mothering Jordy. And Harriet, though Kylie's helping there now. Some kid's going to get very lucky someday."

"You're buttering me up for something. How much money do you need to borrow?"

"Hah! I'm flush. You know that. I save most of my paychecks. And I have a pension coming soon. But I feel like life's slipping past me. Coming home will help me figure out who I am. What I want. What living a real life means."

"You have a real life, Den. You built an honorable career."

"Can't do this much longer, though. My body's strong, but there really is a point where you time out."

"Mom will be overjoyed if you move back home."

"I know. So don't tell her. Not yet."

"I can keep a secret, even if I can't keep a boyfriend."

"That's harsh." Dennis got very, very quiet. It set her nerves on edge. "Mom said the other day that you might be secretly dating someone."

"MOM!" she blasted through the call.

Dennis snickered.

"Thought so. Mom swears Nadine Khouri is the biggest gossip in town, but..."

"I hope she's not telling my secrets all over Luview!"

"Maybe only to *other* Luviews," he replied, letting silence reign for a bit, pulling her to talk.

"You're coming home and I might leave. Aren't we a pair, Den?"

"Don't leave if you're not leaving on your own terms."

Bluntness was always Dennis's strong suit.

"Does Randy hump trailers?" In the town of Luview, this had become code for *Does a bear crap in the woods?*

"I know."

"And don't leave just because you're butthurt."

"That's a plenty-good reason to leave."

"I've been away from home for more than twenty years and it's still in my cells. You're so intertwined with every person in Luview that I can't imagine you elsewhere."

"Doc Blythe thinks I'd make a great nurse practitioner or physician assistant."

"You would."

"Can't get those added degrees without leaving."

"*Temporarily* leaving."

"Maybe forever, if I find the right guy."

"Who says Moore isn't the right guy?"

"Who ever said a word about Moore? Mom told you *all* of it?"

A loud knock at her door almost made Colleen drop the phone.

"COLLEEN!" It was her mother. "COME HERE!"

Dennis and Colleen looked at each other onscreen, his eyebrows raised, as Deanna walked right into Colleen's living room.

"What's going on?" Colleen asked, flashing her phone at her mom. "I'm FaceTiming with Dennis."

Deanna took the phone.

"Oh! Hi, honey!" she said brightly to the glowing screen. "Colleen has to go now. Sandwich is pooping balloons."

As Dennis made noises of surprise, Deanna ended the call and grabbed Colleen's hand, trying to drag her outside. Colleen shot to her feet, shoving them quickly into her boots, then lunged across the room for her coat.

"Did you just say my cat is *pooping balloons?*"

"It's either that or her intestines are falling out, and I didn't want to get too graphic with poor Dennis."

"MOM!"

As her mother began to jog toward the lodge, Colleen huffed along with her, wondering what Dennis must be thinking right now. Hampered by her aching wrist, she'd given up trying to shove her arm through her sleeve and was now half in and half out of her coat.

"Something's wrong with Sandwich."

Her mother's words didn't make sense to Colleen. Twenty minutes ago, it was her day off and she was in the middle of her favorite fantasy series, lost in a bookworld of prophecy and unexpected journeys. Then her older brother called and told her he was coming home to take over the family business.

Now her cat's intestines were falling out.

Colleen pieced the words together and ran them through her mind again.

"Why didn't you bring her to me?"

"We got hissed at, and her claws extended. She's acting funny."

"What do you mean something's wrong? What's she doing?"

"Acting funny."

"Sandwich always acts funny. That's Sandwich."

"I think she's sick."

"Sick? She's been fine all day."

"When was the last time you saw her?"

Pausing to think that one through, Colleen had to confess that she hadn't noticed her cat for the last half a day. It was one o'clock in the afternoon on her day off. Last time she remembered seeing her cat was a few hours ago. "Where is she, Mom?"

"The lodge."

"Maybe she got a bad mouse. Is she bleeding?"

"No. Nothing like that," Deanna assured her. "She's just walking funny and dragging her butt."

"Dragging her butt?"

"Yeah. You know." The way her mom tried to mime what she was describing made Colleen's stomach twist.

"Mom, Sandwich isn't a dog. She doesn't drag her butt on the floor like she has anal glands."

"Colleen," Deanna said flatly.

"What? It's basic anatomy for canines. I'm not being vulgar."

"I know that. I'm telling you something's wrong with Sandwich."

"Deanna," her father's voice boomed. "Get back here. Something's *really* wrong with her."

Her dad was standing on the porch, her mom joining him before Colleen could even reach the lodge's front steps.

"Everything okay over there?" Luke shouted from far across the compound. Colleen turned around and craned her neck to see him. He and Kylie were standing on his porch, Luke in his red uniform jacket, Kylie in a tight black ski coat. Steam rose from mugs they both held in their hands.

Colleen knew that Kylie had spent the night last night because her car had been here when she woke up. Luke and Kylie were working on getting Harriet accustomed to her living with them.

"Something's wrong with Colleen's cat," her dad shouted.

Oh, great. Now Luke was going to come over and interfere.

She turned and went inside the lodge, her dad right behind her.

Sandwich was a calico cat with an adorable auburn line along her belly, her legs a mishmash of dark white and reddish chaos. She was standing on all four legs in the middle of the enormous lodge, glaring at them, tail up in the air. Sandwich looked up at Colleen, then slitted her eyes.

Colleen tried to step closer to her poor kitty, who only hissed in warning and gave her the evil eye. For Sandwich to act like that toward her, she must be in pain.

"She seems fine to me."

"There it is again," her dad said, pointing.

"There's nothing wrong with Sand..." Colleen's words cut off as her cat blew a balloon out of its butt.

A *balloon*.

A balloon the color of–

"Is that part of her intestine?" her dad hissed.

Adrenaline shot through her, like when an ambulance arrived at the trauma bay, that moment you were suspended between knowing and not knowing, touching the patient and not having that connection.

The suspension between two realities.

"Something's wrong with Sandwich's butt," she heard her mom yell across the compound.

"Could you repeat that?" Kylie called out, her voice incredulous.

"NO!" Luke shouted. "No one needs to repeat a sentence like that."

Colleen heard footsteps pounding up the wooden steps, and Luke appeared in the doorway, Kylie on his heels, carrying their coffee mugs. Both looked down at the cat, then at Colleen.

"What's wrong with her?" Kylie asked sweetly as Sandwich bore down and–

"What the hell?" Luke said in a low, shocked voice. "How is that poor cat alive?"

"I don't see anything wrong–"

The... *thing* came out of the cat again.

Crouching, Colleen rested her hand on Sandwich's back. Sick animals were part of choosing to have pets, of course, but her range of animal crises was limited to cats fighting with squirrels, cut paws, and that one time her old cat, Hearty McHearterson, had drunk some Gatorade everyone thought might be antifreeze and Darren had lectured them all on proper storage of equipment fluids in the garage bay.

And leaving containers of electrolyte drink laying around, too.

"I just got off the phone with Darren," her dad said, invoking the name of the town veterinarian, Darren Chassi. A longtime friend of Luke's, he was cranky but fair, compassionate but blunt.

And he was their only option.

"He's on his way. Happens to be about ten minutes from here."

"If that poor little thing's intestine falls out, it won't have ten minutes!" Deanna worried.

"Please stop talking about Sandwich like that!" Colleen hollered, her voice carrying throughout the loud, echo-y room. Sandwich reeled back slightly, turning in a half circle, her body tensing and–*yep*.

A tan-colored, translucent ball popped out of her butt, then went back in, like a bubble-blowing contest gone horribly wrong. Sandwich moved about two feet away from Colleen with tight, painful-looking steps, then hissed when she tried to touch the cat again.

"The poor thing," her mom whispered, voice shaking with emotion. "That must hurt."

Shuffling at the main door caught her ear, then the sun was blocked by Kell's massive body.

"Why is everyone staring at the cat?" he asked, walking over to Sandwich, who arched and looked at him like she wanted to turn him into Kell coleslaw.

Kellslaw.

Her brother was a cat owner and knew instantly to back away.

"Her intestines are falling out," Luke said slowly between sips of coffee.

"I think she ate a balloon?" their mom suggested.

Dean looked at Luke's steaming mug and asked, "Got more of that at your place? Looks like we'll be here a while."

"I do not need," Colleen said, performing a head count, "six adults plus Darren to help me with a sick cat."

"I am just so curious to know what that thing is!" her mom said.

"That thing" made its appearance again, a clear bubble emerging, then contracting back in.

All six of them were staring intently at Sandwich's butt-hole when Rachel walked in, halting quickly on her heels.

"Um, what are you all–OH, WHAT IN THE UNHOLY MESS IS THAT?"

"A balloon," Deanna called back.

"Intestines," Luke announced.

"We need a grid. Luke's got five dollars on intestines, Mom's got five on a balloon," Kell called out to her as Rachel skittered backwards to get away from the cat.

"Don't joke about this!"

"Can't think of anything else it might be," Kylie said in a contemplative voice.

"Broken amniotic sac?" Dean mused, reaching for his wallet and pulling out a five-dollar bill.

Deanna and Colleen looked at him with identical withering expressions.

"Cats don't give birth out of their butts, Dad," she finally said.

"I know that! I just thought–"

The crunch of rubber on gravel made them all turn, Darren Chassi's beat-up old work truck driving right to the front door. Why not? There was just gravel leading up to the building, and in an emergency, you do away with niceties anyhow.

"Thank goodness," Deanna said with a long, relieved sigh. "Whatever's wrong with Sandwich, Darren can fix it."

"Don't turn me into a god, Deanna," Darren said from the doorway. "I haven't even touched the cat yet."

"Good luck with that," Colleen announced to him. "She won't let any of us near her."

"She's spayed," Darren muttered to himself. "I did the operation. So no worries about pregnancy. Dean said something's coming out of her–"

Voice trailing off, they all watched as the thing re-emerged from her poor kitty's butt.

"Huh." Darren approached the cat like the pro that he was, and Sandwich let him. Placing one already gloved hand on her back, he reached for the thing and tugged gently.

"He's disemboweling her!" Rachel said in horror, turning away to bury her head in Kell's chest.

"I'm doing no such thing." With a gentle, tender touch, Darren tugged.

Some of the tan tube emerged.

Tugged again.

The cat arched her back.

Slowly shaking his head, mouth twisted in his signature

curmudgeon look, Darren pulled one more time. A long, thin string emerged, like folded skin with a rimmed edge.

It was not an intestine.

"Balloon! Told you!" Deanna crowed.

Colleen felt all the blood in her head migrate to her toes.

Because it was *not* a balloon.

"Nope," Darren said, his mouth curling up in amusement. "This isn't a balloon. Not exactly."

"Intestine?" Dean asked, confused.

"No. It's a condom."

The entire room went silent, as if the word itself were cursed.

Luke looked slowly around the room, like he was interrogating murder suspects.

"Who here uses condoms?"

Kylie began choking on her coffee.

"Because we don't," Luke said for the whole world to hear.

Kylie smacked him.

"What?" He seemed genuinely mystified by her. "We don't!"

Dean shook his head lightly as Deanna laughed and said, "My ovaries closed up shop two years ago, so we're good."

"Ugh, Mom," Luke said as Kylie snorted.

"So it's gross when your mom talks about it, but not when you do?"

"Yes," he said simply.

Kell's eyebrows went up and he said nothing. Rachel began peeling herself off him. Darren picked Sandwich up and stroked her, walking over to a trash can, tossing in the obstruction, and stripping off his gloves.

Sandwich just purred in his arms the entire time, occasionally rubbing her chin on his arm in apparent gratitude.

As Luke turned into the Torquemada of errant condoms, Colleen quietly pulled out her phone and texted to Moore:

When we slept together here at my house, what did you do with the condom?

I... wore it ;) he replied.

She let out a low growl, earning a strange look from her mom.

I mean after! Did you flush it?

Why?

I'll explain later.

Of course I didn't flush it. Your camp runs on septic. I threw it in the trash.

A thin headache, clear and growing, began right between her eyes.

Thanks.

Why are you asking me about a condom from two weeks ago?

I'll explain later.

Is it–are you worried it broke? Are you pregnant? Because I inspect condoms after I use them, and it was intact.

She looked away from the screen. Ah, the details Moore was revealing to her. Of course he did. After what happened to him at seventeen, he'd learned young–and the very, very hard way–how a single broken condom could change his entire life.

The car accident had led to some wounds that had some signs of infection. She'd gone on antibiotics, which could neutralize the birth control pills she was on. So that day, Moore had worn a condom.

Which, apparently, seemed like a tasty snack at some point for poor Sandwich.

"Who're you texting, Colleen?" Luke demanded to know, damn near making her drop her phone in surprise.

"None of your business. Work stuff."

Bzzz

She ignored the text, knowing it was Moore, likely very curious after her odd question. She'd probably sent him into a panic thinking she was pregnant, and that was the last thing she needed to do to the poor guy.

"Darren, give me my cat," she insisted, walking away from Luke, hands outstretched. Sandwich was transferred and, turning around, she found herself the object of everyone's attention. It was almost like she was onstage, and they expected her to entertain.

"What? Sandwich found a condom somewhere in the woods. You know teenagers roam out there and–"

"Sandwich is an indoor cat," Luke pointed out, crossing his arms over his chest and giving her a pointed look. "At most, she walks between the buildings here."

Darren shot Luke a sidelong glance that said he knew something was up but not the details.

Good. That meant Luke hadn't told him about her and Moore. As of now, Darren was the only person in the room who didn't know.

"Then whatever, Luke. Someone here is having great sex and using a condom."

"How do you know it was great?" Kell asked, earning a rib poke from Rachel. She and Kylie wore open looks of sympathy aimed straight at Colleen.

"Aidan Forsythe's pet beaver needs its anal glands cleaned out, so I gotta go," Darren declared. The look on city-girl Rachel's face as she processed that sentence was enough to make Colleen crack a smile.

But it faded quickly under Luke's steady, flat gaze.

"Thank you so much, Darren," she said, knowing he'd bill her later. "I appreciate all you did."

"I spent ten seconds pulling a condom out of your cat's butt, Colleen. It's not like I earned a Nobel Prize."

"Do you need to examine her more?"

"For what? To see if she ate the wrapper? Drank a bottle of lube? You said you thought she found it in the woods.

Anything you want to tell me?"

Now it was Luke's turn to grin.

"Nope. Thanks." Colleen followed Darren out the door, her face aflame but her cat soft and happy in her arms.

"Watch her. Any more strange behavior and just bring her in. I can x-ray her if we have to, but let's go the low-intervention route and wait and see."

Darren climbed in his truck, waved, and took off. Luke was on her heels, his hand on her shoulder. She brushed it off and kept walking.

"Colleen."

"What?"

"Come on. It's obvious. Sandwich ate a condom in your cabin."

"I see why they made you police chief. You really know how to dig into the complex, nuanced details of situations."

"That's two. Better stop there."

"Huh?"

"Two times you've slept with Moore."

"How would you know how many times we've slept together?" She wasn't about to admit he was right. Once in the cabin in New Hampshire and that one afternoon here, before Jordy flew in.

"I'm guessing. But stop now."

"You can't tell me who I can and can't sleep with."

"I can warn you, though."

"Warn me away from your own best friend?"

"More like warn *him*, now that I think about it. Don't sleep with him a third time."

"Stop trying to control my life!"

"Remember what happened to Tim. Gerry. Slicer."

"You really think if Moore and I sleep together a third time, he'll end up in my emergency room?"

"You *are* Third Date Colleen, after all. Moore doesn't have some magic exemption."

Her hand itched to slap her own brother.

But she didn't need to add assaulting a police officer to her list of problems right now. That list was long enough on its own, thank you very much.

"You are such an ass."

"You only say that when I'm right."

"You seriously think something bad will happen to Moore if he and I are together? Do you hear yourself, Luke? Do you know how much that hurts?"

"Truth often does."

"What truth? You're suddenly superstitious? You think I'm really, actually cursed?" Walking away from him, she went into her cabin, dropped Sandwich off, and turned back to her stupid brother, who was almost in her house. As she descended on him, he took two steps back, both of them on the porch.

Her finger went straight to his face, wagging like his golden retriever's tail.

"And before you make some snarky comment, let me tell you what a jerk you're being. You have no idea how important Moore and I are to each other. You have no business being up in *our* business."

"I do when I don't want to see either of you hurt."

"That's not your job!"

"I know damn well what my job is, Colleen. I'm not policing you two. I'm trying to warn you both."

"Both? Have you warned Moore away from me?"

He didn't answer that. Instead, he responded, "Moore's been married and divorced twice. It didn't work with Cammie, and Gia was a train wreck. You two are sneaking around like you're addicted to the secret."

"We're being private because Jordy isn't ready yet."

"That's why you haven't gone public? Oh, sure," he said, his voice dripping with derision.

"It's true! You of all people should understand."

"Me? Since when have I snuck around town hiding a relationship?"

"You won't let Kylie move in until the wedding."

"We're doing that out of respect for Harriet! Easing her into having Kylie as a stepmother."

Colleen gave him a triumphant look.

He gave her a disgusted grimace.

"You're comparing you and Moore to Kylie and me?"

"No. I've been daily friends with Moore all these years. I'm already very close to his son. Jordy's been expressing a lot of feelings about not wanting stepfathers and stepmothers as things get thorny for him back home. Moore was just about to tell him and his parents, but–"

"I don't want to talk about this anymore. You know my feelings. I think the two of you are bad for each other. You're deluding yourself about not going public."

"Which is it, Luke? We shouldn't be together at all because we're bad for each other? Or we should be totally open about being together? You're not making sense."

"Because your relationship doesn't make sense!"

"TO YOU! Not to us! Can you for once try to be happy for me? For Moore? Can you think about the fact that the same happiness you had with Amber, and now with Kylie, might be what I want in my life, too?"

"And you think Moore will give that to you?"

"I'd like the chance to find out!"

"I wish you were right, but I have a bad feeling about this."

"No man will date me because of this Third Date Colleen nonsense. Moore can't go public about us because of Jordy and YOU. What am I supposed to do, Luke? You're making it so my only option is to leave Luview!"

"I never said that!"

"You didn't have to!"

With that, she stepped back into her cabin and slammed the door in her little brother's face.

He didn't come after her.

Just as well. If she were really going to have to move away, she'd be the one leaving.

Might as well start practicing.

Chapter 18

Colleen

The Cupids were losing.

This wasn't unusual, but it was always depressing.

Cheering for the underdog came as second nature to Colleen. It had to. When you were a die-hard Love You Cupids fan, the local AAA baseball league team, you got used to generating an endless supply of manufactured hope.

Which was not unlike being 'just friends' with Moore.

Luke was sitting a few rows away and shoved his fingers into his mouth, the piercing whistle cutting through her thoughts. Normally, he'd sit with her, but a gaggle of eight-year-olds surrounded him, all girls. They all wore their adorable Girl Scout uniforms and sat in a giggly, ragtag row.

The score was 0-1, and the Cupids were down.

"Hey."

Jordy stood next to her, holding a soda the size of his head and a popcorn the size of Colleen's ample butt.

"Hey, yourself," she said, taking the popcorn tub out of his hand. "When did they start making *this* size?"

He shrugged. His long hair covered his eyebrows and slanted over his left eye, giving his face the appearance of a cave in the shadows, the entrance in the sun but the rest of it a mystery. As he sat next to her, his head dipped down but his eyes darted up, scanning the area.

What was he looking for? People he recognized? Old friends from the years of coming to visit?

Baseball and video games were their shared passions, and as the announcer did his required sponsorship commercials, she let herself relax a little.

This was home.

The benches were painted white with red accents at the ends of each row. Players donned pink uniform shirts with red and white lettering, their white baseball pants allowed to conform to normal standards. Pink baseball caps with the Cupids logo on them adorned every player's head, and two-thirds of the crowd as well.

The opposing team was the Lawrence Panthers. The crowd was thin today, maybe a hundred people on the home side and another forty or so in the stands to cheer on the opposing team. It wasn't the size of the crowd that mattered, it was the amount of heart they brought to support their team.

And Love You, Maine, had heart in spades.

"Where's Moore?" she asked Jordy, ignoring the flutter of her heart at the mention of the man.

All she got for an answer was a shrug, Jordy's mouth full of popcorn. He mumbled something close to *I don't know,* and Colleen had to be satisfied with that answer.

Moore's attendance at baseball games was hit or miss. They never knew when he'd have a business issue that would pop up and prevent him from attending. Jordy had made it clear to her one night that he was actually happier when

Moore didn't attend, because it was, in Jordy's words, "more fun that way."

Colleen had kept this detail from Moore to spare his feelings.

A few years ago, Moore had confessed to her that he was jealous of her relationship with Jordy. Unable to conjure an answer that would simultaneously make him feel better and honor Jordy's privacy, she had realized that there was no good answer. Platitudes had come out of her mouth and Moore had accepted them, the two awkwardly moving on from the topic.

Navigating an emotional landscape where she wasn't Jordy's mom and yet she wasn't just an acquaintance meant taking on the role of an auntie.

Aunties were good. Aunties were solid.

She adored her biological niece, and Harriet adored her right back. If it weren't for the Girl Scouts meeting, Colleen would've invited her along, giving Jordy an extra dose of fun. He was the closest thing Harriet had to a sibling, although that would change soon.

She knew Luke and Kylie planned to have more kids.

With Cammie pregnant and soon to marry Locke, there were major changes going on in both kids' lives. Being an auntie to both, whether symbolic or real, meant that she had to ride the transitions, too.

Kylie joined Luke and the girls. She stood looking around, catching Colleen's eye, a big, friendly wave following her recognition. Colleen waved back and nudged Jordy.

"There's Kylie," she said.

He grunted. "Okay."

"Wave back."

"Why? She's waving at you, not me."

"Because you're in Love You, and this is what we do. Just lift your hand three inches and pretend you care."

He rolled his eyes, but he did it.

"Good to see your arm isn't broken."

"Feels like it. That was an epic *League* game last night."

As Jordy waved to Kylie, the crowd began chanting. Instantly, Colleen knew what was going on. She looked at the jumbotron and saw her brother and Kylie in the frame.

"KISS! KISS! KISS!" the crowd chanted.

Jordy rolled his eyes, and Colleen stuffed her mouth with popcorn. Obliging the crowd, her brother and Kylie kissed, leading to cheers that lasted for ten seconds before the camera cut to the next victims.

The bleacher seats made a thumping sound one stack above them, and then the surface beneath Colleen's butt began to shake. Moore popped down next to her, holding a paper tray filled with nachos, bright yellow cheese sauce dripping over the edge. Colleen swiped it with her thumb.

"Mmm," she said.

"Yay," Jordy muttered, "Plastic cheese."

She elbowed him in the ribs. "Your fake cynicism doesn't fool me."

"The cheese is fake. My cynicism is real." Jordy smiled as he said it, leaning across her to grab a perilous stack of nachos coated in cheesy goodness. Somehow the kid managed to move it over to his own lap without dripping, using his left hand as a makeshift plate.

While he chomped, Moore handed Colleen a lemonade and leaned over to ask both of them, "Do you have a heart on?"

"Dad!" Jordy screeched.

"What?" Moore tapped his chest, where an enormous red heart was pinned to his shirt, part of a promotion to show patrons had donated to the team's special charity. "Your *heart*. Do you have a *heart* on?"

This time, he emphasized the *T*.

Jordy was a furious shade of red. Colleen just shook her

head. The joke was ancient here in Love You, Maine, and just as juvenile and puerile as it had been when she was Jordy's age.

Baseball games were a study in empty space. Where else could you sit and watch men in uniforms take the longest possible amount of time to complete a sequence of steps that added up to a win or a loss?

Golf might be a rival, but baseball was significantly more fun.

Colleen loved every minute of every game she had ever attended. The smell of popcorn and hot dogs, the roar of the crowd, the shakiness of the bleachers, the goofy mascot (Marty Martinez, Selena's younger brother, in a Cupid costume), and the sight of familiar faces trickling in around her. Every bit of it made her attend every single game she possibly could.

No, the Love You Cupids were not the best team in their league. Not even close. But they were her team, and they did what they did for love of the game, and that mattered more than anything else.

Seated between Jordy and Moore, Colleen passed nachos and popcorn back and forth, smiling on the inside as she watched Jordy thaw, minute by minute, play by play.

Every year for the last six years, Jordy had come back and gone to this very same game with her. Every year, he began his trip with a visceral disgust for Moore that lessened with time. The baseball game seemed to short circuit it, blending its own form of magic with the companionship that Colleen added to the outing.

Moore had taken Jordy to plenty of games, and both of them always told her that the ones when she was there with them were the best. It was a source of quiet pride for Colleen to know that she could enhance their relationship.

A bridge, of sorts. She helped the two navigate an awkward relationship that deserved to be stronger than it was allowed to be.

In a way, the relationship between Jordy and Moore was a wound that Colleen was tasked with nursing through recovery and healing.

They were just on a very, very long timeline.

Suddenly, the crowd got loud.

"OH, NO!" Jordy bellowed, then folded in half with laughter. Colleen and Moore looked up.

They were featured on the kiss cam.

Twisted in his seat like a pretzel, Luke was glaring at her as if he could wield some obsessive control over her by telepathy. The crowd began to chant "KISS! KISS! KISS!" as Jordy turned a delightful shade of Love You Red.

Colleen froze.

"What do we do?" she asked Moore, leaning in as her gaze pinged between him and the giant screen.

"I want to kiss you," he said softly, making all the hairs on her neck stand up, body flushing. The cacophony of the ballpark receded, fading into nothing.

There was only her, Moore, and the question of a kiss.

That's all she wanted the world to be.

"EWWW! Don't you dare!" Jordy finally choked out. "It would violate the laws of physics or something!"

The crowd grew louder and more frenzied, denied the emotional payoff they so desperately demanded.

Sheer anxiety made her turn toward Moore and kiss his cheek just as he turned toward her, their lips brushing for a brief, frustrating moment.

Then the jumbotron flashed to another couple.

"That was hilarious! As if you two would ever be together," Jordy screamed, his gut practically busting wide open and spilling onto the seat. "I can't believe that happened!"

"Same here, kid," Moore muttered.

Colleen was too stunned to say a word, a vortex of emotion taking over. All the reasons why they weren't going public with their relationship made sense, even if "all the reasons" were really just one giggling teen boy.

A very important boy.

Jordy's reaction was completely normal, but it hurt.

It hurt a lot.

Between Luke's bizarre reaction to the condom incident three days ago and now Jordy laughing at the idea that Moore and Colleen could be together romantically, a funk descended like a dark mist, enveloping her.

Sitting in her happy place while her cells changed mood was not how she envisioned this day.

"Would someone pass the tub of popcorn that's the size of Luxembourg?" Moore asked, reaching over to take it from Jordy. His hand brushed Colleen's leg as the transfer took place, and it made her gasp.

She'd been holding her breath.

John Shanley was the longtime baseball announcer, and Selena Martinez from the local radio station was broadcasting the game as well. WLUV was thriving and baseball season was a major reason. Between the new radio tower that allowed their broadcasts to reach Massachusetts and improved tourism that got people interested in listening on the internet, life was good for Selena.

"Line drive!" John called out. Colleen grounded herself in the moment again, Jordy leaning forward to watch and stuffing a candy bar in his mouth. Moore munched popcorn and pretended they hadn't just been forced to kiss in front of a hundred of their friends.

And then pretend it was a joke.

"Beautiful," Moore said.

Colleen looked out on the field to see what he was talking about, then noticed he was staring at her. She looked up at the crystal blue sky. "Sure is."

"I meant you." The sincere tone in his voice made her heart

leap into her throat. The fake kiss was embarrassing enough, but Jordy's words had cut to the bone. Now here was Moore, scrambling her signals even further.

His hand reached for hers but paused, pulling back. He leaned in and whispered softly, "I'm sorry. I wish it were different."

It could *be different*, she thought to herself but didn't say. That funk caught her tongue.

"Hey, batter batter batter," Jordy called out, using his pinkies to set off a light whistle. Luke was the master whistler among their circle of friends, and Jordy had studied carefully last summer under his tutelage. Anemic, but still, his whistles were better than nothing.

"This is so hard," she hissed in Moore's ear. His jaw tightened.

"I know. I'm not sure when to tell him."

"He's only here for four more days," she reminded Moore, who nodded.

"We'll have to tell him before he goes," he promised. "And not the day he actually leaves. I wouldn't want to dump that on any kid. He needs time."

"Day after tomorrow?" she ventured. Maybe some of the depression that was settling into her would lift if she knew there was an end date to all of this.

Moore's eyes drifted, going unfocused.

"That works," he finally said, nodding slowly.

The crowd jumped to their feet, Jordy screaming as the batter got a triple and brought the man on first base home. Suddenly, the game was tied.

"Go Cupids!" Moore shouted.

Jordy sat, reaching for the popcorn and grabbing a fistful. They all settled back down. Baseball was like this.

Endless dull stretches of time punctuated by sudden bursts of excitement.

Looking over, she watched Harriet, Luke, and Kylie all laughing hysterically. Seeing her brother and niece so happy helped to ease some of her dread. This was a good place. These were good people. Her roots ran deep in Luview, but the confrontation with Luke had led her to do some digging.

Doc Blythe had been right. There were plenty of scholarships out there to help her get a BSN or even go on to complete a nurse practitioner's program. Becoming a physician assistant felt like too big a reach, too much time spent in school compared to what she would be able to do and balance in her life.

But these were individual steps.

First, finish her bachelor's degree.

Then she could make decisions about more.

And about *Moore*.

"LOOK OUT!" Jordy screeched, and she looked up to see a baseball flying straight at her head. Too shocked to react, she barely registered Moore's instinctive move, his body in front of her as he shoved her aside.

The impact of the ball against his breastbone made a resounding thud, her ear pressed against his shoulder blade.

"Oof," he said, the sound so understated, she couldn't quite believe it. The crowd roared and John Shanley called out:

"Foul ball!"

Coming to her senses, she wiggled out from under a deflating Moore, who held the pink and white ball like it was a gold nugget.

"Here," he wheezed, "I got you something."

"Dad's so lucky! Keep it, Colleen. He caught one for me two years ago."

"Your chest!" she gasped, knowing full well Moore would have a huge, ugly bruise after an impact like that. Luke was climbing up the stairs, a worried look on his face. All traces of irritation at her or Moore were erased.

"Hey, man. Need me to get a paramedic?"

"I'm a nurse, remember?" Colleen said tightly, now standing and pivoting Moore into his seat. His hand covered the spot that had been hit. As she moved, she dropped her ball and Jordy carefully picked it up, holding it loosely in his lap.

"I'm fine," Moore said with a huge inhale that expanded his ribcage, taking the exaggerated breath to make a point. Extending his arms fully, he lifted his head, neck muscles tight, shoulders dropping.

As he exhaled, his eyes flared, but he turned to her with a smile.

"See? Fine."

Her hand went to his forearm, the rest of her wanting to hug him, be held by him, connect so she could calm down.

"Geez, Dad. That was one heck of a hit."

Jordy. Right.

Jordy was here.

A hundred people were watching them, including Luke, who stood in the aisle talking to Mark Insfield, a nineteen-year-old EMT she'd known since he was a baby, and who just graduated from the vocational school program. He carried a medical bag and wore an expression of determination to help, but was as green as could be.

"I've got this," she called out, reaching up to Moore's neck, her hand going to his chest. "How does this feel?" she asked him, pressing a bit with her fingertips.

"It would feel a lot better if we were alone and naked," he whispered.

"Not here. Not now," she hissed back, pulling away. In a loud voice, she called out, "He's fine!"

"I told you all," Moore informed them weakly.

"You sure?" Mark asked, uncertain. Luke clapped him on

the shoulder and said something to make him back up, nodding.

The field cleared as the inning ended, Colleen's eyes struggling to comprehend the board. Bottom of the third, heading into the fourth.

"Here," she said, digging through her purse for a small bottle of ibuprofen. "Take two of these."

"A beer would loosen me up better."

"No beer. You really do need to watch that hit. Take the pills. Hydrate. Maybe I should ask Mark for an ice pack," she said to herself, reconsidering.

"I might even need a nurse to watch over me in bed."

"Stop!"

His laughter made her join in, wishing they could hold hands, put their arms around each other, lean against one another.

For now, they were maintaining the image of being just friends. Within the next two days, that would all change. Looking to her right, she observed Jordy without drawing attention to herself.

Stepmother.

Thinking that word was a leap–a huge one–but not out of the realm of possibility. She'd cared for Jordy since he was born, and their kinship had remained strong through his moves, the long distance, and his anger toward Moore.

Maybe this was who she was meant to be: his stepmother, someday.

At the same time, her research into scholarships for advanced training loomed large. Getting a BSN would be somewhat easier than she'd thought, given a program she'd recently discovered in New Hampshire, one that would let her do all the classes online.

They even had an MSN program.

Other programs, though, with more hands-on experience

required, meant she'd have to leave town. Balancing what might be with Moore versus what might be outside of Luview weighed heavily on her.

One glance at him made her frown.

"You look like you're in pain."

"Waiting for the ibuprofen to kick in."

She stood, moving past him toward the aisle. Luke was still talking to Mark, but down near the row where Kylie and Harriet were sitting.

"Where are you going?" Moore asked.

"Getting you an ice pack."

As he stammered, she moved swiftly, jogging lightly down to her brother and Mark, who looked at her with mild alarm.

"Does Moore need assistance? I knew I should have helped."

"Just an ice pack. I gave him ibuprofen and I'm watching him carefully."

"Bet you are," Luke muttered, making Mark frown at him.

"I can do my job!" Mark said in a high, defensive tone. Dressed in a pink EMT uniform and carrying a red medical bag with the Love You Cupids logo on it, he fit right into town.

It took a moment for Colleen to realize Mark thought Luke's snarky comment was aimed at him and not her.

"You're a great EMT, Mark. No problem there. Hand me an ice pack," she said with a smile.

Mark did as told, giving her a questioning smile.

"You'll call me if something goes wrong?"

"Sure will."

Moving a bit more slowly back up the stairs, she cracked the pack open, releasing the cold. She reached their seats and slapped the pack on Moore's chest.

"Oof!"

"Hold it there."

As she sat down, Jordy handed her the prized ball. She bounced it in her hands a few times, shaking her head, hostility pouring out at the inanimate object that just tried to break her face.

And yet... it was a prized souvenir now.

"Attention, fans! The Luview High School flag line has joined forces with Love You Dance for a rousing performance of 'Cups'!"

"I didn't know they did performances during games!" Jordy gasped, leaning forward to watch.

"It's new," she told him. "Started at the end of the season last year."

"This is great!"

"Bet they'll partner with the new performing arts high school next year, too."

As the opening beats of the song began, played by the high school drum line, the crowd began clapping along, the groove fun to fall into.

Moore started clapping, but Colleen made him hold the ice in place. He sighed and sat back, shooting her a grateful smile.

For the next minute, everyone's body was infused with the beat, joy filling the stadium.

"Don't you feel that, Moore? The rush?"

"The rush?"

"It's—oh, it's so hard to describe. I guess because words don't matter? I don't know. It's just this feeling like I'm in their body and they're in mine, and when they move, I move, and it's all just—body. The rush. You know? Don't you feel it?"

He looked at her, cheeks flushed, eyes crazy excited, her whole heart into this.

"I do. I feel it, too."

Barely able to contain herself, she wanted to jump to her

feet, run onto the field, and join the dancers, the feeling so freeing.

As the song ended, they all rose to their feet, including Moore, though he didn't clap. The rush inside her was so strong, she nearly kissed him.

Nearly.

How much longer would *nearly* be enough?

As the game resumed, her pulse slowed, her limbs calmed, and her mind refocused. A tug in her heart turned to a dull ache, nothing compared to the pain in Moore's chest, she imagined, after that sacrifice to save her from the ball's impact.

But it hurt. A lot.

Today, she was at a baseball game with her friend.

And that was all she was allowed.

For now.

Chapter 19

Moore

For as much as he couldn't stand his ex-wife, her extended family welcomed Jordy back with open arms every time he was in town. The Forsythe family had strong roots in Luview, Maine, almost as strong as the Bilbees or the Luviews themselves, and with a passel of uncles and cousins who ran Love You Handy Jobs, the handyman business in town, Jordy could always be kept busy with some sort of project.

Right now, Slicer Forsythe was building a trebuchet, and Jordy was enthralled.

This gave Moore an unprecedented night out while Jordy was in town. Every moment that he wasn't working always spent with Jordy, even if his son wasn't his biggest fan. He'd always absorbed every drop of time with him as if it were his last, a parched father seeking what he could.

But now? Now he could relax, even if just a little. Jordy

was older, wiser, and determined to come back to Luview and live here for the rest of high school.

That call with Cammie hadn't been just a minor conflict. Warning shots had been fired. Moore's lawyer, Grant Otterbein, called to tell him her lawyer had threatened a custody battle if he tried to keep Jordy longer than the agreed-upon visit, and he had explained the whole mess.

Grant's succinct reply: "I'll go into bulldog mode. And this time, we'll win."

That had been his final call before heading here to Bilbee's, giving him a spring in his step and a sense that all was right with the world.

What more could he want? His son was about to come live with him. *Wanted* to live with him. He and Colleen were going to hang out with the gang at Bilbee's, and soon—achingly soon—they would go public with their relationship.

Life was good.

So good, he couldn't believe it.

"Moore!" Rider Bilbee greeted him as he walked in, approaching the bar. Head shaved clean, and wearing an eye patch, Rider could be mistaken for a man cosplaying a pirate, but you didn't ever say that to him. "The usual?"

"Am I the first one here?"

"You are!" Even Rider seemed surprised by that. "But we held the table."

"Thanks. I'll take a dirty vodka martini and all the usual fried crap Colleen orders for us."

"No beer?"

"I'm experimenting."

"Edgy. I love it. Show us your wild side, man."

"Not too wild. I have Jordy this week."

As Rider began making his drink, he glanced up, the single eye disconcerting yet familiar at the same time. "Heard he might go to the new high school?"

"That's what I'm hoping."

"Would be nice to have him back. He's a Mottin and a Forsythe, through and through."

"His uncles and cousins are indoctrinating him over at their workshop."

Rider snorted and groaned at the same time. "Oh, boy. Slicer?"

"And Trey."

"Of all the families to combine. He gets the steady, calm Mottins and the, uh–"

"The Forsythes. You don't need to say another word about them, Rider. I get it."

"At least you didn't have a kid with a Morgenstern," Rider whispered, making Moore laugh.

"How is Lyle doing these days?" he asked. Luke and Lyle Morgenstern had a longstanding feud, which culminated in a huge blowup here at Bilbee's a while ago, but Moore hadn't seen Lyle in ages.

"Hell if I care," was Rider's tidy reply, one that echoed Moore's own thoughts.

"Thanks," he said as he took the drink out of Rider's outstretched hand.

"Apps coming in platters to the table. How many of you tonight?"

"Six? Eight? Not sure."

"We have some new spicy breaded shrimp."

"Bring it on, man. Bring it on."

"Living large?"

"Something like that."

As Moore took his first sip of his martini, the front door opened and in walked a laughing foursome:

Luke, Kylie, Kell, and Rachel.

At the sight of them, a piece inside of him tightened and loosened at the same time, craving Colleen's presence. This would be the first time that they'd ever hung out at Bilbee's as something other than friends.

He wanted to be a couple. A couple like Rachel and Kell. Luke and Kylie. Sheila and Blake, when they came in.

Dean and Deanna.

His parents would never come to Bilbee's for darts and hanging out. Too standoffish, they were more the type to attend a string quartet concert than trivia night at the local tavern. Sure, they'd come here for lunch, or one of Rider's new pop-up bistro dinners, but not this.

Beer, booze, laughs, and killing time together.

"Want your peanut butter cheeseburger?" Rider called out to Moore as the gang descended on the large circular table set aside for them.

"Of course!"

""Peanut butter on a cheese burger? How can you eat that?" Kylie asked with a shudder. Her judgment always made him bristle.

"With my mouth."

Kell and Rachel moved over to the darts section, where Maisy Bilbee was sitting with a group of friends, her eyes tracking Kell as he passed. They were distant cousins, something like fourth cousins twice removed, but Maisy's crush on Kell was legendary.

Colleen appeared. "Place is quiet tonight, isn't it?" she said.

"Most of the Forsythes are back at their shop, hanging out with Jordy and a bunch of the kids doing the trebuchet."

"Great. That makes darts so much easier tonight."

Bluegrass music began to play softly over the music system in the old bar. Bilbee's Tavern had been around since 1788, longer than the town itself had existed. Colleen's ancestors had founded Luview, Maine, but the Bilbee family had been here long before. While they'd all intermarried over the years, there was still a rivalry. The Luviews embraced the tourist-town concept of love that dominated, while the Bilbees were curmudgeonly grumps, who tended to reject it.

It was no accident that the tavern's sign was a depiction of a large goat chewing on a red heart, and their slogan, *If we don't have it, you shouldn't drink it.*

"You ordered a falafel plate, right?" Rachel called out to Moore, who raised his hand, two fingers indicating how many he'd ordered. She smiled back as Kell wrapped his arms around her from behind and helped guide her through a throw that would at least land somewhere close to the target.

The sound of pool in the back room filtered into Moore's ears, the crack of balls being racked and cues against ivory a familiar sound. He looked at Colleen, wishing that he could mimic Kell and wrap his arms around her with such public confidence.

Instead, he took another sip of his dirty martini and dealt with her inquisition.

"No beer?" she asked, clearly surprised.

"I'm trying something different." Plucking the toothpick with olives on it out of his drink, he sucked lightly. One of her eyebrows went up.

"Seems to be a theme for me in life, too." She snuggled up to him, though it had to be a platonic move.

He felt her restraint as dueling parts of her fought for dominance.

"Can we tell Jordy tomorrow?" she asked, her voice so earnest, it cracked something open inside him.

"Yes," he said, desperate to be done with living in two worlds. "Yes."

She sagged against him in relief and then put a foot of distance between them, looking up at him with soulful eyes.

"I can't play pool or darts with this wrist," she noted, holding it up as if he didn't know which one had been broken.

She licked her lips, and he wanted to kiss them so badly, he nearly broke his own rule.

His phone buzzed in his pocket and he reached for it. A text from Jordy.

Can I spend the night here at Uncle Slicer's? Reggie, Tori, and Nathan are staying and we want to have an overnight.

Moore reeled back in surprise. Jordy had never asked for a sleepover with his cousins before.

He held the phone out to Colleen, who had a similar reaction as she read the text.

"Wow." She said slowly. "Are you going to let him?"

"Of course I am. Why wouldn't I? He's never asked for this before."

"Maybe he never asked for it because he knew you wanted to spend every possible moment with him."

Moore had never considered that.

"He could have if he wanted to."

"You know that," she replied, "but maybe he didn't. Maybe now that he knows he wants to move here and live here permanently, he feels a sense of freedom to ask for more. More that ties him to Luview."

"That's so paradoxical." Moore replied, taking a long sip of his drink. The implications of all of this were coming at him fast and furious.

It was simultaneously wonderful and overwhelming.

A new text appeared.

Dad?

No problem buddy. Have fun. What time should I get you in the morning?

Quickly, Jordy's response appeared.

I'll text you.

Do you need clothes?

I'm fine, Jordy wrote back. *If I need pajamas, someone can lend me some. And Uncle Jake says they have extra toothbrushes for guests. I'll just use one of those.*

"Is this normal?" He consulted with Colleen. "Do fifteen-year-olds just spend the night spontaneously at other people's houses?"

"Of course they do. You used to spend the night at our house all the time. You and Luke were thick as thieves."

"I know, but that was twenty years ago."

"Childhood hasn't changed that much, Moore."

"It has for me. I feel like I'm being handed a fifteen-year-old and expected to parent him without having the fifteen years of experience behind me."

"You're doing fine. Let him have fun. Let him be connected to his cousins. You're giving him a gift."

"I am?"

"Yes. The fact that he trusts you enough to even ask means that you're getting closer. He'll appreciate you even more tomorrow."

A sudden rush of desire ripped through him.

See you in the morning, kid. Have fun, he texted, then tucked the phone away in his pocket. Racing thoughts filled him. Did he need to ask Cammie about this?

No, damn it. *No*. He wasn't going to let her dictate every detail of how he parented.

And just like that, Moore had a free night. Jordy was here, but he wasn't spending every second in his orbit. Like a normal parent.

And then there was that desire.

Colleen looked up at him and it took every bit of restraint not to tuck his hands along the fine edges of her jaw, thread his fingers in her hair, and pull her in for a kiss. A kiss that would lead to pressing against her, their heat mingling, their tongues dancing.

He could see it in his mind's eye. The scent of Bilbee's,

wood smoke and sour beer. The sound of his friends laughing and telling stories around them. It was a movie in his head of what the next thirty seconds could be.

But if he did that, they would be going public before Jordy knew. And he worried that this extraordinary relationship he was finally building with his son would be undone by a single kiss in the wrong place.

Colleen's eyes reflected his own need right back at him. She stood on tiptoes, one hand going to his shoulder, and he bent down to put his ear close to her lips.

"You have a free night," she murmured. "What do you plan to do with it?"

"Do you know how weird it feels to be here with you?" Moore asked.

Luke walked by carrying two beers, giving them a grumpy look that made him look like a nun carrying a yardstick at a middle-school dance.

"Weird?"

"Yeah. Everyone here thinks we're just friends. And next time we're here, we'll show them we're more. But for now, we have to hold back, and that feels–"

"Weird."

"Right."

"What if we leave?"

"Leave?"

"You said it yourself. You have an empty place. We have all the time in the world, for once. Why not use it?"

"Skip out on darts?"

"They can manage without us."

"And go back to my apartment to make love?"

"Is that really an option?"

"I wouldn't have suggested it if it weren't."

"Then what are we still doing here?"

She reached for his hand, but he dropped it quickly. At

that exact moment, Rider showed up at their table with an enormous tray filled with appetizers.

Moore downed the rest of his martini. Bilbee's Tavern was within walking distance of his apartment over the store.

"Where did you park?" he asked her.

"Out back."

Years of desire pumped through him, the frustration of the last couple of weeks coming to a head. Yes, they'd made love back at her cabin shortly before Jordy came, but that had been almost tentative, an exploration to see if what had happened at the cabin was just a one off.

This would be their third time, and with plenty of hours stretched out before them to see what was real and what wasn't.

As more patrons came into the bar and Rider went back behind the counter, he realized Colleen hadn't had even a single drink.

"I've got wine and beer back at my apartment," he told her.

"Are you serious?"

"More serious than I've ever been."

"Besides," she whispered, "We've already christened my house. It's time to do yours."

Moore didn't need to be convinced.

"What kind of excuse do we come up with to get out of here?" he muttered through the side of his mouth. "Everybody's just beginning to play darts."

"Food poisoning?" she ventured.

"Can't start a rumor like that. Rider would kill us."

"Something's wrong with Sandwich?"

"Luke will just send Darren over."

"Jordy?"

Moore made a face.

"He's over at the Forsythes. Word will get out."

"How about using me as an excuse?"

"What do you mean?"

"I'll just say something's wrong with my wrist and I need a ride home."

"If I don't come back, people will wonder."

"People like who?"

"Luke."

"Let him wonder."

Moore's eyes went soft, watching her with a newfound appreciation.

"We're so close, Colleen," he said as his phone buzzed.

Dad?

The text from Jordy made him sigh.

Yes?

I need my rubber bands. Can you bring them?

Instantly, a plan formed.

Sure, bud.

"Hey. Jordy needs his rubber bands for his braces."

Colleen perked up.

"And you drank too much!"

"No, I didn't."

"Yes, you *did*," she stressed. "But I haven't had a sip of alcohol yet. You need a driver!"

"I need... a driver! Yes!"

For once, Jordy's forgetfulness was going to pay off.

"Where are you two going?" Kell called out as Colleen and Moore began shrugging into their coats.

"Jordy!" she yelled back. "He needs Moore to deliver something."

"You're not Moore!"

"I drank," Moore explained, earning looks of instant understanding from his friends. "She'll drive."

"Hurry back," Kylie called out, munching on an onion ring the size of her thigh. "Or we'll eat all the food."

"That a threat or a promise?" Moore joked. "You can have

my cheeseburger, Kylie."

"With peanut butter on it?" She made gagging noises. "I'd sooner get trapped in a metal donation box again!"

Laughing their way out the door, they raced around back to Colleen's car, but before they could even reach it, he stopped her, their kiss dizzyingly hot. His hands went under her coat, seeking the warmth of her skin, finding her breasts as his tongue slid between her lips and opened to her exquisite taste. Warm and soft, she pressed back against him with a full abandon that made him desperate enough to have a quickie right here in the alley.

But she deserved a bed. Sheets. Privacy.

And they deserved all of each other.

"Let's deliver the rubber bands and get back to my place ASAP," he murmured against her neck, licking her ear as she giggled, then kissed him until they were both breathless.

Her small SUV was typical Colleen, with thermoses in both cup holders and a half used roll of breath mints cluttering the console tray. As she drove the short two minutes to his apartment, he wondered if they should have just walked, but then he remembered the errand they still had to run.

Maybe they could quench their thirst quickly upstairs, deliver Jordy's orthodontia needs, and return for round two.

She pulled into one of the parking spots reserved for the store, behind the main drag. It was a routine she knew well after years of being his friend, but it felt different now. They were about to go upstairs into his living space, his private sanctuary, and make love. Whether they did it now or after dropping the item off with Jordy didn't matter.

What mattered was that they were finally going to have all the time they wanted to connect.

His phone buzzed as they took the back stairs up to his apartment.

It was Jordy.

Never mind. Nathan has some I can borrow.

Moore read the text to Colleen. Before the words were completely out, she was on her tiptoes, kissing him, his back slammed against his front door from the force of her need.

If the first time they made love was one of crossing a line, and the second was one of exploring their bodies, the third time was all about lust.

Pure, unadulterated *lust*.

Naughty and slick, hot and wet, this was a quickie, Moore peeling out of his clothes, shirt off, belt off, pants unbuttoned and unzipped as Colleen pulled her own clothes off and they raced to the bed, their teeth banging against each other as they kissed, fingers flying *everywhere*.

"Tell me what you want," he demanded, mouth on her breast, fingers between her legs, conjuring the magic that seemed to work last time. All he wanted was her, so much of *her*, and giving her pleasure counted so much.

"I'm *sooooo* ready. I hate hiding. I hate not having you."

"Whatever you're feeling, I feel it ten times over, Colleen."

He rolled over to his nightstand, finding a condom, putting it on fast as she grabbed him and before he could say a word, guided him in.

"Colleen," he rasped. "Don't you want–"

"This," she cried out loudly, her voice tense, body primed as she moved him, making him understand she wanted to be on top. He pulled out and repositioned her, the wet cocoon of her making all his edges merge with the word.

"You're so luscious," he said, hands going to her hips and leading her into a rhythm. Her head tipped down, loose hair tickling his chest, and he reached down to touch her.

Which made her pick up the pace, her lips parting, an unfocused look taking over her features. Colleen was always so controlled, with a hard shell. Penetrating that–penetrating her, literally–was an achievement. If he could give her the kind of unadulterated, unleashed ecstasy that connected them in bed, he felt whole.

And now, his orgasm rising in him, he worried he couldn't hold out.

"Moore!" she called out. "I'm so close. This feels so good."

"*You* feel good," he said, just as she bent down to kiss him, their mouths loose and frantic. She made a low, deep sound, one that came with a fierce tightening, as if he were being milked from the inside out.

Heart bursting with love and lust, he came in her, half dazed by the suddenness of it, loving every second of spontaneity and unexpectedly raunchy sex.

Until his phone interrupted them.

It actually *rang*.

"Damn," he groaned, rolling over to find his pants, the phone going on and on. Colleen gasped and sat up, pulling her knees in and wrapping her arms around them.

"Jordy? What's wrong?" he barked into the phone, his already rapid heartbeat speeding up.

"Can I watch an R-rated movie?"

"Excuse me?"

"I, uh, Dad. Look. I'm really mature, okay? I'm not that scared little boy who had nightmares after watching *Frankenweenie*, you know?"

"What are you talking about?" Moore looked down and realized he was naked except for the condom and his socks. Colleen was still wearing her shirt.

And socks.

And... shoes?

Head spinning, erection gone, he struggled to make sense of his son's words.

"Dad! I mean it! I can totally do this!"

"Do... what?"

"Watch an R-rated movie! Reggie's allowed, and he's fourteen! A year younger than me!" An angsty, defensive tone was winding up in Jordy's voice, confusing the hell out of Moore.

"What's wrong?" Colleen asked.

He hit mute on the phone before talking to her. "Jordy wants to watch an R-rated movie and he's freaking out about it with me."

"That's Cammie's fault."

"Huh?"

"Jordy didn't tell you? She's banned him from watching R-rated films. Not allowed until he's seventeen."

Barely able to breathe, he panted for a few breaths, until Jordy screamed, "DAD!"

"WHAT?" Moore snapped back, startling Colleen and eliciting a weird squeak out of his kid.

"Um, uh, can I?"

"What's the movie?"

He named a psychological horror film. Moore repeated the name to Colleen, who gave a thumbs up.

"Sure."

"Really?" Jordy's voice cracked with joy. "It's okay?"

"Just tell him to call you to come get him if he gets scared," Colleen whispered.

"Call me if you get scared," Moore paraphrased, grateful for the advice. "I'll come get you."

"You're the best! Hey, guys! My dad says I can watch! Quit calling me a baby!"

The call ended.

The bed began to vibrate as Moore stared at his phone, utterly perplexed. Colleen was laughing so hard, she sounded like a hyena, and Moore felt like he was living in a Salvador Dali painting.

"Did we just slip out on our friends at the bar to have a mind-blowing quickie and get interrupted by my kid asking to watch a horror film his mom banned him from seeing?"

"Yes."

"And I just had to negotiate that while still wearing a condom."

"YES!" she shrieked.

He threaded his fingers in his hair, pulling back on his scalp in disbelief. "Real life can't get any weirder."

"Don't tempt the gods, Moore!" Colleen cackled, nearly falling off the bed as she hooted, her bare ass gleaming in the moonlight.

She rolled away and he caught her, happy to have that ass in his hands.

Again.

"You," he said fiercely, kissing her laughing mouth, "are perfection."

"Me? Are you confusing me with someone else?"

"You knew what to say."

"I knew what he wanted to hear."

"You're amazing."

"So are you. Best sex I've ever had."

His hand went to his heart. "Really?"

"Really."

"And I'm not even playing my A game."

"You're holding back?"

"No. More like warming up."

She got up on her knees and kissed him, hard.

Both of their phones buzzed.

Exasperated sighs filled the air where moans had been two minutes ago. They checked their phones.

Where are you guys? Darts tournament starting.

It was Luke.

"He's such a spy!" Colleen groaned as Moore went to the bathroom, cleaned up, and began finding his clothes, getting dressed as Colleen did the same. By the time they were finished, they looked like they felt.

Sexed out and ready for an imaginary post-coital cigarette.

"We *soooo* look like we just banged each other's hearts out."

He placed his palm over her chest.

"Nope. Still there. And as big and loving as ever."

Bzzz

"Do not look at that!" she demanded, grabbing her purse and heading for his door. "Let's go back to Bilbee's and get him to shut up."

"You want to go back?"

"I don't want to. But if we don't, it'll look suspicious, and we're keeping up the friendship ruse until we tell Jordy, right?"

Pain shot through him, emotional and physical at the same time. He didn't want to hide anymore.

But he followed her to the car anyhow, climbing in, taking her hand.

"I love... *this*," he said slowly, instantly regretting the pull back at the last second.

He wanted to say *I love you*.

"I love this, too." Starting the car, she backed up, a smile on her face.

Whew. He hadn't offended her.

"But," she said as she turned right on Main Street, headed back to Bilbee's, "I can't hide any longer. We have to tell Jordy."

"Of course."

"You're amazing in bed, you know. So responsive," he said to her as she drove, her expression changing as he said the words.

"You make it easy."

"Sex should be easy."

She let out a huffy laugh. "I agree, but it isn't always."

"You've had a lot of bad sex?" Now he was intrigued.

"I've had a lot of *no* sex. Third Date Colleen, remember?"

"We're going to break that curse, then," he joked, her face changing again as she seemed to realize what had just happened.

"Third time. That was our third time."

Moore held up his hands.

"I'm still alive!"

She pulled into a parking spot close to Bilbee's, killed the engine, and gave him a stark look. "You are."

"It's fine, Colleen. Don't let other people's weirdness get into your head."

"Oh, I know that. Are you sure you're okay?"

"Why wouldn't I be?"

"Slicer could tell you. Or Tim Fields. Or–"

Looking around, he made sure no one could see them, then kissed her.

"I'm not them," he said firmly, ending the conversation by opening his car door and getting out. She joined him and they walked to the main door of the tavern.

"You ready?" he asked, looking in at their friends.

"No, but here goes."

"Wondered if you got lost and took a wrong turn into Canada," Luke joked as they rolled into Bilbee's, hoping they didn't reek of sex and secrets. Doc Blythe, chatting with Kell by the dart board, gave them a double take.

"I'll mingle. See you later," she whispered, putting distance between them, making him ache with the desire to be public. So close. They were so, so close.

But not quite there.

Doc held up his glass, a pint of what looked like a dark beer, and smiled. Moore walked on over and blended in with everyone, his body one live wire, the quickie turning every circuit inside him aflame.

Because *that?* He wanted more of that. So much more.

A lifetime of more.

Chapter 20

Colleen

Colleen woke up in her own bed, in her cabin, to the sound of an electric saw.

It was not an unfamiliar noise.

When Luke had approached the entire family with his idea to buy the old camp near Luview, they'd all reacted differently. Colleen had been more skeptical than anyone. Her biggest concern hadn't been living so close to family, but rather the renovations that would be required to make the place truly livable.

Three seasons out of the year, the cabins and lodge were fine, but winter revealed some harsh truths about the structures at the camp.

And every weekend, every repair, every patch reminded them of that fact.

Weekends and days off weren't relaxing like they used to be when she lived in her small house in town, because they were all spent on the fixer-upper part of owning the camp. Envying Dennis for a moment, her older brother's long-distance ownership made her reconsider whether living here along with everyone, with people all up in her business, was the right choice.

When Luke had proposed the idea, it had felt like her *only* choice.

Her phone buzzed with a text from Jordy.

Be there soon. Dad says we're helping you renovate the camp, then you're coming over to our house for dinner before your night shift.

Dinner? I thought we were just getting pizza, she wrote.

He says Mountain Dragon. Bi bim bap.

Ooooo, fancy.

I'll just get ramen. I don't like those gross eggs you pour on your noodles.

They're not gross!

She got back a puking emoji as a reply.

A thrill of happiness ran through her as she thought about Moore. Kell asked him a while ago to come help paint, and Jordy agreed it could be fun. Colleen was certain that Kylie's promise of fairy muffins had drawn him in. Fifteen was the magic age when a teen's stomach was an influencer in his life.

A text came through with a picture, both of them dressed in ratty, paint-splattered work clothes, both grinning at her.

They looked so much alike for a second that she did a double take.

You two look way too chipper for me. I need a lot more coffee before I can even look at those smiles.

Mine is radioactive. Shield your eyes. Hide your children and pets, Jordy shot back, making her laugh.

So much for trying to sleep some more.

Padding into her kitchen, she found her pre-programmed coffee pot nice and full of hot coffee, waiting to nourish her.

In the distance, her dad called out to Kell, then a thumping sound cut through the morning air.

Harriet squealed with happiness. Luke whistled for Jester.

Simple sounds, but deeply good ones. Mornings like this reminded her of why she chose to come into the family compound, invest herself and her future in it.

Would Moore consider moving here with her? Would Jordy?

The thought took her breath away, leaving her staggering toward the dining table, plunking into a seat.

Sex with Moore last night hadn't just been earth shattering, it had opened up a portal into an imagined future that she had never let herself consider before.

Colleen felt like a bag of puzzle pieces. Everything she needed was there, either as part of her or part of her life, but she hadn't figured out how to put the parts together into a whole that made sense.

Being with Moore did that.

Closing her eyes, she sipped her coffee and let her imagination run wild, to a future time when Moore lived here with her, with Jordy in his own room. They could go to breakfast with the family down on the dock by the lake, walk in the wildflower fields that her father mowed mazes into, help Kylie with the future fairy camp she so desperately wanted to start and maybe even give Jordy a sibling.

After all, if Cammie could do it, so could Colleen.

At her age, there wasn't much time for babies, but she hoped that Moore might be open to the idea. It was a topic that hadn't come up yet.

Yet.

Having found the online nursing program, she felt less of a pull to leave Luview but more of a draw to change her future. She had options—more than one—but the only option she really wanted was Moore. A life with him and Jordy, here at the compound with her family, would be a dream come true.

Every time she inhaled, she remembered his mouth on her breast, his body over hers, the intensity of his gaze, the taste of him still in her mouth, his scent on her skin. She wondered whether she would be able to smell their sex from last night on his hands when he arrived.

Perhaps when they had Korean takeout for dinner, they would finally tell Jordy.

That was the goal, after all. First, they would help with the renovations, which would root the Luview family more deeply in the camp. Then she and Moore would tell Jordy the truth about their relationship, which would root them even deeper in their shared experience in the town.

What better future could she and Moore have than to be together in a place where so much love had been given to them? Giving love to each other surrounded by community would be so healing.

Tap tap tap

The knock on her front door startled her enough to spill a tiny bit of coffee onto her hand. She set the mug down, stood, and tightened the sash of her bathrobe. There at her front door was Kell, carrying a ladder.

"We're thinking about doing pizza for dinner tonight, you in?"

She shook her head.

"I'm going over to Moore's. We're playing *League* with Jordy and getting Mountain Dragon."

He nodded once and continued on, carrying the twenty-foot ladder as if it were a feather.

Colleen looked at the calendar where all of her notes for her schedule were stored. That dinner with Jordy and Moore was scheduled for around four o'clock because she had a six o'clock shift at the hospital. There was no way to change it, so she knew they'd have to squeeze in their talk with Jordy.

Keeping it brief made sense, though. No fifteen-year-old wants to talk for too long about his father's romantic relationships.

And how would he react to learning that *she* was the woman in question?

Timing was everything, and Jordy's recent comments about being glad Moore was a bachelor clashed with the nineteen years of restraint they were breaking. An aching wrist reminded her that the crash was just last month.

Not much more than a month ago, they crossed a line they'd spent half their lives holding.

And today, they would cross another line, one that she thought would be so much easier. Moore was too concerned about Jordy's reaction. She was close enough to the kid to know he was tender and needy underneath the shell of contempt showed the world.

Her phone buzzed. Expecting another text from Jordy or Moore, she was surprised to get one from her cousin, Sandy, who worked at the hospital in administration.

Jill called off. Any chance you can come in at noon today instead of six?

No, she replied instantly. *I've got plans.*

Shift bonus if you can, Sandy wrote back with a pleading emoji.

Sorry, but thanks. Good luck! Colleen replied.

While she felt plenty of sympathy for Sandy's plight, she also needed to protect her day. Going into work at six would be hard enough, pivoting from what she expected to be a deeply emotional moment to the more clinical approach required for helping patients.

Cutting off the majority of her day for work was a no-go.

For the next hour, she showered, chopped vegetables for a

veggie tray for lunch, and puttered around her cabin, tidying. The vacuum cleaner always scared poor Sandwich, who deftly slipped under a dresser.

This time, sex with Moore had taken place at his apartment, so no worries about stray condoms, thank goodness.

When she was finally done, she walked over to the lodge, plastic food tray in one hand and a refreshed hot coffee in the other.

"Hey, slacker," Luke said as she shuffled into the lodge, the scent of paint and freshly cut wood in the air.

"Slow start?" her mom asked, a thick roll of blue painter's tape in her hands.

"Something like that," Colleen muttered. Sipping her coffee, she took a seat in a battered old chair. "Moore and Jordy are on their way," she called out as she watched her parents, Luke, Kylie, and Kell all moving around in synchronicity.

Buying the old camp had been a financial stretch for everyone, the hundreds of acres giving them privacy but also coming at a cost. Doing so many of the renovations themselves had been a key part of the calculus of buying the sprawling property.

Her nerves were getting the best of her, and it wasn't just about telling Jordy and how he would react. Once Jordy knew, it would be time to go public.

Braced already for the hundreds of comments about how everyone knew that they were meant to be together, and how could they have missed what was right in front of them all these years, she didn't relish the town's reaction.

There would also be the handful of women who had pursued Moore all this time.

Handsome and charming, he was a catch. And although he lived modestly in the apartment above the jewelry store, Colleen knew that he had investments. Moore wasn't rich by any means, but he was comfortable, smart, and careful with his money.

And had spent his adulthood trying to prove that he was more than the single mistake he made at seventeen.

As the new dose of caffeine entered her bloodstream, she perked up, but her heart stayed soft, her stomach fluttering.

Today was a big day in her life. Today was a turning point, one that no one in this room understood. In an effort to find connection and love, Colleen and Moore would have to violate a protective boundary yet again. Keeping Jordy unaware of their relationship made sense until it didn't, and now it was time.

"Are you going to be a potted plant or an actual helper?" Luke sniped at her as he walked by, carrying a gallon of paint.

"Give a girl a minute to have some peace and caffeine."

"We were all up late partying at Bilbee's, and *we're* here on time."

"That's because you're perfect, Luke."

He grinned. "Good of you to finally notice."

The sound of a car outside made Colleen look out the window. It was Moore with Jordy in tow, the two of them looking exactly like the photo that Jordy had texted her. Soon the entire crew had settled into their respective jobs, with Dean acting as project manager. Colleen was a worker ant in this project; whatever her father told her to do, she just did.

Jordy asked to be paired with Colleen, so the two of them worked on painting trim while Kell and Luke handled filling in holes.

"How's it going?" Colleen asked. "You have fun at the Forsythes' last night?"

Jordy smiled. "Yeah. I've never done that before, had an overnight with my cousins. It was cool. When I move here, I want to do that again."

"That's great," Colleen said, momentarily wordless at how casually he said that.

His face went dark.

"But Mom called me this morning. She heard I spent the night there and yelled at Jake."

"Why?"

"She said I should have told her, and Jake and Dad should have checked in with her."

"You're here though. No one needs to ask her permission for you to do things when you're here."

"That's what I said."

"Did Moore talk to her?"

"She doesn't want to talk to him, says everything has to be through lawyers now."

"Oh."

"But that's Dad's fault."

"What do you mean?"

"He's the one who started with all the lawyer stuff. That's why Mom never has any money, because she's always paying for lawyers."

The casual way Jordy said this triggered a giant defensive response in her. Lines were being crossed today. Big ones.

"You know that's not true," she informed him, unable to stop herself.

Jordy jolted. He looked up at her but pressed his fingers in place on the blue tape around the molding.

"What?"

"It's not true that the lawyers are your dad's fault."

"Mom says Dad's always using lawyers to make her life miserable through me."

"He does hire lawyers, but it's more to protect his time with you."

"Mom says he's always using them like a weapon, to try to bleed her dry."

"Do you know why he started using lawyers?" She bit her lower lip and glanced over. Moore was gone from the spot where she had just seen him. Should she say something? Was it time? She knew Moore didn't want Jordy to know the truth about what happened when he was five, and yet he held these opinions of his father that were so volatile and ignorant of the goodness she knew was at Moore's core.

Jordy's eyes narrowed. "What do you mean? You act like you know something–why *did* my dad start using lawyers?"

"It happened when you were five."

He blinked, then he blinked again. Suddenly, a rapid spurt of them turned his face emotional. His eyes filled with pain.

"When I was five? That's when Dad kicked me and Mom out of the house."

Something in the way he held himself made her suspicious. It was just a sense, not rational.

"Jordy," she whispered, "has someone been talking to you about this?"

Chewing on the inside of his cheek, he avoided eye contact.

"Nathan. Reggie. They, uh, said something when I was at their house. No one agreed on what really happened, and then they all suddenly shut up. It was weird."

"Weird?"

"Nathan said something about Mom taking me. Then Reggie and Tori said Dad was the one who was in the wrong. I tried to ask what the hell they were talking about, but... It was like they all knew something about me I didn't know. I almost texted Dad to come get me, but then we started watching anime and I just chilled."

All the air in her lungs disappeared, as if someone had come up from behind and struck her twice. Her gut tightened, pushing up on her diaphragm, forcing her spine to straighten.

"Okay," she choked out, touching his hand. "Let's go talk outside."

"Why can't we keep talking in here?"

"Because what I need to tell you is private."

"Oh."

A worried look passed over his features, settling in for the duration, and her heart nearly broke. No, Jordy wasn't her child, but she felt so connected to him. Never being able to tell him the truth of what had happened to him had kept them apart, a secret she'd held out of respect for Moore that created a distance between her and the teen.

Now, finally, she was going to close the distance.

They headed out toward a bench near the flagpole, but Colleen decided on the fly that sitting would be a bad idea. Talking to a teenager was awkward enough. Movement would be key here, so she kept walking.

"Your dad didn't kick you and Cammie out when you were five."

"That's what Mom said he would say."

"Have I ever lied to you?"

"Uh... no." Astonishment flooded his voice. "You never have."

"I need you to listen. And try to understand. You're fifteen now, not five. And you've been lied to for years by your mother."

"What?"

"When you were five, she took you. Just... disappeared. No one knew where you two were for months."

He just blinked.

"Moore hired investigators and lawyers to track you down. And eventually, they found you and your mom, living in California with Mike."

His eyes drifted to the ground.

"Cammie fought your dad in court, over and over. He flew

to California to see you and she called the cops. It was ugly, Jordy. I'm not going to tell you all of it right now, because this is a lot, but you can always ask for details whenever you want."

"My mom said Dad kicked us out. Said he never tried to see me. She said that it was his fault I'm a grade behind. Said–"

"She said a lot of things, Jordy, that aren't true."

"I can't believe this. Do–is there proof?"

"Proof?"

"Yeah. Like, if Dad tried to get custody of me, where's the proof? Papers? Something like that?"

"You mean documents? Your dad has plenty of those."

"I don't want to ask him. Would Grandma and Grandpa have them?" He pulled out his phone and began texting.

"What are you doing?"

"We learned in critical thinking class that when someone tells you something you don't believe, ask for proof. Then validate the proof. I'm doing that now."

Jordy stared glumly at his phone, then looked at her.

"This is real?"

"It is."

"Then why didn't Dad tell me?"

"He never wanted to say anything bad about Cammie in front of you."

"That's–but–but–"

His phone buzzed. He read the screen, frowning.

"Grandpa says it's true. And he took pictures of some of the court paperwork. Said I could ask Nadine Khouri or Chief Anderssen for details about the missing child case." Jordy stared hard at the screen. "I was a missing child?"

"For a time, yes."

"Like an Amber Alert?"

"No. It never rose to that level, but something like that."

Leander had taken about ten pictures, reacting quickly to Jordy's request. She imagined him in his home office, the polished oak desk shining as he sighed to himself and pulled from one of the drawers full of legal paperwork the Mottins had subsidized. A good portion of their retirement savings had gone to fighting for Jordy.

"This is a lot, Colleen."

"It is."

Tears made his eyes glisten as his jaw began clenching.

"Why didn't you tell me?"

"Because Moore asked me not to."

"I thought you were *my* friend!"

"I am!"

"Friends don't keep secrets like this from each other. I feel like such an idiot! Does everyone in town know? Uncle Slicer? Uncle Trey?"

She took in a long, deep breath to buy herself time as he turned to her, red faced and furious.

"They do! I'm a joke here in Luview, aren't I? Just some sad little kid who doesn't even know anything about his own life! Grandma and Grandpa, Dad, *you*–" he spat out. "And Mom, all of you are liars! ALL OF YOU!" he screamed, turning and running along a path into the woods, down toward the dock on the lake.

Adrenaline coursed through her, her body an ocean of fear.

That had not gone well.

At all.

A burst of laughter from the lodge was a bizarre moment of cognitive dissonance. The rush of her own tears made her shoulders shake, her hands flat against her thighs as she tried to control the tremors building in her.

In an effort to stop Jordy from being mad at Moore, all she'd done was alienate him from all the other adults in his life, too.

Including her.

The front door to the lodge swung open, Moore's fast footsteps a gigantic clue that he somehow knew what had just happened between her and Jordy.

"Colleen!" he called out, his voice tight. "Where's Jordy?"

"He ran off into the woods." She leaned against a small potting table outside the greenhouse and fought her tears.

Moore showed her his phone screen. It read:

You lied to me all these years.

Then a two-word expletive.

"Did you—did you tell him about us?"

"No."

"Then why is he... oh, no. No, no, *no*. You told him? About when he was five?"

"I—he asked."

"He *asked*? He specifically asked, 'Did my mother steal me?'"

"Not in so many words, no, but the topic came up and—"

"I CANNOT *BELIEVE* YOU!" Moore bellowed, sounding so much like Jordy, she suddenly thought she was reliving his outburst.

"I don't understand why you're so upset."

"That's the problem, Colleen—you don't understand!"

"I do, though," she conceded, reaching for his arm, needing the tactile connection to be able to navigate this difficult conversation. "And I've kept this secret all these years, I've respected what you wanted. But Jordy came to me to ask about it, and—"

"And *what*? And you decided to violate what I had asked you to keep confidential?"

"I decided that, in that moment, I would give him what he needed. That I would give *us* what we need."

"Us?" he asked. "What do you mean by *us*?"

"We matter, Moore. You keep pushing back when we're

going to tell him about us. That poor kid lives with so many secrets."

"I can't believe you told him! Damn it, Colleen, that wasn't yours to tell!"

The way he slammed his palm, hard, on the scarred table made her feel it in her gut, as if he'd dropped an anvil straight through her body and it caught in her belly.

"No, it wasn't. And I'm sorry. But I'm also not sorry, because he needed to know! It's his history, too."

"It's *mine*. *My* story. *My* choice. You go on about how people should have autonomy and how no one else can tell you how to live your life and then you go and decide the direction mine should take. Hypocrite!" he hissed.

This was completely new.

Moore was pissed at her. Really pissed. Not like that time when they were ten and eight and she broke his new robot toy by accident. Or the time she refused to let him win at Monopoly and played until he cried when they were eleven and nine. Or even the time when he ate a worm on a dare when they were thirteen and eleven and she didn't give him the promised chocolate bar from Love You Chocolates.

Oh, no.

This was earth shattering.

Soul destroying.

Relationship ending.

Dull with fear, her tongue wouldn't move. All she could do was stare.

"Now Jordy knows. And he's going to ask Cammie." He snorted and began to pace like a caged, angry animal. "Not ask. *Confront*. And knowing how he is with me, it'll get ugly, *fast*. Kid's got one hell of a mouth on him."

Moore said it with pride.

Colleen kept hers shut.

"And Cammie will just lie to him. He'll believe her. And then it'll all be worse."

"No."

Jerking up, his eyes met hers.

"What?"

"No. She can lie, but he won't believe her."

"How do you know that?"

"Because I told him all about your court cases. And he went to your dad, who confirmed. Showed him some of the files."

"You got my *father* involved in this?"

"Jordy did. He went to Leander and asked. Texted him, and Leander texted back photos."

"This all just happened? Just now? You've only been outside for ten minutes!"

"It's been a whirlwind, for sure," she tried to joke, but Moore was having none of it.

"Because of you."

"I started the ball rolling. Jordy asked the right questions to keep it going. "

"My dad didn't say anything to me."

"Jordy asked him not to? I don't know. It's only been ten minutes!"

"What have you done? What have you unleashed? I didn't want this, Colleen. Cammie is going to–"

"QUIT TALKING ABOUT HER!"

Slamming down her own palm, her voice came out like thunder.

Moore reeled back. Good.

"You don't get to yell at me!" he roared back, storming her with a sudden movement, their faces inches apart.

"YES, I DO!"

"Why?"

"Because you're so damn afraid of her when it comes to Jordy. She's a paper tiger!"

"A paper tiger with very real custody rights that can make my life a living hell!"

"He's fifteen now, Moore. He can decide. And that means he can choose to live with *you*."

"Maine law doesn't have a cutoff age for the judge to consider the rights of the child. You just put everything in jeopardy!"

"I was trying to help."

"I can't believe you did this to me!"

"I did it for Jordy! He said Nathan made an offhand comment last night about Cammie taking him away. Jordy said *you* were the one who made *them* leave, and the cousins all went silent. Nathan said Cammie took him. Reggie and Tori defended Cammie. He came to me and asked for the truth."

"He should have come to *me!*"

"But he didn't, Moore. He *didn't*. Is that why you're so mad at me? You're really mad at Jordy for trusting me more than you, and you're taking it out on me?"

"ARE YOU *KIDDING?*" he thundered, bearing down on her with a ferocity she didn't know he had in him. "You're going to deflect and turn your betrayal into *my* problem?"

"Betrayal?" she choked out, the word so dangerous, like a hand grenade that he'd lobbed at her, an emotional hot potato she couldn't hold. "Telling Jordy the truth about what happened is a betrayal of... what?"

"Of my *trust*," he yelled back.

"Why are you so angry?"

"Because I'm afraid," he confessed, slumping into a chair, the change in him so great she felt like her heart ricocheted against her ribs over and over.

"Afraid of Cammie?"

"No. I'm afraid of losing Jordy. What if he doesn't want to come now?"

"Why wouldn't he want to come now?"

"I don't know."

"Moore, everything you want is right here in front of you. Jordy. Me. We can let go of all the secrets. We can live freely."

"That wasn't your secret to tell, and now he may change his mind. You don't understand what it's like to walk through life as a giant loser, always having to prove myself, over and over again. I made one mistake—*one*—and I've paid for it for half of my life. And just when I think everything's going to finally turn around, that Jordy will come live with me, that maybe I have you, that maybe I'm not constantly walking a narrow line where I can't make a single mistake, you go and do this. You go and upset the delicate balance."

"I was trying to help Jordy."

"I don't think you were, Colleen. I think you were trying to help yourself."

"What?"

"You could have told him about us, if you're so worried about keeping secrets."

"You told me not to."

"I told you not to tell him about what happened when he was five, too, but you went ahead and just ran roughshod over that one."

All she could do was blink. They were past the point of no return now, every word out of their mouths just another cut that bled.

"I thought we could have a reasonable conversation about this. I knew you'd be upset. Jordy was upset! I was about to come to you and tell you so we could both go talk to him and help him to calm down. Absorb the truth. Re-organize himself inside and be supported."

"I'm his father. You're not his parent. You don't get to make that kind of unilateral decision."

"I know I'm not his parent, but I am close to him."

"Maybe that's clouded your judgment, then."

"Are you intentionally hurting me, Moore? Is that your goal? Because I'm over here trying so hard to talk this through and come out on the other end, and it feels like you're just going for the jugular."

"I'm so tired of being told I'm wrong!"

"Then stop *being* wrong!"

"I AM ALWAYS WRONG! Wrong for you. Wrong for Cammie and Gia and Hannah. Wrong for working in my family's company until I proved myself beyond a shadow of a doubt. Wrong for Jordy until now. Wrong, wrong, *wrong*. Now I finally have my kid ready to move here and you tell him the truth about the one thing I've spent ten years hiding from him for his own good. He hates me all over again. I never have any good choices! I'm always cursed, either way."

"Cursed."

She let the single word hang in the air, like a chime you strike once and hear forever.

He said nothing, panting hard, watching her like he expected her to say something magical to make this all go away.

"You think I've cursed you."

"I was cursed long before you, Colleen. Wasn't allowed to tell you how I felt when I was younger. Turned to Cammie in desperation. Screwed that up with a broken condom. Fought like hell to make a stable financial life for my wife and kid. Wife took my kid–"

"I know your entire life story, Moore. I'm part of it!"

"Then act like it, for once!"

"I'm trying! I've been trying all these years. But I'm done! Too many years, too much trying, and never enough!"

"*You're* never enough? Try being me!"

Furious and hurting, she started toward her cabin, unable to continue talking to him right now.

"I have to go to work."

"What about our early dinner? We were going to tell Jordy about us."

"What *us*, Moore? I don't even know what your idea of *us* is!"

She ran up the path to the quiet haven of her own home, blindly grabbing her bag and keys. Then, slamming the front door in frustration, she stormed out to her car and pressed the starter, tears filling her eyes as she tried not to imagine her family's stares, grateful they were all inside the lodge.

Once she was down the road, she'd text Sandy and take that early shift after all.

Why not? It would be nice to go somewhere where she was allowed to be herself in public.

She had to get away.

Had to escape.

Had to leave the man who yelled at her because she crossed a line.

Cursed. He used the word *cursed*. Maybe he was right. Maybe she really was cursed.

And maybe she and Moore weren't meant to be after all.

Chapter 21

Colieen

When you worked in an ER and you heard the sound of running in the hallway, you ran, too.

As two people in scrubs shot past her, Colleen heard words no one ever likes to hear:

head injury
  long fall
  complex fracture
  not looking good

But as she raced to join the team, an alarmed Doc Blythe stopped her mid-run, his grip on her arm so strong, she felt her biceps tear slightly with kinetic force, her hip slamming into the wall.

"What are you doing?" she snapped at him, the old man surprisingly strong, a pen clattering on the tile floor as it fell out of his front coat pocket. "Ow!" Thankfully, he'd grabbed her good arm.

His gray brows knitted together, kind eyes sharp. "Colleen. No."

"No, *what?*"

"Don't–don't go in there. Not yet."

The grip remained iron tight.

"You're hurting me, Doc. Why not?" And then she froze, because the only reason Doc Blythe would stop her was if she knew the person. The patient.

And the only people she knew who might have long falls, head injuries, and complex fractures were her Dad and Kell.

"It's not Dad? Kell?" she whispered in horror. "Tree accident?"

He shook his head.

"Not Luke?" she guessed.

"No."

"Then stop playing Twenty Questions with my damn heart, Doc, and tell me what the hell you're doing?"

Doc cleared his throat as cacophony reigned around them.

"It's Moore."

"MOORE?" she half screamed. Her eyes bugged out of her head. "*MOORE?* What was Moore doing in a tree?"

"Tree?"

Her mind struggling to piece this all together, she heard someone call for a crash cart.

"No tree. He fell, Colleen. Off a tall ladder while painting the lodge. Fell a good fifteen feet. Bad hit to the head."

She moved to the left, enough to peek in and see blood soaking the discarded gauze on the floor, a team working fast and furious to stabilize him.

"Moore. *Moore Mottin?*"

"Yes."

"*My* Moore?"

"Honey, yes." Something in Doc's eyes made terror shoot through her.

"*Oh, my God,* NO!" Wrenching herself out of his grip, she sprinted into the room, stopping short at the sight of him. His right leg was splinted, the fracture forcing her to go into clinical detachment. If she could triage him, assess the wounds, know that the best doctors at Luview Medical Center would care for him and–

"Colleen!" Luke's messy paint clothes clashed with the pristine medical equipment, white coats, and green scrubs as he rushed into the trauma area, glancing over at Moore's prone body, then turning back to her, fast. "I came to find you. I was at the hardware store, buying more primer. Heard the 911 call and–"

She collapsed into his arms.

"You were right," she sobbed into his shoulder as she watched Doc join the team around Moore.

"What?" Luke's hand caressed her hair, soothing her. "*Shhh.*"

"You were right. I did this to him."

"You–no! He fell off the ladder. Kell says he insisted on doing the high section because he had so much painting experience and–"

"We slept together, Luke. Last night. And now here he is..."

They both looked over.

"...in my emergency room." She felt a sound rise up in her, the vibration deep and lonely, a mourning tone that turned into wordless feeling.

"I cursed him."

"That–it's just a–no. No, no, *no*. You didn't do this to him, Colleen. You can't think that you–"

Doc peeled away from Moore's side and looked over her shoulder, forcing Colleen to follow his gaze. In the distance, she saw Leander and Francine at the ER desk, Moore's father's voice rising, louder and louder.

She caught, "...demand to see him!" before Luke pulled her close again, shuffling them out of the way of the team.

Medical terms she used daily floated through her consciousness as Luke held her, Francine and Leander running past them.

"Where's Jordy?" she gasped, looking up at Luke.

"Back at the camp. Mom has him. Told Francine and Leander to just come straight to the hospital and she'll manage him for them. She'll bring him over if it's bad enough."

"Bad enough?"

"He hit his head bad, Colleen. Fell on a paint can with a scraper on it."

Blunt words, but anchoring words. Colleen knew what those words meant. Plenty of people survived worse falls completely intact, though with scars.

But plenty didn't.

Injuries like Moore's were crapshoots, and for someone so unlucky in life, the odds weren't in his favor.

"He never falls! He's so sure footed."

"I know. Shocked the hell out of us."

"You saw it?"

"No. Kell and Kylie. Dad and Mom were in the work shed with Harriet getting some trim and—"

"Get him into surgery!" Doc said urgently, the attending, Dr. Singh, pulling with the team as Moore's gurney went in the opposite direction.

She wanted to go to him, hold his hand, kiss him, tell him she was sorry—oh, so sorry—because she was. Their argument earlier today was so stupid, an aberration in what should have been a healing moment, but instead was nothing but unnecessary conflict because they were in pain.

Pain they should have talked through together, instead of using it as a weapon against each other.

She knew running after the team would only slow them down, and time was of the essence. Rational and clinical, she let that part of her take over, the tears slowing as she folded her fear into a small, neat square of terror that she tucked into a corner of her mind.

Wiping her face, she looked around, a bit startled. Luke's frown deepened, his blue eyes now worried for her.

"Are you in shock?"

"Shock?"

"You've gone flat."

"Flat?"

"Colleen." He closed his eyes, but didn't move his hands from her shoulders. "If anyone in the world know what it's like to—"

"He's not dead like Amber."

Her voice carried, and a handful of her colleagues looked up and stared at them like deer caught in headlights.

Luke's face was a mask of shocked pain.

"No," he said slowly. "He's not. But he might die, Collie. He really might die. And—"

Reeling from his words, she lost control of her legs. He held her up.

"If you want to try to see him before they put him under—" Luke began, but she cut him off.

"No. I don't want to delay his surgery. But Luke, we had a big fight right before I left for work."

"We heard. Haven't seen you yell at Moore since we were kids, other than chewing him out for eating the last mozzarella stick on a platter at Bilbee's."

She gave a sniffly, snotty huff of laughter.

"We were about to go public."

"Yeah?"

"Yeah."

"When you skipped out on us at Bilbee's? That wasn't really about Jordy?"

"No. It was. And then it wasn't."

"What was your fight about?" he asked gently, leading her down the hall to the nurse's lounge. As they entered the room, two of her fellow nurses, Sara Mosk and Colleen's friend Yulia, gave them sympathetic looks, momentary surprise crossing their faces as they took Luke in.

"You two need anything?" Yulia asked.

"Moore's in surgery," Luke explained. "Head trauma."

"We heard." She gave Colleen a half hug. "We know how close you all are. We're here if you need us."

"Sandy's calling around to get your shift covered," Sara added.

"I'm fine," she said out of habit, then burst into tears.

Because nothing was fine.

And if her last words to Moore turned out to be *What us, Moore? I don't even know what your idea of us is...*

...she would never forgive herself.

* * *

"Being a nurse has its perks here," Yulia said, accompanying Colleen into the recovery room.

Moore was one of three patients and Dr. Singh gave her a skeptical scowl.

"You shouldn't be here," he said, but then turned away. "I don't see anything for twenty seconds."

Years of working with patients hooked up to IVs and ventilators had numbed her to the sight, or so she thought. Turned out she was wrong.

Nothing prepared her for the sight of Moore's hospital bed. His head was wrapped in a white gauze helmet. Various tubes were bringing liquid in and taking liquid out of his body, a fine-tuned system.

A team was required to make all of the outcomes as positive as possible. Much like raising a child, helping a patient recover after surgery took a village.

"Moore," she whispered, touching just the very tips of his fingers, not wanting to harm him in any way or wake him too quickly. Coming out of anesthesia was a delicate process.

She scrolled through her memory and couldn't find another instance when Moore had ever undergone general anesthesia. She hoped he would sail through with no complications.

Yulia pulled a curtain around them for privacy, then patted her on the back.

"One minute," she said quietly. That was all Colleen got, her time with Moore partitioned and restrained, even here, in the place where she belonged.

"I love you," she whispered, her lips trembling as the words flowed so easily out of her mouth. "I know you can hear me somewhere in there. I'm so sorry."

A lump in her throat made it hard to talk, but she forced herself, knowing that time was limited.

"This won't be the only time I tell you. I swear to God, it won't, Moore, but I have to say it now in case..." She interrupted herself, unwilling to entertain the thought of what "in case" encompassed.

"We didn't need to fight like that and I shouldn't have told Jordy without talking to you first. You're right. I just did it because I love you so much and all I want is to start what's left of our life together. I feel like I've lived half a marriage with you, only we weren't actually married, now I want the married part. I want the love and the babies and the daily life and living together. All of it with you. I don't want to be cursed anymore. I want to break the curse. I want to break the curse with *you.*"

She squeezed his hand, knowing that he was unable to give back. That didn't matter. She just wanted to fill him with her love.

"When this is over and we have a good laugh about it, you're never allowed near a ladder again. Do you hear me, Moore? I mean it. No ladders."

The rustle of the curtain was her cue. She bent down, kissed him softly on the cheek, stroking his face.

Who would he be when he woke up? She loved him no matter what and would take him however he emerged from this.

And then she walked out into the hall, pressed her back against the wall, and slowly crumpled to the floor.

Within seconds, four hands were on her, Yulia on one side, Luke on the other, holding her.

Doing the only thing they could:

Just being there.

* * *

She was greedy.

Refusing to leave the hospital, she abused her personnel privileges by making sure she had as much access to Moore as possible.

They moved him into his room right around the time that his parents left to go take care of Jordy and to settle in for the long haul. This meant that she had Moore all to herself. Yulia was working his case, and though she knew the doctor was impatient, she took what she could get.

For obvious reasons, Dr. Singh refused to put her on the

case, so she gave up all pretense of trying to be a nurse. All she was now was the girlfriend.

The unofficial girlfriend, stuck in limbo.

Not sure what Moore would say when he finally woke up, if he ever woke up.

"Honey," her mom said, handing her a bag, "you need to change your clothes."

"I have clothes in my locker."

"I know you do, but these are comfortable. Leggings, sweatshirt, that kind of thing. If you're going to be here for Moore, you need to be as comfortable as possible." Deanna shook the bag. "There are some protein bars in there, too."

"There's plenty of food here, Mom."

"For people who work here. You're a family member now, waiting for your loved one."

"Not technically a family member, Mom."

Deanna came in for a hug that caught Colleen off guard, her body melting into her mother's warm embrace. She felt childlike, cared for, supported. The waiting was the hardest part and she knew professionally that this would take a while, but personally, every second felt like a year.

"Go change," Deanna said pointedly. "I'll stay with him. If he wakes up, I'll come get you. But I mean it, honey. Take care of you. Moore is going to need you to be as strong as possible when he gets out of this. It's going to be a long recovery."

"Mom, I said some horrible things to him. We had a fight and..."

The sad smile on her mother's face made Colleen's heart skip a beat.

"I know. We heard you guys arguing and then you drove off and Moore came back into the lodge angry. He tried to hide it, but he's always been terrible at covering his true self. That man is so good, to the core. He was a wonderful little boy, a marvelous teenager, and now an amazing man and father." She squeezed Colleen's biceps. "And a perfect partner for you."

"I may have ruined it."

"Even when two people love each other and want what's best for each other, so many things can get in the way, Colleen. Trust me. Love is never ever easy. It's also never perfect. People aren't perfect. You're both deeply flawed. Moore is coming into this relationship with you from a weaker position."

"What is that supposed to mean? I'm Third Date Colleen. I'm the cursed one."

"And he was married and divorced twice by age twenty-seven. He was shamed by his own parents for what happened with Cammie. Moore has plenty of his own ghosts when it comes to love, honey. Whatever conflict you had, you'll patch it up."

"I told Jordy about what happened when he was five. Moore didn't want me to but I did, and then I got defensive. I dug in. We fought and we were supposed to tell Jordy the truth about our relationship today. But I stormed off to work, picked up an extra shift and just thought I would bury myself in emergencies. Instead, I created one."

"You did not hurt Moore."

"Of course I did. I said terrible things to him."

"You didn't make him fall off that ladder."

"I know. I'm not cursed in that sense. But everyone in town's going to talk about it. Especially when they find out that yesterday, we..."

"You what?"

"We slept together for the third time, Mom. Third time's the charm, right? And now here he is in my ER." She threw her hands up to the sky. "It's not funny, but it's funny. It's not funny because it's sickening."

"It's not funny," Deanna said slowly. "At all. I wish I could take all your pain away. When you kids were little, it was so easy. I'm sure you told Jordy the truth for a good reason."

"I did. But Moore had a good reason *not* to tell him and I decided that my reason was better than his."

"You two will solve this."

Colleen took the clothes and went down to the locker room, changing mindlessly. Instantly more comfortable in her casual clothes, she had to admit her mom was right. Sweats really were made for waiting in the hospital.

When she got back, Yulia was there, giving her a comforting smile.

"He's coming out of it," she said. "His parents won't be here for a bit. Do you want some time with him?"

Colleen nodded and walked past.

"I'll go fill in the family," Deanna told her.

Colleen shut the door and faced Moore's body again. Hooked up to machines, she could see his status at a glance, his heart rate, oxygen level. Everything going on inside him physically was there for her to read. But his heart? She knew what the electrical signals were saying, but she had no insight at all into how he felt.

Sitting on the edge of the bed and taking his hand in hers, she watched his chest rise and fall, grateful for the steady rhythm. The surgeon had relieved pressure on the brain and sewn up the deep wound in his scalp but he was still unconscious.

"I said it in the recovery room," she began, "after you made it through surgery. So I'll just keep saying it. I love you. I love you and I want to be with you. I want us to have Jordy here and to enjoy what's left of his childhood. I want babies with you, sweet children we raise together in our blended family. I want more nights at Bilbee's with you, every festival, every dip in the hot springs. Please, Moore. Please wake up. I love you and I can't imagine life without you."

Hearing a sound, she turned and realized that the door was open. There stood Jordy in the doorway, Moore's parents behind him.

"Colleen," he said. "What did you just say?"

"Jordy! I thought you wouldn't be here for a while."

"Grandpa wanted to come now. Wanted me to see Dad again."

Leander tapped on the doorway, clearly embarrassed at overhearing what Colleen had just said.

"Hi."

"Come in." She waved them both in, but only Jordy entered, focused entirely on her.

"Did I hear you tell Dad you love him?"

"Yes."

"Like, as a friend? You know, like 'love ya!'"

"Jordy, I–"

He frowned. "Or like you're actually in love with him? Did you say you want to be my stepmother? And have *babies* with Dad?"

Time to bring out all the truths.

"I'm deeply, hopelessly in love with your dad, kiddo," she said, her voice going airy and pain filled at the end. Jordy reached for her, his hand on her elbow, teen boy emotions covering his face as he grappled with how to respond.

But instinct made him reach out for connection.

"Colleen," Leander said softly. "Good for you. We wondered when you two would finally come to your senses."

A wet, sniffly laugh bubbled out of her.

"Moore said everyone would feel that way."

"My son was right."

The way Leander said "my son" made her cry harder.

"Why didn't you tell me?" Jordy asked, the question adding another layer of pain for her.

"Because you said you didn't want your dad to bring anyone into your life. Remember?"

"*I* sure do," Leander said, eyes jumping between Moore and Jordy. "You made your feelings perfectly clear, young man."

"That was when I thought it was Tissue Lady! I never dreamed Colleen and Dad would be together!"

She wished Moore were fully awake for this. Somewhere deep in his unconscious, she hoped he was registering this.

"I don't know if we are," she confessed. "We had a fight right before he fell."

Jordy let out a groan.

"It was about me, wasn't it?"

"Yes."

"Because you told me about what happened when I was five."

"Yes."

"It's my fault Dad fell."

"No!" she and Leander said loudly, forcefully.

"Absolutely not!" Jordy's grandfather insisted. "It was a simple accident."

"I yelled at Dad. Right after you left. He found me in the woods and I screamed at him. Said he should have told me. I called him some, uh, bad names. He went back to the lodge and started painting. Then I guess he fell. I wasn't there to see it. I just got a bunch of texts from Harriet telling me to come back."

"Harriet?"

"She was the only person with my cellphone number. On her new phone. The one for emergencies that Luke got her for her birthday?"

"Colleen?" Jordy's voice broke. "My last words to Dad were really terrible. If he doesn't wake up..."

"Mine were, too, bud. Mine, too. How about we not

think about that? Let's focus on how much we both love him."

Jordy nodded and Leander pulled up a chair, the three of them surrounding Moore's bed.

Each asking for forgiveness in their own way.

Chapter 22

Moore

He couldn't open his eyes, but his ears worked just fine.

Except they couldn't believe what they were hearing.

Luke Luview, his best friend since they were babies born three days apart, was sitting on the edge of his hospital bed, holding his hand.

And *crying*.

"I'm so sorry. I'm a jerk. And an idiot. Or, as you said back in fifth grade, a *jerkidiot*. Remember how you made those hand-drawn bumper stickers with the word on it, and tried to sell them at one of the summer love festivals? And old Stan Petrinelli drove you off because it violated the emotional tone of the town's products? 'No negativity,' he said. You got a lecture from him, but my dad came along and bought every one of those bumper stickers from you." Luke laughed through tears. "I should slap one on my forehead. How could I have been so stupid?"

If Moore had the energy to grunt in agreement, he would. But he didn't.

"You love Colleen. She loves you so much. It's obvious, and I think it's been in front of my face all this time and I was too stubborn to accept it." He sighed deeply. "Nothing about you is wrong, Moore. You're not a screwup at love. Cammie hurt you, and so did Gia, but none of it was ever your fault. And here you are, hurt and suffering because you tried to help my family and do the dangerous part of the paint job."

Moore just inhaled and exhaled.

He had a vague sense that he should respond, but everything that made up his body felt like it was floating ten thousand feet in the air, like his skin was helium.

"I said some bad things to you. I never meant them. Pride and surprise do so much damage. I don't know why I made you take that pledge when we were fourteen. I think because... we were fourteen." He laughed lightly, then sniffed. "And when I found you two in bed in that cabin, I lost it. I lost it because I'd just waded through a pond at the truck crash and expected to haul you both out of the water, dead. And instead, I found you naked and very, very much alive. Never in all my life did I expect to experience that." He sniffed again. "When Kell and I spotted Dad's truck, it was like reliving that moment with Jude DiPalma when we found Amber's body on Thanksgiving. I just couldn't find another... another *body*... of someone I love. Two someones I love, this time."

Moore wanted to squeeze his hand. Tell him it was okay. Say *something*.

All he could do was breathe, but given his current status, that seemed like an achievement.

A sob ripped out of Luke, his weight shifting on the bed. Moore struggled to open his eyes, succeeding just enough to glimpse his oldest friend curled into himself, his free arm wrapped around his belly. He was clad in a windbreaker, jeans, and a navy sweater, and his jaw was covered in scruff.

How long had Moore been in here?

"Just... live, man. Have your whole brain. I want you to be Moore again. I want my sister to have the kind of love she deserves. The kind I have with Kylie. What my parents have. You and Colleen–life better not rob you of that."

The door opened, and Moore heard a gasp.

"Luke." It was Colleen. "Oh, Lukie."

"Collie," Luke whispered. "He can't. He just–he can't."

"I know. I know. He can't. We won't let him."

Let me what? Moore wondered, listening to the sound of two people he loved so much crying in each other's arms, until consciousness drifted away.

* * *

"Dad?"

"It's okay, Jordy. You can sit on the edge of the bed. Hold his hand. He likes that." Colleen's voice made Moore want to smile but instead, he let out a sigh.

"Is–is he trying to talk?"

"I think he has too much medication in him right now, honey. Remember? They're trying to give his brain lots of rest."

"He looks so weird. Like Dad but not like him. Better than right out of surgery yesterday, though."

"When people have been injured like that, or they're really sick, they can look different. But he's not different. Moore's one hundred percent in there, and he knows you're here, too."

"I don't know what to do." Jordy's voice broke, snapping off with a gasp. "I–"

"Hold his hand again. Like last time." The weight on the bed changed slightly.

Moore let out a groan and opened his eyes. Jordy's face was bright red, eyes bloodshot as he caught his father's gaze.

"Dad?" He stood and took a step forward, peering at Moore, who was working hard to open his eyes more. "You–you awake?"

"Honey," Colleen cut in. "He'd have to be a lot more healed to be able to–"

"Jor?" Moore croaked out, using every drop of energy he had.

"Daddy?"

Hadn't heard that word in years.

"'S me."

"You're awake!" Colleen gasped, running to the door, calling down the hall. A rush of medical people appeared and Moore felt sad to be interrupted, Jordy stepping away from him and letting go of his hand.

"Stay," he whispered, but no one heard him.

And then he went quiet again.

* * *

"I think God had us fly up here so we would be here for him, Francie."

"I don't know if it was God, but I feel blessed to be here. For Jordy, too."

"He'll be fine, right?" Moore heard his dad ask his mom, the old man's voice cracking in a way that Moore didn't know was possible. "He said Jordy's name earlier today."

"Dr. Singh and Doc Blythe said his brain activity looks fine. And he squeezes our hands when we say his name, so..."

"He's such a good man, Francie. We raised a good boy."

A prickly sensation filled Moore's sinuses, his father's words going straight to a pain center in his brain that connected to his heart. Years of shame opened up inside him, flooding his bloodstream, all of it leaving his body.

"All that tough love nonsense the therapist told us to use," his father went on. "Maybe it was wrong."

"We turned to experts and did what they said."

"I've never seen a man who works so hard to do the right thing. But if he does it out of fear, we failed as parents."

Moore's head began to spin. Was this really his own *father* saying this? Or was he hallucinating from the pain meds?

"Dad?" he said, keeping his eyes shut, hearing his father gasp, then the sound of his parents moving to his side, the pressure of them leaning against the bed. Cool, smooth skin, papery and soothing, touched his hand.

"We're here," his father said somberly.

"Mom?"

"Yes, honey. Right here."

"Colleen? Jordy?"

"They're coming back in a bit. How do you feel?"

"Like I could do a really bad rendition of 'I Will Always Love You' at the festival," he joked, earning shocked sounds from his mom, and a snicker from his dad.

"No permanent brain damage, I see," his dad said with a chuckle. "That's the most you've said since you've been coming to. Should I go get the doctor?"

Leander stood. Small crying sounds came from his mom, forcing him to open his eyes.

"Not yet," Moore begged. He took in a long breath. "Give me time."

His mom squeezed his hand.

"Don't you ever do that again!"

"Fall off a ladder?"

"Nearly die!"

"We all die someday, Mom."

"Parents are supposed to go first. It's the natural order of things. You're too young."

"Don't feel young." Any time he opened his eyes, the pain in his head worsened. He pressed the pain medication button on his IV.

"You are, though. And you're going to be fine. Jordy, too."

"I'm sorry," Moore whispered. "Should have done better."

"Better?"

"Got into a fight with Colleen and Jordy before I climbed that ladder. Distracted. I fell."

"Was the fight about Jordy's search? He texted me to ask for court papers. I assumed you'd finally told him."

"Colleen did."

"We always respected your choice to stay above the fray and not criticize Cammie, but I have to admit, I was relieved when he texted me," Leander confessed, earning a surprised look from Francine.

"You were?"

"She doesn't deserve to be protected from the impact of her own actions," his dad said. He patted Moore's leg. "But now is not the time for this conversation."

"You did fine," Moore said softly.

"What's that?" Francine asked, leaning in.

"You did fine," he repeated. "If the expert told you to use tough love, it's okay."

They both froze.

"You heard that?" his father finally said as his mom's hand went limp in his.

"Yes. And I get it. Parents—we never know whether we're making the right decision, do we? I thought not telling Jordy was the best path to protect him, but I was wrong. You thought being tough on me when I made a mistake with Cammie was the right thing, but you were wrong."

"Son—"

"Let me say this," Moore insisted, exhaustion threatening to strip him of words.

"Of course."

"Since I was seventeen and had to tell you I got Cammie pregnant, I've spent every waking moment trying to make up for it. My life is split in two, the time before that broken condom, and the time after. I'm all done with that."

"Done?"

"I did it. I proved myself. I'm worthy of love and respect."

"Moore, darling, no–" his mother began, but he cut her off.

"You never said I wasn't. But that tough love left its mark. Made me afraid to take chances. Made me worry more about losing what I had than what I could gain."

"I'm so sorry," his father said, gravelly voice vibrating into Moore's seventeen-year-old soul. "We could have done better by you."

"Maybe it worked, though. I'm stronger than I might have been otherwise."

His father cleared his throat.

"It didn't work out because we were tough. It worked because *you* were so tough. You taught us a lesson in how to be tough *and* be loving."

"You're a wonderful father!" his mother exclaimed. "So good with Jordy. So persistent, so... unwaveringly devoted to him."

"I know," he said. The words sounded arrogant but he didn't care. It was time to own his honorable actions instead of constantly churning out more to justify his existence. "It's a lot of effort."

"Hard work well rewarded. You've raised a good boy."

"With my fifty days a year."

"You fought for every single minute. And now look at what's happening."

"What do you mean?"

"Jordy is moving here."

"That's for the courts to decide," Moore said, feeling weaker as the topic changed.

His parents shared a look across his hospital bed, a gaze that sent dread rumbling through his gut.

"What?"

"Uh, well..." his mother stammered, her affect unusual. "It's confirmed. Jordy is moving in with you."

"Grant confirmed it? Already?"

"You won't have a tough legal battle this time," his father said in a mysterious voice. Was he... crowing?

"Say it straight out, Dad."

"Jordy confronted Cammie. He must have something he's holding over her, some information we don't know. She caved. Instantly. He's free to move here. She just wants visitation."

"Whoa." The room swam. Exhaustion filled him, competing with elation.

"Sleep, darling," his mom said, kissing his cheek as the pain meds kicked in. "Sleep. We love you so much."

* * *

Her hand slipped into his, palm against palm.

"Hey there, sleepy guy."

Hearing Colleen's hushed, comforting voice made him open his eyes, her bare face smiling, blonde hair pulled into a practical ponytail. She wore a Love You Cupids pink hoodie and was holding a coffee in her other hand.

Inhaling slowly, he found the aroma delightful.

"I remember caffeine," he said, pretending to be sad. Implementing his closest expression to puppy dog eyes, he mooned for a sip.

She obliged, bringing the to-go cup to his lips.

"*Shhh*. Don't tell the doctor."

"Lying at work. I love integrity in a nurse."

She smacked him lightly, grinning wider.

"I see your brain is truly recovering."

"I don't know. But my stomach sure is." It growled as if he'd cued it. "When can I get a loaded brownie from Greta's?"

"When you're back home."

"Jordy leaves tomorrow," he said, suddenly remembering. "Doc says I won't be out of here before then."

"Leander and Francine have it all covered. And you heard the custody situation is all clear?"

"I heard. How the hell did Jordy blackmail his own mother?"

"Don't look a gift horse in the mouth."

"I like *your* mouth."

"Are we flirting? Recovery has reached that point?"

"I don't know. Are we?"

"Is it time for this conversation? I thought we'd wait until you're discharged and at home."

"I don't think there's a better time to talk than now."

"Fine. You start."

"Okay. I love you. I'm sorry. Can we make up and put this all behind us?" He was intentionally direct, knowing it would shock her.

He was right.

"You don't mince words. At all."

"After that fall, I'm lucky to *have* words. At all."

"That's it? Just… you love me, you're sorry, let's have a future together?"

"What more am I supposed to say?" He squeezed her hand. "That's all there is to say."

And it really was that simple. Moore had decided during his middle-of-the-night insomnia that this was how he wanted to clear the air with Colleen.

Like a grown up.

"I love you," he said again, the words feeling so good in his mouth.

"I love you, Moore."

"No, you don't."

"Of course I do!"

"You can't love me more than I love you."

"I was saying 'I love you, Moore.' Like if you said 'I love you, Colleen.'"

"Ah! Then we love each other."

"We do."

"You were right in front of me all along."

"I was. This feels too easy," she said, kissing him, completely in control. His body was still broken, brain healing, tissue knitting itself together, swelling needing to be controlled.

In more ways than one.

Their kiss was chaste, his bandages too cumbersome, and as she kissed him again, he felt wetness on her jaw, his fingers tracing the fine lines of her face.

"You're crying."

"I almost lost you just as I found you."

"And I almost lost you because I couldn't get over myself. You've been the best thing that's ever happened to me, aside from Jordy. My best friend's sister—we grew up together. I grew attracted to you. We had a misunderstanding and I took Cammie to homecoming, and it changed my life forever. But you stayed. You helped. You helped me so much those first five years of Jordy's life and I didn't even know. You've been a silent partner all along, unrecognized and loyal. Loving. Stable."

"I was being a friend."

"No, you were being a life partner, but without any of the romantic benefits."

"I wouldn't go that far."

"I would! And I'm so grateful. I'm so sorry I never saw it all in full until now. And now, I want an *us*. Before I fell, you said you didn't know what *us* is. I do know. *Us* is *this*. Being there for each other, cheering each other on. Making a life together."

This time, their kiss was one big, long *yes*. A yes that covered all their years together, all the unacknowledged longing, and all the hope that lay before them.

"I love you," they said in unison.

"Jordy approves, you know. He says it's gross, but he says if he had to pick someone for his dad, it would be me."

"Smart boy."

"Wonder where he gets it from."

Moore pointed to his chest, to a spot over his heart. Colleen rested her head on it, carefully edging onto the bed with him, cuddling up.

Where they fell asleep together, wholly relaxed.

And together.

Forever.

:)

Epilogue

The auditorium smelled like new furniture and teen flop sweat.

Moore and Colleen took their seats in the sixth row, the tickets torn by a fourteen-year-old kid with electric-blue hair, half their head shaved. The student wore a white shirt, black bow tie, and black pants, using an exaggerated sweeping arm gesture to usher them to their seats. Smack in the middle of the row, they were crammed like sardines in the sold-out theater, Moore beaming like the super-proud parent he was.

For once, he could watch Jordy at a performance and not have to take two planes to get there.

For once, he'd been part of Jordy's play from start to finish, from tryouts to curtain call.

And for once, he was here with Colleen, holding her hand, who was as proud as Moore and as beautiful as ever.

For the last six months, he'd felt complete. Jordy moved in back in August and started school. Colleen and Moore went public with their relationship. His parents traveled back and forth to Florida on their seasonal migration, but they were here for Jordy's role in *Brigadoon*.

And today was the one-year anniversary of the horrible car accident he and Colleen had been in.

"You happy?" she whispered, squeezing his hand as people milled about, settling into seats. Clad in a red cardigan, navy turtleneck, and jeans, she wore snow boots and a scarf, her blonde hair in a thick braid.

Her eyes glowed.

"Always, when I'm with you."

She tilted her head toward the stage.

"I mean about this."

"Of course."

Colleen looked around, catching people's eyes, waving over and over to people she knew. The performing arts high school was a good thirty minutes from Luview and at first, Moore had made the drive nearly every day. Within a month, though, they'd made a decent carpool arrangement with two other families.

Jordy expanded Moore's world, exposing him to new families in different towns in the western Maine area, all united by love of theater, dance, and music.

All offering their children a chance to explore what they loved most.

This was Jordy's first performance, though there would be another in May. Cammie had sworn she'd come to that one; she was watching online tonight, on the streaming channel the school set up for parents and family members who couldn't attend.

Their dueling lawyers had come to a decent agreement; his dad's comment about not having a legal battle had been a bit too optimistic, but in the end, everything favored Moore, for once. Cammie would have Jordy for eight weeks in the summer, Thanksgiving, and Christmas, as well as February and April school breaks.

Moore got him the rest of the time.

And Jordy was happy with it all.

Moore's phone buzzed with a text.

Dad?

I'm here. Sixth row, center, with Colleen.

Awesome. I need help.

Anything, kiddo.

Can I borrow your tie and belt?

"He wants my tie and belt?" Moore said to Colleen, hopelessly confused.

Her hand went to his knee, gliding up, fingertips playing.

"Mmmm. If it gets you undressed, I like it."

"Don't make promises you can't keep," he growled in her ear before standing, his bad leg protesting slightly. The fall off the ladder last year had taken its toll. His dark hair was missing along a thin scar line on his scalp, though he wore his hair a bit longer now to cover it.

The compound fracture in his leg took longer to heal than he liked. Skiing was no longer a daredevil sport for him.

But he had more than enough to keep his leisure time occupied now.

Looking down at Colleen, he had to take a deep breath to control himself. The last thing he wanted was to walk around with an erection at his kid's high school play.

"I never make promises I don't keep," she retorted, and he had to give her that.

"Fair enough. Let me go find Jordy and I'll be back."

Winding his way through the crowd, he was stopped four different times by fellow parents he knew, either folks who had bought jewelry from the store or people he'd come to know because of Jordy's involvement at the school.

Sights and scents in the auditorium made him reflect back on his own high school years, the building in Luview older but really not that different. He couldn't think of a single memory from those formative years without Luke in it, and most of them included Colleen, too.

Which made him smile.

"Dad!" Jordy rushed down the small flight of stairs off stage right, his hair pulled off his forehead by a headband, some kind of covering taped to his head. Jordy wore a wig for his performance, and Moore stifled a laugh. "You wore a tie! Whew!"

The relieved grin had no metal in it. Seeing Jordy smile with his pearly whites, straight and aligned, was still a jolt.

"I came straight from work."

"You're a lifesaver! The person in charge of my costume in Act II left her bag on the bus and now we need some stuff." Jordy touched Moore with an ease that had only developed since they'd started living together. He toughed the knot at the base of Moore's throat. "Can you just loosen the tie and I'll put it over my head?"

"Why?"

"I don't know how to tie it the right way."

"I'll teach you."

"Not now! No time!"

"Fine. No problem. Take a deep breath."

Moore flipped his collar up, loosened his tie, and pulled it over his head, taking care around the scar tissue from his surgery. Then he put it on his kid and tightened the knot.

"Colleen's here, right?"

"Yes, why?"

"We need a pair of women's high heels, size ten."

"Sorry. She's wearing flats."

"Are Grandma and Grandpa here?"

"They're coming to tomorrow's show."

"Okay, Dad. Thanks!" Jordy fled, disappearing backstage.

Mission accomplished.

Shuffling back to his seat, tieless and beltless, Moore

laughed when Colleen looked up at him and said, "Keep your pants on, buddy."

Settled in his seat, he whispered, "Only in public."

They held hands, fingers intertwined, until his phone buzzed again.

Cammie.

What's the live-streaming link? Locke, Soria, and Zelda and I want to watch it.

Moore had already sent it to her three times this week. He knew this was Cammie's way of intruding in his life, especially mentioning Soria, Locke and the baby. Getting Jordy here had been a struggle, with Cammie using every trick she could think of to make it hard for Moore.

All he replied with was the link.

Then the house lights blinked three times and he shut off his phone.

"Ladies and gentlemen," the announcer began, "welcome to—"

Welcome to the rest of his life.

Because the best was yet to come.

<3

Thank you so much for reading Love You More, Colleen and Moore's book.

But you're not done! How about a FREE BONUS EPILOGUE, with a flash-forward a year or so into the future? Take a look at what Colleen and Moore are up to RIGHT NOW: https://mybook.to/LYMbonusepilogue

Trust me. You want to read. :) And find out more about the elusive fourth Luview sibling, Dennis...

Acknowledgments

This book was written (and delayed) as so many issues hit my life at once: multiple family members and friends getting COVID, my husband's eye surgery to recover his sight (it was a success!), a schooling crisis with my thirteen-year-old with special needs – and it all meant pushing the release back by a month.

Thank you for your patience.

I have to thank Maria Connor, who came to my home in late 2019 for a much-beloved business trip and introduced our family to chaffles. If you haven't tried them, they are so easy and good. One egg, 1/4th cup of shredded cheese, and a waffle iron are all you need (maybe cooking spray so they don't stick). Mix egg and cheese. Pour into waffle iron. Cook until crispy. Add seasoning, bacon, chives, etc. if you like. I wanted to feature them in a book, so here we go.

Many, MANY thanks for MacKenzie Johnson and Reilly Zoltan for their extraordinary help with any and all *League of Legends* references. Both are on the eSports team at Clark University in Worcester, Massachusetts (red team!) and both helped me in a line-by-line conversation that was so much fun, as I explained the emotional tone and plot movements I was going for while Jordy, Colleen, and Moore play *League* together, and how to make sure the conversations and game developments would be accurate and authentic.

My understanding of video games stopped with *Centipede* and *Frogger*, so... I bow before their awesomeness.

As always, my husband Clark and my editor Elisa Reed

were of tremendous help (see my social media for examples of Clark's edits on my books). Elisa tolerated many delays and a last-minute rush, and she's the best. <3

Like Luview, Maine, it takes a village of support to write my books, and I'm always appreciative for my beta readers, my regular readers, family, and all the people who make it easier for me to do my dream job: make stuff up in my head all day and laugh while doing it. My gratitude knows no bounds.

Other Books by Julia Kent

SUGGESTED READING ORDER

Shopping for a Billionaire Boxed Set (New York Times Bestseller!)

Shopping for a Billionaire's Fiancee

Shopping for a CEO (USA Today bestseller)

Shopping for a Billionaire's Wife (USA Today bestseller)

Shopping for a CEO's Fiancee (USA Today bestseller)

Shopping for an Heir (USA Today bestseller)

Shopping for a Billionaire's Honeymoon

Shopping for a CEO's Wife (USA Today bestseller)

Shopping for a Billionaire's Baby (USA Today bestseller)

Shopping for a CEO's Honeymoon

Shopping for a Baby's First Christmas

Shopping for a CEO's Baby

Shopping for a Yankee Swap

Shopping for a Turkey

Shopping for a Highlander

Little Miss Perfect

Fluffy (USA Today bestseller)

Perky (USA Today bestseller)

Feisty

Hasty

Love You Wrong

Love You Right

Love You Again

Love You More

Love You Now

Our Options Have Changed (USA Today bestseller)

Thank You For Holding

Her Billionaires (New York Times Bestseller!)

It's Complicated

Completely Complicated

It's Always Complicated

Random Acts of Crazy (New York Times Bestseller)

Random Acts of Trust

Random Acts of Fantasy

Random Acts of Hope

Randomly Acts of Yes

Random Acts of Love

Random Acts of LA

Random Acts of Christmas

Random Acts of Vegas

Random Acts of New Year

Random Acts of Baby

Maliciously Obedient (USA Today bestseller)

Suspiciously Obedient

Deliciously Obedient

Christmasly Obedient

About the Author

Text JKentBooks to 77948 and get a text message on release dates!

New York Times and USA Today bestselling author Julia Kent writes romantic comedy with an edge. Since 2013, she has sold more than 2 million books, with 4 New York Times bestsellers and more than 21 appearances on the USA Today bestseller list. Her books have been translated into French, Italian, and German, with more titles releasing in the future.

From billionaires to BBWs to new adult rock stars, Julia finds a sensual, goofy joy in every contemporary romance she writes. Unlike Shannon from *Shopping for a Billionaire*, she did not meet her husband after dropping her phone in a men's room toilet (and he isn't a billionaire she met in a romantic comedy).

She lives in New England with her husband and three children where she is the only person in the household with the gene required to change empty toilet paper rolls.

She loves to hear from her readers online.

Visit her at http://jkentauthor.com